Hidden Truths

Muna Shehadi

H
REVIEW

First published in Great Britain in 2020
by HEADLINE REVIEW
An imprint of HEADLINE PUBLISHING GROUP

4

Cataloguing in Publication Data is available from the British Library

ISBN 978 1 4722 5873 1

Typeset in Sabon by Avon DataSet Ltd, Bidford-on-Avon, Warwickshire

Printed and bound in Great Britain by Clays Ltd, Elcograf S.p.A.

FSC
www.fsc.org
MIX
Paper from responsible sources
FSC® C104740

Headline's policy is to use papers that are natural, renewable and recyclable products and made from wood grown in well-managed forests and other controlled sources. The logging and manufacturing processes are expected to conform to the environmental regulations of the country of origin.

HEADLINE PUBLISHING GROUP
An Hachette UK Company
Carmelite House
50 Victoria Embankment
London EC4Y 0DZ

www.headline.co.uk
www.hachette.co.uk

For Mark, my husband, best friend,
and really good time.

At Headline Publishing, I'd like to thank my wonderful editor, Kate Byrne, whose unfailing cheer and astute literary judgment has made working with her such a joy, and my hero Nathaniel Alcaraz-Stapleton, who helped sell the Fortune's Daughters trilogy far and wide. Special thanks to talented architect Meg Baniukiewicz, who not only helped me with this book, but designed a gorgeous addition to our house. Much appreciation also to Charlotte Lukes, who answered seasonal wildlife questions about Washington Island, and to Cindy Kasper, who provided a wealth of interesting information about technical writing, most of which I regret I was unable to fit into the book.

Hidden Truths

Chapter 1

September 4, 1970 (Friday)

I haven't been writing as often because now I have Daniel and don't need to talk to you so much, my dear diary. Yes, I've been cheating on you! Today, not only have Daniel and I been married exactly six blissful, wonderful months, but I'm also writing to mark the occasion because I, Jillian Croft, née Sylvia Moore, from the nowhere town of Jackman, Maine, have landed a part in a Steve McQueen movie! I even have a line: 'Will that be all, sir?' I memorized it already, as you can see.

I have an agent and am already getting so many auditions that I started feeling like I was spending all my time either in an airplane or in LA. Daniel and I love New York, but LA is the place for movies, and I've decided that's where I want to make my career, then come back to the stage when I'm Someone To See. So we're moving! Daniel is already looking for teaching jobs in theater. He's so well known and successful I know he'll get snapped up. Maybe UCLA or CalArts. I think he should open his own acting studio, but he says he's not ready for that.

Next trip to California we are going house-hunting in . . . Beverly Hills! I still can't believe it. Daniel says it's better to buy a big house right away, because we'll get a stinking lot of money for his New York apartment and should put it back into real estate to avoid taxes. He is so smart.

And I am so so so excited! I wrote to my parents, telling them I'd be moving and that maybe I'd come visit sometime. They didn't answer. I guess I didn't expect them to. They haven't responded to my letters since I ran away. Two years and still no forgiveness, except from my sister? At times the pain chokes me. What kind of mother can wipe a child out of her life as if she never existed?

If I had a baby, I'm sure they'd want to meet him/her. I don't know how I'll ever make that happen with my deformed, barren body, but I swear to almighty God, someday I will figure out a way. I desperately need the chance to give my children what my mother never gave me.

I suppose we all live our lives trying to fix whatever went wrong in our childhoods.

Love,

Me

'Happy birthday!' Eve echoed the voices around the blue-cloth-covered dining table brought into her father and stepmother's retirement cottage on the occasion of her father's eightieth birthday. Or, if you counted precisely, since Daniel Braddock had been born February 29, his eightieth year, but only his twentieth birthday. Eve and her two older sisters and their stepmother were hoisting champagne flutes to honor the family patriarch.

'Thank you all.' Their beloved tyrant had recovered much of the weight he had lost last summer, and his ability to speak had improved dramatically, but the stroke had clearly accelerated his aging. 'I wasn't sure I'd make it to this one.'

His wife, Lauren, just turned sixty, took a tiny sip of champagne. She'd do that a few more times, then put the glass down and not touch it for the rest of the evening, claiming alcohol brought out the devil in her. Given her personality, Eve would expect maybe a minor imp – one who'd leave the last teacup unwashed.

'You're getting better every day, Daniel.' Lauren patted his back. 'Another few months, you'll be your old self again.'

'Another few months I'll just be myself *older*.' He raised his glass and nodded to the table. 'Thank you for coming, girls. It's nice to be together again.'

'Hear, hear.' Olivia, the eldest, beamed adoringly at her father. She looked thinner than usual, and tired, though impeccably dressed and made up as usual. 'I bet you make it to your twenty-first birthday. Then you can drink legally.'

'Looking forward to that.' Her father chuckled fondly. 'Rosalind, I keep meaning to ask, how is that young man of yours?'

'He's fine.' Rosalind's face glowed, brown hair in a flattering pixie cut that emphasized her pretty eyes. She'd stopped dyeing her hair bizarre colors, though her Rosalind-designed clothes still reflected her crazy patchwork take on life. 'He's working on sculptures of me.'

'With clothes on?' Her father managed to make the question a threat.

'Of course, Daddy.' She put on a cherubic, eye-fluttering smile. 'I would never, *ever* let Bryn see me naked.'

The table erupted into laughter. Rosalind had always been strong, but finding her birth mother last fall and meeting Bryn seemed to have changed her strength from stoicism into an irresistible self-assurance. For once, the self-described hummingbird was the most settled and content of the three of them.

'It's not *him* seeing that worries me.'

'He does very tasteful work.' Rosalind reached toward her

father's hand on the table. 'The sculpture will be PG-13 at worst.'

'Hmph.' Her father put down his glass and pointed emphatically. 'I'd like to see you marry this one. Your mother would have approved too. She so wanted to see each of you happy and settled, with babies of your own. You all brought her so much joy.'

'That's sweet. Thanks, Dad.' Rosalind's expression tightened, mirroring what Eve felt on her own face and saw on Olivia's. Not long after their father's stroke, the Braddock sisters had stumbled over information revealing that their mother – Jillian Croft, the on-screen epitome of female sexuality – had been born with complete androgen insensitivity, which meant that she had no reproductive organs. In spite of three very public, and apparently fake, pregnancies, well documented in family photo albums and celebrity magazines, she could not have given birth to any of them.

Last fall, Eve had followed Rosalind's brave journey to find her birth mother with interest, then with relief over how well it had turned out, but she still had no desire to search for her own. Olivia had bought a one-way ticket to planet denial and refused to talk about any of it, either then or since.

'Olivia.' Lauren looked across the room and back, a peculiar shy gesture, as if she couldn't bear to make eye contact for long. 'How's the show going?'

Eve tensed. Olivia had recently admitted to her sisters that while her TV cooking show had at first drawn viewers curious about the offspring of their favorite movie star, lately ratings had been dropping like a failed soufflé – ha ha.

'You know, I'm thinking of getting back into acting.' Typically, Olivia revealed no vulnerability to her father, and especially to Lauren, whom she still hadn't forgiven for daring to show up in her adored mother's place. 'My agent has me up for three parts. Cougar, old maid and a MILF.'

'What is a MILF?' Lauren asked.

Dad smirked. 'I'll tell you when you're older.'

Olivia leaned forward, giving the impression of being right in Lauren's face even from across the table. 'It stands for "mother I'd like to—"'

'Fondle.' Eve smiled sweetly at her sister, whose teeth were still biting her collagen-plumped lip, ready to give the F-bomb plenty of punch.

Lauren's pink face wrinkled in disgust. 'That is horrible.'

'Maybe.' Olivia drained her glass of champagne and reached for the bottle. 'But at thirty-eight, that's what I get.'

'Soon to be thirty-nine,' Lauren said.

'Oh, *thanks*.' Olivia filled her glass, not meeting Lauren's eyes. 'Like I really needed a reminder.'

'And we should raise a glass to you, Lauren, for your sixtieth.' Peacemaking was usually Rosalind's job, but Eve decided to take this one on herself.

'Which she spent by my bed instead of on the Mediterranean cruise we'd planned.' Daniel glared at no one in particular. 'I owe you, Lauren.'

'All you owe me is to work on getting your strength back.' Lauren gazed adoringly at her husband. 'The Mediterranean will still be there.'

'Didn't you and *Mom* go on that cruise to—'

'So, Eve.' Rosalind very wisely interrupted Olivia's bid to stir up trouble. 'I want to know what the latest is with your big architect job in Wisconsin. Is it still happening?'

Eve felt the usual adrenaline rush that hit her whenever the subject came up. The chance to design a house – even a small one – and to work with a client instead of fellow students, then to see her vision built rather than simply graded, was thrilling. And overwhelming. Since she'd graduated from the Harvard

School of Design and started work at Atkeson, Shifrin and Trim Architects, her design work had been frustratingly limited to hotel bathrooms and elevator shafts.

She accepted more champagne, knowing she'd probably had enough, but not in the mood to be sensible. 'I don't know. It's been weeks since I've heard anything. Apparently Shelley was ill, and then—'

'Then she ran into trouble getting financing for the project. Banks are so fussy these days,' Lauren said. Shelley Grainger was a close friend of hers from Machias, Maine, where they had both grown up. 'But I was saving this to tell you in person, Eve. Shelley called me a few days ago. She put in a new application and thinks this time the loan should go through. She'll be contacting me soon with more details.'

'Really.' Eve lifted her brows, her thrill at the opportunity mixed with fear that she'd be in over her head. Shelley Grainger owned a six-bedroom family house on Washington Island, a little dot on the map off the tip of the Door County peninsula that pierced Lake Michigan like a nearly detached splinter. She wanted Eve to design a cottage she could escape to both when her kids and their families visited, and when she rented the big house to summer tourists to supplement her retirement income. She also had a friend who wanted a sunroom added to her own house.

Lauren had first mentioned the jobs to Eve last fall. Eve's boyfriend Mike hadn't exactly jumped up and down at the idea of her leaving for the weeks it would take to complete the designs, and her boss would undoubtedly have felt the same way. Eve had been excited by the idea of being able to design something substantial, but wasn't sure she was ready. Then Shelley seemed to run into one delay after another, and Eve had been able to shelve the idea with guilty relief.

Now that the offers were back, there was a new complication. On Friday, she had been told her immediate supervisor was leaving, a post she'd been all but promised two years earlier when she was hired. Agreeing to the promotion, then asking for a month's leave to travel out of state – not a great move.

'It's a great opportunity.' Her father cut himself another slab of cake, ignoring Lauren's disapproving look. 'Especially for a beginner.'

Rosalind bristled. 'Eve has worked in firms since high school and has a master's from Harvard. I wouldn't call her a beginner.'

'What has she built? She *is* a beginner.' Her father fixed his intense brown gaze on his middle daughter. While their mother had disciplined her children with words and volume, all it took from Dad was that look and his eternal threat, '. . . or else'.

He might be older and weaker, but he was still Daniel Braddock.

'It would be a challenge,' Eve admitted.

'But challenge is good. That's what you want.' Olivia gestured to her. 'You've been stuck in that firm arranging sinks and toilets since you graduated.'

'That's true.' Eve toyed with her cake, heart thumping oddly. She hadn't told anyone about the promotion – superstitious, but her right. Olivia wouldn't understand her inadequacy fears anyway. Her eldest sister had been born anxiety-free. If she decided to do something, *voilà*, in her mind she was immediately qualified. That kind of confidence hadn't come to Eve from whoever gave birth to her. She'd made strides in conquering her shyness, but it was a constant and insidious battle.

'Well, ya can't beat northern Wisconsin in early spring, eh?' Her father's voice was thick with a fake Wisconsin accent and sarcasm. 'Everyone will still be ice-fishing or whatever it is they do there. Eating cheese.'

'And bratwurst,' Olivia announced. 'And pasties.'

'What's a pass-tea?' Rosalind cut herself a third nearly transparent sliver of cake.

'Spelled like pasty. Pronounced pass-tee. It's a meat and vegetable turnover. They originated in England – in Cornwall – invented for miners so they could hold lunch in their hands.'

'Thank you, Miss Food Encyclopedia,' Eve said.

'You're welcome.' Olivia beamed sweetly at her. 'Would you like to know about chicken booyah?'

'I definitely would not.'

'How about fish boils?'

Eve made a face. 'Is that a dish or a skin disease?'

'Gee, Olivia, you're selling this hard,' Rosalind said.

'Just doing my job, ma'am.' Olivia proffered the bottle. 'Who wants more champagne? Dad?'

'I think he's had enough.'

'Do I not have a working tongue?' Daniel glared at his wife. 'I would love more, Olivia.'

Lauren shook her head, *I give up*. 'You'll fall asleep at the table.'

'I will do no such thing. It's my birthday and I am going to enjoy it.' He held out his glass defiantly. Olivia poured him a healthy dose.

Ten minutes later, he was snoring over his half-eaten cake and had to be woken to go to bed. The girls wished him happy birthday one more time, then Lauren took charge of him while the sisters cleared up, chatting and laughing. But even when the last dish had been loaded into the dishwasher, the last flute washed and dried, Eve was not remotely ready for the evening to end. As the family's biggest introvert, she was usually the first to retreat.

'This was so fun,' Rosalind said.

'It's not even nine yet.' Eve dried her hands. 'Want to get a drink at Marlintini's? Even if it's coffee?'

'Absolutely.' Olivia snapped off her rubber gloves, which she'd used to protect her manicure. 'But screw coffee. It's only six in LA. Time to get started.'

'Rosalind?' Eve raised her eyebrows hopefully.

'I'm in. For coffee.' Rosalind held out her hand. 'And the car keys.'

They bundled up and drove the short distance – every distance in Blue Hill, Maine, was short – Olivia complaining about the cold weather, when the real problem was that her coat wasn't warm enough for winter. Eve didn't even make fun of her, just told her to turn up the heat in the car.

They pulled into the restaurant parking lot, carved out of the forest of birch and evergreen that blanketed the state. Emerging into the frosty air, Olivia rubbed her arms, then spread them to embrace the scenery. 'Look at this! Trees, trees everywhere. I never realize how tired I am of brown hills, drought and palms until I come back east and everything is so green! Even at this absolutely horrendous time of year.'

'Such a California girl. You should visit us more often.' Eve was surprised to find herself meaning it. She and Olivia had been remarkably friendly this visit. At Christmas, the family gathering had included significant others, with fairly disastrous results. Rosalind's boyfriend Bryn had been an immediate favorite with Dad, but Olivia's husband Derek and Eve's boyfriend Mike had never made Daniel's Good List, so he'd not had one pleasant thing to say to either of them.

Therefore, it was hard for either Derek or Mike to say anything pleasant back.

Therefore, everyone was horribly tense during the holiday, and exhausted after.

Therefore, the men had stayed home this weekend.

'I wish I could visit more. Sometimes I regret we sold the house on Candlewood Point.' Olivia whirled in a blissful circle. 'I love this state!'

'What state?' Eve grinned at her sister's uncharacteristic goofiness. 'Maine, or champagne buzz?'

Olivia scowled back, hands on her hips. 'So very not—'

'Race you to the door!' Rosalind took off for the restaurant.

Eve followed at a sprint, her longer legs overtaking her sturdy sister just as they reached the front door of the low brown building, brightened in front by a row of white-silled windows. Panting, they turned back to see Olivia laughing wildly back by the car, in a hopping struggle to remove a high-heeled shoe that seemed not to want to come off.

Eve draped an arm around Rosalind's neck. 'Look at her. She's crazy.'

Rosalind sighed. 'I worry about her. She's way too skinny. I think she's in trouble.'

'Me too. But you know her, she'll have to collapse completely before she admits she needs help.'

'Just like Mom. They're practically identical.'

'If I didn't know for sure Jillian couldn't have given birth to her . . .'

They watched in silence as Olivia finally got her shoe off and speed-walked toward them in her stockinged feet. 'Total humiliation. I *always* used to win.'

'Brought low by Manolo Blahnik.' Eve rubbed her shivering sister's bony back. 'You makes your choices, you pays your price.'

'A helluva price if they're Manolos.' Rosalind opened the door and ushered them inside.

In the crowded bar area, the women managed to grab a just-vacated table. Olivia ordered a glass of Pinot Noir, Rosalind a decaf coffee and a glass of water. Eve hesitated, then went for a draft Sam Adams. She didn't need more alcohol in her system, but she was feeling reckless, worked up. Maybe the prospect of a promotion. Maybe finally having to decide on the jobs in Wisconsin. Maybe she was just having a great time with her sisters. Lately, at home in Boston, great times had been in short supply.

'Dad seems to be doing well.' Rosalind pulled off her pink and purple scarf, taking a look around the bar. 'Even better than at Christmas.'

Eve nodded. She was still upset by the changes in him, but given that he'd nearly died and could have remained seriously impaired, she was also incredibly grateful. 'We're lucky he's come back as far as he has.'

'The doctor says he'll recover further.' Olivia was using her eldest-knows-best voice, which had driven Eve crazy since she was old enough to recognize it. 'The biggest improvement is in the first year, but even for years after that he can get better. It's only been five months.'

'Six,' Eve said. 'Late July to late February.'

'Okay, six. The point is, he'll still get a lot better.'

The waitress brought their drinks and left the tab.

'That *is* the point, you're right.' Eve lifted her glass, wondering when she'd last conceded anything to Olivia. 'Here's to Dad.'

The three toasted together, then sipped their drinks and put them down nearly in unison, Eve's in the exact middle of her coaster, a silly superstition she'd adopted as a kid, telling herself that if she set the glass down too far from center, the earth would tilt.

'Olivia, are you really going to try acting again?' Rosalind looked at her elder sister in concern. 'You were so miserable doing it before.'

'Ah, I don't know.' Olivia let her chin fall on to her hands, long chestnut hair spilling over her forehead. 'Honestly, things are worse than I made it sound. The ratings stink, and I have no idea what to do differently, nor does anyone else. And I'll tell you, but only because I've had so much champagne, that it absolutely *sucks* to be the daughter of the most successful woman in showbiz history and be a failure.'

'You are *not* a failure.' Rosalind shook her finger at her sister. 'You only *think* you are.'

Olivia straightened, simultaneously tossing back her hair, a signature move Eve could try a thousand times and look cool maybe once. 'You're just trying to cheer me up.'

'No, no, she's right. You have to look at what you *have* accomplished, instead of what you haven't. None of us is going to be Jillian Croft.' Eve forced a laugh, the familiar resentment resurfacing. 'Which is a good thing.'

'That wasn't kind,' Olivia snapped.

'Come on, Olivia.' Eve knew better than to argue, but she didn't seem to care. 'Our mother had demons that made other people's look like Disney princesses.'

'Yes, okay, that's true.' Olivia followed her surprise retreat with a dramatic sigh. 'If I could just get *pregnant*, I'd feel I'd achieved at least *one* goal in my life.'

Eve's annoyance vanished into sympathy. She'd been hoping for good news this month, but even though every test Olivia and Derek took showed no obstacle to pregnancy, it didn't seem to be happening. 'You will.'

She wished she could sound more sure.

'Maybe if you stopped worrying about it so much?' Rosalind said. 'A lot of people have kids once they give up trying.'

Olivia snorted. 'Yeah, I don't think it works when you tell yourself you're giving up just so you have a better chance of getting pregnant.'

'You're right.' Rosalind looked miserable. 'I'm really sorry you're having to go through this.'

'I shouldn't have brought it up. We're here to continue Dad's celebration.' Olivia waved the subject away, eyes wandering toward the bar, then back. 'Let's talk about something else. Politics?'

'*No!*' Rosalind and Eve objected in unison.

'Okay, not that.' Her eyes darted to the bar again. 'How about . . .'

'How are the Allertons, Rosalind?' Eve couldn't resist teasing Olivia – she couldn't renounce hostilities totally. Their conflict was too deeply ingrained.

Olivia's attention came back to the table. 'Who?'

'My other family.' Rosalind sent Eve a disapproving look. 'Half-sister Caitlin and birth mother Leila. The ones you don't want to hear about.'

'You're right. I don't.' Olivia pushed back her chair. 'While you talk, I'm going to the restroom, then I'm going to hit on that adorable guy over there.'

Rosalind gasped, even while turning to look. 'You are *not* going to . . . Ooh, is he cute.'

'No kidding.' The preppy look wasn't Eve's type, but she still snuck another peek.

Olivia grinned and tousled Rosalind's hair as she passed. 'Wish me luck.'

'You wouldn't dare.'

'You're right. Though Derek doesn't deserve me.' She wiggled gracefully over to the bathroom for their benefit, in the process catching the eye of the guy at the bar. Of course. Olivia slayed them in packs. Always had. Eve attracted plenty of interest – when Olivia wasn't around – but thanks to her mother, she'd had expert lessons at keeping unwanted people at a distance, a talent many celebrities cultivated. Except Jillian had embraced her fans and used the technique on her family, her youngest daughter in particular.

'The Allertons are fine, thanks for asking.' Rosalind finger-combed her hair to smooth it after Olivia's attack. 'Caitlin's going to business school in the fall. Her ex-fiancé is still touring on his motorcycle. He's stopped texting her so much. Fingers crossed she can move on. Leila's singing with the Princeton Opera this summer and in Seattle in the fall. She's happy. I'm happy. Life is good.'

'I only need to look at you to know that.' Eve reached across the table to squeeze her sister's arm, squelching a flash of envy. 'I'm thrilled for you. Think there's a proposal in your future?'

Rosalind shrugged, but her enormous smile and shining eyes gave her away. 'Early days yet.'

'I'm betting yes.'

'Maybe.' Rosalind buried her nose in her coffee in an utterly failed attempt to hide her joy. 'What is going on with you? My spidey sense is telling me you're still not happy. At Christmas you said Mike's depression was better after he got into therapy. But you're not jumping on the jobs in Wisconsin. Mike isn't still being an ass about that, is he?'

Eve hesitated, wishing she hadn't confided to Rosalind last fall that Mike was convinced she was considering the work only to get away from him. A deep and frightened part of her worried that was true. 'He's still taking it personally.'

'*Are* you trying to get away from him?'

Irritation flashed. *Maybe*. 'No, of course not.'

Rosalind's eyes narrowed. 'So . . . what is your instinctive response?'

'Confusion.' She didn't want to talk about this. She didn't want to talk about anything real or serious. She wanted to get up and dance. 'There's no right or wrong involved, it's just two possibilities, go or don't.'

'Maybe.' Rosalind took a careful sip of her coffee and made a face. 'Why did I order decaf?'

'Didn't want to stay up all night?'

'Hardly worth it.' Rosalind put the cup down. 'You know, Bryn helped me realize that I was avoiding moving forward out of fear. Do you think you're afraid?'

'Afraid this isn't the best time or place for my first solo jobs, yes.' Eve replaced her beer in the center of the coaster. 'And don't you think it's a little weird that Shelley has enough money to build an entire house, but she wants a totally inexperienced architect to design it?'

'She's seen your portfolio, right?'

'Yes. But I mean . . . I've never done anything like this on my own.'

'I think you're being paranoid. And too down on your talent.'

Olivia joined them at the table, flinging her hair behind her shoulders in a gesture startlingly like their mother's. 'Why paranoid?'

'Thinking it's weird that this Shelley Grainger and her friend would be willing to hire someone like me.'

'I don't think you're paranoid at all.' Olivia picked up her glass. '*I* wouldn't hire you.'

Eve pointed at Rosalind, who looked exasperated. 'See?'

'Seriously.' Olivia moved wine around in her mouth and swallowed. She made everything she did look sexual. 'Not that I don't think you can do it, I know you can. But if I were her, I'd want someone who had plenty of experience, plenty of recommendations, plenty of everything you haven't got.'

'Exactly.' Eve thumped a triumphant fist on the table. 'It's weird.'

'How many architects could there be on the island? You're being paranoid. Do it, Eve. I've been saying that since this came up last fall.' Rosalind pushed her coffee away. 'You need a change. Mike needs to get over himself.'

'That is *definitely* true,' Olivia said.

Eve bristled. 'Lay off Mike, or I'll get Rosalind to do her Derek imitation.'

'No one can imitate my husband better than me.' Olivia pulled her hair back tightly from her face and let her beautiful features relax into dullness. '"Are we outta beer? I can't get another one, it's fourth quarter. Please? Just this once, baby? Pleeeeeeeeeease?"'

Eve and Rosalind dissolved into helpless laughter. Olivia had nailed his deep, slow voice and inflection perfectly.

'He's not *that* bad,' Rosalind said.

'Of course not. Good imitation, though, huh?'

'Right on.' Eve lifted her hand for a high-five, even though she hated high-fives. It was that kind of evening.

'Oh my God.' Olivia put on one of her TV smiles, speaking through it without moving her lips. 'He's coming over.'

'How do you do that with your mouth?' Eve stared in fascination.

The smile remained undisturbed. 'Years of practice cussing people out while I'm on camera.'

'*Who* is coming over?' Rosalind turned to look.

'The cute guy from the bar.'

Eve got a chestful of adrenaline and a great view of him headed to their table, staring directly at her.

'Hey.' The guy was clean-cut, dark-haired, probably in his late twenties. As he reached the table, he turned to Olivia. Eve was used to that. Her sister was not only a knockout, but took care to emphasize that fact. Eve dressed down to minimize her looks, wore subtle makeup, kept her long blond hair in a ponytail and didn't stick her half-covered boobs out at every opportunity. 'I'm Chez.'

Of course he was. No doubt his Beemer was parked outside.

'Hello, Chez,' Olivia purred.

Chez directed a stunning grin at Eve, who remained cool, shocked at the scattering of sparks his interest produced.

'Listen, uh . . .' He turned back to Olivia. 'This sounds like the oldest line ever, but you look familiar . . .'

'Ah.' She put a modest hand to her not-modest chest. 'Given that I'm internationally renowned, I'm not surprised.'

Rosalind and Eve let out simultaneous snorts of amusement, making Chez glance over again. 'Yeah?'

'Nope.' Olivia's TV smile turned natural. 'Making it up. I'm Olivia.'

'Olivia!' His face lit. 'Olivia Croft. From *Crofty Cooks*.'

Olivia's expression dropped into astonished delight. 'You must be from LA?'

'Yeah. Yeah, I'm here visiting friends.' He tipped his head toward the bar. 'My girlfriend's family actually. She loves your show.'

'Oh, that's so nice.' Olivia scanned the room. 'Is she here?'

'Actually . . . no. I'm kind of in the doghouse right now.' He gave Eve a sheepish look. 'Can I buy you a drink? Uh . . . I mean all three of you.'

'Of course you do.' A touch of acid in Rosalind's tone. She was a beautiful soul, but it was Eve and Olivia who had always attracted the male attention. Men were fairly shallow creatures.

But this particular shallow creature was making something a little wild bloom in Eve's chest, an urge toward recklessness she thought she'd left behind in her mid twenties. What would one drink hurt?

'You know, Chez, that is so sweet, but we were talking about something kind of important.' Olivia patted his shoulder as a dismissal.

'Sure, sorry, sure. But . . . well, my girlfriend would kill me if I didn't get you to sign something. Would you?'

'No problem at all.' Olivia whipped a pen out of her bag without having to fumble to find it. 'What's her name?'

'Jessie.'

'To Jessie . . . your . . . boyfriend . . . Chez . . . is too . . . adorable . . . not to . . . forgive.' She signed the napkin with a flourish. 'Okay? And for your information, the beautiful blond woman you're staring at is my sister Eve.'

His face turned beet red. 'Hi, Eve.'

She couldn't resist smiling. He *was* adorable. 'Hi, Chez.'

He stepped toward her, effectively shutting out her sisters. Panic rose. He was younger than he'd initially seemed. Barely mid twenties, while she was going to be thirty in May. There was a smear of food on his Green Day T-shirt, and it was very apparent his dinner chef had been generous with the garlic.

Eve had been trading in ridiculous fantasy. She didn't want Chez. She wanted . . . something else.

'What do you do, Eve? Are you on TV also?'

'No, no, I'm an architect.'

'Hey, that's cool. How long are you in—'

'And this is my other sister.' Olivia reached over and turned him away from Eve. 'Rosalind.'

'Hi, Rosa—' Chez's eyes widened; he gestured in a circle. 'Wait, the three of you are *sisters*?'

Olivia's perfect eyebrow arched. 'That's what I said.'

Eve groaned silently, knowing what was coming. This was why she'd changed her name to Moore, her grandparents' last name. Rosalind had stuck with Braddock, while Olivia had taken Jillian's stage name for the most attention possible.

'Holy shit, you're *Jillian Croft's daughters*!'

'Shh.' Eve put a finger to her lips, anxious to shut him down before they attracted any more attention. 'It's a secret.'

'Shh, sorry.' He clamped a hand over his mouth. 'Oh my God. You're *her* daughters.'

'We are.' Olivia put her red-nailed fingertips to his arm and pushed gently. '*And* we're having a nice private time here, so you need to go away now.'

Eve was grateful to Olivia for taking charge, but she couldn't help snarkily wondering how quickly her sister would have sent Chez away if he'd been coming on to *her*.

'Right. I'm gone.' Chez backed up, waving the napkin. 'Thanks for this. Sorry to bug you.'

When he turned, Eve gestured to Olivia. 'Well, looky there. You're famous even in Blue Hill, Maine.'

'How about that?' Olivia went to put away her pen without looking. Eve heard it clatter to the floor and felt a tiny flare of satisfaction she was immediately ashamed of. 'But he was totally into you, Eve.'

Eve knew better than to agree. 'Trolling for whatever he could get.'

'Maybe I shouldn't have discouraged him. You could have had a fling.'

'Oh what uncomplicated fun *that* would have been.' Eve snorted, annoyed that she'd ever considered it. For some reason tonight she'd broken free of her usual personality. 'What were we talking about before?'

'You and the job in Wisconsin,' Rosalind said patiently. 'I was going to say that we're not going to tell you what to do, but—'

'Of course we are,' said Olivia.

'But if you don't do this . . .' Rosalind leaned forward gravely, brown eyes dancing, 'We will have to call you a hopeless super-sized weenie.'

'Not that!' Eve clutched her chest. The phrase had been Rosalind's ultimate insult as a girl, most often hurled at her younger sister, of course.

'*Vicious*.' Olivia tsk-tsked.

Eve lifted her beer. 'Or else!'

'Or else!' The three girls clinked and took another drink.

Eve laughed with her sisters and continued to chat as the subjects changed, but the evening's events and her uncharacteristic thoughts had shaken her. Being with her family had been a joy this weekend, where it was usually complicated and tiring. An attractive stranger's interest had been exciting and energizing where it was usually merely annoying.

She thought back to the rare nights when she and Mike went out, how often now they did things separately. How her job in Boston had kept her back instead of moving her forward. How even the promotion didn't hold much appeal to her tonight. And now the jobs in Wisconsin, which she'd all but decided to refuse, were back on the table, newly tempting as well as anxiety-inducing.

When their next round of drinks had been mostly consumed – Eve left half her second beer untouched – Rosalind drove them back to the Blue Hill Inn, where they hugged goodnight, still giggling at shared memories and teasing, promising to get up and meet at Dad and Lauren's for an early breakfast before they flew home, Eve to Boston, Olivia to LA and Rosalind to New York City.

In her unfamiliar bed, Eve lay awake for a long time, worrying, brooding, tossing, turning, then turning back.

By 3 a.m., mind still spinning, it hit her with a jolt of self-awareness that there had been two other times in her life when she'd started behaving out of character. The first, easy to understand, was in the years after her mother had died. Adolescent Eve had started hanging out with troubled kids, adopting their uniform: black hair, black lipstick and nail polish, black clothes, leather and metal. Three years later, when she was the only daughter left at home, Dad remarried. In Lauren's quiet presence, Eve had felt her goth getup reflected back at her not as rebellious cool, but as an ill-fitting costume she was desperate to own. That and their shared shyness meant Eve was closer to her plain-vanilla stepmother than either of her older sisters, who had had more time with their every-fruit-flavor-plus-chocolate mother.

The second time Eve had stepped outside her natural reserve, she'd been back in LA after graduating from Cornell, working in the same firm where she'd started as an intern in high school, hanging out with the same friends, going to the same places. She found herself drinking and partying way too much, crawling into work in the mornings feeling like hell, and doing it all over again the next night.

When Dad and Lauren sat her down and accused her of wasting her life the same day her boss suggested graduate school, Eve realized that party girl didn't fit her any better than goth, and promised from then on to be true to her real self.

Until tonight, she'd been convinced she'd done just that.

By 3.15, she was able to admit – painfully, reluctantly – that her sisters were right, and that she could no longer ignore the neon flashing signs of tonight's feelings. Promotion or not, Washington Island or not, somehow her life needed to change.

Chapter 2

February 11, 1971 (Thursday)

Holy Mother *of God, two days ago we had an earthquake. Terrifying. Horrible. It made me want to run back to Maine. Daniel said it's the earth adjusting, and now it's done there won't be another big one while we're living here, but I don't know. I dropped to my knees and prayed and prayed to God to save me, which I found out later was stupid. Not the praying part – I should have gotten out of the house! But He didn't let me die, even having been stupid, so that's something.*

Our house! It's beyond description, so beautiful and so elegant and so pink! *Christina didn't believe me when I told her where her big sister was living. I'll have to send her a picture. We have a pool and palm trees on the property. I feel like a queen here. Daniel makes me feel like a queen. He says I make him feel like a prince. And the weather! Let's just say this isn't the type of February I'm used to. Daniel will teach at UCLA. We're really truly settled here! Now we just need to make friends so we feel like real Californians.*

I got another bit part, in a Mel Brooks movie. I want more, more, more! *Bigger parts and bigger still! Daniel says be patient, that I'm doing all the right things. I'm not patient! Never have been. I want what I want when I want it. It makes me sound such a spoiled brat, but it comes from deep-down fear that things might not go the way I want them to, so the sooner they do, the better I feel, and calmer.*

Besides, how can I be a spoiled brat with the curse I was given and with how hard I've had to work to make this life happen? Except meeting Daniel. With that I was just lucky lucky lucky!

I just this second *got a call from my agent. I'll be reading for a big supporting role in a movie about a crime boss's secret family. My first! I can't stand it. I want this so badly.*

Love,

Me

PS I read with everything I had. They loved me, I could tell. When I got home, my agent called again with another audition. I am so excited I'm just floating all over our house. I dance, I leap, I spin, I shriek from the joy. I think life is about to get extremely busy.

I am ready*!*

Eve poured herself a glass of wine from a bottle on her kitchen counter that had probably been open too long to taste good. Her flight back from Maine had landed late due to a brief but intense snowstorm – few things were more annoying than late winter snow. Having to drag her suitcase up her unshoveled driveway had soaked her unprotected feet and further dampened her spirits. Usually coming home was a relief, back to her familiar bed and routines, not to mention her best friend Marx, who'd been waiting impatiently at the front door, wagging his fluffy tan tail. Marx was never in a bad mood. Marx's life was blissfully uncomplicated.

Now he nudged at her side, reminding her that she owed him a weekend of retroactive adoration.

'I missed you too.' She squatted to embrace him properly, allowing a few sloppy dog kisses, then took her wine into the living room. The house felt empty but peaceful. Mike was at his Sunday-night basketball game; he'd be home soon.

She opened the door to their new sunroom and stepped in without turning on the light, wanting to decompress from the travel, the busy social weekend and the annoyance of having to run the snow blower through the wet, heavy snow when she was so tired. Around her on three sides, the same snowy view that in November was shivery-enchanting, in December cheerfully festive, in January okay-it's-winter, in February pain-in-the-ass and by March just-shoot-me claustrophobic.

Meanwhile, she'd been thinking of traveling farther north. Wasn't Wisconsin under a white blanket from October to May? She'd have to check.

Even without Mike's objection or her possible promotion, it was easier not to go. Easier to have negative thoughts, convince herself it wouldn't work out, that she might not be able to handle the work, that she might not get along with Shelley, that she might irreparably harm her relationship with Mike.

And yet she was being pulled inexorably toward the job – by Lauren, by Shelley, by her father and sisters, by her lifelong ambition and creative itch, further stirred by her studies in college and graduate school, then left to stagnate in the confines of her current position. And by the forgotten seed Rosalind had planted last summer as they'd sat together in the kitchen of the Candlewood Point house, confirmed during last night's lack-of-sleep revelation at the Blue Hill Inn. She needed a change.

Eve hated change. It made her want to fist her hands, clench her teeth and dig in her heels like a toddler. *You . . . can't . . . make . . . me*. Probably why she'd clung to this job, hoping to be booted up the ladder instead of having to strike out on her own.

She heard the front door open and glanced at her watch. Mike must have come home right after the game.

Her heart sped at the same time as faint resentment warmed her chest. Didn't that just quantify how she felt about so many things these days? This wasn't like her at all. Her mother's mother, Grandma Betty, who still lived in the tiny town of Jackman, Maine, would call her wishy-washy. Namby-pamby. What else?

Milquetoast.

'Hi, Mike.'

'Hey.' He met her at the sunroom entrance with open arms. 'What are you doing standing here in the dark?'

'Standing here in the dark.' She went on tiptoe to kiss him, then slid her arms around his broad torso, relieved that her initial hesitation had vanished. Mike had showered and shaved at the gym and smelled soapy and sexy. 'Nice to see you.'

'Same here. Thanks for doing the driveway. Sorry you had to.'

'Not a problem. How was your game?'

'Real good.' His voice rose proudly. 'I scored twenty points.'

'Twenty! Impressive.'

'Thanks.' He released her and stepped back to turn on a light. 'You had a good weekend, huh?'

'I did. An entire three days together without any scenes.'

'Also impressive.' His sandy curls were still damp, his cheeks flushed from having exercised, making his Irish-blue eyes pop. 'Rosalind still blissed-out with her new boyfriend and family?'

'Apparently. She still seems to like us, though.'

'Olivia still a diva pain in the—'

'Yep.' Eve frowned. 'But . . . more fragile than I've ever seen her.'

'Fragile? Her! Ms I'm-all-the-universe-I-need-in-my-universe?'

'Ah-ah-ah.' She waggled her finger. 'She's my sister.'

'Half-sister.'

Eve felt her lips tighten, a jolt to her midsection. She didn't like thinking about that. But Mike was nothing if not precise. 'I guess that's true.'

'Dad's doing okay?'

'He is.'

'Lauren?'

The news from Shelley leapt into Eve's brain. She looked down at her feet. 'Lauren is Lauren, and forever shall be Lauren.'

'What happened?'

Her eyes jumped back to his face. 'What do you mean?'

'You just tensed, your whole body. Something happened with Lauren.'

She sighed, not in the mood for one of Mike's inquisitions. His insecurity could be sweet – it kept him from arrogance – but also exhausting. 'Nothing bad.'

'Okay, but . . .' he stepped forward and took her shoulders, 'you might as well tell me now.'

'I'm sorry, Mike, I don't want to talk about it now.'

His warmth chilled. 'We've discussed this. It's not fair to keep stuff back.'

'It's not fair to force me to talk about something when I'm not ready.' She wanted to cry. How long had he been home? Five minutes, and already they were fighting.

He let go of her, walked halfway across the room, hands on his hips, then turned. 'So I just sit around and wait until you choose to drop whatever this bomb is on me?'

'What makes you so sure it's a bomb?'

'Isn't it?'

'No. It's nothing like a bomb.'

'Then why the wait? Why not tell me now?'

She had no idea how this had happened to them. Where was the easy-going relationship they'd fallen into and maintained for so long? After the torrid intensity of her first two relationships, both of which ended abruptly when her older boyfriends graduated – Sam from high school, Dale from college – life with Mike had been like plowing a field with a tractor instead of a team of oxen.

Had he changed? Had she? Why did he no longer seem to trust her? She'd never given him any cause not to. But over the past several months she'd been feeling increasing pressure from him to spew up her innermost thoughts – which only made her work harder at hiding them. The worst kind of reaction.

Three years into their relationship, two years dating, one living together, she couldn't help feeling they should have built a solid enough foundation that this kind of conversation would be unnecessary.

I'm not ready to tell you.

I understand. I'm here when you need me.

She gave in, as she'd given in countless times, on the theory that if she was as transparent as possible, he'd no longer have cause to pry.

Wasn't the first sign of insanity trying the same thing time after time and expecting a different result?

'Shelley Grainger, Lauren's friend from Wisconsin, got over whatever illness she had, and has found the funding to do the project. She still wants me to come up and look at the job. And the one for her friend.'

Mike's full lips compressed disapprovingly. 'I thought we'd settled this.'

'No.' She tried to speak calmly, ending the word on a higher pitch to soften its impact. 'You said you didn't want me to do it, and then the project seemed to go away, so I dropped the subject.'

'I thought you said—'

She held up a hand to stop him. 'Mike, sweetie, I don't want to talk about this late on a Sunday when I'm exhausted and still in a happy place from being with my family. I want to process it for a while, maybe ask tomorrow at work what kind of time I could get off.'

'You were going to let your boss decide our relationship issues? Without checking with me first?'

It was almost as if he *wanted* to find something insidious about her choices. She couldn't explain this change. 'If I can't get the time off, then my decision isn't—'

'Our decision.'

She took a deep breath, annoyed to feel her legs trembling. 'This one is mine, Mike. It's my career. If you decided you wanted to switch schools, that wouldn't be up to me. I'd never dream of interfering.'

'Not the same. If I switched schools, I'd still be here every night in this house.'

'You don't need babysitting.' She crossed the room and put a hand to his cheek, hoping to steer the conversation back to an affectionate place. 'What is this really about?'

He held her gaze. 'You are leaving me. Piece by piece. This is the next one gone.'

Eve resisted the urge to escalate. She dropped her hand to his broad chest and looked up at him – the only guy she'd dated who was tall enough that she had to. 'There's one way I can convince you that's not true, and that is to go and come back.'

'If you go, you won't come back.'

Eve let out a sound of exasperation. She was all about escalation now. 'You can't tell me what I'm doing or feeling. You're being unreasonable. And melodramatic.'

'Actually, I'm seeing this very clearly and staying totally calm, which is very different from how I'm feeling inside.'

'How *are* you feeling inside?'

'Like you've turned to liquid or sand and you're running through my fingers. No matter how much I scoop up in one spot, you're slipping away in another.'

She felt a deep-down burn of guilt. Was she? Had she been? 'I love you, Mike. But you're wearing me down with your insistence that I don't love you enough or in the right way or whatever else you seem to think I'm—'

'That's not what—'

She shot up her hand to stop his interruption. 'This problem turns up behind every argument we have, and we have too many. I don't know how to combat that. Maybe this break will help us.'

The second she said the word 'break', Mike jerked as if she'd struck him. Eve had to fight a wave of panic. Why had she said that? She loved him. Their relationship was worth fighting for. The mantra came automatically, as if she were still trying to convince herself.

'You need a break.' He spoke slowly, sounding triumphant. 'There it is. Exactly my point.'

'Not like you're saying it. Not like it came out.' She turned away from his skepticism to keep her thoughts clear. It was snowing again, big, fat, slow flakes that drifted lazily on to the patio and lawn. It was rarely this still so close to the ocean. She'd bet that outside it was incredibly silent, incredibly peaceful. 'All I'm saying is that it seems as if lately we're driving each other crazy. Maybe it's just this godawful time of year, snowy and cold when we're ready for spring. I don't know. But don't you want that to stop? Turn off the engine and let it cool when it keeps reheating? Come back fresh and new to each other again and try—'

'No.'

She turned back, gesturing at nothing. 'Then what *do* you want?'

Mike set his jaw, legs solidly apart, arms folded, her great immovable object. 'I want you to *want* to stay here.'

Eve sighed and put a hand to her forehead. 'I'm sorry. I can't have this conversation again. It's the same circle we keep traveling around. I'm going to bed.'

He let her leave without comment. She looked back once and saw him, a scowling male statue, fists frozen to his hips. Marx sniffed his leg a couple of times, then followed Eve up the stairs.

Unpacked, showered and teeth brushed, she lay in their bed, thinking of her fantasy on the plane, in which Mike met her at the door the way he used to, dragging her squealing and giggling on to the sofa, where they'd make frantic love, desperate for each other after her absence.

Couldn't they do that anymore? Not even once in a great while? Maybe she should have jumped him when he walked in through the door. Maybe that was her mistake. Maybe he was right, and the chill between them was coming from her.

She turned on her back, staring up at a ceiling she couldn't see. No matter how deeply she trusted her thoughts and feelings, no matter how carefully she worked out her arguments, more and more often his point of view could make her feel unmoored from her instincts.

Had the shift started last summer when her dad had had the stroke and she'd found out about Jillian's condition? Mike had been in the depths of his depression then; she couldn't recall if her shock had made it worse, or whether emotional fallout she wasn't aware of had changed her since.

It was also possible that after starting in therapy, Mike had become more anxious, more needy as he confronted trust issues from his own upbringing. His parents had made expecting the worst from their youngest son into an art form. Maybe he was covering up that new vulnerability by becoming more controlling. In which case, she owed him rock-solid support, of the type Lauren had offered their father after his physical collapse. Her stepmother had hung in there for Dad, absorbing the worst of his temper and frustration on the long, slow crawl back from helplessness. Eve needed to do the same for Mike while he wrestled with his demons.

She groaned and flung herself over on to her stomach. This was *exactly* why she hadn't wanted to talk about this tonight. She was too worked up now to sleep, and she needed a clear head in the morning to make sure she was first in line for Tim's role, and to feel her boss out on the possibility of taking time off for the jobs in Wisconsin.

Of the three sisters, she'd always considered herself the most practical, the daughter with her feet most firmly on the ground. The one who'd known what she wanted from when she was old enough to conceive of an architecture career. The one who'd waited two years to be sure she and Mike were solid before he moved in with her. Not for her Rosalind's tendency to throw herself in with whatever man showed interest, then move out of state when she got bored. Nor would she be like Olivia, getting engaged three weeks after meeting Derek and never stopping to ask herself if she'd made a mistake, even now, so many years later, when she clearly had. Eve had done this the right way. Sanely. Intelligently.

But how sane or intelligent was it when she could no longer

tell if she was being selfish considering this job opportunity or if Mike was being selfish wanting to prevent her?

After more infuriating tossing and turning, wondering whether Mike would come upstairs or sleep alone in the sunroom, she finally drifted off – and embarked on one of her rage dreams.

In her twenties, the dreams had been about her trying to get a very emotional point across to her mother while Jillian sat calmly putting on makeup, not even pretending to listen, no matter how loudly Eve screamed or begged.

This one starred Mike, making basket after basket, some of the shots going through her as she yelled and ranted, failing even to get a glance. As far as he was concerned, she simply wasn't there.

When her alarm went off, Eve dragged herself out of bed and into the shower. The rumpled covers on Mike's side showed he had come to bed at some point, which meant he'd gotten even less sleep than she had. He'd be out running now, his usual dawn habit.

Eve was an early riser as well, but not *that* early. She generally ran also – a shorter distance than Mike – and they met up for breakfast before work. Today, however, in a display of spectacular cowardice, she skipped her run and left the house earlier than usual, so she'd be gone when he got back.

Bad, Eve, bad. But she needed her boss's input before she felt comfortable making a decision about going to Wisconsin, and before she encountered Mike again, who might insist on knowing if she'd made any decisions in her sleep.

She drove to the train station and took the Newburyport/Rockport line into North Station; then, because the air was chilly, the snow slow to melt, she skipped the twenty-minute walk in favor of taking the T green line to Park Street. Out in

Boston Common, she crossed to the building that housed Atkeson, Shifrin and Trim Architects, and bounded upstairs to the third floor, nervous energy keeping her away from the elevator.

Inside, she greeted the temporary receptionist who'd started three weeks earlier – Eve had forgotten her name, and by now was too embarrassed to ask her to repeat it. The firm had adopted an open-workspace concept, which made the large central room populated by workers sitting at L-shaped white desks feel bright and open, but meant privacy was pretty much non-existent, except for the bigwigs' offices around the room's perimeter, which had actual doors, walls and windows.

At her very own L-shaped white desk, Eve sat and turned on her computer, feeling jittery and thick-headed at the same time. She called up her current bathroom project and stared at it stupidly until her boss, Frank Trim, opened his office door, indicating that he was off whatever call he'd been on when she arrived.

Go.

She got up, pulling the hem of her olive-colored tunic to lie evenly over her black pants – she must own ten pairs – and strode over to Frank's door before anyone or anything else could distract him. She needed to get this conversation over with so she could relax. She hoped.

'Morning.' She fake-knocked on his door jamb. 'Got a second?'

'Hey, yes. Absolutely.' He beckoned her in. 'Have a seat.'

Frank was one of those middle-aged men whose face refused to wrinkle, whose jowls refused to sag, whose waist refused to thicken, because he was of good Long Island breeding stock and would have none of this aging business! When Eve had started at the firm, she had a crush on him for about two minutes, which was as long as it took him to open his mouth.

She took the chair in front of his desk, which she'd always suspected he used because its seat was unusually low. Even from her height – five-ten – she had to look up at him, feeling like a fourth-grader. 'Nice weekend?'

'So-so.' He leaned back in his chair, resting his elbows on the armrests, turning a pen in circles between his fingers. 'You?'

'Very nice. I was in Maine with family. Dad was celebrating his eightieth.'

'Yeah?' Frank clearly could not have cared less; not that Eve expected him to, but she didn't want to jump right into her request until she could gauge his mood. 'May we all be so lucky.'

'No kidding.' She smiled tightly, glad she'd never told anyone in the office who her father actually was. Being able to mention her famous parents without gawking and intrusive questions was very soothing. 'I wanted to talk to you.'

'Obviously.'

She'd let that go. 'A job opportunity has come up in Wisconsin.'

His eyebrows flew up, and she realized how that sounded.

'No, no, not permanent. One-time projects for a friend of my stepmother's, and a friend of hers. I'm considering going up there to give it a shot.'

'When?'

'Early April.'

'We can't spare you.'

'I have some vacation—'

'Sorry.' He shook his head.

'Okay, but . . . we're not that crazy these days. Seems like I could take some work with me and—'

'You were hired to work in this office. We're a team. We work as a team. This isn't a telecommuting job.'

'Right. Okay.' She watched him calculatingly. He was bullshitting her. Did that mean she was getting the promotion but he couldn't let her know yet? 'So Tim is leaving.'

'Yep.' Not the slightest change of expression, but the pen rotated faster.

'When I was hired, I was told I'd be moved up quickly.' She was about to state the obvious – *that hasn't happened* – but decided against it. 'With his job opening up, I was hoping I'd be first in line.'

'Yeah.' Frank shifted to a more upright position in his chair. 'I figured you'd want to be in contention.'

She waited. He watched her. What an asshole, making her squirm like this. But her hopes were rising. 'And?'

'The job is going to Robert.'

'Robert?' Eve stared. She couldn't believe her ears. 'He was hired last *month*.'

'Yes, he was.'

'Was I even considered?'

'Not for this job.'

'Why not?'

'He was more qualified.'

Eve was suddenly and blindingly furious. Robert was a disgusting suck-up, just talented enough to get a position, but no threat to Frank, who as far as she was concerned was the weak link in the company's partnership. She'd help *train* him, for God's sake. 'My work is as good if not better, and I've been here a lot longer. What's the real reason?'

'He's also good with clients.'

'And I'm not?'

'I'm saving you for something bigger.'

'What is it? And when is it coming?' She got to her feet, body shaking. An inner still-sane voice told her to sit down and stop talking. Or leave until she could calm down.

She did neither.

'You said when I was hired that I was too good for this job. You said I'd be at Tim's level within a year, maybe sooner. That hasn't happened. I was hired to—'

'You were *hired* because we had to hire a woman.'

She gaped at him, outrage momentarily sucked out of her by the shock, though it didn't take long to come crashing back. 'Tell me you did not just say that. You *had* to hire a woman? What kind of caveman crap is that?'

He gave her a condescending smile, white-knuckling his pencil. 'It's complicated.'

'No, it's actually very simple. Maybe I can explain.'

'I don't want to hear this.' He put down the pencil and folded his hands, which she was even more infuriated to notice were as still and calm as his freaky-young face.

'Fine. You need a woman in this office? You're going to have to hire another one.' Eve leaned across his desk, stabbing her finger on his blotter. 'Because I quit.'

She straightened in utter shock. What the hell had she just done?

'No. Don't do that.' Frank had the decency to look nervous. 'You don't mean it.'

Of course she didn't mean it. This was her job. Her livelihood.

A job she didn't need for the money.

A job she didn't need for her career.

It was just a job. And she was suddenly utterly sick of it.

Just as suddenly, she became absolutely calm and deliciously certain.

'I'll send my resignation to HR. Not that nice working with

you.' Smiling pleasantly, she turned and walked out to her desk.

'Hey. Eve.' Frank was calling from his office. 'Could you come back in, please?'

'Nope.' She turned off her computer, opened a drawer and yanked out her purse. 'I don't work here anymore.'

Co-workers turned shocked faces away from screens toward her. Eve was the quiet one, never raising her voice. The last one they'd ever expect to make a scene. What was she doing? What had happened?

'*Eve*.' His voice sharpened, authority figure needing to seem in control in front of the underlings.

She grabbed the picture of her father, Lauren and her sisters taken at Thanksgiving several years earlier, her only personal item in the place. As if she hadn't ever really wanted to feel settled there.

Seemed as if she needed to run into brick walls before she could see them.

She strode toward Frank, seeing his face relax and the beginnings of a smarmy victory smile. At the last second, a foot from his shiny, too-tight blue suit, she turned and made a beeline for the exit.

Chapter 3

August 22, 1971 (Sunday)

I'm so exhausted, I just want to lie in bed in a dark room and sleep and sleep and sleep. Why doesn't the world go away and let me do that? I don't want to be an actress anymore, I just want to be a normal wife and a mother. I can't stop crying because I never will be a mother, and now I'm not even a good wife. What is the point of being a woman if I can't do what I'm supposed to do? Why was I born into this gruesome, flawed body? Daniel keeps trying to get me to see a psychiatrist.

So now I'm crazy, too?

Eve got off the train and found her car in the parking lot. She'd spent the day in the city, first wandering distractedly through the Museum of Fine Arts, then in the Boston Public Library reading room, leafing through a book on the development of Back Bay's townhouses. After a listless lunch, she'd shopped unenthusiastically in boutiques on Newbury and Charles streets, finding nothing, mostly because she had no idea what she was looking for.

Now back in Swampscott, she wouldn't be expected at the house yet, and still didn't feel like going there. First, Mike would have a fit that she'd quit her job. He still had trouble understanding that thanks to her inherited third of Jillian Croft's fortune, being out of work didn't mean financial ruin. He wasn't a fan of abrupt changes and would think she'd acted rashly and irresponsibly, which she might have, but so far with few regrets. In fact, apart from dreading Mike's reaction, Eve mostly felt relief, a sure sign she'd done the right thing.

Second, having left Atkeson, Shifrin and Trim meant there was no longer any reason not to take the jobs on Washington Island, except that Mike didn't want her to go.

Two good reasons to expect more fighting.

When she reached the turn on to Puritan Road that would take her toward the house, she kept going, needing to feel a sea breeze on her face, to stand in the damp sand watching the waves come in and freezing her ass off.

Ten minutes later, she turned on to the appropriately named Beach Street, and pulled into the nearly empty parking lot at Devereux Beach, part of the town of Marblehead. A gust nearly blew the car door out of her hand. She slammed it shut and turned to walk down toward the sand, pulling up the hood of her navy jacket.

Waves rolled in, breaking in foamy sprays. The tide was turning to go out, having left wavy lines of seaweed at its peak a foot or so from the current waterline. One other person shared the beach with her, a guy walking his dog a fair distance away.

Eve folded her arms and stood, wind buffeting her back, gazing out at the whitecaps and the horizon, listening to the surf pounding the sand. The light was dimming – the sun would be setting soon, though its rays were hidden by clouds.

So.

She'd quit her job.

'Ha!' The syllable burst out of her, barely audible over the insistent tumbling water.

The mature and sensible adult part of her was still a bit stunned.

The girl who had grown up chafing under paternal authority and rejecting her mother's slavery to her career image was incredibly proud of her.

Eve took a deep breath, and with that strange certainty that came from subconscious decision-making, she knew.

If she could get Mike to agree, she'd go to Washington Island. The opportunity for real, meaningful work of the type she hoped to spend her life doing had dropped into her lap. She'd be a fool to give into the fear and turn it down. Worst case, she'd do a crappy job for nearly no money, and Shelley would have to hire someone else to draw up plans she liked. The change of routine would do Eve good. Maybe it would do both her and Mike good. They'd gotten to such a bad place after such a great beginning.

During her second year at Harvard's GSD – Graduate School of Design – romance hadn't been on her radar. She'd spent her senior year at Cornell single after Dale dumped her, finding it lonely but so much easier to manage her course load and her extracurriculars – theater tech, intramural soccer, cycling club, and Habitat for Humanity. After graduation, intimidated by the idea of starting at Harvard, she'd decided to stay single until she earned her master's and had established a career.

As her dad would say: *Famous last words.*

After surviving their first year at the GSD, Eve and friends had been out celebrating at the exquisitely retro and very popular Trina's Starlite Lounge in Somerville. Packed bars were not generally Eve's thing, but some of her friends thought standing elbow to elbow shouting over people who were shouting over other people, all shouting over the ridiculously loud music, made for an excellent time. That night she'd gotten into the spirit of the evening enough to convince herself she didn't mind the crush.

While making an undoubtedly profound point, so profound she couldn't remember it, Eve had gestured expansively at exactly the same moment someone jostled her arm, which sent most of her beer cascading down Mike's back.

Horrified, she had apologized profusely, trying to use a tiny cocktail napkin to blot up the mess, expecting him to be furious. Instead, he'd grinned and shrugged, holding her gaze. 'It'll dry.'

She was used to guys hitting on her. She had the kind of blond, slightly exotic look men noticed, which until last summer Eve had assumed she'd inherited from her stunning mother and handsome dad. She'd never expect sympathy for having something so many women were sure they wanted, but the type of male attention she got never ceased to appall her. As if they thought she lived in a constant state of wanting immediate sex from whomever approached. In other words: as if she were a man.

That night she'd insisted on buying Mike an I'm-sorry drink. As they chatted, she'd waited for him to start the preening, the puffery, the swagger and all the other peacock-like behaviors that would indicate he was ready for mating.

Nothing. He talked, she talked. He made her laugh. She made him laugh. They found things they had in common – movies they hated, restaurants they loved – and plenty they didn't. When her friends had been ready to leave Trina's, he'd given her a slip of paper with his phone number and the phrase *If you feel like it* scrawled in black ink, then nothing but a friendly goodbye. Her last look that night had been at the drying back of his shirt when she glanced to see if he was ogling her ass as she walked away.

As she'd said so often, Mike was a surprise.

Eve had spent a week looking at his number, turning over reasons to call and reasons not to, then finally gave in. School was out. She'd be interning at a low-key firm in Cambridge – a summer fling would be fun. When fall started and classes resumed, she would explain to Mike that she no longer had time for a relationship, but that she'd enjoyed knowing him and goodbye.

Yeah, that part hadn't happened.

'Lovely evening.'

She turned with a start, not having heard the beach's dog-walking occupant's approach over the wind and waves, and not having seen him around her hood. 'Oh. Not really.'

'Good for brooding, though.'

She wasn't biting. 'Hen or mare?'

He looked confused, then his face cleared. She'd put him at forty, maybe younger, the kind of unremarkable features that probably looked awkward in adolescence but had matured into an attractive balance. 'Oh, I see. Brood hen, mare. Slow on the uptake here.'

'S'okay.' She half turned away, hoping he'd take the hint.

He didn't. He stood next to her, his dog sniffing suspiciously at the hem of her jacket, undoubtedly picking up scents of Marx.

Eve sighed. Was hugging herself in the middle of a deserted beach in crappy weather not enough of an indicator that she wanted to be alone?

'It'll get better.'

She gave him a startled look. 'Sorry?'

'I said it will get better. You'll come through and be fine.'

'What are you talking about?'

'I have no idea.' He grinned, wind pushing his wavy hair forward into chaos. 'Just thought you might need to hear that.'

'How do you know I'm not here celebrating a gigantic victory?'

'Because the beach for victories is Preston. Devereux is for misery.'

She smiled in spite of herself. 'I did not know that.'

'Dumped? Fired? Diagnosed?'

'Do you always ask strangers such personal questions?'

'Always.' His blue eyes were amused, which made him even more attractive, though she had the distinct impression he was gay, for no reason she could consciously identify. 'I'm a therapist.'

Eve cracked up, first real laugh of the day, and felt some of her tension loosen. 'So you come to the beach of misery looking for people about to hurl themselves into the drink?'

'God, no. I'm walking my dog.'

She laughed again, then stood with him watching the charging waves curl up and up before tripping over the sand and tumbling into foamy defeat.

'I quit my job this morning.' Why had she told him that? 'Wasn't planning to. I just did.'

'How do you feel now?'

'A little freaked out. But not too bad.'

'Are you looking behind or ahead?'

'Ahead. I've been offered a temporary job out of state, designing a house and a sunroom.' The words came easily, and with them a burst of pride. She turned to him, having to hang on to her hood to keep it from blowing back. 'I haven't even told my boyfriend yet. You must have therapy superpowers.'

'Much easier telling a stranger big news. No connection. No fallout. Poof, I'm gone in . . .' he looked at his watch, 'two minutes. Without knowing anything really, it sounds to me like you did a wise and brave thing. Will your boyfriend be supportive?'

Eve shrugged out of loyalty to Mike, eating up the words of praise.

'Are you afraid of him?' The therapy-stranger watched her intently. 'Any violence in the relationship?'

Eve recoiled. 'No, God no, nothing like that.'

'It happens.'

She was annoyed now, wanting him and his piercing eyes to go away. 'I'm safe with him.'

He fished a card out of his wallet. 'If you need to talk more. Otherwise toss it.'

His card had an oak tree on one side, a willow on the other, his name in between. Joseph Simington.

'Thank you.' Eve put the card in her pocket. She'd toss it. 'And for your . . . kindness.'

'Sure. Nice to meet you.'

She watched him walk away, wondering how he could stand listening to people's problems all day, wondering how he'd gotten her to admit to even the tiniest bit of her own.

Darkness was falling in earnest now. One more breath of the salty, bracing air and she turned and trudged back to the parking lot, where Joseph's car was just pulling out.

Feeling lighter after her time by the sea, Eve left the beach and drove back to her house, her determination to have a pleasant conversation with Mike deepening the closer she got, along with the determination not to let him gaslight her this time.

As she turned off Puritan on to Littles Point Road and saw the cars gathered around her driveway, her positive feelings wilted. She'd forgotten. First Monday of the month, Mike's poker night, and his turn to host. Her house would be full of his friends, men she liked fine individually, but who when they got together turned into a group of stupid-guy-movie extras.

Dread mounting – unreasonably; their fun was loud but harmless – Eve opened the front door just as the yelling started. She turned the corner into the dining room in time to see the guys gathered around a laptop with a video playing.

She moved to one side and caught a glimpse. A woman on a low table on all fours, naked except for a spiked dog collar and leash, and a man behind her in a black suit, pants around his ankles. Once Eve registered what the couple were doing – *ouch* – she started backing out of the room, hoping to escape notice.

Then the camera pulled back to reveal the difference in their ages. The man was in his fifties. The woman turned her head, revealing herself to be younger than Eve had initially thought. No longer a girl, but not yet a woman. Too young.

Eve's gasp couldn't have been loud enough to penetrate the yelling, but one of the guys – Bill, she thought his name was – caught sight of her. His expression of fierce, almost violent rapture morphed into shock. He reached to slam down the lid of the laptop. The men's howls of protest fell silent as they realized why he'd cut the fun short.

'Eve.' Mike had the good sense to look embarrassed. 'This isn't . . . We don't usually . . . It was just—'

'Disgusting. It was just disgusting. If you want to play poker in my house, you are welcome. If you want to watch that *crap* –' Eve gestured contemptuously to the laptop – 'find somewhere else.'

She left the room, face hot with fury, and climbed the stairs, figuring that once she was out of sight, they'd try to get their dick-dignity back by dissing her. She could only hope Mike would be on her side.

Guys will be guys, she got that, especially guys in a group. She'd like to think none of the men downstairs – or at least not all of them – would watch something like that alone at home.

But she couldn't rationalize away the shock and the outrage, not all of it.

Not enough.

Head pounding, she walked into the bedroom, which she'd taken pains to decorate in a way that would fit Mike as well as herself, muted colors, straight angles in the furniture layout. Traditional art.

Still shaking, she downed three ibuprofen and two glasses of water. The last half of the second glass was hard to swallow. She felt cold, suddenly, then weak.

Her breathing and heartbeat accelerated.

Aw, hell.

It had been so long, she hadn't recognized the symptoms, though she did remember how to handle the attack.

There is nothing wrong with me. I'm not in danger. I'm fine. She knew it was true, even if the rest of her body wasn't convinced. *There's no one else up here. All the guys are downstairs with Mike.*

Breathe slowly. Relax. What was the other advice?

Hold something. She ran to the bed and grabbed a pillow, sat on her side of the mattress, closed her eyes and talked to herself like the lunatic she resembled.

There is nothing wrong with me. I'm not in danger. I'm fine.

Downstairs she could hear the guys leaving. She'd broken up their party and couldn't feel bad about it, except it meant Mike would be up soon.

He couldn't find her like this. She didn't want to explain, though there were worse things than admitting you had panic attacks sometimes.

Like admitting why.

Quitting her job was a convenient explanation, though her

obvious misery would put a wrench in trying to spin her leaving as a positive step.

Breathe. She buried her forehead in the comforting softness of the pillow, leaving her nose and mouth unobstructed, and told herself again and again that she was fine. This was a dirty trick her body was playing on her. Nothing more.

Dammit, she thought she'd gotten over this craziness years ago.

Five minutes later, the attack had subsided to the point where she could cope. Her heart was still pounding too hard, but Eve was confident she could function normally enough.

Two minutes later, Mike's heavy tread came up the stairs – slowly. He must be as unenthusiastic about seeing her as she was about seeing him.

Eve lifted her head. This would be over soon. She'd be fine. Today's trigger was an aberration. She had this under control, had worked through the problem on her own and was fine.

Mike's tall form appeared in the doorway. He'd lost the extra weight gained over the summer during the worst of his depression. Some he'd put back on in recent weeks, but he still looked good. 'Hey. Eve. I'm sorry you saw that.'

'Not sorry you were watching it?'

He gestured helplessly. 'Dennis put it on. It's not my thing, but I would have looked like a dork trying to stop it. We're guys. We're all assholes. We can't help it.'

'That's it? You're off the hook for whatever other disgusting things you do?' She let her hand plop back down on the pillow, telling herself to calm down, not to make him suspicious. 'Women joke about guys being led around by their dicks, but in spite of all evidence to the contrary, we still keep hoping it's not true.'

'It was harmless fun.'

'Harmless? Did you see the age difference? She was barely legal.' Her legs had started shaking again; she clenched them together, reminding herself that she was okay, that she didn't need to get so upset.

'Okay. I already explained. What more do you want? It was gross and I won't do it ever again, Mommy? Speaking of which, I asked you not to call this *your* house in front of the guys, like I'm some kind of kept man.'

Eve stared at him, mouth open, stunned by his anger, though she had previously been on the receiving end of that kind of temper when he'd been drinking or felt humiliated. In this case, both.

Her rage receded, rational thought took over. Mike was correct that he'd asked her not to mention that the house was hers. Eve had agreed, but in the heat of the moment, she'd forgotten. This was a little thing. If an apology calmed him down, he might do better with the rest of her news. 'I did promise. I'm sorry.'

'Thank you.' He put his hands on his hips, frowning at her. Such a handsome guy, her big Irishman. She wanted to experience the usual rush of love to warm her through, but felt hardly anything. Maybe a trickle. 'So what happened today? Have you been promoted?'

'Nope.' She put the pillow back on the bed, then felt too exposed and grabbed it again. 'This time I quit.'

Mike's expression sagged into disbelief. 'Tell me you're joking.'

'I'm not joking. This is the second time they've passed me over.'

'You can't just quit like that.'

'Mike, of course I can. I'm not slave labor.' Her voice cracked. When had he stopped taking her side? When was the last time he'd been her champion? 'I deserved that job. Why are you more upset at me for quitting than at them for not promoting me?'

'Oh, sorry.' He laughed bitterly. 'Once again I'm not the boyfriend you wish I was.'

She blinked. What was this hostility about? Guilt for what he'd been caught participating in downstairs? She wanted to say what she was thinking: *Does it always have to be about you?*

Instead she said what she always said.

'Sorry.' She wasn't sorry. How had that word become so meaningless? She should save it for when she actually meant it and invent another one for times like this: *Aw, honey, I'm splorcher*.

'I was upset about you quitting because it was a bigger shock than you not being promoted. Okay? I'm not a terrible person, Eve.'

But he'd just made her feel like one. Again. 'I know.'

'Come on.' He sat down next to her on the bed and took her hand. She hoped he didn't notice how clammy it was. 'I don't want to fight like this.'

'I don't either.' She put the pillow aside, still feeling cold all the way through. Cold and numb. A coping mechanism, she supposed, to help her recover from the attack.

'I guess now you're free you'll take that job in Wisconsin.'

Eve pulled her hand away and stood, shaky but okay. 'I met a guy at Devereux Beach today.'

'What, so you're leaving me for *him* now?'

'Ha ha.' She folded her arms across her chest and managed to look at Mike. 'He said I'd done a wise and brave thing. That made me feel really good.'

'He's a total stranger!'

'He's a therapist.'

'Who doesn't know you from Adam.'

'Eve.' She gave an absurd giggle.

'Not funny.'

'I know. Sorry.' Sorry again, always sorry. She remembered their first nights together, how they'd laughed and laughed over everything, giddy with a happiness she'd never felt before.

Back then if she said she was sorry, his answer was always the same: *You don't have to apologize to me for anything.*

She stepped forward, bringing her legs in contact with his. 'Can we start this over?'

'Yes.' He pushed a hand through his hair, making the curls stretch and fight each other. 'Yes. C'mere. We'll start over. You just got home . . .'

Eve climbed into his lap and wrapped her arms around him, trying not to be dismayed at the smell of alcohol coming off him. 'Gee, Mike. It seems you're watching porn.'

'The guys had it on. I thought it was gross. I should have put a stop to it. But when you walked in, you reacted like you didn't know who I was anymore. That hurt.'

'The video freaked me out.' *Because I was molested when I was young by a man in his fifties* . . . Such simple words. She couldn't say them, had never said them.

'So, how was your day at work, dear?' He spoke in a goofy artificial voice.

'I didn't get promoted, so I quit.'

'They didn't *promote* you!?' His big-time outrage made her laugh. 'That's *terrible*. I don't *blame* you for quitting.'

'But you don't like it either.'

'No.' He was serious now, stroking her hair in a way that seemed designed to comfort him more than her. 'It scares me.'

'Why?'

'I don't know. Maybe because Dad was out of work a lot and the family really suffered.'

'We won't suffer.'

'I know that. Rationally.' He kissed her, softly, sweetly, over and over until she felt herself coming to life again, responding, pushing him back on to the bed and climbing on top of him.

They made love, slow and tender, the way she liked it best, hands and mouths never resting, sharing each other's pleasure. Afterwards he gathered her up tightly against him – she never managed to be comfortable that way, but the break from their battling was so lovely she didn't care.

'Eve?'

'Mmm?'

'Tell me why you want to go to Wisconsin.'

'It's weird.' She traced the defined lines of his pectorals, sweeping down and back up. 'It's like I have to. There are things I have to figure out.'

'You sound like your wacky sister.'

She snorted. 'Which one?'

'Rosalind. What do you need to figure out?'

'If I can handle the job. How I function independently.' She put a soothing hand on his cheek. 'Professionally, I mean. Not without you.'

Though maybe that was part of it too.

'Okay. Then you should go.'

She lifted her head and studied his face. 'Really? You mean it? It's okay with you?'

'It's not fair of me to hold you back.'

She heard his therapist's voice in his answer, wondering if he'd seen or called her today after their discussion last night. 'You're sure?'

'No, I'm not sure. It still makes me crazy.'

If he'd said anything else, she wouldn't have believed him. 'I've been designing bathrooms and elevator shafts for a long time, Mike. I want to challenge myself with something worth doing. See how good I am, make mistakes and fix them. Work with clients, one on one, listen to what they need and try to design something to fit. I'll be gone two or three weeks. Maybe longer, not sure.'

'Wis-*kahn*-sin, eh?' He did a pretty good Midwestern accent. Not like Bostonians had any right to make fun. She still couldn't figure out how people made 'short' and 'shot' sound like the same word.

'The Cheesehead Nation.' She poked him, hit by a great idea. 'Hey, if this takes a while, I might be gone during your spring break. Why don't you go visit your brother in Florida like you've wanted to forever? Play a bunch of golf. Lounge by the pool . . .'

'I don't know.' His hopeful expression belied his doubtful tone. 'I've been saving for a new car.'

Eve made a sound of exasperation. 'Do I have to say this again? If our positions were reversed, wouldn't you pay for me?'

'Yes, but—'

'But nothing. Stop being such a caveman.'

He grunted, *oogh*. Rolled her over and grunted again. This was when they were good together. The fun times.

The easy part.

'Go on.' He grabbed her phone from beside the bed and handed it to her. 'You know you want to.'

'What? What are you talking about?'

'Call Lauren right now and tell her you'll do it.' He grunted again, scowling. 'Before your caveman changes his mind.'

Chapter 4

June 2, 1975 (Monday)

Dear Diary,

I'm writing again because my head doctor told me I should record my thoughts and feelings. Yes, doctor, yes, doctor. The crazy woman does what she's told. Good, crazy woman! Gold stars, crazy woman!

What great news! In addition to my barren, half-male body, I also have a deformed mind! Manic-depressive. Bipolar. Such ugly terms.

Daniel calls me a handful, which is so much kinder. He is the reason to take the meds and suffer their awful consequences – unless I'm working on a film, then I won't take them. Because when I am in front of a camera I can't be some dumbed-down Stepford Wife version of Jillian Croft. I have to be me, in all my radiant glory.

So on the one hand, I have success beyond anything I ever imagined. And on the other, I am foully and shamefully cursed. The Lord hath given to me and the Lord hath snatched back with both hands, the greedy bastard.

Apart from the love of a wonderful man, which I found in Daniel, I have only ever wanted two things in life: the chance to share with the world what I am meant to do on stage or screen, and the chance to try to make up in some small measure for what my parents did to me. To nurture and love the way mothers are supposed to, instead of judging and pushing away. To watch a child grow without ever making him feel he isn't human the way you'd like him to be.

I am no longer so enamored with God's plan for my life. Wouldn't it make more sense to give this twisted body to a woman who hates children? To give the crazy brain to someone who works in obscurity where it doesn't matter so much?

O Lord of Lords, to thy blue and ample heavens I cry foul. Fie on thee for this cruel bullshit.

The drive from Swampscott to Washington Island took three days. After an awkward and painful goodbye to a stoic, resigned Mike, Eve left on March 25 in her beloved forest-green Mercedes, which she'd bought eleven years earlier when she went to college. Before starting the trip, she'd spent a couple of weeks back at the office part-time, wrapping up her job, then a week just for herself, during which she took Marx for long, chilly beach walks, caught up on some reading, made a couple of romantic dinners for Mike and researched Wisconsin building codes and the existing types and styles of housing on the island.

Marx was a good passenger, sitting contentedly in his crate, his need for potty breaks and water keeping Eve from spending too many consecutive hours behind the wheel. She made it to Buffalo the first night, and nearly to the Indiana/Illinois border the second, after a distinctly less scenic drive that included a glimpse of the RV/Motor Home Hall of Fame on Route 80. For several miles after passing the building, she entertained herself wondering what qualified a person or vehicle for such an honor. Length of ownership? Miles traveled?

Wisconsin's I-94, less truck-filled and trafficked, led to

Milwaukee, a smaller, more attractive city than Eve had expected. In a surprisingly short time she was past and into the northern suburbs on I-43, through flat fields and birch-heavy woods, passing Sheboygan then nearly to Green Bay, home of the famous Packers football team.

She couldn't resist overshooting to stop in the city for a quick lunch and a peek at Lambeau Field, where she took a couple of stadium pictures to torment Mike, a diehard Patriots fan. Backtracking slightly, she picked up Route 57, which ran the length of the Door County peninsula. Her first view of the lake astounded her. Big. Ocean-like. Back in Swampscott researching travel routes, she'd discovered a high-speed ferry – which didn't start running until April – that bisected the caterpillar-shaped lake from Michigan to Milwaukee. At thirty-four knots the trip took two and a half hours.

As she said, big.

Once she'd crossed the harbor bridge at Sturgeon Bay, the first largish town on the peninsula, she left Route 57 for Route 42 in order to travel the more populated northern shore of Door County. The rural highway was dotted with billboards for cherry and apple orchards, roadside farm stands, restaurants, ice cream stores, antique shops and other attractions, most closed now during the off season. Eve could guess that the mostly deserted road was packed with tourists during the warmer months, and was glad she was coming this time of year, even if late March meant colder temperatures and, except for evergreens, a rather bleak landscape.

Towns came and went, identical, at least to her, in their old-town summery quaintness: Egg Harbor, Fish Creek, Sister Bay, Gills Rock. As she drove toward Northpoint Pier, her destination at the very tip of the peninsula, where she'd catch the ferry to Washington Island, civilization all but disappeared, and the highway, for no apparent reason – so bizarre, she started laughing – began curving back and forth as if the planners had been drinking too much Door County cherry brandy.

Toward the end of the narrow two-lane road she slowed behind a row of stopped cars, not sure if there was a traffic problem or if she'd reached the line for the three o'clock ferry. No signs to give her a clue, and she couldn't see the lake, though her phone's GPS insisted it was just ahead. The Washington Island Ferry website had indicated that tickets were first come, first served, but she had no idea how many cars were ahead of her or how many the ferry held.

She put her car in park and emerged into air much chillier than it had been in Green Bay to spring Marx from his crate and snap on his leash. Up the line of cars she walked, counting fifteen ahead of her until the road ended in a paved lot with a small blue drive-up ticket booth roughly at its center. Beyond that, the pier and a ferry currently unloading its cargo of passengers and cars.

Eve bought a round-trip ticket, then, in spite of the damp chill, took a moment to watch waves splashing against the stacked-stone breakwaters, on which were perched gray and white herring gulls, birds very familiar to her, but in an ocean context. There were other similarities to Maine, but the abundance of deciduous trees made the land here look as if it had molted. The air was light, crisp, clean, but curiously devoid of scent, like a sterile version of the Atlantic she loved so much. At the shoreline, no seaweed, no shells, no signs of thriving marine life.

Disappointing.

A frigid gust sent her shivering back to her car, where she waited, petting Marx in the passenger seat while he sniffed excitedly out the window, praying she made it on to this boat and wouldn't have to wait two more anxious hours for the next ferry before she could meet Shelley and get started. Anticipating was much more nerve-racking than doing.

The brake lights of the cars ahead of her lit as their engines came to life. Eve followed suit, and was able to move forward surprisingly quickly. The men loading the ferry had the job down to a speedy science. Not only did Eve make it on, but so did three cars behind her.

Needless worry. She was expert at it.

The Mercedes set in its berth, Eve and Marx climbed up to the top deck to watch their journey in the open air, for as long as they could stand the cold. As the boat started chugging out of the quiet harbor, enough cloud cover lifted to allow a ray of sun through, lighting the island in the near distance like a beacon of welcome. Eve grinned at the very Rosalind-like thought that it must be a good omen.

The trip was short, less than half an hour over respectably rough water. That, and the wide, blank horizon, made Eve constantly have to remind herself she was not on an ocean. She hadn't previously known much about the Great Lakes other than the grade-school acronym all kids memorized to remember the five names: Huron, Ontario, Michigan, Erie, Superior – HOMES.

When the ferry entered the calm-again waters of a large cove on the southwestern part of Washington Island, Eve and Marx returned to the car, chilled but refreshed after the long drive. Unloading was accomplished quickly, and Eve left the ferry terminal behind, following Shelley's instructions, allowing a delighted Marx the chance to ride up front with her on the nearly deserted roads. She drove north through thick woods, then turned right on to Lakeview Road and crossed the island to its easternmost side before heading south on Hemlock Drive until she reached Shelley's driveway, marked by a mailbox painted with the distinctive red-patched head of a sandhill crane.

She'd made it.

Immediately shyness showed its annoying head, making her palms sweaty and her heart thud. For heaven's sakes. She wasn't heading for the gallows. Lauren had assured her that while Shelley wasn't a woman of many words, she was kind and thoughtful. After a brief email exchange, initiated by Eve when communicating through Lauren started feeling middle-school bizarre, she had quickly understood the 'few words' label, Shelley's abruptness making her use too many exclamation points in her responses. 'Kind and thoughtful' remained to be proven.

Shelley's driveway, unpaved like most Eve had passed on this part of the island, traveled quite a ways through the cedar-heavy woods. None of the houses here were visible from the road, and given the thick forest, likely not from each other, preserving for the residents precious privacy and the illusion of isolation.

A curve widened the driveway into a parking area at the back of the house, which faced the lake. Eve got out of the car, again expecting the intoxicating Maine blend of Christmas tree, salt water and life, and being disappointed. The air here was too clean, too pure. The lake smelled like . . . water.

Marx bounded out, as thrilled to be somewhere new as she was anxious, and began sniffing for an appropriate tree to become acquainted with. Eve grabbed her suitcase from the back of the car, and the smaller bag containing supplies for Marx – her computer and wide-format printer could be retrieved later. She slammed the trunk and headed toward the house. A woman who must be Shelley was just stepping out of the door.

Shelley wasn't smiling, which sent Eve's grin wider, as if she could force a responding one by trying harder.

It didn't work any better than her exclamation-pointy emails.

Her client was shorter than Eve had imagined, and on the heavy side, though she moved easily. Her salt-and-pepper hair was cut close to her head, and she wore wire-rimmed glasses, a plaid shirt and faded jeans.

'Shelley?'

'Eve.' In a surprisingly deep voice, she announced the name as though she'd just decided what to call her, and stared rather fixedly, which made Eve have to struggle not to look away. 'Yes, I'm Shelley.'

'Nice to meet you.' Eve put down her case to shake hands. 'Your place is beautiful.'

Shelley twisted around as if just noticing there was a house behind her, then went back to her staring. 'Yes.'

Marx came up to her, tail wagging, and put his nose exactly where he shouldn't.

'Marx.' Eve held her breath. Shelley had said she liked dogs, but everyone had limits, and Marx was certainly testing one.

'Well, aren't you friendly.' She firmly pushed the dog's snout away and patted his golden flank.

'This is Marx. He's usually well behaved. You won't have a problem with him.'

Shelley looked down at Marx's friendly face, a relief after the intense inspection she'd made of Eve's. 'I don't have problems with animals.'

Her slight emphasis on the last word made Eve wonder if she had problems with humans. 'That's good. He's a great dog.'

'Come in.' Shelley turned abruptly. 'I'll show you the house.'

'Thank you.' Eve followed her up the steps into the small, nondescript foyer. Keeping a brisk pace, Shelley led her into the kitchen, which had clearly been modernized. The room was clean and sleek, cool and subdued in white and gray with stainless appliances. At the lake end of the room, a breakfast nook with a small table and chairs, and beyond that, the porch, which looked to be closed in with storm windows for winter use. Glimpses of a dining room showed a comfortable, minimally furnished space with lovely views of the lake.

Next to the kitchen, a living room, done in muted colors – olive, beige, taupe – which gave an equally detached impression as the kitchen, and was equally as spare as the dining room. A sofa, a chair, a coffee table, and an upright piano against one wall.

With a start, Eve realized she'd done her own house in many of the same colors, but felt she'd accomplished understated sophistication. Did people find her house cold?

She paused to look around again, trying for new eyes. Maybe Shelley's place seemed dull because Eve had expected the interior of a lake house to have a bright, summery feel.

Still silent, Shelley strode toward a wooden staircase, passing a room containing a large desk and chair, then up to the second floor, and straight into one of the bedrooms, all sunshine yellow and royal blue, a stark contrast to the muted shades downstairs. Near the bed, made up with a blue and white polka-dot comforter and a yellow blanket at its foot, was a large dormer with a cushioned window seat where it would be impossible not to sit and gaze out at the lake.

'Here's your room. My daughter's.' Shelley looked around blankly at the two bright yellow walls and the two painted royal blue. 'Her colors, her room. She insisted you have it.'

'That's nice of her.'

'She's a nice person.'

Eve was going to have to get used to Shelley's way of talking, as if she were being forced to admit to a series of blunt and uncomfortable facts. 'It's a beautiful room.'

'You can use the office downstairs to work. The room we passed at the foot of the stairs. Anything else you need? Towels are there.' She pointed to the folded yellow stack on a white chair. 'Use either bathroom up here.'

'Thank you.'

Shelley headed for the door, then stopped. 'Dinner's at five thirty. In the dining room.'

Five thirty? At home, she and Mike ate at seven at the earliest. Thank goodness she'd had a small lunch. 'Can I help?'

'Rest today. You can help tomorrow.'

'Sure. Oh . . .' She pointed to Marx. 'Anything about Marx you want to restrict? Rooms he shouldn't go in? Other house rules?'

'He's fine.' Shelley looked down at the dog, hands on her sturdy hips. 'You can put his bowls in the kitchen.'

'Thanks.' Eve stood smiling while her hostess left, then abandoned the effort. Shelley would take work. Like Lauren, she was from the Maine coast north of Bar Harbor, the area known as 'Down East'. Eve had spent enough time in New England to recognize people who epitomized its famed reticence.

But.

Making conversation wasn't Eve's strong point, and it obviously wasn't Shelley's either. Eve couldn't imagine the two of them chatting away like old friends over dinner. Possibly not even if they *did* become old friends.

If God was feeling merciful, Shelley would serve a lot of good wine with whatever she was cooking. Wine helped shy tongues move more easily.

If He was feeling even more merciful, Shelley would be a decent cook.

Eve took out her phone to call Mike, as she had done the two previous evenings. He'd been mostly mopey, rattling around the empty house, missing her, missing Marx. Mike was an extrovert to the point where he was uncomfortable unless he was actively engaging in conversation with another person. Eve loved her alone time. It had taken a while to work that balance out between them. Luckily he'd made several plans already for the time she was gone, though he still wouldn't agree to a Florida trip.

'I'm here. In one piece. Marx is fine too.'

'How's the place?'

'It's a beautiful house. Big Federal, added on to a couple of times and updated fairly recently. Gorgeous porch with a view of the lake. Gorgeous lake. My God, it's huge. Have you ever seen one of the Great Lakes?'

'Sure. My family visited Mom's sister in Chicago once. Big.'

'Big! I mean I knew that, you can tell on a map, but until you see the size, nothing but horizon on the opposite side . . . you really have no idea.'

'Yeah.' He made his stretching noise. She could picture him watching TV with a few beers for company before dinner. 'What's Shelley like? Have you talked design yet? What about her friend?'

'I only just got here. Shelley . . . she seems nice. Very . . . Maine, don't know if you know what I mean. Says only what she needs to, smiles only when something's funny . . .'

'Same types in New Hampshire and Vermont.'

'Yes.' Eve sank to the bed, suddenly tired, homesick for familiar surroundings. 'What are you doing?'

'Well. Let's see.' His voice rose a notch. 'Watching TV. Going to grade some papers later. The usual. I miss you.'

'Same here.' *Sort of*. 'But the time will go quickly. Then I'll be back.'

'Yeah.' He wasn't convinced. After he'd told her to go ahead and take the job, they'd had a miserable three weeks together, Eve anxious, Mike sullen, regretting his decision but not enough to change his mind, not that it would have made a difference after Eve told Shelley she was coming.

'I need to go.' She glanced at her watch. 'It's dinner time around here soon, and I haven't unpacked yet.'

'Soon? Aren't you an hour earlier there?'

'Uh-huh.' She found herself smiling, waiting for him to figure it out.

'Wait, dinner time is *soon*? How soon?'

'Five thirty.'

'Five-thirty dinner.' He started chuckling. 'You're in the Midwest now, babe. What's on the menu? Deep-fried tuna casserole?'

Eve rolled her eyes. Californians might be snotty about the middle of the country, but Northeasterners were worse. 'I'll let you know.'

'Call me tomorrow?'

A kick of irritation in her stomach made her feel guilty. They talked every day at home; it wasn't as if his request was out of line or a big impediment to her day.

The little voice that had been whispering inside her grew louder: either they had to break up or resolve to go to counseling and put everything they had into refreshing the relationship.

She'd wait until she got back home to make that decision. In the meantime – RELIEF! She was out of the house and its tension.

Eve said goodbye, then unpacked her suitcase, which consisted mostly of jeans and various tops and sweaters. From what she'd heard and read, temperatures up here could vary widely at this time of year – sometimes a spring tease, sometimes a continuation of winter. The one nice outfit she'd brought – a long-sleeved tunic top with a swirling blue design that matched her eyes, warm enough for chilly spring with a sweater, cool enough without it for milder days, and a pair of black rayon pants – she hung in the closet, though she still couldn't imagine what she'd need it for.

Apparently she hadn't been able to shake all her mother's influence. Not long before Jillian Croft died, she'd summoned the girls to her bedroom, where she was packing for a weekend trip. She'd been in one of her moods that required an audience. This little drama had involved teaching her daughters how to pack a good suitcase. Eleven-year-old Eve could not have been less interested as her mother had droned on and on about stuffing socks into shoes to save space, about putting belts around the perimeter of the case . . . it was amazing that she remembered any of it.

The final lecture item, a black sequined mini dress, had been carefully folded into Jillian's Louis Vuitton weekender, while she gravely instructed her daughters always to travel with at least one nice outfit, because you never knew when you'd need to look pretty for some gentleman.

Olivia had listened closely with her usual starry-eyed expression around Jillian. Rosalind had been good-naturedly attentive, but clearly uninterested. Eve had stared at their mother, promising herself that she would never, ever dress for anyone but herself, *least* of all for some *man*.

Not two weeks later, she'd been forced to wear the jailbait dress her mother had picked out for the Braddocks' holiday party, held annually between Christmas and New Year's Eve, and had been led upstairs by the revoltingly named Mr Angel, famous Hollywood producer, while her mother did nothing to stop him.

Will you come with me? Please, Mom? I don't want to be alone with him.

Eve drew in a sharp breath and closed the closet door on her current outfit and the memory. She had better things to think about. Like which bathroom to use.

She chose the closer of the two, charmingly done in navy and white tile with a white wallpaper on which glided small blue sailboats, wondering if Shelley's daughter had made those choices too.

After a quick shower to freshen up after the long drive, Marx waiting patiently outside the bathroom door, Eve blew her hair dry and pulled it into its ponytail, then dressed in jeans and a pink sweater, deciding to forgo makeup and jewelry. Given Shelley's totally natural look, she doubted her hostess/client would be offended.

Back in her room, planning to go out to survey the property with Marx, she glanced at her watch and realized it was nearly time to eat.

Oh boy. Eve would have to come up with plenty of chatty topics to get through this first dinner. After that, she and Shelley would become more comfortable with each other.

She hoped.

Picking up Marx's bowls and his bag of food, she descended the stairs, sniffing to try to identify the source of the aroma. Some kind of fish? In spite of her dread of the meal, she found herself hungry.

Outside the kitchen, she hesitated, Marx bumping his head at the bowls in her hands.

C'mon, Eve. The sooner she got to know Shelley, the less awkward this would be.

She turned the corner, wide smile in place. 'I'm all settled. The room is great, thanks.'

Shelley nodded, standing at the stove.

Eve took a few more steps, reminding herself, as her mother so often had, to stand straight, enjoy her height, not hunch her shoulders like she was trying to disappear. 'Something smells great.'

'Whitefish.' The deep voice startled Eve again. 'A Midwestern specialty.'

'Whitefish as in whitefish salad?' The only way she knew the fish.

'Yes. But that's smoked. This is fresh.'

Eve looked around the kitchen, hoping for an obvious out-of-the-way spot to keep Marx's food. 'Is it okay if I put the dog bowls in this corner? By the dishwasher?'

'Sure.' Shelley uncovered a saucepan and adjusted the heat. 'I suppose you drink alcohol.'

Absolutely.

'I do . . . sometimes, yes.' Eve poured food into Marx's bowl and went over to the sink to get him water. It didn't sound as if Shelley had a fabulous wine cellar she was dying to share. 'But I'm fine without it.'

'I have wine. I bought some in case.' Shelley grabbed mitts that went all the way up to her elbows, and took a sheet pan of foil-wrapped packets out of the oven. 'Pinot Grigio.'

'Are you having any?' Eve bent to pet Marx, who'd interrupted his meal to sniff the air curiously.

Shelley put a packet on each plate and slit them with a sharp knife, releasing clouds of steam that made Marx sniff harder. 'I'll have a bit.'

Thank you, God. 'Then I'd love some, thank you.'

'Glasses up there.' She pointed to a cabinet out of her reach.

Eve took down two of the glasses, chunky and heavy, each emblazoned with an enormous overly ornate *G* in gold.

'Wedding presents from my husband's family.'

'Oh.' She tried to sound polite. 'They're . . .'

'Hideous.'

'Maybe a little.' Eve took them out to the dining table, on which Shelley had laid two settings with placemats showing maps of the island and a basket containing slices of white sandwich bread.

'I hardly ever use them.' Shelley peeked into the saucepan and turned off the heat, then from it spooned on to the plates green beans in some kind of sauce. 'Haven't bothered buying new.'

'And after a glass or two, who cares, right?'

Shelley stiffened. Her mouth set.

Eve tensed. Wrong thing to say. She'd keep her drinking to one glass around Shelley. At home she'd been drinking too much anyway, to keep Mike company and, frankly, because of the nearly constant tension between them. It wouldn't hurt to cut down.

'We're ready.' Shelley picked up the plates. 'Can you bring the butter?'

'Sure.' Eve opened the refrigerator and searched – upper shelves, lower shelves, door shelves – but couldn't find any. 'I'm not seeing it?'

'Right in front. In the red tub.'

'Oh. Right.' Feeling foolish, she pulled out the container of 'Buttery Spread' and brought it to the table, where Shelley had poured two half-glasses of wine from a bottle with one of those cute labels that usually meant the contents were horrible. This one said: *Kicky Cat*.

Eve sat and spread her napkin in her lap. 'Everything looks delicious.'

'I expect you'll want meals on your own sometimes.'

'Uh . . .' She froze. Was Shelley implying she *wanted* Eve to eat by herself? Or was she assuming Eve didn't want to eat with her? 'We'll see. I'd love to cook for you too. You don't have to feed me every night.'

'Least I can do. I'm aware you're barely charging me enough to cover your expenses.'

'That's not a problem. This job will be great experience for me.' She made as if to reach for her fork, and then realized Shelley hadn't moved and snatched her hand back, hoping the move had gone unnoticed. Hostess was supposed to take the first bite, right? But maybe Shelley operated differently, and she was waiting for Eve to take the lead.

She reached for her fork more openly.

'I see you don't say grace.'

Aw, hell. Eve grimaced apologetically. 'Not . . . usually. But I'm fine if you want—'

'I don't either.'

'Oh.' Eve nodded too many times. 'Well, okay then. We can agree on that.'

'Yes.' Shelley picked up her fork and helped the fish off the foil on to her plate.

Eve copied her, uncovering a peppered fillet under thin slices of lemon. The fish was moist, delicate and flavorful. 'This is wonderful.'

'Mann's doesn't always carry it, but they had it today.'

'Is Mann's the fish market?'

Shelley's mouth curled; not quite a smile, but almost. 'Mann's is the everything market. If they don't carry it, you order it or get on the ferry and buy it yourself on the mainland.'

'How many people live here year-round?'

'About seven hundred.'

Ugh. Eve couldn't stand that much coziness. Everyone knowing everyone else's business. Swampscott was substantially larger, big enough to mostly disappear into, with the total anonymity of a major city nearby. 'That is small.'

'Yes.'

She ate another bite of whitefish, not sure she'd digest anything this evening.

Maybe not this month.

Shelley cleared her throat. Eve glanced over hopefully, but she was still absorbed in her meal.

'I assume this fish is local?' Eve gestured out at the lake.

'Probably from Lake Superior. Cleaner if it is.'

'Cleaner?'

'Less polluted.'

'Ah.' Now there was a nice thought. Eve tried the beans, some commercial combination Shelley had heated up. Not fancy food, and the wine was too light for her taste, but she was too nervous and hungry to care.

'So, Shelley, I'm curious to know more about what you're thinking for the new cottage.'

'Tomorrow. When we're outside.'

'Oh.' Eve found herself nodding again. 'Okay. That makes sense.'

Darn it. That was her ace-in-the-hole conversation piece.

Click of utensils on plates. Thump of heavy glasses on table.

'Lauren said you two met in grade school?'

A mouthful of beans. Chewing. 'That's right.'

'You were best friends.'

'We were.' Shelley helped herself to a slice of bread and pushed the basket toward Eve.

'Thank you.' She selected a soft slice and spread it with the yellow spread. Not delicious, but the type of salt/fat/carb combination that made it taste good anyway. She would try not to think about the fresh wholegrain rolls from her and Mike's favorite bakery slathered with the extra-fat European butter she splurged on.

Another mouthful of fish. A gulp of wine, nearly emptying her glass, while Shelley had barely touched hers. After Shelley's reaction to her joke in the kitchen, Eve was not going to ask for a refill. She forked up more beans. 'How long have you lived here?'

'I don't like talking during meals.'

Eve barely kept from gasping in surprise. But a quick look at Shelley's troubled face made her realize the sentence had been more confession than blame. That didn't stop Eve from blushing like a child called out on bad behavior.

'Okay. That's fine.'

'Just saving you trouble.'

'Right. Sure. Thank you.' She ate the rest of her fish and green beans and bread in a humiliated silence she hoped Shelley found comfortable.

Everything she'd experienced since early childhood had taught her that meals were not just for food, but for sharing conversation, for forging and tightening social bonds. Granted, her family's table at times became a battlefield, but at least that was some kind of social interaction. At home, even if she and Mike were exhausted, they made an effort. Or she did. Or they agreed not to try and watched TV or a movie.

No wonder Shelley wanted a house for herself. Lauren said she had three grown children with kids of their own. It must be a nightmare for her when they were all here.

Shelley laid her fork across her empty plate. Eve hurried to shovel down her last mouthfuls and did the same. The second the utensil hit the porcelain, Shelley stood and collected both plates.

Eve jumped to help, bringing the bread and not-butter back into the kitchen. 'I'm happy to do the dishes.'

'You don't want dessert, then?'

'Oh. Yes. I'd love some. I didn't realize. Thank you.' She groaned inwardly. Even if it meant she'd wake up in the middle of the night starving, Eve didn't want to sit there a second longer.

She perked up slightly when a plate of brownies appeared, but they turned out to be from a commercial mix, satisfyingly chewy in texture, but tasting only faintly of chocolate.

Yes, she was spoiled where food was concerned. Her mother had been into natural ingredients decades before farm-to-table was fashionable, though it was easy for her since they had a cook and Jillian could afford whatever she wanted from wherever it grew. Still, Eve had been brought up eating from-scratch baking and high-quality, healthy meals, lots of vegetables, fruits and grains. In the Beverly Hills school system, she'd plowed doggedly through her brought-from-home lunch, crunching each bite of carrot stick, negotiating thick-crusted wholegrain sandwiches of goat cheese, prosciutto and olives, envying kids who inhaled peanut butter and jelly and Snack Pack chocolate pudding in five minutes, leaving her alone at the table with half her meal still uneaten.

She and her sisters had regularly begged their parents for commercial candy bars, soda, Jell-O, TV dinners . . . The forbidden evils were allowed only during their summers at the house in Maine, and occasionally when their parents went out to dinner and left them with a sitter. Eve remembered swearing to herself that when she grew up and was out on her own, she'd eat all the bad-for-you foods denied her as a child.

But needless to say, she hadn't fallen far from the organic apple tree, though sometimes Mike, who'd grown up on Kraft macaroni and cheese and Hamburger Helper, would whip up a batch of one or the other for nostalgia's sake.

After her brownie, Eve waited for Shelley to make the first move, not wanting to screw up again. She didn't have to wait long.

'After the dishes, we can sit on the porch if you want to chat.'

Eve's stomach sank. This evening had already contained more minefields than she had imagined. Here, already, was another one. Did Shelley *want* to chat or did she think she owed her guest conversation after denying it during dinner?

Eve would test the waters. 'Sure. I should walk Marx, though. He's had a long day in the car.'

'Go ahead. Plenty of time for both.'

Yes. There was. Because dinner was over and it was only *six fifteen*!

But that seemed to answer her question. Shelley did want to talk. So Eve would give it a try.

Clearing up didn't take long. Shelley put everything in the dishwasher: pots, pans, kitchen knives – shudder – even wooden-handled utensils, all things Eve took care to wash by hand.

She had to admit, it made the process quicker.

'Any recommendations for a nice walk?'

Shelley shrugged. 'Not a lot of excitement around here, but not a lot of ugly either. Any way you go is pleasant.'

'Okay. I'll wander close to home tonight, then. Thanks.'

Upstairs, she grabbed Marx's leash out of his bag, causing him to practically turn himself inside out with excitement. New smells! New trees. New squirrels! Ohboyohboyohboy!

She started for the stairs, passed by a doggy lightning bolt who waited at the bottom, tail wagging. Shelley stood next to him, as impassive as Marx was impatient, arms folded across her chest.

'We're off.' Eve clipped the leash to Marx's collar, then had to plant both feet to keep him from pulling her to the front door. She wasn't sure if Shelley had something to say or was just being polite seeing them out. 'Back soon.'

'Take your time.'

'Thanks.' Taking that as a signal to go, Eve pulled on her jacket and let herself be dragged through the front door.

Outside, the air had turned nippier as the sun was on its way down, though it wouldn't set for at least another hour. At the end of Shelley's driveway, Eve checked the map on her phone and found a loop that would bring her right back here: a little more than two miles, about half an hour if she walked briskly. Probably enough for her first time out, since she didn't know when Shelley went to bed, and didn't want to keep her waiting long.

At the end of the driveway she turned left and walked along the side of the deserted tree-lined road while Marx checked out new scents. In Swampscott, crocuses were blooming, daffodils on their way up. Soon bare tree branches would mist over with buds, though closer to the ocean, still cold from winter, the process took longer. Here it was clear the island still had a wait for spring.

A tangle of trunks, branches and evergreens, mostly cedar here too, blocked her view of the lake, but she could hear the swish of tumbling water, calmer here than what they'd crossed on the ferry.

As she walked, letting Marx explore in his zigzag pattern of search-and-sniff, Eve took in deep lungfuls of the clear, chilly air, starting to relax from the somewhat unsettling first meeting with her client. She and Shelley would work it out. Each day would get easier, especially once Eve started work.

She turned right on Old Mill Road, which turned out to be a sand and gravel track, and followed it until it met up with Hemlock again, where she turned south toward Shelley's house, unhooking Marx's leash. Not a single car had passed, and he was well trained. If she was violating some strict leash law, she could plead newcomer ignorance.

Here there were a few more driveways, though the houses on the lake side were still invisible from the road. A casual peek down one turned up a man carrying a bag of trash. Eve had been so lulled by the isolation, she was startled to come across another living being. As she drew level with the driveway, the guy caught sight of her and waved, his face lighting in a grin, obviously mistaking her for someone else. Eve kept going without responding – and heard feet thudding down the driveway behind her.

This would be embarrassing.

She gave him a quick nod, without stopping, assuming that once he saw her face and realized his error, he'd turn around and go home.

He didn't. His eyes widened, as did his grin, and he came after her, still carrying the garbage. 'Hi there.'

'Hi.' She gave the syllable an extra dose of New England curtness, not slowing her pace.

He was tall, probably about her own age, dark hair and eyes, long nose keeping him from being classically handsome, big teeth making him look a bit horsey. 'Are you by any chance staying with Shelley?'

She was startled enough to stop walking. How did he know that? 'Yes.'

'Lucky guess.' He gestured with the garbage. Marx sniffed it with interest. 'I'm Clayton Marshall.'

She took a step away to communicate that she was planning to resume her walk, not settle in for a chat. 'Hi.'

'Have you got time for a drink? We can get to know each other a little. I can show you around my place.'

Eve gaped at him. Was this how things happened between men and women in Wisconsin? Because it wasn't how it happened back home. 'No, thanks.'

'Okay. Sure. Okay.' He seemed surprised by her lack of enthusiasm. 'Not a good time, I guess. Tomorrow would also work for me. Would that be better?'

Tomorrow? What made him think she'd want to have a drink with him at *any* time? Annoyance and adrenaline spiked. She started walking again. 'Not interested in drinking with you.'

'O-*kay*.' He gave the word the drawn-out emphasis of the very offended, as if *she*'d barged into *his* walk.

Clueless.

Eve increased her pace, resisting the urge to break into a flat-out run. She could never handle unwanted advances calmly, even having been fending them off her whole life.

Recently recaptured peace having made another escape, she stalked back up Shelley's driveway, no longer in the mood for a strained chat on the porch. She wanted to go up to her room and disappear into a book, or plan what she'd cook for tomorrow night's Vow of Silence Dinner.

Back inside, she shut the front door, feeling at least some sense of safety return by locking it. Marx ran to the kitchen – smart dog, remembered already – to lap up water from his bowl. Eve wandered into the living room and saw Shelley waiting on the porch. She got herself a glass of water, briefly wondering if Jesus would mind turning it into wine – or better still, slyly colorless gin – and joined her.

The porch ran the width of the house. Natural wood rockers, a wicker love seat and low tables paid homage to the magnificent but rapidly dimming view of the lake. Heaters worked hard to warm the space. Eve left her jacket on and sat in a rocker to Shelley's right.

'Nice walk?'

'Yes, except on the way back I ran into a weird guy who wanted me to come into his house for a drink.'

'Really?' Shelley looked mildly curious. 'What did he look like?'

Eve pulled up a mental picture. 'Tall. Dark. My age. Big nose. About three driveways up.'

Shelley's face cleared. 'Well, that's Clayton. He was just being friendly.'

Friendly? Apparently this *was* how things worked in Wisconsin. 'Okay. Where I come from, asking someone you don't know to come into your house is not friendly, it's creepy.'

'Creepy?' She looked genuinely confused. 'I don't understand. Because you'll be working for him?'

Eve blinked. Dread invaded her stomach. '*Working* for him?'

'That's Clayton Marshall. Your other client. He wants a three-season room on his house. I thought I told you.'

Eve closed her eyes in a silent groan. 'Yes, but not his name. For no particular reason, I assumed it was a woman.'

'Well, now you know.'

Eve shook her head ruefully. 'I'll have to apologize.'

'Why?'

'I thought he was trying to . . .' She blushed fiercely.

'You thought he was trying to pick you up!' Shelley burst into a high cackle, not a sound Eve had expected, given her speaking voice. 'That's what happens when you're so beautiful.

You think every guy who talks to you is trying something.'

Eve took a breath to keep from bristling visibly. 'It happens.'

'That's what I meant. Probably all the time.'

She exhaled, realizing that Shelley hadn't been passing judgment, but in her rather odd way stating fact. 'He never mentioned the job. He just invited me in.'

Shelley shook her head, still grinning. 'Poor Clayton. I'll have to tell him what you thought.'

'No!' Eve checked her outburst, feeling herself blushing. 'No, thank you. I'll talk to him.'

'He'll think it's funny.' Shelley spoke fondly. 'Clayton's a good person. He's had a rough run with women. He's divorced now. The house belongs to his family. I think he uses it as a refuge sometimes. He can work anywhere.'

'Ah.' Eve hated to cut short Shelley's longest speech to date, but she didn't want to talk about Clayton, at least not until she got over her mortification with an apology. 'How long have you lived here?'

'A little over a year. I'm still fixing the place up. My uncle had no family. He left it to his brother, my father. Dad gave it to my sister.' Shelley had reverted to emotionless recitation. 'She died some years ago, and I got—'

'Oh, I'm so sorry.' Eve couldn't help the grief in her voice just at the *thought* of losing Olivia or Rosalind. She could hardly imagine the extent of Shelley's.

'Yeah, she had it coming.'

Eve froze, clutching her water glass. She had no idea how to react to that. 'Oh.'

'I got her estate, which included the house. Moved in after I retired.'

'Hmm.' Eve managed to bring the glass to her mouth and sip. Swallow. Put it down. 'Retired from . . .'

'I was a corporate trainer. I had to earn *my* retirement. Every penny.'

'Right.' Eve forced herself back to polite interest. Not her business whether Shelley thought her sister deserved to die or not, but her brain had immediately gone looking for a reason and come up with melodramas involving adultery and other forms of punishable-by-wishing-death betrayal. 'Before that you were a teacher, Lauren said.'

'Elementary school in Machias.'

Eve nodded. 'Your hometown. You and Lauren.'

'Yes.' Shelley's lips pressed shut. She folded her arms, staring out at the lake. 'It was good of her to recommend you.'

'I'm curious why you would want to hire someone with so little experience.'

Shelley turned to her. 'You don't have any experience?'

'I . . . Not . . . I haven't . . .' *Aw, hell.* Maybe she should go upstairs, grab her case, whistle for Marx and get out of there.

'I was joking. You should have seen your face.' Shelley cackled again. 'Lauren says you're brilliant and I can afford you. That's enough for me.'

'Okay.' Eve let her head fall back against the rocker. This day had worn her out. 'Well, thank you. I hope I can come up with a design you like.'

'You don't have to sit out here.' Shelley spoke almost kindly. 'If you're like me, people wear you out, especially strangers.'

'I *am* tired.' She found it oddly comforting that as different as they were, at least Shelley understood that part of her. Mike could immerse himself in a new crowd every evening. After a couple of hours, Eve wanted to curl up and rock. 'Thanks for dinner. I'll cook tomorrow. I really enjoy being in the kitchen.'

'I won't say no. I don't care for it much. Breakfast is help yourself. Toast, eggs, cereal, whatever you can find. Tomorrow we'll talk about my new house. I'll introduce you to Clayton if that's easier. You can also tour the island, not that there's much to see.'

'Okay, thank you.' Eve stood, rolling her stiff shoulders to loosen the driving kinks.

'Oh.' Shelley slapped her thigh, tightly rounded in denim. 'A package came. I meant to have it on your bed when you arrived, but I forgot. It's there now.'

'Thank you.' Eve had no idea what that could be. Only her family and Mike knew she was here. Just like her sisters to pull some gag. A Cheesehead hat or a Packers jersey made for a dog.

She took one last look at the darkening sky over the lake and went upstairs, trailed by Marx. Once she got used to Shelley, once she made things right with Clayton, once she was grounded in the projects she'd been brought here to do, she *might* get used to this.

On her bed, as Shelley had said, lay a small package wrapped in brown paper secured with plenty of tape. No return address. Postmarked Saratoga Springs, NY. Eve knew no one there.

But something started nagging in the back of her brain, some association with that city . . .

She opened the package and stared in disbelief at a blue leather-bound book with the word *Diary* embossed in gold.

The memory came into clear focus. Rosalind had also received a package, mailed to her New York apartment. No return address. Postmarked Saratoga Springs.

Inside had been a diary, written by their mother.

Chapter 5

June 4, 1977 (Saturday)

Daniel and I have been married almost seven years. I crave babies constantly. I want to be an integral part of a family, a thread of its very fabric, unlike the one I grew up in, where I was so entirely left out. I didn't – still don't – understand how my sister and parents could hold in so many emotions, joy and passion and love. How they could be satisfied by such tiny lives lived in such a tiny town. I want children who are an extension of me and of Daniel, who enrich our marriage by weaving themselves into the happiness we already have. What a precious gift a child is, and how cruel Fate is to withhold it.

My shrink says such grief is normal, that we should adopt. But if we adopt, everyone will know I can't have children. Some people might blame Daniel, but most people will assume it's me, I know they will. The shame would kill me. I can't give up the dream of having my own children, even though it makes no sense, no sense at all. But I believe in my heart of hearts that there must be a way, or why wouldn't I accept the inevitable? Maybe God is trying to tell me something. Maybe I'm just crazier than I thought.

That idea terrifies me.

I'm weeping and I can't stop. Daniel just came in to beg me to take my meds. He says it gently and with love, but he probably wants to grab me and force the pills down my throat. Two more days of shooting and I will, I promise.

This hell will end one way or another.

Eve woke with a start and lay blinking up at the unfamiliar white ceiling. All night she'd been tossing and turning, a mess of anxiety after opening the package containing her mother's diary. As soon as she realized what it was, she'd picked up her phone to call Lauren, then stopped. Lauren would deny sending it, of course she would, or why would she try to make it look like it had come from some anonymous source in New York State? Plus she'd get all annoyed and defensive, the way she did every time Jillian Croft was mentioned.

When Rosalind had received what now turned out to be only one of Jillian's diaries, it had seemed fitting. She had been on a quest to find her birth mother and learn about the circumstances surrounding her own conception and delivery. Even having appeared under such mysterious circumstances, the diary's arrival in the midst of her journey made perfect sense.

But Eve didn't want to know, had never asked to know, and had never considered what she would do with information like this.

As far as she was concerned, her mother's life had been a train wreck – a train far too wide for its tracks, which took out everything that came too close. As the youngest daughter, Eve's memories consisted of Jillian's worst struggles with mental illness and addiction. While Olivia pretended nothing had gone wrong, and Rosalind tried to fix everything, Eve had coped by shutting it all out, until the nightmare of Mr Angel at the holiday party. Even that she'd managed to put on the shelf, albeit a slightly unstable one. Seeing the video Mike and his friends were watching had been its latest seismic shift, but for the most part the memories and lingering anger at her mother had stayed obediently out of the way.

Last night Eve had taken the diary out of the box and stared at it for a long time, at the shining gold letters, at the contrast between its textured leather cover and the pink skin of her thumb, wondering about its contents, wishing they could jump into her head without her having to read them, dreading the discovery of any other dark part of this confusing and exhausting woman she'd both loved and feared. Whose betrayal of Eve had happened less than a week before Jillian died, robbing her youngest daughter of any chance to understand her choices.

I can't come upstairs with you, Eve, I have guests to take care of. Don't be so shy and silly. Mr Angel is harmless.

Eve had put the book back in its box and stuck the box in her empty suitcase, shoved way back in the closet. Maybe Rosalind would want to read this one too.

There. Done.

Of course it hadn't been that easy. Sleep had been difficult, not only because of the strange bed and unfamiliar night noises. Jillian Croft had returned from a long, peaceful respite to haunt her. Her mother's legendary beauty, her remarkable talent as an actress and her equally remarkable failings as a parent. Take a dash of bipolar disorder, a soupçon of narcissism, add a healthy splash of alcoholism and a heaping tablespoon of Valium addiction, and what do you get?

Not Mother of the Year.

Eve threw off the blue and white comforter, splashed water on her face in the blue and white bathroom and grabbed the running clothes she always laid out next to her bed at night so she'd be too guilty to change her mind about going. Marx was ready – *he* never tried to find an excuse. She pulled on tight compression pants and an exercise bra, a couple of layers of shirts and a fleece to ward off the forty-degree chill and dampness, then gathered her hair into a ponytail. Downstairs, she hunted for orange juice, grimacing when she saw it in a plastic pitcher, made up from concentrate. She and Mike had been spoiled by their supermarket's juice machine, which made reasonably priced fresh-squeezed orange juice an everyday luxury.

Eve poured a glass and gulped it, needing the jolt of sugar to get her going. A glance around the gray and cream kitchen showed no bananas, another of her early-morning habits, but she could buy those. She opened a few cabinets and helped herself to a handful of raisins, which would work fine for now.

'C'mon, Marx.'

She thought about leaving Shelley a note, then decided against it and let herself quietly out of the front door. She'd barely be gone twenty minutes. Shelley would probably think she was still asleep.

Three minutes into the run – the same loop she'd walked last night – she stopped trying to push herself to maintain her usual pace and let herself slow to a comfortable jog. It was one of the bad exercise days, when she felt as if she were dragging a ten-pound weight. Someday she hoped experts figured out the details of the mind–body connection, because she was convinced it held the clue to operating efficiently. If she hadn't gotten the diaries last night, she probably could have knocked off a couple of nine-minute miles.

As she turned the corner back on to Hemlock, Eve kept a wary eye out for Clayton, in case he was an early riser as well. She owed him an apology, but she'd rather not deliver it to him panting and sweaty.

No sign of his tall form, but opposite his house, or near to it – she couldn't be sure which driveway was his – a teenage boy in a red hoodie stood staring, arms folded around himself. As she approached, he must have heard her footsteps – more like foot thuds – because he glanced over, then turned abruptly and walked ahead of her along the road.

She passed him soon after. 'Morning.'

'Hi.' The soft voice surprised her. She'd expected a deeper sound from a boy his age.

Several steps later, Eve realized she was running alone, and turned to see Marx shamelessly eating up attention from the kid, who was bending over to pet him.

'*Marx*.' He came bounding back. 'If I dropped dead you'd barely notice as long as someone else was around to love you.'

Instead of looking suitably ashamed, Marx dashed ahead, pausing at the entrance to Shelley's driveway, looking back as if to make sure he'd gotten the right place.

Feeling better for the run – the main reason she'd forced herself to go when she felt least like it – Eve let herself quietly into the house and took off her shoes to tiptoe upstairs. On the day's agenda: shower, breakfast, talk to Shelley about her project, apologize to Clayton, get to work.

When she came back downstairs, clean and feeling much better, she found Shelley in the kitchen making herself toast with peanut butter. Eve glanced around for the coffee maker and saw instead, with true coffee-snob horror, a jar of instant on the counter.

Another item for her shopping list.

'Good morning, Shelley. Hope Marx and I didn't wake you.'

'No.' Shelley gestured to the instant. 'Do you drink coffee?'

'Yes.' Eve eyed the brown granules dubiously. Did that even count as coffee? She'd developed a taste for the brew at a young age, when Dad would let her sip his, to her mother's eye-rolling disapproval. He was the original coffee snob, buying only from Tanzania, Nicaragua and Sumatra.

'There are coffee shops on the island, a couple of them. Red Cup is good. There's instant to tide you over this morning. Or I can make you tea. That's what I drink.' Shelley gestured to a box of Lipton. Eve made a mental note to order her a special treat of her favorite loose-leaf from MEM Tea Imports back home in Cambridge as a thank-you gift.

'This is fine.' She made herself toast and spread peanut butter thickly, starving after the exercise and her minimal meal the night before. The silence during breakfast was much easier than the night before, not yet companionable but not as excruciating. Eve had brought down her phone so she could read the *Boston Globe* online, instead of not being sure where to look.

'Well.' Shelley put down her tea mug after what must have been her last sip, signaling that speaking was again allowed. 'When do you want to talk about the cottage?'

'Now is good.' Eve stood and gathered her plate and mug to put in the dishwasher. 'I'll get my notepad and we can talk about the basics before we go outside to look at the site.'

She helped clear the kitchen, then ran upstairs for pen and paper, taking a moment on the landing to pause and recognize that after so many years of theoretical designing, she was embarking on her first big solo project. If she didn't screw this up, she'd be able to come back next year and see something created from Shelley's need and Eve's imagination, a physical manifestation of the talent she'd felt inside her from such a young age, more interested in picture books of houses than animals, more interested in where her Barbies lived than what they did.

If she didn't screw this up, she could gain the confidence necessary to take on more and larger projects. Someday she might look back at this moment as the true launch of her career.

Or she might wish she'd never crossed the Wisconsin border.

Out on the chilly porch, Shelley turned on the heat, and she and Eve settled into the same seats they'd sat in the evening before.

'I've made a list of questions, mostly about your tastes, habits and expectations. But first, I wanted to know what *you* were thinking for the space.' Eve waited, pen poised, adrenaline humming. Best scenario, Shelley would have thought a lot about what she wanted, and be articulate and exact in her descriptions. Worst case, she'd say . . .

'Mostly I want your ideas.'

'Sure.' Eve kept a confident smile on her face. 'Why don't we start with the questions. How much time do you anticipate spending in the new place?'

'All my time. That's why I'm building it.' Clearly she thought Eve was a moron. 'So I don't have to be in here.'

'Right. Right.' Confidence slightly punctured, Eve scribbled something meaningless and moved on. 'Which rooms do you think you'll spend the most time in?'

Shelley scratched her elbow, frowning. 'I guess I'll eat in the kitchen and sleep in the bedroom.'

'Right.' Eve felt sweat prickle under her arms. 'What about other spaces? Living room? Porch?'

'Yes.'

Yes. 'Are you an early riser or a night . . . owl.' She sighed. She knew those answers. 'If last night and today are any indication, early riser, right?'

'And early to bed.'

'Were you thinking of a two-story house?'

'I don't like ranches.'

That was something. 'Did you want two traditional floors with stairs, like in this house? Or a more open concept inside?'

'I don't know.' Shelley rubbed her plump thighs through the denim. 'Why don't you do plans for both? Then I can decide.'

'I could . . . try.' Except that would be a massive amount of work and take forever. 'What about the exterior? Did you want it to match this place?'

'I guess. Maybe. At least not look wrong next to it.'

Not wrong. Okay. 'Fireplace?'

'Yes.'

'Air-conditioning?'

'I suppose with climate change I should. I can't sleep when it's hot.'

Inspiration hit. 'Any other houses you like on the island that I could take a look at?'

Shelley frowned, thinking, while Eve figuratively crossed her fingers. 'Not really.'

'Okay.' Eve wrote more notes, trying to quell her panic. She and Shelley would be able to come to some solution, she was sure, but the more she had to pull answers out of her client, the longer this project would take. She wasn't anxious to be on this odd little island with her odd little hostess any longer than she had to be.

After asking a few more questions and getting half-answers, Eve nodded as if she had the whole thing figured out already. Maybe seeing the site would give her ideas Shelley couldn't. 'Shall we go outside and look?'

At least Shelley had a definite answer to that question, and a definite site chosen for her cottage. Out of sight of the main house through the trees, but still close, where a small natural clearing had already defined the space.

Immediately the beginnings of ideas started buzzing around Eve's brain. The cottage of course would take full advantage of the view, and match the big house exterior with dormers and color. Inside . . . a warmer personality, maybe simple, old-fashioned, much like Shelley herself.

Yes, Eve agreed, with massive relief, the site would work well.

With that, her first meeting with her first client was over, and she was desperately in need of a decent cup of caffeine. Google directed her to Red Cup Coffee, not far from the ferry harbor where she'd landed. She could sit and think some of this over, pick up groceries from Mann's and then perform the dreaded apology to Clayton and be back for lunch.

One problem: she couldn't take Marx with her. Red Cup politely didn't allow dogs inside, and she doubted the grocery store would love him either. She could keep him in the car, but . . .

Happily, Shelley seemed genuinely fine with having him stay in the house with her.

A light drizzle was falling as Eve pulled into Red Cup's dirt parking lot. She grabbed her pad and laptop, and hurried to the front porch of the brown-shingled building, where a huge red coffee cup dangled from the ceiling, then into the funky space with its brightly colored walls, comfy-looking couches, chairs and tables, and local arts and craft items for sale.

Behind the counter, the menu board listed sandwiches, quiche and breakfast items. Eve sniffed appreciatively. Bacon was on the premises. Yum. But then the scones looked delicious too . . .

She settled on a currant scone and coffee with a shot of espresso, figuring that would get her through the next couple of hours until she could buy some to keep at Shelley's.

The scone was delicious, moist and crumbly, the coffee definitely the real thing. She'd picked a table at the front of the store, near shelves of pottery and a display case of CDs. She loved the idea of lounging on a couch, but lounging wasn't conducive to work. She wanted to start thinking about Shelley's cottage, maybe look up a few ideas online.

The door opened to admit another customer. A flash of red caught Eve's eye – the boy she'd seen earlier on her run. He ordered a breakfast sandwich and coffee in that same high, soft voice. It wasn't until he turned and showed a distinctly feminine face that Eve realized her mistake.

He was she. Or . . . maybe he was a they. Or . . .

Whatever.

She bent back over her laptop aware that the girl/boy had chosen the table next to hers when there were plenty of empties further away. She hoped that didn't mean he/she/they – the *person* – would want to start chatting.

The person sat and attacked her sandwich as if she hadn't eaten in days.

Eve pulled up the Houzz website, logged in and typed 'lake cottage' to see what came up. Some exteriors and some interior shots as well. She scrolled down, studying them, stopping to write down features that caught her eye.

'What's your dog's name? I saw you running with her this morning.'

'Him. Marx.' Eve barely looked up, but it was long enough to register that the person was female enough to be thought of as a girl and that she was younger than Eve had originally thought. Fifteen? Sixteen? The older Eve got, the harder it was to tell. When *she* was fifteen, she'd been in her rebel goth phase, sneaking out at night to get high with her best friend Cornelia, copping a sullen, superior attitude about everything that didn't apply to her. Even with all that bravado, though, she never would have struck up a conversation with an adult stranger.

Come to think of it, she still wouldn't.

'Marx? Like the philosopher? Or the brothers?'

Eve didn't look up this time. 'Yup.'

'What kind is he? Is he out in your car?'

'Some shepherd, some collie maybe. He's at the house.' She made a show of bending forward, staring earnestly at her screen, hoping that would clue the girl in.

'How old is he?'

'Five.'

'Have you had him since he was a puppy?'

'Yes.' Her teeth were practically gritted by now, except it was her own fault for not just politely saying she was busy. It was so hard to, at least for her. Her sister Rosalind would find some funny way to say it. Olivia would come right out and tell the kid to go away. Eve couldn't do either. Not well, anyway.

'I love dogs.'

Eve finally looked up and registered that the girl was quite pretty. Her short hair with its sweep of bangs suited her pixie features, still rounded with youth. She looked vulnerable and a little sad.

Eve relented. 'Do you have a dog at home?'

'No.' The girl scowled and looked down at her breakfast, left leg jiggling. 'My *stepdad* won't let me.'

'Sorry about that.' She grimaced sympathetically. 'Maybe when you leave home to get a place of your own.'

The girl bunched her mouth tightly and ducked her head.

Was she *crying*?

Wonderful. More than Eve could handle.

She went back to her laptop. A sniff at the next table, then another one.

Eve glanced over. The girl looked miserable, and sweet, in spite of her masculine getup and swagger.

Okay, okay . . .

She pushed her laptop back a few inches. 'Do you live on the island?'

'My dad does.' She made a face. 'My . . . *real* dad, that is.'

Eve cringed. The subject of what made a dad 'real' was a little too topical in her own life. Daniel Braddock was her father, but the jury was still out, and might stay out forever, on whether he was her birth father too, though from what Rosalind had discovered, it sounded as if her parents had picked out surrogates to carry all three girls, women her father proceeded to impregnate.

Ew.

'So you're visiting?'

'Spring break.' The girl tipped her head awkwardly, as if she were trying to look at Eve and away at the same time. 'I'm Abigail, by the way.'

'Eve.'

'Do *you* live here?'

'Visiting.'

'Who?'

'A client. Do you always ask this many questions?'

'Yes.' The first sign of spirit brightened her face. 'Are you always so stingy answering them?'

'Yes.' They shared a smile. 'I suppose you're going to ask who the client is and what I do.'

Her grin, showing slightly crooked teeth, was heart-stealing. 'Yup.'

Eve gave an exaggerated sigh. 'Her name is Shelley. I'm designing a house for her.'

'You're an architect! That is so cool.' Abigail's pleasure dimmed quickly. 'I was thinking about doing that someday. I love to draw. My . . . friend and I . . . were going to . . .'

Eve drew herself up stiffly. Abigail was trying not to cry again. Times like these, Eve wished she had the natural warmth of her sisters, or Mike. But whether she'd conditioned herself in childhood to retreat from emotion, or whether she was simply born that way, the outcome was the same. Another reason she'd decided long ago that children probably wouldn't be on the cards for her. Being around kids didn't seem to produce the same maternal longings in Eve as it did in other women, nor could she picture herself happily and eternally at the beck and call of little beings with such big needs and feelings. Given her self-absorbed, complicated parents, she wasn't sure how to be a good one herself. A job like that wasn't the type where she could say, oh what the heck, give it a shot and see.

'Are you okay?' The words came out as stiff as her body, making her want to try them again.

'Yeah, fine.' Abigail tried to sound disgusted with herself, but the pain was still there. 'I was going to say a friend and I are totally into design. She's into landscape more than buildings. I think I'd be more of an urban planner.'

'Well, that's cool.'

'Can I watch you work?'

'No.'

Abigail smiled again and took a sip of her coffee. 'Just so you know, I'm not usually like this. My home life is pretty grim right now.'

'Ah.' Eve nodded politely, afraid she was about to hear the whole story. 'Sorry to hear that.'

'It's . . . whatever.' Abigail stared at her plate, empty except for crumbs. 'I'm pretty bored around here. Nothing to do. I don't know why my dad would have a house here.'

'Hmm.' Eve took a lingering sip of coffee to avoid saying more.

'So . . . I don't know, I was wondering, like, if you're going to come back here.' She gestured to the tables around them. 'Or if you'll be doing work somewhere I could maybe . . . watch? I'd like to learn all I can.'

Eve put her cup carefully back on the table in the middle of her napkin, trying to find a nice way to say not-in-a-billion-years.

Then she remembered how at that age, during her summer internships at Blue Design in LA, she'd hang around the architects incessantly, so she could hear and absorb as much as possible about the process, thrilled to bits when the owner, Kathryn Blue, offered to take her out for lunch one day to talk. It was undoubtedly the last way Kathryn wanted to spend a precious hour or so, but Eve's first and finest mentor was unfailingly generous with her time and her advice.

Apparently Eve wasn't Kathryn.

'I know, it's weird. You don't know me, and . . . Well, I figured it didn't hurt to ask.' Abigail's voice cracked. 'I wouldn't get in the way. I mean, talking too much and everything.'

So much pain in such a young kid. Eve remembered how that felt, too.

'Maybe.'

The young face brightened. 'Really?'

'It would have to be on my terms.'

Abigail darted a glance to the side, as if sharing disgust with an imaginary friend. 'Well, *yeah*.'

Eve laughed and made an impulsive decision she would undoubtedly regret later. 'If you promise not to be a pain in the ass, I will walk you through some of the software I use and talk about my design process.'

Once she was more sure what that was.

'Wow, thanks!' Abigail's smile was so wide, Eve felt like a jerk for having hesitated. 'Starting when?'

Eve gave her a version of Olivia's famous stink eye. 'Not now.'

'Jeez, okay.' She was still smiling.

'How long are you around?'

Abigail looked away, grin fading. 'Not sure.'

'I thought you said spring break.'

'I did. So . . . a week probably.'

Probably? She didn't know how long her spring break was? Eve's caution reinstated itself. She'd meet with Abigail once, see how that went. 'Why don't I show up here tomorrow, same time. About ten. That okay?'

'Yeah! Cool, thanks.'

'But right now . . .' Eve gestured to her computer.

'Got it.' Abigail jumped up as if she couldn't contain her happiness. 'See you tomorrow. And thanks.'

Eve stayed another half-hour, unable to concentrate as well as she wanted to. As much as she told herself Abigail wasn't her problem, she couldn't help wondering what was going on, why some instinct told her the girl hadn't been totally forthcoming. Eve had come to Washington Island partly to escape her own emotional messes; she didn't want to take on anyone else's.

Speaking of messes, since she wasn't able to concentrate on work, she might as well go grocery shopping, then get the dreaded apology to Clayton over with.

Mann's was a small, old-fashioned supermarket with worn wooden floors, deep blue walls and what looked like an original tin ceiling and crown molding painted fresh white. For its size, it was remarkably well stocked, and Eve was able to find everything she needed for a simple dinner that night as well as breakfast and lunch items more to her taste than those Shelley stocked.

Which meant all too soon Eve was headed for Clayton's house, heart in her throat, hoping, as Shelley said, that he was a nice guy who would understand her confusion.

She turned into his driveway, long and graveled like Shelley's, drove several yards and parked. The woods were so peaceful and quiet, she couldn't bear announcing her invasion by driving right up to his house. Walking would feel more casual, more neighborly.

Following the track, she reached a clearing next to a sprawling ranch painted gray, like the surrounding tree trunks, its grim color relieved by a teal front door and a line of large teal diamonds stenciled on to each black shutter.

Clayton was outside, with a rusty metal contraption that looked like the wheels and axles of an ancient go-kart slung over his shoulder. When he saw her, he stopped walking, letting her approach, the guilty party awaiting her sentence. He was taller than she had thought from their earlier encounter, six-two or three, lean and right now expressionless.

Eve stopped three feet away and cleared her throat. 'I came to apologize for yesterday.'

He leaned down and let the metal drop, then straightened and put his hands on his hips. 'Yeah, that was weird.'

'See . . . no one told me your name.' She felt herself blush under his severe stare. 'I didn't know who you were. So when you introduced yourself and invited me in . . .'

His dark brows went up, then he let out a guffaw that startled her. 'You thought I was hitting on you.'

'Yes.'

'*Really* creepily.'

'Yes.' Eve was incredibly relieved he found this funny instead of insulting.

'That is hilarious.'

She wrinkled her nose. 'It wasn't last night. And it got much worse when Shelley told me who you were and I realized how rude I must have seemed.'

'Let's start over. I'm Clayton Marshall, and I'm only after

your architectural expertise.' He held out a grimy hand, then noticed the dirt and curled it into a fist. 'We'll shake when I've cleaned up. Let me put this piece o' junk into my truck and I'll show you the house and what I'm thinking of doing.'

'Sure.' She eyed the filthy metal dubiously. 'Need any help?'

'Nah, I got this.' He hefted it up on to his shoulder again. 'I'm clearing out the garage. There's crap that's been in there for decades, probably some of it when my grandfather bought the house. It would be nice to use the place for something useful. Like cars. Wait here, I'll be right back.'

'Okay.' She folded her arms against the chilly drizzle that had started again, watching him stride out of sight around the garage to where he must have parked his truck. The encounter had made her a little uneasy, and she wasn't sure why. He was perfectly friendly and seemed genuine. Maybe she hadn't quite shaken off the shock of their first encounter.

A metallic crash told her Clayton had managed to toss the go-kart into his truck. She turned toward the lake so they wouldn't have to stare at each other while he walked back toward her.

'Come on in.' He passed her on the path to the teal front door.

Eve followed, sizing up the house. She'd never been a huge fan of ranches. They seemed unfinished, like making only one layer of a cake.

'My grandfather, my dad's dad, bought the house in 1969. I'm the only one in the family using it anymore. Mom and Dad moved to Spain, and my sisters live in Seattle and Portland. I figured that while I'm up here I'd do some cleanup and renovation.'

'Sounds good.'

She stepped into the foyer, wondering why he was here at

this chilly, drab time of year, and was immediately struck by the unexpected sophistication of the interior. Mottled green wallpaper above oak wainscoting over a slate tile floor. On an antique table stood a tall black vase of rust, cream and brick-colored silk flowers. Glimpses into neighboring rooms showed similar elegance, muted colors and expensive furnishings. Clearly there was not only plenty of money in the family, but good taste, certainly closer to Eve's than her own parents' house had been. The pink Mediterranean in California was a mix of antique and modern, whatever Jillian and Daniel collected during their travels around the globe, with very little thought to how they'd look in one space. An ostentatious mishmash.

'Very nice house.'

'You think?' He was clearly unconvinced. 'I'd like to shake things up a bit. Or down, as the case may be. A little museum-y for my taste, especially for a summer lake house. But that's not what you're here for.'

He led the way to the back of the house. The living room fronted the lake, with floor-to-ceiling windows and French doors that led out to a deck running nearly the full width of the house. '*This* is what you're here for – a deck big enough for all the huge parties we never have. I'd prefer to enclose the space outside the living room so it can be used year-round. I'd want it to have a summer feel, though, casual furniture, maybe a hammock. Windows all around, with screens for maximum air flow. Ceiling fan. Heat and air-conditioning. What else?'

Eve walked toward the French doors, tried one, and, since it was unlocked, stepped through to the deck, checking both directions, north and south. 'Have you thought about having the room at one end of the deck instead of here in the middle?'

'No.'

She glanced at him. Tricky business suggesting other ideas.

You never knew whether someone would get offended. She pointed south. 'Which room is down at that end?'

'Bedroom.'

'That way?' She pointed north.

'Kitchen.'

'Can I see it?'

'Sure.' He led her back through the living room – complete with an ornately carved and painted baby grand piano – through a small dining room with a crystal chandelier and into the spacious kitchen built around a large island with a smooth-top five-burner hob, hardwood floors, dark-wood cabinets and black appliances.

For all its finery, this did not feel like the house of the happy-go-lucky. Certainly not a relaxed anytime retreat.

'What do you think?'

Eve peered through the door from the kitchen out on to the deck. 'How much do you want to spend?'

'How much do I *want* to spend? Nothing. What can you give me for that?'

'For that . . .' She pretended to calculate. 'My trip home.'

'I figured.' He tipped his head and scratched behind his ear, reminding her fleetingly of Marx. 'The house is worth a few hundred thousand. So less than that.'

'Okay.' She dug out her phone. 'Why don't I take some measurements and pictures, work up an idea and see what you think?'

'That sounds reasonable.'

She headed out to the deck, a little surprised when he followed her.

'How are you liking Washington Island?'

'I haven't seen much of it.' She held up her phone and started her picture-taking.

'There's not much to see. Nice beach, nice harbor, cool Norwegian wooden church, that's about it.'

'Your grandfather must have seen something.'

'Quiet. Peace. Tradition. Family.' He stood at the railing, gazing out at the lake. 'I love it here too. I come up when I can.'

She took more pictures, only half listening. This would be a challenging project. Building outside the living room as he'd suggested would leave a disjointed deck on either side. 'Come up from where?'

'Chicago. I'm a technical writer, so I'm able to work remotely. My apartment is being renovated right now. There was a massive leak, so they're tearing out floors, walls and ceilings. I'm staying away from the dust.'

'Don't blame you.' Building the new addition outside the kitchen, which had more public access, seemed better than bisecting the deck or putting it outside the bedroom on the other side. But a structure jutting out from either end would threaten to take the house out of balance. 'How did you get into technical writing?'

'My degree was in journalism, but that field isn't easy to be in right now. I started at the *Chicago Sun-Times*.' He turned to lean against the railing, folding his arms across his chest. 'I thought I was going to take the newspaper world by storm. Two years later, I was laid off.'

'Ouch.' She took another picture, then dug out her laser and started taking measurements, jotting the numbers down on a quick sketch she'd made on her pad.

'You're from Boston?'

'Yes.' She'd need to see if there was a basement under the house. Maybe she could—

'Have you left anyone back home?'

She turned to focus on him. 'Have I *left* anyone? Like by mistake?'

He grinned. Nice smile, big with the teeth, one that warmed his face appealingly. 'Boyfriend? Husband? Kids? Pets?'

'Boyfriend, yes, a dog at Shelley's.' She turned away, disappointed. She'd been enjoying the fact that he seemed uninterested.

'I'm divorced. Two years now – no, God, three. We agreed we wanted kids, then she changed her mind. Back then it was a deal-breaker.'

Why was he telling her all this? 'That's a shame.'

'It's okay. Neither of us was all that happy in the marriage anyway. Ironically, in the meantime I've become somewhat less sure I want a family after all.' He made a jerky circle with one of his shoulders as if it was bothering him – maybe from hauling the go-kart. 'You get to know someone and it seems like it's going to be perfect in that first wave of passion, then the wave rolls back and leaves you alone on the sand, with crabs in your suit.'

Eve gave him a look. 'Crabs.'

'Aquatically speaking. Marine crabs. The kind you eat. Make soup from. Those.'

'Got it.' He reminded her of John Cusack in that movie *Say Anything*, unable to stop talking. Only he wasn't as cute as John Cusack, though he had the actor's charisma and charm.

She went to the edge of the deck and took more pictures. Straight down was a drop of about fifteen feet, then the land flattened to a more gentle slope. 'Do you feel strongly about keeping the room attached to the house?'

'You mean put it out there?' He came to stand next to her. He smelled of hard work and herbs, like he'd been writhing around in a patch of oregano.

'Not necessarily. Just checking in case I'm inspired.'

'I don't know. It might work. I'd want to see your idea.'

'Sure.' She'd thought designing the house for Shelley would be the harder of the projects. Not so sure now.

'So listen, I was about to have lunch; can I convince you to hang out with me a little longer? I'm waiting for approval of a presentation before I can move forward, and there aren't that many people around this time of year. As you can tell by the way I've attacked you with conversation, I'm pretty sick of talking on the phone and to myself.'

'Oh.' Her immediate instinct was retreat. 'I think I'm expected . . .'

She wasn't sure why she trailed off. Maybe because it made it sound as if Shelley was her mother and Eve was Abigail's age.

'Still need convincing I'm not a creep, huh?'

'No, no, I'm . . .' She met his eyes, kind and devoid of judgment, which emboldened her to speak the truth. 'I'm a little . . . awkward around strangers at first.'

'I get it.' He accepted her statement so naturally she wondered why she didn't go around all day telling people she was shy. 'No pressure. But I'm pretty easy to talk to. And last night I made too much Somalian chicken soup, which is, frankly, delicious.'

Ooh. That might do it. At Mann's she'd bought some plain ham and a can of tuna fish for lunches, since all she'd seen in Shelley's meat drawer was a package of bologna.

Clayton hadn't put out a single predatory vibe all morning, Shelley had been obviously fond of him, and this was the Midwest, where people were renowned for their friendliness. It wouldn't kill her to have lunch with a client.

Besides, the longer she stood here thinking about it, the more of a dork she'd appear to be.

So she put on her big-girl pants and smiled. 'Thanks, Clayton. Lunch would be nice.'

Chapter 6

October 4, 1978 (Wednesday)

It happened again today. It happens all the time! It is so hard to stay smiling and polite. When are you and Daniel going to have children? You'd have the most beautiful children. Such handsome boys and such beautiful girls.

For God's sake, of course we would! I want to say, 'Tell you what, I'll have a baby when you shut up. I'll pop one out right here on the sidewalk. Good enough?'

I can't stand the gossip I know is going on. Why can't they have children? Is it her? Is it him? It can't be her. Or can it? Maybe it is. What could be wrong with her? We need to find out.

I must, must, must think of something.

Our sex life is good. It was worth the agony and shame of the stretching so I'd have something resembling a decent vagina for Daniel. Men need vaginas, sorry to say. If I was to have any hope of being everything to him the way he's everything to me, I had to have one, or as close as my traitor body will give me.

But a vagina isn't any good if it doesn't have a cervix and uterus attached. It's just a tube, and might as well be in a blow-up doll.

Love and gooey kisses to me,

Still-childless Jillian

* * *

'To the kitchen.' Clayton led Eve back into the blessedly warm house through the living room, which had what appeared to be original artworks crowding all four walls: still lifes and portraits, one canvas a nearly life-sized geisha surrounded by falling petals that looked like snow.

'The decor in here is amazing.' And the longer she was there, the more strangely uncomfortable she found it.

'My parents' taste. Want to use it in the new room too?' He glanced at her, eyes dancing. Had he deliberately put her in a tough spot?

'Everything is exquisitely worked out.' Eve chose her words carefully, arriving in the grim kitchen, itching to redo it with a pink refrigerator and yellow and pink polka-dot linoleum – just to piss it off. 'It isn't what I would have expected in a lake house. And to answer your other question, I think this kind of decor would be a little jarring in a sunroom.'

He nodded approvingly. 'I hate it too. It's on my list to change.'

Maybe he would *like* a pink refrigerator. 'Your parents won't mind?'

'I'm the one using the house, so I can't say I care. It's not like I'll be throwing things away.' He frowned at a large print of a black and white owl. 'Put them in storage maybe.'

'So will the sunroom be used mainly in the summer, or are you planning to spend time here all year round?'

He opened the Darth Vader refrigerator door and contemplated its interior. 'That becomes a surprisingly complicated question.'

'Oh?'

'Tell you what. I'm going to shower and get the stink off while the soup heats. If you're still here when I get out, I'll tell you.'

She found herself smiling. 'Fair enough. Anything I can do to help?'

'Can you chop radishes and cabbage? Use a microwave?'

'Yes to both.'

'Then you can do that.' He took out a covered saucepan and put it over a low heat on the stove, which fired up bright orange within a few seconds. Then he pulled out two radishes, a couple of cabbage leaves, and a bowl of rice. 'Chopping board . . . knife . . . microwave is over there for the rice. And thank you. I'll be quick.'

He wasn't kidding. She'd sliced the radishes and cabbage, heated the rice so it was steaming hot, and managed to find a couple of bowls and spoons by the time he came back in, wearing jeans and a sweatshirt, feet bare, his dark hair curling from the wet, smelling soapy and masculine. Sharing his kitchen turned suddenly intimate. Eve should have turned him down and gone back to Shelley's for tuna fish and ham.

But not bologna.

'You're still here.'

'Apparently.' She retreated to the other side of the kitchen island, pasting on a smile. 'Tasks complete. I was looking for napkins.'

'That drawer.' He pointed, then went over to the refrigerator again. 'I have sparkling water, beer, and an already open bottle of Chenin Blanc. It's fairly low-alcohol if you worry about that. Goes great with the soup.'

'I shouldn't.'

'No?'

She came up with two napkins that felt like linen. Black, of course. 'It doesn't seem . . . professional.'

A mere raise of his eyebrow reflected her words unflatteringly back to her ears. 'I won't tell if you don't.'

Eve set the napkins next to the bowls, annoyed at herself for coming across as amateur and uptight. 'Half a glass. And a sparkling water too, please.'

'It's a deal.' He took the wine bottle out of the refrigerator and held it up for her consideration. 'Underdog, from South Africa. I discovered it recently.'

'You know about wine?'

'I know about my wine merchant. He knows about wine.'

She liked that he didn't pretend to be more than he was. 'My dad was a collector of sorts.'

'Yeah? What did he do?'

'Teacher.' She hurried on before he could ask more. 'What about yours?'

'What did he teach that he could collect wine? I'm guessing not kindergarten.' He poured out two glasses, both only marginally less than full, and handed one to her.

Eve took it reluctantly, though it did look refreshing. She didn't have to finish it. 'He taught theater.'

'Yeah? Where?'

'Los Angeles.'

'I would have guessed New York.'

'He started there. What about your dad?'

'My dad took over his father's advertising business. That's where he met my mom, when they both started there in their twenties. She became an account executive. Dad made it his life's work to get rich and stay rich. He did this very well, as did my mother.' He set a blue can of LaCroix seltzer in front of Eve and held up his wine glass. 'Cheers. Here's to the project.'

She clinked glasses with him, then took a tentative sip. The flavor was crisp and delicious, much more interesting than last night's Pinot Grigio. 'I don't know if Shelley said anything, but . . . I haven't done many big projects yet.'

'I was warned.' He shrugged. 'But the island isn't exactly crawling with architects, and I can't say no to Shelley. Worst case, I don't like what you propose and we work it out.'

'That's fine.' She could feel herself blushing, annoyed that she hadn't been cagey enough to hide her lack of confidence around him. Mistake number two. 'You said your parents are in Europe. Are they working there now?'

'Retired. Do you want to eat here or in the dining room? Less formal here, nicer view out there.'

'Here's fine.'

'Good. In that dining room, I feel like I should be wearing velvet knickers.'

She laughed and helped him set the round wooden table by the windows with arty placements and ornate silverware.

Clayton put a scoop of hot rice into each bowl, then ladles of the nearly clear broth, generously studded with shredded chicken. 'Here's the soup, and . . .' Darting back to the refrigerator, he retrieved two small bowls, one containing a red paste, one a green sauce. 'The red is this recipe's version of *berbere*, primarily spices and lime juice. The other is a salsa of lime, garlic, tomatoes and serrano peppers. It's good and hot. Add those to the soup in whatever quantities you're brave enough to try, then put the radishes and cabbage on top.'

Eve was practically drooling. 'It sounds amazing. Do you have a connection to Somalia?'

He sat opposite her. 'I subscribe to a cooking magazine and this recipe was in it; does that count?'

'It makes you an expert.' Eve inhaled over the bowl. Some citrusy flavor in there. Lime? Lemongrass? She stirred in a bit of the *berbere*, then salsa, and added a small handful of the raw vegetables, suddenly ravenous. Stress plus low-fat, white-flour breakfast equaled empty stomach much too quickly. She tasted a spoonful and rolled her eyes ecstatically. A fascinating tangle of flavors, and a satisfying contrast between each cold crunch and hot sip. Addictive. She'd have to work not to tip the bowl down her throat and be done in under a minute. 'This is *so* delicious.'

'Thanks.' He dug into his own soup, clearly pleased.

There was no noise for half a minute but dainty slurps and surreptitious crunching. Eve wished Clayton would put on a heavy-metal soundtrack, praying her stomach wouldn't gurgle. At least the silence wasn't as hideous as the previous night with Shelley.

'You were telling me about your family?'

'Right.' He stirred more salsa into his soup. 'I'm the baby.'

'Ah. So am I.'

'Yeah? How many others?'

'Two sisters.'

'Same here. Mine are a lot older. Mom had just sent Lisa, the younger one, off to college when she found out she was pregnant with me. So my siblings are more like aunts than sisters.'

'And you became essentially an only child.'

'Uh-huh. An only child whose parents kept him because they were Catholic and didn't believe in abortion.'

Eve looked up from her soup. He didn't sound bitter, didn't look bitter either. But that had to be a nasty burden. Her own parents' secret adoption scheme was epically messed up, but at least Eve and her sisters never questioned that they were wanted – if only as a way for Jillian to pull off the lie that she was fertile. 'I'm sorry.'

'Yeah, I was quite the inconvenience.' He smirked humorlessly, blotting his full lips with black linen. 'Their empty-nest plan had been to move to Europe. Of course they were much too smart to let me ruin their lives. They hired a nanny, who pretty much raised me during the school year while they bounced back and forth over the ocean.'

'Wow.' Eve didn't know what else to say. He seemed completely at home divulging his story, which was fine, but she wasn't sure how appropriate it was for her to comment on it, especially when she wanted to say: *Your parents sound like selfish dirt-bags*.

He swirled wine in his glass and took a sip, the movements unselfconscious and practiced. Her father used to do the same, but in his hands it always struck her as designed to impress. 'I'm making it sound more dire than it is. I did get to go abroad a lot. Nearly every summer.'

'I don't feel that sorry for you anymore.'

'Few people do. So what about you? Your dad was a teacher. Did you get to travel? I had a friend whose professor father was always taking sabbaticals abroad with the whole family. Pretty great way to grow up.'

'We did travel, yes. We were lucky that way too.' Eve took a small sip of wine and followed it with water, wishing Clayton was more typical of his gender and happy talking only about himself. She'd developed standard avoidance answers over the years to questions about her parents, but there were times when the hedging felt dishonest rather than socially necessary. This seemed to be one of those times. Maybe because Clayton had been so disarmingly forthcoming.

'Where did you grow up?'

'Los Angeles.' Her stock answer instead of Beverly Hills. 'I live on the Massachusetts coast now, just above Boston. You can't get me away from water.'

He looked out toward the lake, his arched nose impressive in profile. 'You do get used to having a horizon handy. Did your mom work?'

'In the movie business. You can't get away from showbiz in LA. Showbiz or surfers.'

'Surfers? Really?' He looked astonished. 'That's not like, I don't know, a myth?'

Eve nearly choked on her soup, picturing the black-suited dots bobbing up and down along the coast practically every day of the year. 'A myth! No, they're everywhere.'

'I thought it was just a cliché.'

'Like cows in Wisconsin?' Eve couldn't stop grinning.

'I know nothing about that. Nothing. I'm from *Illinois*.' He chuckled when she looked blank. 'Classic neighboring state rivalry. We call them Cheeseheads. They call us FIBs.'

'Fibs?'

'Illinois Bastards. I'll let you figure out what the F is for.'

'Got it.' She had a little more wine. Its chill was a perfect way to soothe the soup's heat. 'Did you always live in Illinois?'

'In Chicago. A two-story apartment right next to the lake; what's called the gold coast.' He rolled his eyes. 'Poor little rich boy.'

She shrugged. 'Money doesn't get rid of all pain. You still bleed. You still get sick. You still have to live. Life can suck for anyone.'

'You sound as if you know what you're talking about.'

'Yes.' Eve wasn't planning to say more. 'You didn't have a close family, then.'

'No, I did not.' He smiled pleasantly. 'I'm sure I'm massively screwed up.'

She barked out a laugh. 'You hide it well.'

'Thank you.' His smile made her reach for her wine again, though his eyes were nothing but friendly.

'My family was a little on the dysfunctional side too.' Immediately Eve regretted letting the comment slip. She'd been seduced by his openness. Inevitably, too many questions would follow.

'Ah, sorry. We get what we get.' Clayton lifted the bottle. 'More wine?'

'No, no.' She still had plenty left.

He poured another inch into his own glass. 'Tell me one thing your family has made impossible for you, and one thing it's made possible.'

Eve leaned back warily in her chair. 'Are we playing Truth or Dare?'

He gave her a quick look, putting down the bottle. 'Was that too personal?'

'I don't know.' She blotted her lips self-consciously. His questions had been unusual and interesting. But any attempt to find out about her family felt like a dangerous intrusion. Her mistake for inviting this one. 'I'm probably just too private.'

Clayton didn't show even a hint of disappointment. 'No problem. We can talk about something else. Do you want more soup?'

'Just a little, thank you. It's so good.' She was relieved and touched by his sensitivity to her reticence. While he ladled rice into her bowl and poured the soup over, she thought about what he'd asked. Thought-provoking questions, bringing up new territory around an old and often painful subject. What had her family made possible? What had it made impossible?

Clayton put the steaming bowl in front of her and helped himself to more.

She stirred in the red and green, watching their Christmas colors mix to disappointing brown, and scattered more radishes and cabbage over the hot surface.

A sip of wine for courage.

'I'll take a stab at it. At your questions.'

'Sure.' His calm response strengthened Eve's theory that anything she said would be accepted and processed as part of getting to know her, whether he agreed, approved or neither.

How different from the Day of Judgment discussions she and Mike had been having lately. The ones she'd had with her father, with teachers at school, often with her boss as well, in which fragile egos meant that being right, coming out on top, was more important than listening or fostering a respectful exchange of ideas.

'Let's see. My family made it *im*possible for me to want children. The dysfunction put me off. My family made it *possible* for me to become an architect. I believe I was wired to be one, but I also needed something to be good at that had nothing to do with either my parents or my sisters.'

'Interesting.' He put his spoon down and folded his hands together, elbows on the table. 'This is my theory of dysfunction and misfortune in the world. Too much black-and-white thinking. Every character trait has both a positive and negative aspect, as does everything that happens to you. There is no absolute good or bad. This isn't new thinking, obviously, but I have been obsessed lately with applying this philosophy to my life. Very liberating.'

'How so?' Eve reached for her wine, relaxed now and no longer caring if she finished it. This had turned out to be a really nice lunch. She was not attracted to Clayton, he wasn't hitting on her, they had no baggage and no expectations other than client and architect. Just two people talking about whatever interested them. 'Give me an example.'

'Example, okay.' He turned to look out at the lake. 'As you can see, I tend to be very open. I can put people off by sharing too much – that's bad. I can also get close to people more quickly – that's good. You had a dysfunctional family – bad.

Separating yourself from the crazy landed you solidly in what you were born to do – good.'

She finished her second helping of soup, wishing she had room for more. 'Looking for the silver lining?'

'Sort of. That's more a reaction to something bad that's happened. This goes beyond that. It frees you not to expect that life will be good or bad. You throw away those labels, accept that it's life, and get through it.'

She frowned. 'I'm not sure that's really inspiring.'

'I think it is. Inspiring and freeing.' He grinned at her. It seemed absurd that they'd only just met. 'You think I'm flaking out.'

'No, no.' Eve wrinkled her nose at his skeptical look. 'Well . . . maybe.'

He finished his soup and got to his feet. 'Would you like to try a spiced fruit bar? I made them yesterday. With coffee?'

'Yes to both, thank you.'

'Coming up.' He moved around the kitchen, clearly in his element, working with concentration and efficient grace. Eve put her elbows on the table – her mother wasn't there to yell at her – and watched him openly. Heat water, measure beans – real coffee! – grind beans, serve fruit bars.

'Milk in your coffee? Cream? Half-and-half?'

'Black is fine. Tell me more about what you do when you're up here.'

'I'm usually up for a week or two in the summer.' He rescued the kettle just as it started to shriek. 'Mom and Dad show up at some point, and my sisters come over from the West Coast when they can. We bike, kayak, read, cook. Then I come up alone for long weekends in the fall, longer if I can swing it. Sometimes I work, sometimes not. That may change soon.'

'Why?' It didn't strike her that now she was the one asking

too-personal questions until the words came out of her mouth, feeling totally natural, as if she had every right to his secrets.

'A midlife crisis,' he announced firmly.

'Oh come on.' She shook her head. 'You're not in midlife yet.'

'I'm nearly forty.'

Her eyebrows lifted. 'I would have said much younger.'

'Okay, thirty-two.'

Eve cracked up. 'That's not "nearly forty".'

'I know, I know.' He sat and put her coffee in front of her. 'Truth is, lately I've been feeling confined in Chicago. A little like I've been there my whole life.'

'I thought you had.'

'Oh, right.' He grinned mischievously.

'And this place is what you'd pick for a second choice? After Chicago?' She tried not to sound appalled, and failed.

'It's a transition time for me. I need to get away from . . . someone.' His grin faded. 'Someone I have gone a long way toward getting out of my system, but . . .'

'She works in your office.'

His look of astonishment nearly made her giggle. 'How did you know?'

'Actually a lucky guess. A person at work is hard to get away from unless you quit. Or work from your house in Washington Island. Does that mean the renovation on your apartment isn't really happening?'

'It is happening, but it's not keeping me away this long.' He sipped his coffee grimly. 'After my divorce, I did the number two stupidest thing by falling for a co-worker.'

'What's the number one?'

'That'd be falling for your best friend's wife.'

'Ooh.' She grimaced. 'Yes. Bad.'

'Actually . . . Christie was part of what precipitated the

divorce, though I didn't ask her out until it was final. Anyway, I fell hard, which is apparently the first thing everyone does out of a bad marriage. I didn't realize she was a typical symptom. I thought it was love.'

'I'm sorry.'

He shrugged. 'It was great at first.'

'It's always great at first.' Eve sipped her coffee, pleased she'd avoided any bitterness in her tone – and that Clayton made a fabulous cup of coffee.

'We connected very intensely. Unfortunately, everything *else* about the relationship didn't work. That's the simplified version anyway.'

'I understand.' She put the mug down and picked up a fruit bar. 'All the pieces have to be there.'

'Exactly. She . . . Well, anyway, we broke up. But then once we weren't dating but still saw each other every day . . .'

Eve nodded, understanding perfectly. 'Everything you loved about her was still there, but you no longer had to deal with the bad stuff, so you needed to get out before you fell for her again.'

'We have a winner – a stuffed teddy bear for the lady!' He threw up his hands, then brought them down abruptly. 'I must be boring you to death.'

'No, not at all.' Not even remotely. She held up the rest of her fruit bar, mouth tingling with ginger, cinnamon and clove. 'These are fantastic, by the way.'

'Easy. I'll give you the recipe if you want.' He helped himself to one. 'It's your turn to overshare.'

'No, not me.' She wrinkled her nose, shaking her head. 'I'm an undersharer. Tell me more about your newspaper career.'

'Ah, that's a sad story. You might have to fling yourself in the lake.'

Eve shuddered. 'Much too cold.'

'In January in Chicago, there's a Polar Bear Plunge.' He shivered dramatically. 'People go right in. Milwaukee, too, on New Year's Day. Totally crazy.'

'They do that even in Swampscott.' Eve finished chewing, embarrassed to have spoken with her mouth full. 'And yes, it's crazy.'

'*Swamp*scott? What a charming name.'

She rolled her eyes. 'You were telling me about your sad life . . .'

'Yes, right.' Clayton took a hasty sip of coffee. 'I studied journalism at Northwestern. Graduated in 2009, which I think makes me older than you.'

'How do you know how old I am?'

'I don't, it just makes me think that.

'Ha. I'm twenty-nine. Go on.'

'My first job was as a reporter with the *Chicago Sun-Times*. No!' He held up his hand. 'I lied, my first job was as publisher and owner of the *Gold Coast Times*, when I was twelve. Hot news and goings-on in the neighborhood. During the summer I owned and operated the *Washington Island Herald*. Fabulous in-depth stories about the mosquito population and what washed up on the beach.'

'That's adorable.'

'Did you know what you wanted early on too?'

'Oh, yes.' She beamed, confident he'd know exactly what she was talking about. 'When I was a little girl, I'd stack and arrange shoeboxes into houses. My mother had an embarrassing number of shoes, so those were always available. I'd cut out little windows and shingle the roofs with colored paper. I was obsessed from way back. Thought I'd be I. M. Pei by the time I was twenty-five.'

'And I knew I was on my way to the top when I was hired

by the *Sun-Times* right out of college. All those people who said being a journalist would be a struggle? Not for me! *My* future was brilliant because I was *that good*.' He scoffed. 'Naïve dork.'

'Aw, you were young.' She put down her empty mug. 'It's important to have that kind of confidence at that age. Otherwise you'd realize you knew nothing about anything and just stay home.'

'Ha! Very true.' He offered her another spiced fruit bar, then took the plate over to the counter when she shook her head. 'Two years later, I married Felicia, and boom, got cut from the paper.'

'Nice wedding present.' Eve stood and picked up her soup bowl and coffee mug.

'It wasn't a happy time. Felicia was in graduate school in Chicago, so I didn't want to leave the city. One of my friends was doing technical writing for JPMorgan Chase, and they brought me on. I liked it okay and did well, and I'm still at it seven years later.'

Eve lowered her dishes into the sink. 'Wait, why is that a sad story?'

'Ah, it's not really. I'm just sad about what's happening to newspapers. Gobbled up by huge corporations that care more for profit than quality. They slash away bit by bit until the paper is unrecognizable as itself. Or anything really. It's the part of capitalism – and technology – that I hate most.'

'But it's also *good* because . . .'

'Oh, right. That.' He poured the uneaten soup into a small glass storage container. 'I never could think of one for that because I get so pissed off my brain stops working.'

Eve returned to the table to finish clearing. 'Everyone has something to be irrational over.'

'What's yours?'

'Hmm.' She stood holding his plate and mug, searching for a safe answer. 'Architectural clutter. Spaces crammed with under-designed buildings it would take so little not only to make beautiful or graceful in their own right, but also to fit in with what's around them. When you're in an area in a city or town that has real coherence . . . it's relaxing and a joy to be in. I also become slobberingly furious about beautiful houses of irreplaceable quality in old neighborhoods that get torn down and replaced by sprawling mansions with every modern convenience and not the slightest hint of a soul.'

He inclined his head. 'You speak the truth, Obi-Wan.'

'Bottom line, people suck sometimes.' Eve turned and crossed back to the sink. 'I'd become a hermit, but . . . no room service.'

Clayton's laughter pleased her absurdly. He put the soup into the refrigerator. 'Changing subjects . . . what does your boyfriend do? Also an architect?'

'He's a schoolteacher.'

'A noble profession.'

'He's very dedicated.'

'I guess he'd have to be.' He was watching her closely. 'How long have you been together?'

'Three years.' She turned to open the dishwasher.

'How did you meet him?'

'Spilled beer on him in a bar.'

'Classic.'

She put their mugs and plates into the dishwasher, then glanced back at Clayton to find him still studying her. 'What?'

'This is none of my business, but when you talk about your boyfriend, your face shuts down, your voice drops and you curl in on yourself.'

Eve straightened without thinking, then realized that was

about as stupid as slowing down after a cop had already recorded your speed. 'I don't really know what to say about that.'

Except that he'd freaked her out, both that she reacted that way talking about Mike and because Clayton had noticed. Did everyone? Shelley? Her sisters? Other friends?

'Sorry. That was out of line.'

She shrugged and turned back to the dishwasher. 'You saw what you saw.'

'I didn't have to say anything.'

'It's okay.' She finished loading their soup bowls and dried her hands. 'Thank you so much for lunch. I should go back. I don't want Shelley thinking I came up here just to drink wine and goof off.'

'She won't think that.' He finished putting away the last of the food and stood with his hands on his hips. 'But if you ever want to drink wine and goof off again, my door is open.'

'Thank you.' She found herself folding her arms and forced them down by her sides. 'I had a good time.'

'I did too.' He walked with her to the front door. 'If you want to come over and measure, look, meditate in the space, ask more questions, whatever you creative types do, feel free. How long do you think you'll be on the island?'

'A few weeks at least. More if I need it.' She stepped out of the door and turned back to face him. 'I left my job, so I'm free to do what I want.'

'That sounds really nice. I'm also available as a tour guide if you're looking to take a break.' He lifted a hand, tall and smiling in the teal doorway.

Eve ambled back down the driveway, checking her phone for text messages – cell coverage was iffy on the island – cheeks still a little hot from the wine. The sun had come out while she was inside; the grass was thinking harder about turning green, though it hadn't quite made the commitment yet.

She found herself humming, a spring in her step, feeling happier and more relaxed than she had in a while. More than happy and relaxed – pumped up, confident, ready to take on the world.

Even if she and Clayton never sat down and spoke again, she had this one clear example of what she most prized in a friendship and what she needed to insist on in a relationship. Real conversation, not one-upmanship. Listening without judgment, respecting opinions that differed.

She could talk like this with her sisters – Rosalind certainly, and Olivia when she wasn't too caught up in being Olivia. A couple of her school friends and her work colleague Barbara. Mike's friends . . . yeah, never mind.

Mike . . .

She had been right that she'd needed this time away from him to gain perspective. Mike judged because he had been judged. A dyslexic kid, he'd battled years of ridicule from his father, who'd told him he'd never amount to anything. Eve still wanted to sock the guy every time she saw him. In response, Mike had worked his ass off and become the first kid in his family to graduate from college. But the damage had been done, damage he was still reckoning with in therapy. Who knew how much of it he could repair?

She put away her phone – some chatter from her sisters about Olivia's birthday on Monday, and Rosalind's in April, nothing that needed responding to now – and was about to get into her car when she noticed a blob of red at the end of the driveway. Her blood ran a little cold.

'Abigail?' She walked up to confront her. Abigail stood sheepishly from where she'd been sitting, leaning against Clayton's mailbox. 'What are you doing here?'

'I was walking past. I saw your car.' Abigail ducked her head. 'Are you working for him, too?'

'Clayton? Yes. So?'

'I was sorta hoping you'd introduce me.' Her discomfort was so intense, it was hard to watch. 'I mean, as your assistant or something. So I could be around while you were . . . talking. And hear the architecture stuff.'

Eve stood watching Abigail's cheeks turn as red as her jacket. Something weird was going on here.

'Hey.' Clayton was jogging toward them holding up Eve's laser measure. 'You forgot this.'

Abigail gave a small gasp. Her eyes nearly popped out of her head watching Clayton approach. She took a quick step back, then another.

Something *very* weird was going on here.

'Thanks, Clayton. I would have been cranky without it.' Eve took the laser and gestured behind her. 'This is Abigail. I met her at Red Cup this morning. She says she wants to be an architect. Somehow she found me here . . .'

'I was walking past.' Abigail glanced shyly up at Clayton and ducked her head. 'Nice to meet you.'

'Yeah, same here.' He looked back and forth between the women, obviously confused. 'So . . . you're Eve's apprentice?'

'Yes.'

'*No*.' They spoke at the same time. Eve sighed, not pleased to be trapped in this situation. 'I said I would teach her a little about what I do. But not an official apprentice, no.'

A car slowed by the awkward trio. The driver, an older woman, peered out at them. Clayton waved. She lifted her hand and moved on.

'Do you ever go to Red Cup?' Abigail was looking at Clayton with a combination of hope and terror.

'Uh . . . not that much. Good coffee, though.' He took a step back toward his house. 'I should—'

'What *do* you do around here?' Her face grew pinker again as she sensed them both staring. 'I'm totally trying to figure out why people like this island. I guess.'

'It's quiet.' He spoke gently, smiling, but took another step back. 'People don't bother you.'

She blushed harder, staring at the ground, looking so miserable, Eve couldn't decide whether to hug her or worry she'd start crying again. 'You mean me. I'm bothering you.'

'No, that's not what—'

'Hey.' Eve took Abigail's arm, exchanging glances with Clayton. 'Let's let Clayton go back to work, okay? You and I can drive over to Shelley's house and talk.'

Eve gave Clayton a head start back to his house, then pulled Abigail toward her car. The second Clayton disappeared from view, Abigail yanked her arm free. 'That *sucked*. Totally sucked. I completely blew it. I didn't say *anything* I planned to. It was a *total disaster*.'

Eve started feeling sick. Clayton was more than twice Abigail's age. She should be crushing on boys in her class. 'Honey, I think you're fishing in the wrong pond here.'

'I'm *not*. I know what I'm doing.'

'Okay.' She was starting to wonder if Abigail was unbalanced. It was not a comforting thought. 'Maybe this is something you should go back and talk out with your dad?'

Abigail gave a short, harsh laugh. 'Oh *that's* ironic.'

'I know, I know. But I thought he might—'

'You don't understand.' She stopped walking, face contorting with misery, tears filling her pretty eyes and spilling down her cheeks. 'Clayton *is* my dad.'

Chapter 7

November 3, 1978 (Friday)

I am so excited. So, so, so excited. I have an idea that I know will work. Daniel says it's crazy, it will fail spectacularly, but I say if we plan and plan and plan and think of everything, everything that could go wrong, and then develop plans for handling that too, I know it can be done. I have to make this happen. The world has been unfair to me for long enough.

I can change Daniel's mind. He'll do anything for me. I would do anything for him, too, but he asks for nothing but my undying love, and, of course, sex. He's a man that way.

If we can just find the right person, it will work. I know it will. My sister Christina can be the midwife and deliver the child in secret. Then I will finally have the baby I want so desperately. A sweet-smelling, cooing little darling who will belong to me. A boy or girl we can give all the love and attention children deserve from their parents.

I still have had no word from my mother or father – no acknowledgment of the letters I've been faithfully writing, all the way back to the week I left, no thank yous for the gifts and money I have sent over the years – but my sister Christina and I stay in touch so I know they are healthy, in their bodies if not in their souls.

The parent–child bond is everything. I've often thought Daniel and I must be playing at it subconsciously when I sit on his lap or he rests his head against my breasts. I heard that kissing originated from mothers passing chewed food to their little ones. So it makes sense that I can't stop trying to repair this break one way or another.

When I have my perfect baby, I will show up at our sad, dark little house in Maine. I dare them to turn their backs then on the mother I have become.

Eve stared at Abigail, who had by now broken down completely. She thought Clayton was her *father*? Hadn't she said earlier that she was staying with her dad on the island? Either Abigail was crazy or Clayton was.

Eve voted for Abigail.

'Abigail. Hon, you need to tell me where your – where you're staying.' If she could find the girl's father, she could talk to him, hand Abigail back into his custody. This was way out of Eve's league.

'Nowhere.'

'Okay.' Bad to worse. 'What . . .. where are you sleeping at night?'

'I had a room, but I used up my money last night,' she wailed. 'I can't stay anywhere now.'

'So . . .' Eve was completely at a loss. She didn't even have a tissue to offer.

Abigail sniffed and wiped her eyes with her hands. 'I came up here to find my father, but it took me days to get up the nerve, and now I just acted like a complete moron. I wasn't ready. He came out of the house and I just couldn't *handle* it.'

'But Abigail . . .' Eve tried to sound patient, 'if he's your father, why didn't he—'

'He doesn't know.' She wiped away fresh tears. 'Mom never told him. When she was pregnant with me she married Glen, who I thought was my real dad until—'

'Wait.' Eve put a hand up, the relaxed glow from Clayton's wine and conversation long gone. 'This is too intense to talk about out here. Let's go to Shelley's, get you calmed down and we can start at the beginning. Okay? It's just a few houses away.'

Abigail nodded, tears still cascading down her young face.

Eve drove her to Shelley's, praying the older woman wouldn't be too upset that on Eve's first full day on the island, she was bringing home a stray adolescent meltdown. Best case, Shelley wouldn't be home, at least until Eve could get Abigail more presentable.

Shelley was home. She took one look at Abigail's blotchy face, plunked her hands on her hips and announced, 'Well. The girl from Mann's.'

Abigail nodded and hiccuped, bending to pet Marx, who was investigating her as a potential new friend.

Shelley turned to Eve, face implacable. 'She and I met there a couple of days ago.'

'I didn't have enough money with me.' Abigail turned red again. 'I'll pay you back.'

'Nonsense. It was two dollars. My treat.'

'Shelley, Abigail. Abigail, Shelley.' Eve grimaced apologetically to her hostess. 'She's having a bad moment.'

'So I see. I'll put the kettle on. Tea and cookies. Box of tissues wouldn't hurt either.'

'Thank you.' Eve could have hugged her. As a mother, Shelley had the advantage in handling this situation. Doubtless she'd seen teenage drama before, though maybe not on this scale.

'You two go out to the porch where you can talk. I'll bring the tea.'

'I can help,' Abigail said.

'No, no.' Shelley made shooing motions. 'Go. You can help clean up later. Eve, turn on the heat out there if you need it.'

'Thank you.' Eve herded the thankfully calm girl out on to the chilly porch, turned on the heat and gestured Abigail to the rocker, then sat two chairs away so as not to crowd her. Marx settled in between them. 'Pretty out here, isn't it?'

'You don't have to make small talk.'

Fine with her. Great, actually. 'Okay. Start at the beginning, because nothing makes sense to me.'

'It doesn't make sense to me either.'

'Try.'

Abigail leaned her head back against the chair, puffed her tear-stained cheeks and exhaled wearily.

'Okay. So we live just outside Milwaukee, in Shorewood, which is a pretty liberal place. Mom and Dad are total born-again conservative Christians. They would have fit better someplace like Waukesha. But anyway, Shorewood High School turned out to be really good for me, because I'm . . .' she sent a quick look to Eve, her swollen eyes painfully vulnerable, 'not straight.'

Eve made sure her expression didn't change; just nodded calmly while her heart broke. Shameful that this beautiful girl had to worry that she would be condemned or rejected because of something she couldn't change.

'My dad hates gays. So does his church. Or, well, they don't *say* that, just stupid stuff like that we can be healed if we just *pray* hard enough.' She blew a raspberry, echoing Eve's feelings. 'Like we're sick, not just different.'

'Got it.' Eve absently watched a gull fight newly risen wind for a wobbly landing on the rocky shore. 'When you said your *dad* hates gays . . . you mean your stepdad?'

Abigail's tears started again. 'I *thought* Glen was my dad until last week. He and Mom never said anything different.'

Eve hunched her shoulders against a burn of anger. She knew what it felt like to discover a parent wasn't biologically related. No true upheaval intellectually, but emotionally it felt like your life had suddenly been translated into a language you couldn't read. 'Go on. Tell it your way.'

'Knock, knock. It's the tea lady.' Shelley brought in a tray on which sat two steaming mugs alongside sugar, lemon and milk, a plate piled high with Oreos, and a family-size box of tissues.

'Thanks, Shelley.' Eve smiled gratefully, though the sudden memory of Abigail wolfing the breakfast sandwich that morning made her want to feed the girl something more substantial than cookies.

The tea was hot and delicious, brewed strong. She watched Abigail crunch through four Oreos, then couldn't take it anymore.

'After we talk, would you like me to make you a sandwich?'

'Yes. Please. Thank you.' Abigail took a cautious sip of tea, then wrinkled her nose and added an amount of sugar that made Eve's teeth ache. 'Anyway, because of my family and church, I've always been totally terrified of coming out. I used to pray to God to change me, or at least let me stay closeted and still somehow be happy. I didn't hang with openly gay kids at school. It was like I thought I could catch coming-out or something. I mean, it was stupid.'

'Given your upbringing, it makes sense to me.'

'Maybe.' Abigail shrugged, but Eve got the impression she was pleased. 'Then I started getting close to this one girl on the cross-country team. Friends-close, not romantic.'

'Either way doesn't matter to me,' Eve said. 'Go on.'

'One day she came out to me. I mean, we both sort of knew, but hearing it out loud was *such* a high and a relief and I don't know what else, but it was amazing.' She smiled briefly, staring down into her tea. 'But it made me really angry at myself for waiting so long. When you're with someone like you, who understands you, and everything you are is out there and accepted, it's the greatest feeling there is. All you straight people get to take that totally for granted. Finally I could stop feeling like I was fatally diseased or whatever. Like maybe I wasn't doomed because of something I was born with.'

'Of *course* you're not doomed.'

'Yeah, tell that to my . . . to *Glen*.' She reached for another Oreo, then stopped herself and sipped more tea instead. 'So anyway, then I came out to this girl, and that was so easy I came out to some other friends. The more people I told, the more I was accepted and the more comfortable I felt being myself. Then I got cocky and started thinking that if all these people were fine with it, people who didn't love me half as much as my parents, then coming out to them had to be totally cool, too. Logic, right?'

'Uh-oh.' Eve braced herself. It wasn't going to be cool.

'I started small with my parents, after church, at meals, whenever I could find the chance, talking about how Jesus loved everyone, prostitutes, tax collectors, lepers, you know, all the old stories. They were all over that. Then I asked, if that were true, why did our church say gay people could only be saved if they stopped being gay? Of course they had some bullshit answer about how people had to fight against their sin. I told them I knew gay kids at school and they were mostly great, and some were very devout, so that didn't make sense to me.

'Dad just looked at me and shook his head, said something like they couldn't truly dwell with the Lord unless they cast out the beast within them, like, I don't know, like it was science fiction. When he talks like that, it's like he's been temporarily possessed, like it's not really him anymore, not a real person.'

'It does sound a little preachy.'

'Right. I was like, really, Dad? But still, at that point in the conversation he wasn't all that upset. So next time I found an opening, I told my parents about my friend who tutors disadvantaged kids and gets straight A's, and oh, by the way, she's gay, et cetera. That went over okay too. They didn't say she was going to hell until she stayed away from other women or whatever. So a few days later, I told them at dinner that I was gay, and that I hoped they'd be okay with it.' Her voice cracked; tears started again. She put down her tea and used both hands to wipe them. 'Yeah, not . . . not so much.'

'Oh Abigail. I'm sorry.' Eve could only whisper the words.

The tears became a torrent, Abigail put her arms over her face and collapsed forward, sobbing in earnest.

Incredibly, Marx sat up, lifted his head and started howling.

Eve leaned over to him, grabbed his head and stroked him soothingly. 'Marx, shh.'

Abigail looked up, still crying, but now half laughing too. 'Oh my God. That was so weird.'

'I know. I'm sorry. I've never seen him do that. Marx, shh.' She drew him over to sit close to her. 'Good dog.'

'He's sweet.'

'You don't have to talk about this if you don't want to.'

Abigail sat up and took a tissue, blew her nose and wiped her eyes. 'It's okay. I want you to know.'

Eve nodded, stroking Marx's soft head, wondering why it was so important to Abigail to tell her. Maybe she hadn't been able to talk to anyone else and just needed to hear her story out loud, in her own words. Inconceivable to Eve, but very like Olivia or Mike. Or Clayton. 'Go ahead.'

'So after I told my . . . told Glen, he *argues* with me, like I'm just trying to annoy him, or like he knows me better than I do. Or like this was a generic teenage rebellion. "You're just going through a phase", blah blah blah. "Those people at school are influencing you", and so on and so on. Basic denial.'

'What did your mother do?'

Abigail rolled her eyes. 'What any good wife in the Church of Idiocy would do. She smiled and shrank down, probably hoping she'd disappear. Or maybe that I would.'

Eve set her jaw, holding tight to another upwelling of rage. 'Hmm.'

'When Glen realized I was serious, he lost it, started shouting these ridiculous things, like "You are a filthy stain on this family, an abomination in the eyes of the Lord", and on and on, *much* worse stuff than I ever heard anyone say in church about it. Then he finally said it was time I understood that . . . that I wasn't his daughter.' Her voice sailed upward on the last syllable. Marx stood, watching her anxiously.

'Oh Abigail.' Everything Eve could think of to say seemed totally inadequate. How did you comfort someone whose bedrock had given way like that? How would she have wanted to be comforted when hers did?

'At first I thought he meant metaphorically, you know – "You're no daughter of mine, you're dead to me", that kind of thing. But no.' She was trembling, voice rising. 'He wanted me to know that nothing as disgusting as me could have come from his sacred Jesus-brand sperm. That my mom got knocked up by some guy she barely knew and he gallantly sailed in to marry her and pretend I was his, which apparently worked out fine until he realized he'd inherited a defective child of Satan.'

Abigail paused for a stuttering breath, then made a helpless gesture. 'And you know what the sickest irony is? Abigail, my name, means . . . "father's joy".'

She burst into tears once more. Marx lifted his voice in another howl of outrage.

Eve grabbed his collar, furious that Glen had been able to rant on and on, spilling so much poison on to his daughter. Abigail's mother should have told him to shut up until he could control himself. 'Abigail, that is so unfair.'

'Then he threw me *out*.' She sobbed again, then her sobs became mixed with more giggles when Marx immediately accompanied her. 'Marx, you are . . . awesome.'

'He's upset that you're upset.'

'I know. I know.' Abigail knelt to hug him, getting tears licked off her face. 'It is so sweet.'

'So what did you do?' Eve sat back, releasing Marx. 'How did you know to come here to find Clayton?'

'Right away I went to stay with my friend and her family. I kept going to school and everything.' She grabbed a tissue from the tray and wiped her eyes. 'A week later, I tried to go back home, thinking he would have cooled off, but he wouldn't take me back. Mom probably wanted to fight for me, but I don't know, maybe she thought it wasn't any use until he calmed down. She told me about Clayton then, and where I could find him.'

She should have come with you. She should have protected you. Several seconds passed before Eve could trust her voice. 'How did your mom know Clayton was up here?'

'She didn't. She had like two seconds to pass me a note while Glen was stomping around threatening to call the cops if I wasn't off his property in two minutes. She'd written down

Clayton's name and the bare bones about what had happened; that Clayton had grown up in Chicago, like she did, and had a family house up here. Then Dad came back into the room and she turned back into the brainless twit she is around him.'

Her last words came out on a howl of anguish, which Marx took as his next vocal cue, neatly bringing Abigail back to semi-laughter. In the midst of her fury, Eve had the absurd thought that her dog was helping both of them get through this, and that maybe she should rent him out to counselors dealing with hysterical patients.

'Where did you go? What did you do?'

'I went back to my friend's house for one more night. Her parents said I could stay as long as I wanted, but I'm not their kid and they had a spring break trip planned. And I had to find my dad.'

'They let you go on your *own*?' Eve was so horrified that Marx turned anxiously toward her, chin lifted in case more howling was required.

'I told them I'd found him, that he was expecting me. They'd done so much and I thought I could manage. Probably stupid.'

'Brave.'

'Maybe.' She fondled Marx's ears, earning another kiss. 'I found his Chicago address online, went down there and asked around until someone finally said he was away because of the construction. So I thought he might have come up here and took a chance.'

'Incredibly brave.'

'If I was brave, I would have gone over to see him the first night. But every time I'd go to knock on his door, I'd freak out. I couldn't do it. I just . . .' her chin wobbled, 'I couldn't take another rejection.'

'I can understand that.'

'So you were like a miracle.' Abigail looked pleadingly up at Eve, eyes swollen red, hair plastered in clumps that fell over her pretty hazel eyes. 'I thought when I went over there to talk to him . . . maybe you could help me.'

Eve felt herself shrinking inside. 'Help you . . . ?'

'Talk to my dad. To Clayton. Tell him who I am. I'm hoping maybe he'll at least . . . I don't know, maybe he'll want me. Maybe eventually he could be some kind of dad to me . . . I don't know. Maybe this was a stupid idea. But it's all I have.'

Eve couldn't move.

'Will you come with me, Eve? Please? I don't want to do this . . . alone.' Her eyes were miserable, pleading.

Will you come with me? Please, Mom? I don't want to be alone with him.

Panic threatened. Eve felt frozen in place.

Abigail's crumpled face turned stony.

Eve closed her eyes and put a hand to her forehead. She knew that look. She'd worn it for most of her teenage years, her conditioned response whenever she was faced with indifference to her pain.

You are fine, Eve. This is just feelings. You are in control.

Dammit. How long would she be hijacked by this one hour of her life that had happened nearly twenty years ago?

'Everything okay in here?' Shelley stood in the doorway, frowning at Marx. 'Someone torturing the animal?'

'He's upset that I'm crying.' Abigail managed a tiny smile. 'He's adorable.'

'Well, if that's all. You're both all right?'

Eve turned her head, hoping she was wearing something close to a smile. 'Fine.'

'You, Abigail?'

'I'll be okay.'

'All right then. I'll take those tea things.' Shelley lifted the tray and went back out as if it were just another normal day in paradise.

Eve got up and paced toward the lake, stood staring through the glass at the distant white-capped waves. She wanted to get out on that wild water, away from people and problems, battle the waves with oars or a paddle, or a tiller.

She heard Abigail get up and come to stand next to her.

'I'm sorry, Abigail.'

'What does *that* mean?' She'd retreated into hostility.

'It means I'm sorry.'

'Will you help me?'

'I'll try.'

Abigail burst into tears again. At the same time, they both turned expectantly to Marx, and started giggling together.

'You didn't know he did that when people cried?'

'I had no idea.'

Abigail looked at her strangely. 'You've never cried around him?'

'I don't really cry.'

'You don't?' She looked astonished. 'My mom does. I mean, not all the time, but I've heard her.'

'Ah.' Eve didn't know what else to say about that. She was still too angry at Abigail's mother to care if she was unhappy. Especially since the woman had the means to feel better: leave the bigoted, narrow-minded jerk and do the right thing by her daughter. 'Let's get you that sandwich.'

'I'm too upset to eat now.'

'We'll make it anyway.' She started for the kitchen. 'Maybe you'll change your mind. You like tuna fish?'

'Who doesn't?'

It took longer to make a simple sandwich in a strange kitchen than at home, but Eve managed. By the time she'd finished, added one of the apples she'd bought at Mann's, and poured a glass of milk, Abigail was looking distinctly interested.

Eve brought the meal over to the breakfast nook and sat opposite while Abigail practically lunged for the food.

In an astonishingly short time, the sandwich was gone, apple crunched to its core, milk downed.

'Feel better?'

'Yes.' Abigail heaved a big sigh. 'I was totally starting to feel desperate. Last night I was standing at the end of his driveway and I couldn't make myself walk down it *again*, and I thought I might have to kill myself.'

'God, no. That fixes nothing.'

Eve's blood ran cold in an instant, picturing her mother's deathly still body lying on her bed. The doctor, Dad, Rosalind and Olivia had called it accidental overdose, but Eve had no doubt Jillian had killed herself. After years of agony over her career slipping into the Dumpster used by all no-longer-young Hollywood starlets, the day before she died, Jillian had found out that in spite of sending Eve upstairs with Mr Angel at their holiday party, the producer had given the comeback part of a lifetime to another actress.

'If you kill yourself, you have no chance to fix anything. Ever. You want to get back at your mother? Do it by—'

'Huh?' Abigail's face wrinkled in confusion. 'What was it about the story I told you that makes you think I want to get back at my *mother*?'

Eve stepped back, appalled at herself, at her rage and at the words that had come out of her mouth. 'Your father, then. Glen, or whatever his name is.'

Shelley appeared in the doorway. 'You want to spend the night here, Abigail?'

Abigail's face lit hopefully. 'Can I?'

'Plenty of room.' She lifted a finger and pointed it sternly. 'But no killing yourself in my house. You need to do that, you go somewhere else.'

A faint smile appeared on Abigail's lips. 'Yes, ma'am, I will.'

'Good. That's settled, then.' Shelley folded her arms across her plump middle.

Eve caught Abigail's eye. At the same moment, for some absurd reason – release of tension? – they both started laughing, making Marx stand and wag his tail.

'Crazy girls.' Shelley shook her head. 'Anything you need, Abigail? Toothbrush? Nightgown?'

'My stuff is still at the Airbnb.'

'Where were you staying?' Eve asked her.

'A room over by the ferry. Kind of a dump, but it was cheap.'

Eve put her arm awkwardly around Abigail's shoulders and gave her a squeeze that felt as self-conscious and artificial as it did instinctive, as if the warm and cold parts of herself were fighting. 'Come on. We'll go together.'

Chapter 8

January 10, 1979 (Wednesday)

A horrible thing happened today. It happens to all women in Hollywood, a rite of passage for starlets wanting to make it to the big time. Being already in the big time, I'm supposed to be over that hurdle. I did my time on the way up, pleading periods and soothing ruffled feathers as many ways as I could, of course telling Daniel everything immediately. After he stopped wanting to kill the men involved, I got him to understand. It's how the business works. He knows I will never cheat on him, not only because I love him desperately, but because I would rather bleed to death on the side of the road than let anyone but him and my doctor see me naked below the waist.

I handled it okay. Creepy balding guy as wide as he is tall. Why are the least attractive men always the most convinced that beautiful women will want them? And why don't people taste their own horrible breath? But the script he's offering is fabulous, so I managed oh-how-I-want-to and you-are-tempting-me-you-little-devil, and got him to calm down.

My mother taught my sister and me, in harsh words and by example, to be ashamed of our bodies and to hide them, to dread and hate what men were to do to us. She was wrong. God would not have invented such beauty and joy merely to torment humans. The first time I felt that excitement and pleasure, and the first time I let a boy touch me and saw those same feelings in him, I was sure of it. God intended us to enjoy what He made us for. Why would we deny and cower in shame over something He created?

If I have a daughter, a real woman, unlike me, I will teach her about the power her body has. I will teach her how to use that power, never to give it cheaply to men who don't deserve it.

From knowing her father, from understanding the depth of his honor and integrity and respect for women, my daughter will be aware that fine men exist.

But the snakes . . . she will encounter the snakes because there isn't a woman alive who hasn't. I will teach her at the youngest age possible never to feel she's a victim, but to look down on these pathetic men who come to us because we are goddesses and they are nothing. I will teach her how to handle herself, how to detach emotionally, how in those situations she can use her beautiful and fully female body as a weapon of triumph while not compromising herself and her beliefs.

I will teach her that the true power lies with her.

Abigail set her spoon down and looked first at Eve across the dining table and then at Shelley, sitting at its head. Her eyes were still swollen, but no longer red, and she'd showered and changed into fresh jeans and a blue plaid shirt while the rest of her clothes tumbled around Shelley's dryer. 'Do you really not talk at *all*?'

Shelley looked up sharply from her spinach and tortellini soup – the quickest thing Eve could think of to throw together for dinner. 'You can talk if you want.'

Eve cringed. On the way to pick up Abigail's things, she

had briefed the girl on Shelley's preference for silence during meals.

Abigail colored at the look on Eve's face and jerked her head to toss back her bangs. 'No, it's fine. I just wondered. I mean, Eve told me, but I didn't, I mean, I didn't expect *total* silence.'

'I'm an introvert.' Shelley looked suspiciously at the glass of wine Eve had poured from a relatively inexpensive bottle of white Bordeaux. 'Having to make conversation while I eat makes me anxious, and if I'm anxious, I don't enjoy my food.'

'Okay. I'm not saying it's bad or anything. It's just weird.'

Shelley took a sip of wine and her eyebrows rose over the rim of her glasses, but whether she'd been insulted by Abigail or the taste of the wine, Eve couldn't tell. 'It's not a gag order. If you want to talk, talk. I'll listen and be fine.'

'I shouldn't have said anything.' Abigail wore a sullen look to hide her embarrassment, a look so familiar that Eve could remember exactly how it had felt on her own features. She had to work to remain straight-faced. Did her own parents also have to work this hard when she got in one of her moods? Back then, unable to compete with her chatty and vivacious sisters, Eve had felt her glower to be a thing of power and control. What a joke that seemed now.

'Abigail, if you want to talk and Shelley doesn't mind, why don't you tell us something about yourself?' Eve couldn't imagine a teenager who wouldn't enjoy that offer. And several adults she could think of.

Abigail frowned harder, and for a moment Eve thought she'd miscalculated and that the girl would stubbornly hang on to her grumpiness. Then her face cleared. 'I guess I could. Can I have some wine?'

'Nope.' Shelley didn't even look at her.

Eve hid a smile. 'There's your answer.'

'Okay.' Abigail had obviously been expecting the turn-down. 'What do you want to know?'

Eve shrugged. 'Where you come from, your family history, what you like to do . . . whatever you want.'

'Okay. So . . . I was born in Chicago, where Mom grew up. She told me that she and Glen, my *fake* father, fell in love at first sight, got married right away and conceived me on their wedding night.' She snorted. 'Lies. Glen was older, already out of college and graduate school, and she was a knocked-up teenager.'

'It happens.' Shelley took another sip of her wine.

'That is really tough.' Eve sent over a look of sympathy. Jillian Croft had gone to great lengths to prove her daughters were hers – including a so-called 'pregnancy bible' with pictures of each of her fake pregnancies, elaborate details of their births, and articles in *People* magazine showing the oh-so-happy celebrity mother holding someone else's kid.

'We moved to Wisconsin when Glen got a job with Northwestern Mutual. I was born, I grew up pretty happy, realized I was gay, came out and was told to leave the house forever. End of story.'

'Oh, that's a nice story.' Shelley pulled the bread basket over and chose one of the wholegrain rolls Eve had bought, though she still opted for fake butter. 'I'd say your dad has some issues.'

'He's super-conservative-religious. Thinks I chose to be gay to piss him off. Thinks God hates me. What does he know? He wears slacks.'

Shelley snorted. 'Tiny minds are the hardest to open.'

'Does your mom agree with him?' Eve tried to keep her voice even. 'I know she didn't say anything, but do you think she does? Deep down?'

'What she thinks doesn't matter.' Shelley passed Eve the

bread basket. 'She should have fought him like a cornered cat.'

Eve picked out a roll, trying to remember if her own mother had ever gone mama-bear protective over one of her girls. The only time she could think of was when Jillian was furious that Olivia's high-school director had cast another girl as Reno in *Anything Goes*.

That probably didn't count.

'Mom's not a fighter. Not where Glen's concerned. He rules all.' Abigail's dismissive air was ruined by her voice turning raspy and emotional. 'The mighty king on his holier-than-thou throne.'

'Because your mom lets him.' Shelley put her wine down, then picked it up again and had another sip. Perhaps Eve had weaned her from any more Kicky Cat. 'I wouldn't worry. He'll come to his senses.'

Abigail stared fiercely at the dark wood of the table. 'I can't count on it. I need to figure out a new life.'

'Aw, that won't be hard.' Eve spoke teasingly, but her heart was aching. Abigail should not have to shoulder this much responsibility at such a young age. 'It'll take you maybe ten, fifteen minutes.'

'Tops,' Shelley said brightly.

Abigail managed a wry smile. 'Thanks a lot.'

'Don't worry, you'll have the same life back, but better because you'll be out. You should be proud you had that courage. A luxury of your generation that it's even possible.' Shelley scowled at her soup. 'People didn't dare say anything back in mine. Especially not where I came from.'

Abigail and Eve exchanged glances.

'Are you saying . . .' Abigail trailed off when Eve gave a quick shake of her head.

'What I'm saying . . .' Shelley leaned forward, forcing Abigail to look at her, 'is that your mother will wear your dad down. Moms don't give up on their kids.'

Eve barely managed to hold back a snort.

'All she did was hand over a suitcase and information about my real dad. That was the limit of her rebellion.' Abigail tossed her bangs scornfully. 'She's like Dad's property. Their marriage is totally medieval.'

'From what I'm reading, a lot of guys miss those days,' Shelley said acidly.

Eve picked up the ladle and reached toward Abigail's bowl. 'More?'

'What about you?' Abigail held out her bowl, looking expectantly at Eve. 'What's your story?'

'Oh.' Eve pretended the soup was taking all her concentration. She'd wanted to change the subject, but not to herself. 'Let's see. I was born and raised in LA. I have two older sisters. My mother died when I was eleven and Dad remarried a nice woman. I moved to Boston for graduate school, loved the city and stayed there. I have a boyfriend and a singing dog.' She handed Abigail her bowl, guilty for the lies of omission. 'Not that dramatic.'

Shelley coughed. 'You left out the part where your mother was Jillian Croft.'

Abigail's jaw dropped. '*Jillian Croft?*'

'And her father is the great acting teacher Daniel Braddock.'

Eve set her jaw. Of course Shelley knew, because of Lauren. Stupid of Eve to think she could come up here incognito.

'What's the matter?' Shelley asked her.

'I don't usually tell people.'

'Why not?'

Eve gave a short laugh. How could she explain that what seemed like the best of all possible lives to most people had not been anything like it? 'I don't like the fuss.'

'Who's making one?'

'*Me!*' Abigail's mouth was still hanging open. 'That is so *cool*. Forget my life, I want to hear about yours! You grew up in *Hollywood*! I bet you met every movie star there was.'

'Not really.' Eve was sounding as sullen and bratty as Abigail had. At least, given Abigail's age and circumstances, *she* had an excuse.

'Was Jillian a normal person at home? Or glamorous all the time?'

Eve shrugged. 'She was an amazing talent. Not always the most amazing parent. That's all I want to say about that.'

For a few moments there was only the clink of silverware on porcelain, making Eve feel guilty for torpedoing the conversation.

'Okay, but wait . . .' Abigail looked between Shelley and Eve, frowning. 'If you're an architect in Boston, how did you get here?'

'My stepmother is Shelley's best friend.'

'Eve offered to do the job for next to nothing. I couldn't resist.'

'Oh.' Abigail still looked confused. 'Had you met before?'

'No.'

Abigail's face cleared into something close to delight. 'Then we're all strangers. Not just me.'

'Right,' Eve said. 'You don't get to be special.'

'I'm *very* special.'

Shelley snorted. 'Explain how.'

'Mommy told me so.'

'Ha! I told my kids the same thing every night and they were all rotten disappointments.' During the shocked silence, Shelley took another sip of wine, beaming triumphantly around the table.

'You're kidding,' Abigail said.

'Yup.' Shelley threw back her head for a good cackle. 'Ha! You should have seen your faces.'

Eve grinned unwillingly. 'That was horrible.'

'It was hilarious,' Abigail said. 'How many kids do you have?'

'Three. Keith Junior works as a construction engineer. Kate is a nurse in Ellsworth. Kenny's in the navy, serving in Crete.'

'Keith, Kate and Kenny?' Abigail gave Shelley a look.

'My ex's name was Keith. It was his idea.' She spoke in a voice that left no doubt what she thought of her ex.

'How long have you been divorced?'

Eve gently cleared her throat, hoping to send Abigail the message that she was prying. Unfortunately either she didn't hear or didn't care.

'I've been divorced since Keith decided Cheryl Davis could make him happier.' Shelley finished her wine, but put her hand firmly over the glass when Eve offered more. 'I was pregnant with our third.'

Abigail gasped, her puffy eyes round in horror. 'You married a jerk!'

Shelley snorted. 'Let's just say your mother wasn't the only one who got herself knocked up. Back then you had to get married, to be made into "an honest woman", one of the stupidest phrases ever.'

'I'm sorry you had to go through that.' Eve gave up trying to rein Abigail in, frankly interested. 'I can't think of a much worse reason to marry the wrong man.'

'I wonder what would have happened if Mom had told Clayton she was pregnant and *he'd* married her,' Abigail said. 'I bet if I had to tell *him* I was gay, he wouldn't have kicked me out.'

'If they loved each other, they would have gotten married,' Shelley announced. 'No point torturing yourself.'

'I guess.' Abigail chose the real butter and spread it on her second roll. 'How come you never got remarried, Shelley?'

Shelley looked horrified. 'Go through that again? Forget it. I had three kids to raise, I didn't need another one.'

'You didn't *have* to have another child.'

Shelley raised an eyebrow. 'I meant the husband.'

Eve stood to get the fruit and cookies she'd left on the sideboard. She loved Shelley like this.

'Yikes.' Abigail rolled her eyes. 'You're making me glad I'm gay.'

'Delicious soup.' Shelley rose to clear their bowls. 'Abigail, I can't believe you got me talking so much.'

'And? Have you managed to digest anything?' Abigail asked.

'Not a speck.' Shelley took the bowls over to the sideboard. 'Tortellini still floating around whole.'

'You didn't chew them?'

Shelley gave her a look and stacked the bowls on a flowered tray to take to the kitchen later. 'My turn for the questions now, Ms Smartass. What are you planning to do?'

Abigail's face and body deflated as if someone had pulled her plug. 'I'll tell Clayton who I am. He'll have to help me, right? I mean legally.'

'I don't know how the law works.' Shelley sat back down and took one of the oatmeal cookies from the plate Eve had set on the table. 'Does your mom know you found him?'

'No.' Abigail examined a fingernail before she put it to her mouth. 'She doesn't know where I am.'

'*What?*' Shelley grabbed Abigail's finger away. 'Since when?'

'Since a few days after I left.'

'No. No. You can't do this to her.' Shelley pointed toward

the kitchen. 'Call her right now and tell her you're not dead.'

'She won't care.'

'She cares.'

'I can't.' Abigail wrapped her arms around herself. 'Every time the phone rings Dad wants to know who it is. He'll have a fit if it's me.'

'Text your mother that you're okay.'

'She doesn't have a cell phone.'

A small shocked silence as both women tried to take in this impossibility.

'Then you have to call.'

'Your father might have changed his mind by now,' Eve said.

'If he'd changed his mind he would have called me, or let Mom call me. You don't know how stubborn he is. Or how bad it was. I was dead to them. I was no longer their daughter. I had sinned against God and therefore against them. End of story.' She made a face. 'It was so awful, but also so stupidly melodramatic.'

Eve understood exactly what Abigail meant. The night her mother died, she'd also felt as if the situation was too theatrical to be real. At the same time, it was also so mundane and so ordinary. Jillian was alive at dinner; then, just before midnight on New Year's Eve, in her bedroom, she wasn't, her familiar face still beautiful, her body still impeccably dressed in the blue sweater and linen pants she'd worn to dinner. She'd looked so normal, Eve had shouted at her over and over, ordering her to wake up.

'Who would even *want* to believe in a God that intolerant?' Abigail was nearly apoplectic.

'Too many people.' Shelley took another cookie. 'Non-negotiable, we must let your mother know you're okay. If we can't do it calling, we'll find another way. But you have no other choice.'

'Says who?'

'A mother, that's who.' Shelley spoke in a low, hard tone her children probably still feared. 'Yours is suffering right now, more than you will ever know. Much worse than anything your father ever did or could do to her.'

Abigail's shoulders slumped. 'Okay. But I don't want to talk to her.'

Shelley's face turned stonier. 'That is not—'

'Someone else can call her.' Both women turned to Eve. 'The important thing is that she finds out Abigail is safe. It doesn't matter who does the dialing. Right?'

Grudging agreement from two women who'd obviously been gearing up to fight it out. Eve tried not to smile. Rosalind would have been proud of her.

'How will anyone else get to talk to her?' Abigail reached for a banana, waiting for Eve's answer.

'Uh . . .' Eve didn't remember offering to be in charge of this project. 'Well . . . who would your father let your mom speak to without questions?'

Abigail rolled her eyes. 'Jesus or St Peter.'

'That's it.' Shelley thumped her hand on the table. 'Someone from church.'

'Brilliant.' Eve took a clementine orange and peeled it, trying to keep the skin in one piece.

'I know!' Abigail's eyes lit. 'Mom's in charge of welcoming newcomers to the congregation.'

'Okay. That could work.' Eve started chewing a section of orange, then realized from the silence and the expectation in Shelley and Abigail's eyes that she'd just been volunteered to do the calling.

Ugh.

Tamping down the protests the anxiety part of her brain was forming, she wiped her hands on her napkin and stood, pushing back her chair. Shelley followed her into the kitchen, as did Abigail, who grabbed the cookie plate to bring with her.

Eve crossed to the old-fashioned corded phone mounted on the kitchen wall. 'Do you have caller ID at home, Abigail?'

Abigail gave her a well-*yeah* look, as if she didn't realize phones had ever come without it.

Kids these days.

'She'll see your name if I use this one, Shelley. I can use mine if you'd rather.'

'You go *right* ahead,' Shelley practically snarled. 'If this Glen person tries to make trouble for me, he'll be sorry.'

Eve smiled in spite of the acid pouring into her stomach. 'What's your mom's name, Abigail?'

'Leah Oakes.'

'Number?' She dialed as Abigail dictated, only half sure what she was going to say, feeling somewhat disoriented, as if this weren't really happening.

One ring.

Two rings.

The tension in the kitchen was nearly comic. Even Marx lifted his head and watched anxiously.

'Hello?' A man's voice, high and slightly nasal, but pleasant enough. Eve could already picture the slacks.

'Hi, is . . . Leah Oakes there?'

'Who is this?' The voice sharpened.

'Shelley Grainger.' She tried to sound as meek and malleable as possible, relieved to find that now she was in the fight, her head had cleared. 'I'm moving to Milwaukee with my husband

and baby. I got Leah's name as a contact for . . .'

She opened her eyes wide and covered the mouthpiece. 'Church?'

'Of Higher Faith,' Abigail whispered.

'. . . the Church of Higher Faith.' Eve mimed falling back against the wall with relief and mouthed *thank you*, suddenly remembering Olivia making prank phone calls from Jillian's pink princess phone that had Eve and Rosalind doubled over laughing with terror and excitement.

Except this wasn't the same type of prank.

'Hang on,' said Mr Slacks.

Eve gave a thumbs-up to Shelley and Abigail, who both nodded. Marx put his head back down, as if he already knew how this would go.

'Hello?' The woman's voice was vibrant, warm, not the timid, breathy squeak Eve had expected. She took a moment to swallow a growl. Leah sounded plenty strong enough to defend her daughter.

'Hi. This is Shelley Grainger calling from Door County.'

'Hello, Shelley, what can I do for you?'

'I'm calling to tell you Abigail is here, that she's safe and fine. Keep smiling and breathing normally. And say something like . . . "Oh, yes, okay."'

'Oh . . . yes. Okay.' The effort was obvious.

'Right now she's staying at my house. She'll be in contact with Clayton Marshall tomorrow, but I want you to know that whatever happens with him, she will be taken care of until she can go home again.'

Which you had better make possible soon, or I'm going to drive down there and make you do it myself.

Silence.

Eve gritted her teeth. 'Say something normal. I don't know,

whatever you'd say. Like, "Of course . . . we have a place for you and your family."'

Leah repeated the phrase somewhat mechanically, obviously still struggling with emotion. If she didn't recover soon, this could go badly, because Eve had no idea what Leah would usually say to a prospective church member and didn't want Daddy Dearest to get suspicious.

'Don't forget to breathe. If you cry, say it's because I . . . told you I'd had a previous miscarriage. Or my husband has . . . terminal cancer or something. Okay?'

'Oh, please.' Shelley grimaced from the table. 'Terminal cancer?'

'Shh.' Abigail waved impatiently, eyes trained hungrily on Eve, which made Eve even angrier at the wimp on the other end of the line.

'Thank you.' Leah was speaking more smoothly now. 'We look forward to welcoming you to our community. Give me your email address and I'll send out our standard information.'

'Sure. My email . . .' She opened her eyes wide again, another plea for help.

Shelley jumped in immediately with an AOL address.

Abigail turned in scorn. 'AOL? Are you *serious*?'

Eve repeated the address to Leah. 'And thank you for whatever you can send.'

'We have many programs you might be interested in, as well as daycare during services for your baby. Please don't hesitate to contact me again if anything changes . . . or if you have questions.'

'I won't hesitate.' She bit her lip, wanting to order Leah into the first vehicle she could beg, borrow or steal to get up here and help her child.

'Thank you so much for calling, Shelley.' The woman's voice quavered only slightly.

'You're welcome.' Eve hung up and forced a smile, though she'd rather punch something. She'd been hoping Leah would demand to speak to her daughter while in the background there'd be the sound of a male head being repeatedly smacked against a wall. 'That went fine.'

Abigail's eyes filled. 'Good.'

'Your mom must be a smart lady to go along with the call like that.' Shelley patted Abigail's forearm. 'I'm sure she was operating under some pretty strong emotions.'

'Oh for God's sake,' Eve snapped. 'If she was *smart*, Abigail would be home tonight and her *father* would be sitting miserably in a stranger's kitchen.'

'You young people still think life is black and white.' Shelley spoke mildly. 'That people are either good or bad. It's much more complicated. The sooner you learn that, the better, both so you don't get so hurt by life and so you don't hurt others.'

Eve counted to ten. Then fifteen, while Abigail sat with a cookie halfway to her mouth.

'Okay. But sometimes the bad is *so* bad that the good parts of a person stop counting.' Eve fisted her hands, knowing she should stop, but unable to do so. 'Like when a brilliantly talented man forces himself on a woman. He's still talented, but too bad, because . . . well, just *too bad*. He and everything he touches needs to go away.'

Shelley lifted an eyebrow, watching Eve carefully. 'Those acts don't erase the brilliance. I might no longer love the person, but I can still love what he created or achieved.'

Eve gripped the back of a chair, knowing she should let this go, stop talking. 'No one deserves to get off without paying the full price for their crime.'

'Agreed one hundred percent. But we should not erase whatever he or anyone else achieved or created, because then we all lose.'

Eve was becoming more and more furious, breathing too hard, feeling the familiar trembling taking over her limbs. 'No. It's like people who jump on to the field during ball games. Turn the cameras off them, and people stop doing it. He should be erased from—'

'Eve.' Shelley's calm was even more annoying.

'What?' She forced herself to look at the older woman.

'It wasn't okay. You must understand that I—'

'*What* wasn't okay?'

'Whatever happened to you.'

Eve opened her mouth, then closed it. Abigail was looking back and forth between them with troubled eyes, still holding the uneaten cookie.

Eve should not have argued this case. Not now, not ever, and certainly not when Abigail was in the room, reeling from her own turmoil.

But Shelley had just crossed a line, much worse than outing Eve as Jillian Croft's daughter.

'Now.' Shelley went over to the sink. 'You cooked. I clean up.'

Abigail rushed to the dining room to clear. 'I can help. Thanks for calling my mom, Eve.'

Marx came over and nudged Eve's thigh, looking up at her with quizzical doggy brows while she fought to calm down, to remember where she was, why she was here, who she risked offending or upsetting.

Marx was right. She should apologize. 'Sorry.'

'No need to apologize.' Shelley looked over from the sink with her usual impassive demeanor, but she'd spoken kindly. 'You're entitled.'

But she wasn't. Not in a stranger's house, a client's house, not after she'd kept herself mostly together all these years.

She pulled out a box of plastic wrap to cover the cookie plate, feeling as if her sanity were crumbling. These long-buried feelings wouldn't take her over again. Tonight, after the kitchen was clean, Eve would take Marx out for a walk, then retreat to her room, call Mike and get his deliciously ordinary take on his wonderfully ordinary day as she would if they were home together. Then she'd read another chapter of her book-in-progress and go to sleep. By morning, her world would be back to normal.

'Eve?'

Eve moved out of Abigail's way, unaware that she'd been standing in the middle of the kitchen, lost in thought.

'You'll come with me tomorrow?' Her hazel eyes were full of hope. 'To see my dad?'

Eve tried to keep a pleasant expression on her face. Hadn't she just been telling herself that as of tomorrow she'd be sane again? When she'd left Massachusetts and Mike, she'd been hoping for a change of pace from the circular amble her life had become, but not all the way up to an arms-flailing whirlwind sprint.

In her peripheral vision she could see Shelley's dish towel stop its motion as she waited for her answer.

Dammit.

'Sure, yes. I'll go with you.'

The look of relief and gratitude on Abigail's face almost made it worth it.

Almost.

As soon as she could, Eve fled the house with Marx. On her return, she said a quick goodnight to Abigail and Shelley, who were sitting out on the porch, and went upstairs.

In the blue and yellow room, she yanked out her phone and called Mike. Just hearing his familiar voice pulled her closer to calm. Her shoulders lowered by inches, released from the tension that must have been holding them up. 'Hi there.'

'Hey, stranger.'

She grinned, sat on the bed and took off her socks. 'Whatcha doing?'

'Watching a movie. *Thor: Ra-gna-rok*.' He dragged out the bizarre foreign word like he did every time.

Eve giggled and threw her socks toward the closet, then let herself fall back on to the mattress. 'Haven't you seen that already?'

'Haven't you seen *Casablanca* already?'

'*Not* the same.'

'Why not?'

Eve petted Marx's head, wishing Mike were kidding. 'Having a beer?'

'Having a few.'

Her stomach tensed. A few meant a lot. 'Okay.'

'How's it going up there?'

'Busy.' She wanted to tell him everything that had happened. The diary. Abigail. The discussion after dinner. But she didn't want to get bogged down in another complicated conversation tonight. 'Looks like I'll have plenty to do. The projects are interesting. The cottage Shelley wants built will be exciting. But this other guy wants a sunroom stuck on to his house and there's essentially no good place for it. That will be a challenge.'

'This other *guy*?'

'Yes, Shelley's friend turned out to be male.'

'Okay.' He didn't sound pleased. Eve braced herself. 'You'll do it. I have total faith. You're incredibly talented. And beautiful.'

She smiled in relief, wishing he could say things like that when he was sober, then hating herself for being so critical of every word that came out of his mouth. 'Thanks.'

'You sound kinda down. Anything wrong?'

'Tired. Long day.' She should tell him. That was what life partners did. Told each other everything. 'Feeling in a little over my head.'

'Nah. Not you, Hah-vahd girl.'

She laughed mechanically. The Harvard teasing always carried an edge that was getting old. 'What did *you* do today?'

'Me 'n' Rog went out for a beer after work.' He pronounced it 'beeya'. Funny how strong his accent sounded now that she wasn't hearing others like it all day. 'He thinks his wife is gettin' it from some guy at the office.'

Eve gasped and raised herself up on her elbows. Roger was a great guy, a physical education teacher at Mike's high school. His wife was a high-powered attorney. They'd been dating since middle school. 'Poor guy. What's he going to do?'

'Shoot the bastard. That's what I'd do.'

'I'd vote for counseling first, shooting second.' Eve let herself drop back again, knowing better than to argue rationally with Mike when he was drinking. 'If it's ever appropriate, tell him I'm really sorry and that he's too good for her.'

'I will. When you coming back?'

She put a hand to her forehead. 'I don't know. The situation's more complicated than I expected.'

'Why?' His voice sharpened, reminding her ridiculously of how Glen's voice had changed when Eve asked to speak to his wife.

She screwed up her eyes, annoyed at herself for even thinking of the comparison, and decided to tell him at least some of the situation. 'There's weird stuff happening here.'

'What? What is it? What's going on, Eve?'

His concern was immediate and genuine, making her feel ashamed for having hesitated to confide in him. She was definitely part of this relationship's problems.

'I met this girl . . .' She outlined the story and the evening's events, the phone call, which didn't seem to amuse him as much as she'd hoped, and Abigail's request that Eve be there the next day to confront her father.

'*What?* Are you kidding me? Tell her to fuck off. You don't owe her anything.'

His vehemence shocked her, even with a few beers in him. 'No, but—'

'But nothing. She could be a total con, she could be a criminal, she could be on drugs, she could be a compulsive liar or a total nutjob. You don't know this guy either. Call the police. This is what they're trained for.'

Deep breath. 'It sounds weirder than it is when it's a story over the phone. But—'

'No. No. You listen to me. This girl is no good. I guarantee her story is total bullshit. You're going to get hurt, Eve. If she wants this guy to be her daddy, which I doubt he even is, she needs to pull up her diapers and go by herself. She's using you. Trust me, there is something more going on here than she's telling.'

Eve closed her eyes, praying for patience. 'If you met her you'd—'

'I don't need to meet her. Tell her she's on her own. You have enough to do without taking on her crap.'

Mike was scared for her. She was far away, and he couldn't protect her. She just wished he had a more rational way of showing it. 'Maybe you're right.'

'I'm right.'

'I'll think it over, okay?' She kept her voice light. 'Thanks for worrying about me. I gotta go.'

'Please be careful.'

'I will, I promise.' Eve ended the call and strode to the window, lifted the sash to feel the chilly wind that was tossing up the lake.

The evening had upset her. The call to Mike was supposed to *help*.

She rested her head against the cool glass, closed her eyes and tried to breathe slowly, evenly, in and out.

Tried some more. And then again.

When would she be able to unload the pain of her mother's failings? Eve thought she'd worked through this. She thought she'd been strong enough to handle the fallout by herself. Maybe she should call the therapist she'd met on the beach, whatever his name was. It was intolerable that she kept having to fight the stupid anxiety battle all over again, that she couldn't just function like a normal person. What had set her back like this? The video Mike and his friends had been watching? The hell Abigail was going through?

Jerking herself away from the window, she turned and pounced on her discarded socks, marched over to the closet and hurled them into her suitcase, which she was using as a hamper. They fell on to the box containing her mother's diary.

Eve stared, hand clutching the sliding door as if she were worried the book could jump out and bite her head off.

At this point, nothing would surprise her.

She pressed a hand to her forehead. Took a breath.

Maybe reading it would help.

She leaned down hesitantly, as if it *would* bite her head off, picked up the diary and flipped through its pages, landed on one and started to read.

I have to make this happen. The world has been unfair to me for long enough. I can change Daniel's mind. He'll do anything for me.

Sick to her stomach, Eve slammed the book shut, pitched it back into the closet, and shoved the door closed.

Right. Reminding herself what a selfish nightmare her mother had been would really help. Whoever sent the diary had no idea how little Eve wanted to know about the inner workings of Jillian's twisted mind.

She already knew plenty.

Chapter 9

November 20, 1979 (Tuesday)

I haven't written in a long while. Had a few rough patches, but just finished shooting Dangerous Fall. *We kept having weather delays. It took everything I had for weeks and weeks! Some of my best work, though, I couldn't be more pleased. I wasn't sure how I would be able to act opposite James Coburn. He is so intense, so natural, and I worried he'd be put off by my celebrity status, and not take me seriously as an actress. But it turned out our methods clicked completely. It was so, so beautiful being on camera next to him. Soppy script, my God, I wanted to throw up at half the lines, but the only way to play them was with deep, open honesty, and I managed it.*

Daniel is also crazy busy now, so successful and such a remarkable man. His students love him and I'm so proud of him! He's writing a book about acting. I bet it sells a billion copies. He says he'll dedicate it to me. So sweet!

I have convinced him to give my sneaky route to parenthood a try. Worst case, absolute worst case, if we are found out, we can deny the whole thing or prosecute someone or bribe them. There's nothing you can't do with money. Almost nothing, anyway. I can't be cured with it or I would be by now.

But if I can't be cured in real life, then I can live out a perfectly delicious fantasy that hurts no one.

Daniel has agreed to start looking soon for a surrogate. I told him it's only fair he gets to pick out the woman, since he's the one who will have to – ugh, I can't stand even thinking about that part. It will be yet another terrible hurdle to get over. How many more can I stand? I wish I had been blessed with a life I didn't have to be quite so strong just to get through.

Luckily I am that strong.

Love,

Me

Eve was up early for her morning run, went farther than usual, faster than usual, adrenaline fueling her speed. She hadn't slept well. To say she felt ill-equipped to help an adolescent girl tell a single man in his thirties – who also happened to be her client – that he had a daughter with no place to live . . .

Ill-equipped. The proverbial understatement. She still wasn't sure how she'd stepped into this situation. Her entire upbringing had been one nutty episode after another. Last summer's discovery about her mother's medical condition had catapulted her into uber-crazy. Now this? She must be atoning for some ancestor's sin. Someone who'd sold her children into slavery, or cavorted with Satan.

Back in Shelley's driveway, she paused to stretch, using her shirt to wipe sweat from her forehead. Would it be better to show up at Clayton's house alone and prepare him for the shock? Bring Abigail with her and just let him have it? Would he associate Eve with the upheaval? Not that her career was over if he un-hired her. In fact, it might make life easier. She could focus on Shelley's house and get the hell out of here.

What if her ever-suspicious and overprotective boyfriend was right, and Abigail was playing them?

Too much drama. Olivia should be here, she'd eat this stuff up.

Upstairs, Eve showered and dressed – what was the appropriate outfit for dropping a bomb on someone's life? While she was pulling on a tan sweater, wishing she had something clean in a cheerful color, her phone rang. The call was from her more sensible sister.

'Hey, Rosalind. You're up early.'

'Nope. It's nine here, remember? You're on that weird wrong time.' Her sunny voice was like a comfort blanket. Eve wanted to pull it over her and sleep – maybe when she woke up, all her problems would be solved.

'What are you doing today?' Eve loved hearing Rosalind's answers. Always something different. Painting, a spontaneous trip, this club, that hobby . . .

'Today I'm showing my agent some new paintings I finally finished. Or at least stopped fussing with long enough to let them go.'

'Cool.' She was thrilled her sister had found this new career, rocky and uncertain as it was. 'How's Bryn?'

'He's fine. Working.' Rosalind's voice took on a gooey warmth that made Eve smile wider. Nice to remember that a sane, settled life was possible. 'You sound off, Evie, what's the matter?'

'Not much.' She closed her eyes in annoyance. For God's sake, if she couldn't tell her own sister . . . 'Actually, kind of a strange situation.'

She went through the story, telling the facts plainly, as she had with Mike, hearing Rosalind's gasps and murmurs of pity, trying not to contrast them with Mike's harsher reaction.

'Oh my God. That poor girl. I don't know what is wrong

with her dad. Like finding out she's gay changes her completely from the girl he adored ten seconds earlier?'

'I know. I don't get it.'

'Well, good for you helping her. She'll need someone on her side in case Clayton freaks out.'

'That's what I'm afraid of.' Eve sank on to the bed, buoyed by her sister's sympathy and understanding. Talking to her made the situation less surreal, more manageable. 'I've only met him once and he seemed like a sweetheart, but this is pretty extreme.'

'No kidding. When are you going over there?'

'After breakfast.'

'Are you nervous?'

'What do you think?'

'I know, drama isn't your thing. At the risk of sounding patronizing, I'm really proud of you.'

'For getting involved in something completely insane that is none of my business?'

'Yes.' Rosalind's voice was full of love. 'Exactly. Because I know you'd rather swim in lava, but you're doing it anyway.'

'Not much choice,' Eve grumbled, but her sister's praise felt good. Everything felt good around Rosalind. She made Eve feel she could tell Clayton he had a child he didn't know about and he'd dance the Charleston and never stop thanking her. 'But thanks. I needed your perspective. Mike is worried Abigail's involving me in some scam.'

Rosalind's scornful noise made Eve wish she hadn't told her. 'Has Mike met this girl?'

'No. But you have to admit it sounds a little nuts.'

'How? Like deeply conservative people never kick gay children out of the house?'

'They do. But throw in a father who doesn't know about her . . .'

'And it adds up to totally-sucks. Look at the crap we are going through with Mom. Faked pregnancies? Hiring secret surrogate mothers? Who'd believe that?'

'Good point.' Eve rubbed her temple. This was giving her a headache.

'What does your instinct say about Abigail?'

'Smart, truthful kid in a lot of pain.'

'That's all you need to know. Mike is not a good judge. I think you know that or you wouldn't have run it by me as well.'

'Why don't you like him?' Eve set her teeth, dreading the answer. For all the times she'd wondered, she'd never come out and asked.

'I do like him. I just don't think he's a good match for you.' Rosalind spoke more gently. 'And since you asked me, honestly, I think he kinda drags you down. Lately I'm wondering if maybe he's become a habit rather than a joy.'

Eve bristled. 'Says she in the early, easy days of a relationship.'

'Guilty. But I've been in other relationships, and this one follows none of those patterns. Staying with Mike follows yours. We have classic adult-children-of-alcoholics symptoms. You and Olivia have trouble leaving bad relationships. Until I met Bryn, I was afraid of having a good one.'

Fabulous. Even Eve's love life was defined and controlled by her mother? 'I think it's more complicated than that.'

'You're angry at me.'

'No, no.' She forced herself to sound nicer. Her sister was trying to help. 'I'm just not cut out for this emotional analysis stuff.'

'Yes, you are. Remember when Mom died? I was useless. Olivia was freaking out at the hospital, totally hysterical. Dad was trying to get the doctors to sedate her, remember?'

'God, yes. That was awful. I thought she was going to burst an artery.'

'You totally took charge. What were you, eleven? You planted yourself in front of her and grabbed her in a hug until she calmed down. I couldn't believe you were strong enough. But it was exactly what she needed.'

'She definitely didn't need Dad yelling at her to stop it. Even I knew that. It wasn't like she *wanted* to be out of control.' Eve felt the terrible weight of the memory pressing on her chest. 'That was an awful night.'

'And when we all met Lauren and had that terrible dinner together? Dad was pissed at us for not being nicer and you called him out on it. Remember that? You were totally calm and polite, but it was one of the first times you'd done that, and he backed down. Lauren made him apologize.'

'I'd forgotten that, too.'

'And . . .'

'What, you have a list?'

'. . . at the Academy Awards ceremony in nineteen-ninety-whatever, Mom's last nomination, when Dianne Wiest beat her to best supporting actress. She was about to have a big pouting fit and you saw the camera swinging toward her and said, "Camera." You were like five and you knew exactly what to do. I've never seen her smile that fast.'

Eve laughed. 'She was *so* thrilled for Dianne.'

'That's what the world saw. It was important. She was grateful, too.'

She had been. Eve had been made giddy by her mother's attention – so giddy that the memory clung. Jillian's mercurial nature had been exhausting, but when she was taking her meds, she could be fun. On her own terms, defined by what she wanted, but fun. She'd been so magnetic she could bring anyone into her circle, make him or her feel special, even if it was just for an hour or so. Once you'd tasted that, you were hooked. You wanted to feel it over and over again. Even at a very young age, Eve had recognized the instability of her mother's affection, if not the destructive and selfish patterns that caused it.

'Thanks, Rosalind. This has really helped. You should be registered as an antidepressant.' Eve got up from the bed and opened the closet to find her shoes. 'I'm feeling slightly braver about all this.'

'You know I don't mind. I hope it goes well. Let me know.'

'I will. It will probably—' She stood stupidly at the closet, staring again at the box containing the unknown part of her mother's life.

'Probably what? Did I lose you? Hello?'

Eve turned around and leaned against the wall. 'Rosalind.'

'Ye-e-es?'

She swallowed convulsively. 'Remember that . . . diary you got?'

'The one Mom wrote?' Her sister sounded delighted. 'You want to read it? I can mail it up to—'

'No. Actually . . . I got one too.'

Rosalind gasped. 'You're *kidding*. When?'

'It was here when I arrived.'

'What does it say?'

'I haven't read it.'

'What? Why not?'

'I just haven't.'

Rosalind made a noise of frustration. 'You and Olivia, queens of denial. I couldn't wait to read mine. I stayed up most of that night. Read it, Eve. You'll learn a lot. She was human, she was messed up, deeply insecure, but—'

'I *know* that about her.'

'But there's so much more. Can I tell you one thing? Just one? An example?'

Eve sighed, but she was admittedly curious. 'Okay. Go ahead.'

'When Mom first left Maine, her junior year of high school, she didn't tell Grandma Betty or Grandpa Arnold or even Aunt Christina. She left the house like she was going to school as usual, then took a bus to New York. All by herself. She stayed in a ladies' residence, in this tiny room, and got a job waiting tables at an Italian restaurant while she tried to get into the Stella Adler acting school. She was so convinced that she could be a star. It's amazing to read. So naïve and so confident. And look what happened.'

'Wow.' Eve couldn't imagine her mother as naïve, but it was remarkable thinking of her first sight of New York, having grown up in a town with fewer than a thousand residents.

'It's really interesting to read about what she went through, and who she was at that age. I wonder what period your diary covers, if it's earlier or later than the one I got. Maybe it picks up where mine left off, after she and Dad got engaged.'

Eve made a face, even as curiosity raised its head and beckoned her. 'I'm not sure I want to know.'

'Maybe there's something in there about Helen.'

'Who?'

'Your birth mother? Helen Phillips?'

Curiosity fled in terror. 'How did you know her name? Why did you just tell me that?'

'Oh God, Eve, I forgot, I'm sorry.' Rosalind made a noise of frustration. 'This would all be a lot easier if you'd just let me tell you the whole story. I can't remember what's in bounds and what's not allowed, what I've already told you and what I haven't . . .'

Eve sank down on the bed. *Helen Phillips*. 'I'm not good at coping with this stuff.'

'Her name was in one of the payment ledgers I found way back last summer. That's how I found Leila's name. Olivia's mother was in there too, but her name was crossed out, so I have no idea who she was. Our father paid the women to have us. A nice amount, every month.'

Oh my God. Eve forced her shoulders to relax. She was trembling slightly, unsure whether she wanted to tell her sister to shut up or go on. 'Okay.'

'The weird thing is that payments to Helen stopped in April of 2002. Maybe she didn't want them anymore. Maybe she married someone fabulously rich and didn't need them. Maybe she and Dad made some other arrangement. Maybe she died.'

'You've thought this through.'

'Yeah, Eve.' Rosalind's voice gentled. 'It's important.'

Eve stood abruptly and walked back over to the window, stomach churning as hard as the lake. *Helen Phillips. April 2002*. Paid every month by her wealthy father. How much more did she want to know?

Everything, and nothing.

'Hello? You still there?'

'Yes, I'm here. Sorry, Rosalind. I guess . . . I know you think I'm being unreasonable, but I'm not ready to deal with information about my birth mother. I had a hard enough time coping with the mother we had. And right now, there's enough stress here to go around.'

'I'm sorry.' Rosalind's apology sounded genuine. 'I was so lucky finding my birth mom and her family in Princeton, but yes, it was stressful and exhausting. And you've already got a situation there.'

'You could say that.'

'One thing at a time. I'm positive you'll be a rock for Abigail this morning. You'll be a great mom someday.'

'Thanks, Rosalind.' Eve found her shoes and closed the closet door, shocked at how much the compliment pleased her. 'I hope I'll be able to help her.'

'Let me know everything that happens!' Rosalind chuckled. 'It's so much more fun when the drama is happening to someone else.'

Eve blew a raspberry. 'Tell me about it. Your time in Princeton was one of the best reality shows ever.'

'Take care, Eve. Think positive. It might be a really wonderful thing for Clayton to gain a daughter. Me, I gained several hundred pounds of family and have never been happier.'

Eve ended the call, smiling. Bless her sister. She'd have a first-class seat to heaven for sure.

When she was dressed, still trying to channel Rosalind's positive energy, Eve bounced downstairs to the kitchen, where Shelley was sitting in the breakfast nook, eating a bowl of corn flakes and reading the *Green Bay Press-Gazette*.

'Good morning, Shelley. Did you sleep well?'

'Nope.'

Eve suppressed a smile. 'Me neither.'

'Not surprising.' Shelley went back to her paper. 'No matter what happens, this is a day you'll remember.'

'I guess.'

She made herself coffee from the supply she'd bought at Mann's, and scooped strawberry yoghurt into a bowl, adding cut-up banana and a sprinkle of granola. Next she toasted one of the wholegrain rolls she'd served for dinner and slathered it with peanut butter and jelly.

Fortification she hoped she wouldn't be too nervous to get down.

With no sign of Abigail, Eve tried to concentrate on the sound of the lake and the occasional cry of a seagull as she ate. Sunshine poured over the house and the yard sloping down to the water. The weather would make the day's job easier, if anything could.

How did you lead up to an announcement like this? One sentence that would change Clayton's life forever. Not unlike the way Eve and her sisters' lives had been changed when they stumbled over their mother's diagnosis on one flimsy, misfiled piece of paper. The crucial difference being that if Eve didn't want that truth to be a factor in her life, she could simply ignore it. Clayton would be faced with a living, breathing ball of immediate need.

She finished her last drop of coffee, contemplated making more, then realized she didn't really want the coffee, just the relative peace of drinking it. The longer she put off this mess, the longer it would haunt her. Better to take Abigail over now, introduce her to Clayton and let them work it out for themselves.

Shelley put down the paper. 'Abigail not up yet?'

'Don't think so. Her door was closed.'

'Better wake her. Get this over with.'

'I was just thinking the same thing.'

Shelley's smile softened her blunt features pleasantly. Then, as if she'd been caught doing something she wasn't supposed to, she scowled and got abruptly to her feet. 'Well. You can leave Marx here, by the way. He's a good dog. We'll be fine.'

'Thanks. That's not a bad idea. In case there's any crying.'

'It's quite a trick.'

'Not one I taught him.'

Eve put her dishes in the dishwasher and climbed the stairs to knock on Abigail's door. 'You up?'

Nothing.

Eve rolled her eyes. Teenagers. She knocked again. 'Hey, Abigail.'

Still nothing.

She opened the door and went still with alarm. The room was empty. The bed was made. Had Abigail slept here at all?

Eve checked both bathrooms and hurried back down. 'She's not in her room.'

Shelley got to her feet. 'I didn't hear her leave. Are her things still upstairs?'

'I didn't see them.' They stood and looked at each other.

'Maybe she's gone back home.'

One of Shelley's eyebrows climbed. 'Without telling us?'

'She owes us nothing.'

'She owes us a great deal, and I think she knows it.'

Eve sighed and grabbed her jacket from the coat rack by the front door. 'If I find her, I'll call.'

'If she comes back, I'll call you.'

At the door, Eve paused. 'How did we end up taking care of a troubled teenager?'

Shelley shrugged. 'There are needy people everywhere. God sent us this one.'

Eve nodded, feeling about two inches tall. For whatever reason, she hadn't been born with a caring, nurturing soul. Not like Rosalind. Not like Olivia. When she and her sisters played with dolls, Rosalind had her Heart Family doing all kinds of happy togetherness activities. Olivia had Ken and Barbie dressing up and dating, first-kissing, going steady, talking marriage and children – and often about Ken being supportive of Barbie's fabulous movie career.

Eve had been designing houses, places for her and her sisters' plastic couples to live in and grow their families. She'd always assumed she'd inherited her relative coldness from her mother. Now she didn't know where it came from.

Helen Phillips?

Eve closed the door and strode to her car. What was she going to do now, drive around the island calling for Abigail like she was a lost dog? Abigail was a smart kid; if she wanted to stay disappeared, it wouldn't be hard, even on a small island like this.

But the girl had no money. Nowhere to stay.

Or so she said.

Eve jammed the car into reverse, turned around and barreled to the end of Shelley's driveway.

Two choices. Right or left.

She turned right and saw the flash of red almost immediately. Abigail was sitting opposite Clayton's driveway.

For God's sake.

Heart pounding with annoyance and nerves, Eve parked at the mouth of Clayton's driveway and turned off the motor, then called Shelley and told her the news.

The car door slamming and her footsteps across the asphalt road sounded jarring against the gentle rush of wind pushing waves across the lake. The island was amazingly silent.

She reached Abigail and stopped, folding her arms across her chest. 'Did you sleep any?'

'Yes.'

'Your bed wasn't slept in.'

Abigail sent her a look. 'I made it.'

Oh.

In all the stories, when a neat bed was discovered, it was generally assumed the bed hadn't been slept in. Why didn't anyone think the person might have made it before leaving?

'You took your stuff.'

'It's in the closet.'

Argh. She had only one more outrage card to play. 'You didn't tell us where you were going.'

'The plan was that I'd talk to him myself, then come back.'

Eve's stomach sank. She squatted next to Abigail. 'He didn't take it well?'

'No, not that. I couldn't do it.'

Whew. No burned bridges. The situation was still hopeful. Eve lowered herself to sit on the damp, still-brown ground. 'So what was the next plan? Wait until Shelley and I realized you were missing, panicked and came looking for you? If so, that one worked.'

'Sorry,' Abigail mumbled.

'All right.' Eve patted her awkwardly on the back. 'We survived. But next time, try talking to us before you disappear. We put ourselves out there for you and this was pretty crappy payback.'

'I *said* I was sorry.'

'You did.' Eve took her hand away from Abigail's back and made herself chuckle lightly. 'You're reminding me how much I hated it when my dad's lectures went on and on.'

Abigail turned to her, looking curious. 'Was your dad a total jerk like Glen?'

'Not in the same way, but he had his moments. Like your dad, like a lot of guys, he thought he had the world figured out, or pretended he did. It probably makes them feel safer. More powerful, maybe. In charge.'

'It's ridiculous.'

'That too.' She picked a blade of last year's grass and ran her fingers up its brittle length. 'So are you ready to do this now? With me?'

'No.'

'Thank God. Me neither.' She stood and held out her hand. 'Come on. Let's go back to Shelley's.'

'I can't.'

Eve rolled her eyes, secretly pleased that Abigail wasn't giving up. 'Well, you can't keep sitting out here all—'

'I never *will* be ready. But I've been screwing around all week. I just have to do it.'

'Okay then.'

Abigail stood and faced her. 'Okay then.'

'How do you want to do this?'

'Me?' Abigail's mouth dropped in mock horror. 'I thought you knew how.'

'*Me?*' Eve thumped a hand to her chest. 'Are you kidding? Where would I pick up that expertise?'

'I don't know, grownup school?'

They both burst into nervous giggles.

'Come on.' Eve grabbed Abigail's arm and started her down Clayton's driveway. 'We'll think of something. Worst case, we just blurt it out and watch him die of a heart attack.'

'No.' Abigail pulled back. 'Worst case, he doesn't want me.'

Eve inhaled sharply, trying not to let her pain show. Three parents rejecting Abigail within one month would not be good. Eve should have insisted on warning Clayton first, to get some sense of his reaction. This mistake could end up hurting everyone unnecessarily. She should have gotten more involved, not less.

'You're right. That's worse.' She kept Abigail walking along the narrow drive. 'But not worse than where you are now. You still have Shelley.'

'And you.'

'For some reason, I am here, too, yes.' She was gratified when Abigail giggled at her pretend-exasperation, but something in Eve softened at the girl's trust.

They walked in silence until they reached Clayton's front door.

'Ready?' Eve reached for the bell.

'Not even close.'

'Me neither.' She pressed, and they waited, blinking nervously.

'God, don't tell me he's not home,' Abigail wailed.

'Maybe he's around front?'

'No.' She took a step back. 'I can't do this. Let's go. Before he—'

A window upstairs was shoved open. Eve and Abigail started and clutched at each other, then burst into silent laughter.

'Be right down.' Clayton shut the window.

'*Shit*. He's coming.'

'Shh.' Eve put a hand on Abigail's shoulder to steady her, wishing she could do more. 'It's going to be fine. He's a nice guy. He won't hurt you.'

She hoped.

'Do I look okay?' Abigail put her hands to her face, skin flushed, eyes wide with fear.

Eve smiled reassuringly. 'You look beautiful. I'd adopt you.'

'You may have to.'

'I'd be a terrible mom.' For Abigail's sake, she kept it light. 'Tell you what, though, Shelley has a million kids; she'd hardly notice another one.'

Footsteps sounded, approaching. Abigail grabbed Eve's arm and held on as if she were drowning. 'I like you better.'

Warmth barely had time to bloom again in Eve's chest before the door swung open. Abigail leaned into her.

'Hey, Eve. And . . . was it Abigail?' Clayton smiled warmly, his face flushed, dark hair curling wet around his high forehead. 'Hope you didn't have to wait long. I was showering after my run. Come on in.'

'Thanks. Uh . . . sorry to show up without any notice.' Eve wanted to kick herself. She should have texted him that they were coming. And she should have been thinking about what she'd say to him instead of trying to tease Abigail into a calmer state of mind. 'We were on a walk, and . . . Abigail wanted to look at the site out back, so . . . we thought we'd see if you were here, and if you'd mind. So here we are. If it's okay.'

God. Awful. Mess. She kept a smile on her face, aware that Abigail had turned to look at her, probably thinking she could have done a lot better.

Probably she could have.

'Sure. Help yourself.' He went back into the house.

Aw, hell.

Abigail gave her a *you moron* look. 'He's not coming out with—'

'Sorry.' He was back. 'Had to get the key. Mind if I come with you?'

'No. No. Not at all.' Eve waited while he closed the door, then made a told-you-so face at Abigail, who stuck out her tongue.

Good. *This* was the girl Clayton should meet as his daughter, not the head-hanging mound of misery Eve had encountered by the road.

'I've got chairs set up on the deck. It's chilly, but warmer than it has been, and with the sun out – well, I'm impatient for spring. Every year it's ridiculously slow coming, and every year the whole state complains, like it's some absolute outrage.'

'I can imagine.' Eve wasn't even sure what he'd said. Chairs? Spring? Something like that. All she wanted to do was blurt out the truth and get rid of this terrible dread.

Instead, she went through the motions of showing Abigail

the deck, explaining in basic terms what Clayton wanted and the challenges of integrating a sunroom into the existing structure in a way that would not only make design sense, but work optimally for the family – which at this point seemed to consist only of Clayton.

And very soon, his daughter.

Abigail nodded dutifully, stealing nervous glances at her birth father, obviously not listening to Eve any more than Eve had been listening to Clayton.

When Eve ran out of architectural BS to spout, she turned to Clayton.

Okay.

'Do you mind if the three of us use those chairs you put out?' She pointed to where four dark green Adirondack chairs were arranged around a table, all facing the lake. 'Abigail has something to discuss.'

'Sure.' He looked surprised, but gestured graciously toward the furniture. 'Not a problem.'

Eve put a hand on Abigail's shoulder and gave the poor girl what she hoped was a reassuring squeeze. The girl's rosy cheeks had already surrendered to a deathly pallor.

The trio sat on the spacious porch in the morning sunshine, thick slices of lake visible between clumps of birch and cedars that would afford the house some privacy during the summer months from passing boaters peering inland.

Abigail looked pleadingly at Eve, seated between her and Clayton. Eve shifted straighter in her seat. Apparently this was up to her.

'Clayton . . .' She pretended to be transfixed by the lake view, unable to look at him. 'Abigail has been telling me that you knew her mom.'

Biblically.

'I do? No kidding.' She sensed him leaning toward Abigail. 'Who's your mom?'

'Leah Oakes. Back then she was Leah Billings.'

'Leah Billings, yeah. I remember her. A couple of grades older than me. Wow, small world, huh?' He looked back and forth between the two of them. His face fell. 'Why? Is she okay?'

'She's fine,' Abigail said. 'I guess you and she . . .'

Clayton looked blank. 'She and I?'

'*You* know.'

Eve cringed. 'Abigail, maybe that isn't the best way to—'

'She *told* you that?' Clayton was understandably flabbergasted. And blushing, which was sort of cute.

'Thing is . . .' Abigail stood and walked to the edge of the deck, her back to both of them. 'She got pregnant that night.'

Eve opened her mouth to tell Abigail to slow down, then closed it. This was her show. She was managing things the way she saw fit.

Brave girl. Braver than Eve, who'd dealt with finding out the truth about her birth mother by ignoring it.

Clayton stood slowly, eyes fixed on Abigail's stiff back. 'What?'

'I *said*, she got pregnant.'

'That isn't possible. I used a . . . I mean, I was protected.'

Abigail threw a withering glance over her shoulder. 'I *know* what a condom is. It didn't work.'

'How do you know that? I mean . . .' He looked mortified. 'She didn't tell me. She never told me that.'

Eve held her breath, feeling like an intruder.

'She didn't want to.'

'Obviously.' He looked one way, then the other, restlessly, or as if he were going to be sick and wanted to make sure there was a bathroom nearby.

Abigail turned and stared incredulously. 'Aren't you going to ask what happened to the baby?'

'What? *No*, I'm . . .' He stilled, gaping. 'She *had* the baby?'

'Had *her*.' Abigail looked down, but her voice was still strong. 'The baby was a girl.'

'A girl.' He dragged his hands down his face. 'What . . . Where is Leah? Why isn't she telling me this herself?'

Abigail lifted her chin. 'Guess.'

'She's sick? No, you said she was fine. She's . . . too afraid?'

'It's *me*, dude.'

Clayton stared at her. Eve stared too, and as if Abigail had pulled off a mask, the similarities between father and daughter were suddenly obvious. Take the totality of their features and the likeness was slim, but individually . . . High cheekbones. Big eyes. Strong chins. Large teeth. Abigail had been spared his extravagant nose, and her hair was lighter. Otherwise the resemblance was undeniable.

Clayton got to his feet. 'Jesus.'

'Yeah,' Abigail said. 'How about that?'

'Jesus.'

'You're not the only one shocked by this. I didn't know about you until a week ago.' She spoke recklessly, as if she no longer cared what she was saying. 'I thought the jerk who raised me was my father. Now it turns out he isn't. *You* are. And don't say Jesus again. It's offensive.'

'*Je*—' He made a quick gesture as if to fling the syllable out of the way before anyone heard it. 'This is not happening.'

'Yes, it is, and it gets worse.' Abigail's face turned mutinous. 'My parents threw me out of the house, and now you're all I have.'

'Whoa, give him time.' Eve raised a hand. 'You've had at least a little while to process this.'

'You have . . . nowhere . . . to live?' Clayton spoke slowly, as if the news had damaged his brain.

'She's fine with Shelley and me for now.' Eve tried to make it sound as if Abigail's homelessness was no big deal. 'And her parents might come around and take her back.'

'If they don't?'

'They might not,' Abigail said.

'If they don't . . .' Eve could no longer summon cheer. She wasn't Rosalind. 'Then . . . yes. Nowhere official to live.'

Clayton sank back down into his chair, looking stunned.

Eve went over to the miserable girl and laid a hand on her shoulder, speaking in a low voice so Clayton wouldn't hear. 'Abigail, why don't you let me talk to him for a while? I'm sure you weren't at your best when your dad dropped his bomb on you. Nor was your dad at his best after you dropped yours. Let's all avoid things we might wish we hadn't said, okay?'

'What are you going to tell him?'

'Nothing you don't know. Mostly let him rant if he needs to. You did great, you were really brave.' She pointed toward the water. 'Now you need to go look at the lake.'

'Fine.'

'And don't drown yourself. The worst is over.' She patted Abigail on the back as she passed, hoping that was true. For all of them.

She waited until the girl was on her way down off the deck, then sauntered back to Clayton.

'So.' Eve hugged her arms around herself. 'How's it going?'

He sat with his elbows on his thighs, leaning forward as if he were afraid of passing out. 'I think I'm in shock.'

'I'd be surprised if you weren't.' She was taken aback at how desperately she wanted him to be okay with all of this as soon as possible. For Abigail's sake and for his. Maybe for hers too.

Eve had no idea how she'd come to care so much about two people she'd only just met. 'This is kind of a big deal.'

'Yeah. Kind of.' He rubbed both hands over his face, then through his hair, making it stand up over his forehead. 'How could Leah not tell me she was pregnant?'

'I don't know.' Only one person could answer that truthfully, and she was cowering back in Wisconsin with blinders on. 'From what Abigail told me, Glen, the guy she affectionately referred to as "the jerk", rode in on his white steed, married Leah and adopted her daughter.'

'She's my child. Shouldn't I have been part of this from the beginning?'

'Yes.'

'I could have helped or . . . I don't know.' He shot to his feet, as if he couldn't bear sitting anymore. 'Anything but have her dumped on me like this – "Oh, by the way, you have a kid." It's bullshit.'

'I agree. Maybe Leah felt . . .' Eve threw up her hands. It wasn't her job to make excuses for the woman. Especially because she couldn't think of any. 'I don't know what she felt.'

'It's inexcusable.'

Eve blew out a breath. Yes, but . . . 'People can do a lot of awful things for what seem to them like good reasons at the time.'

'Yeah, I guess.' Whether he realized it or not, he was standing in the same spot his daughter had stood, by the railing, looking out at the lake. In spite of his height and solid build, his bowed head and slumped shoulders painted him as lost and vulnerable.

Eve's heart started thumping. She moved to stand next to him, knots of anxiety warring with her need to help him somehow. 'My parents . . . did some weird stuff, too.'

'To you?'

'To all three of us. My sisters and me. It was . . . impossible to put ourselves in their places and understand. We were never supposed to find out. I guess they counted on that. I suppose Leah did too.'

'So how *did* Abigail find out?'

Eve decided plain speaking was best. 'She told her mom and dad that she's gay. Dad went ballistic and told her she was the spawn of Satan, or whatever, then made her leave.'

'My God.' He turned to her, face screwed up in horror. 'He kicked his daughter out of the house?'

'He also kicked *your* daughter out of the house.' She watched him do a double-take and felt guilty.

'My daughter.' He laughed painfully. 'It's not possible. I mean, biologically, yes, I get it. But . . . I don't know her. I never had that chance. She's a total stranger. Now bang, suddenly I'm supposed to raise a traumatized teenager?'

'Sure looks that way,' Eve said cheerfully, relieved when he grinned.

'You're not helping.'

'I'm trying to.'

'God.' He clenched his fists. 'This is so effed up.'

'Yes.'

'Okay. So.' He relaxed his fingers. 'Does she have money to live on?'

'She's running out.'

'Leah didn't give her any? Didn't figure out some way to help her?'

Eve felt her face tighten. She had to fight to keep her voice steady. 'I gather she's under this guy's thumb.'

'He's an abuser?'

'Controlling, anyway. According to Abigail, he's deep into the Church of Massive Intolerance. Even deeper than the church is.'

Clayton groaned. 'What happened to Leah? She was fun when I knew her. Up for anything.'

'Apparently.'

'I know, I know. But I was *sixteen*.'

'About Abigail's age.' She put a hand on his arm when he recoiled. 'You were a kid. You did what practically all boys do, and probably most men. At least you used protection.'

'Apparently not enough.' He turned his back to the lake, leaning against the railing. 'I can't picture Leah being part of anything that cruel.'

'Maybe she's giving Glen time to calm down, working on him to change his mind. She knows where Abigail is and that she's safe.'

He stood for a few moments, head down. Eve let him be, trying to breathe calmly, pleased that her need to help him surpassed her need to escape. Clayton was taking this about as well as anyone could. She admired him for it.

'Didn't you just meet Abigail?'

'She started talking to me at Red Cup yesterday. Somehow she got me to be the co-bearer of your news. I'm still not sure how.' Eve leaned on the railing next to him, fascinated by the play of emotions over his face as he stared up at the house. He was neither indulging nor suppressing, just letting the feelings come and go.

He turned suddenly, eyes dark and vulnerable, and she had to work not to step back. 'This is really, really nice of you. You came up here to design a porch, and now . . .'

She blinked sweetly. 'Ass-deep in your melodrama?'

His big, hearty laugh pleased her ridiculously, as if she'd fixed the whole problem. Now if she could just feed Abigail a funny line too, they'd be all set and Eve could get back to work.

'God, this is so *crazy*. My whole life I've wanted kids.

Probably some weird compulsion to fix how my parents screwed me up. But after my marriage failed and then the relationship with Christie . . . I thought I'd have to give up that dream. Now I've got a daughter and I . . . I don't even know what I feel.'

'You've known for like ten minutes, Clayton! I wouldn't consider yourself a failure until at *least* fifteen.'

He groaned, sounding slightly crazed. 'Thank you for being here.'

'Wait till you get my bill.' She smiled, wishing she could also be that direct and that emotionally open. Instead she did wisecracks.

'So . . .' Clayton shook his hands and blew out a breath, like an athlete getting out the last kinks before a burst of activity. 'Now what? Consult an attorney? Offer her a place to stay? Where's the manual for becoming an instant father?'

Eve put her hand briefly on his shoulder, trying to reassure him. 'Right now she's fine staying with Shelley and me for a while longer. So that's good. As for the rest, I know as much as you do. I guess spend time with her, right?'

'Yeah.' He pushed away from the railing and started pacing. 'Yeah, I'd like to do that. I guess.'

'We'll contact Leah and see how things are going with butthead. Best case, God tells him he's being a jerk and he calms down and lets Abigail go back home.'

'That would be good.' Looking suddenly doubtful, Clayton let himself sink back into a chair. 'Wouldn't it?'

'Your guess is as good as mine.' Eve crossed to the chair next to him and they sat looking out at the lake in a comfortable silence that made her imagine they were drawing support from each other's presence. Fanciful, maybe. But nice.

'What did your parents do to you? If you don't mind me asking.'

She did mind him asking. There was no way to explain the whole story without revealing who her parents were.

Shelley's voice echoed in her head, asking why that would be so bad.

Eve told her to be quiet. Her habit of hiding her parents was too deeply conditioned to fall prey to logic. 'Let's just say I know how Abigail feels finding out that one of her parents isn't biologically related to her.'

'When did it happen to you?'

She glanced at him, finding only concern on his face, no eager anticipation of good gossip. 'Last summer.'

'Damn. That's intense, Eve. I'm sorry.' He stared so long, she dropped her eyes. 'Did you find out who your birth parent is?'

She moved restlessly. 'No.'

'No desire?'

Eve shrugged, still staring down at his deck. Her hands plunged into her pockets, encountering the edge of a card it took a second to remember was from the therapist on Devereux Beach. 'Not enough.'

'Man, I'd be curious.'

'I'm not you.'

He was quiet so long she looked up, embarrassed to have been so rude. He was watching her speculatively. 'You're afraid?'

'No.' Her voice came out high, defiant; the voice of a child.

'I'm not judging. I get it.' He frowned. 'Actually, no, I don't. If I'd found out about Abigail earlier, I would have wanted to know her. But as you said, I'm not you.'

'That's a different situation.'

'How do you mean?'

She struggled to articulate what she'd never been forced to put into words before, or even into coherent thought. 'Because the nature of parents is to protect their children. Or it should be. The nature of children is to want parents to protect them. So of course you would want to find Abigail. My birth mother didn't keep me. She gave me up.'

'Do you know the circumstances?'

Eve had to look away again, wishing her voice would stop shaking. Yes, she damn well knew. But she wasn't sharing that sordid information with anyone. At times, she wished she could be like Olivia, ignorant of how she and her sisters had been conceived. Then she could imagine a beautiful teenage mother tearfully surrendering the baby she was too young to care for but carrying deep in her heart the image of that little girl for the rest of her life.

Helen Phillips had gotten pregnant with Eve as the result of a business deal. *Here's the baby, now I get paid for the rest of my life*. A win-win situation.

'Not exactly.'

'Then you can't be sure why she did give you up, or whether it was even under her control.' A glance showed he was watching her again in the intent way that made her fight for more rigid control of her body and her emotions. 'Maybe she released you precisely to protect you, and the sacrifice was all hers. I'm not saying you should go looking if you don't want to. But . . . I guess I'm . . .'

'A journalist making me get my story straight.'

He grinned. 'I guess that's right.'

Eve smiled back, throat still thick, hands still clenched, but at the same time astounded to realize that she and Clayton had maneuvered a sticky, complicated and emotional conversation without hurt feelings or blame. She wished she and Mike could do the same. They couldn't. It was about time Eve admitted that to herself.

Dismay propelled her to her feet, even as Clayton was obviously getting another question ready.

'We should go rescue poor Abigail.'

He looked comically stricken, as if he'd just remembered she existed. 'Do we really have to involve her in this whole thing?'

Eve burst out laughing. 'I think maybe.'

He held out his hand for her to pull him to his feet, though he rose easily under his own power. 'Okay. I guess I'm a dad now, whatever that's going to mean.'

'I guess you are, and I have no idea what it means. You'll have to make it up as you go along.' She tried to pull her hand away, but he tightened his grip, making her look up at him, shading her eyes to see his expression, grave but warm.

'Thanks, Eve. I . . . hope you can find some way to make sense of your family mess.'

She was startled, felt trapped there with her hand in his. 'Thanks.'

'I am probably way out of line, given that I don't know you at all, but watching you just now . . . I think finding your birth mother might . . . I don't know, hold some key for you.'

She took a startled breath. 'Well. You're right.'

'Really?' He registered surprise. 'It was that easy?'

'No.' She pulled her hand gently away. 'You're right that you don't know me. Let's go down to the lake and find Abigail.'

Chapter 10

February 25, 1980 (Monday)

We found Woman #1 by holding a publicity casting for a bit part in my next movie, which we're shooting in Maine. I liked the winner. Daniel chose a different woman. She's not the glamorous type I wanted, but pretty enough, and Daniel is right that glamorous types can turn into problems, while the meek can be more easily cowed into doing what we want. She will be well paid for life as long as she keeps silent. We are providing all medical care once she gets pregnant, and will help her with whatever she needs to fit a pregnancy into her life – if she wants to disappear or tell people the baby died or whatever, we will make that possible.

At first I called her (not to her face) my angel of mercy. But Daniel came home yesterday from being with her and I wanted to kill him. I think I tried. I have never felt such rage. For a few minutes I swear I was no longer human. It was terrifying for both of us.

My husband, my love, my reason for being was with another woman, and I had to stay home and imagine it. I told him that if he enjoyed the sex even a little beyond what it took to come, I'd scratch his eyes out. He reminded me that the whole thing was my idea. What does logic have to do with it? Or with any human emotion? You feel what you feel. I had to get stinking drunk or I swear I would have killed myself. I am taking my meds, my only hope of getting through this.

From now on she is no longer an angel of mercy, but an angel-bitch.

At least it's done and my second most precious dream will come true. The world will believe I am a true, whole woman, one who can grow life in her body the way women are supposed to. And I will have a child to love and raise in my image, or Daniel's image, whose life I can make a happy one, full of joy and acceptance. We'll be a real family.

God willing, this one will take. I don't know if I can stand having him screw her again.

Love,

Mommy-to-be

PS I will have to remember that anger in case I ever need to use it in a movie.

PPS (March 10) It didn't take. I want to slit my wrists. What is wrong with her anyway? Daniel has to go again.

PPPS (April 12) And again.

PPPPS (May 13) And again.

PPPPPS (June 15) And again.

Back at Shelley's, upstairs in her room, Eve took off her coat, remembering to dig out Joseph Simington's business card, with its pictures of willow and oak. Over at the white garbage can in the corner of the room, she hesitated. Given the psychological damage that had been unearthed lately, it probably wouldn't be a terrible idea to keep Joseph around. She debated a second longer, then ended up tucking the card into one of the outer pockets of her suitcase.

After she and Clayton had retrieved the prickly and clearly

terrified girl, Eve had waited around until Abigail seemed reassured and Clayton more relaxed before she announced she had work to do. In spite of Abigail's pleading glance and Clayton's haggard expression, she had hardened her heart and left them. This was a father–daughter matter. They'd either work out a solution and a relationship or they wouldn't. She'd only be in the way.

Guilty consequence: she could escape the drama and could get back to architecture.

She settled herself on the window seat, visualizing Shelley's chosen site, trying to imagine a place that would fit the landscape, the island, the existing house and Shelley herself. Her mind kept jumping over the surface of ideas, like stones skipped across water – except unlike a stone, she didn't reach an ending point where she could sink deeply and finally into a concept. Of course today was only a beginning. Too soon to expect the perfect solution. Especially distracted by worry over Abigail and Clayton.

So much for escaping the drama.

Finally she found herself hungry and went downstairs for a bowl of leftover tortellini soup and half a ham sandwich. The day had warmed up to the mid fifties, so she wrapped up in a sweater and sat on the porch with her meal, watching the waves roll in, letting her mind wander again through possibilities for Shelley's house. Tucked away, secluded, filled with private spaces.

The Braddock family's house in Beverly Hills had been a maze of rooms, most much too big to be homey or comfortable. Eve had always felt lost there, swallowed up in luxury and wasted space. Only at their house in Maine did she feel truly at home.

Not for the first time, she regretted that she and her sisters had decided to let that property go.

No wonder, then, that she'd fallen in love with her house in Swampscott the moment she laid eyes on it. It was smaller than many of the houses on the block, and its staid New England profile was about as far from the family's sprawling pink Mediterranean mansion as possible. Close to the ocean, in a safe, quiet neighborhood, with a vibrant bustling city within an hour's commute – her perfect situation. Yet as she sat dreaming about house possibilities for Shelley, she found she was also dreaming of another cozy cabin, in Maine, just big enough for her and Marx.

Her and Marx? This was how she was thinking now?

Suddenly deeply sad, she rested her spoon back in the bowl, staring out at the blue-gray water stretching to the horizon.

'Hi.' Abigail bounced on to the porch, hazel eyes glowing with excitement. 'Oh, you're eating.'

Eve forced out a smile. 'Hungry?'

'Sure.'

'There's more soup and some sandwich stuff. Need help finding things?'

'Shelley's in there, I can ask her.' Abigail stayed in the doorway, grinning at Eve, obviously bursting with news.

Eve leaned toward her. 'Ye-e-es?'

'I just wanted to say thanks. He's pretty great. He wants to take us around the island this afternoon.'

Eve blinked. 'Us?'

'You and me. Sightseeing.'

'I'm here to work, Abigail, I can't—'

'Sure you can.' Shelley walked out on to the porch carrying a lunch tray. 'There's no hurry on the work. Enjoy yourself.'

Eve found herself wanting to say no, searching for excuses. 'What is there to see?'

'Lots of things.' Shelley sat and put her tray on her lap.

'Okay, not lots of things. A few things. The Stavkirke, a replica of an old-style Norwegian church, Schoolhouse Beach, Jackson Harbor, the lavender farms . . . Too early to rent bicycles, but it's a beautiful day for kayaking. Get Clayton to take you on a spin through Death's Door.'

Abigail looked appalled. 'Death's what?'

'Death's Door. What they call the water between our island and the mainland. Lots of shipwrecks. Weather can change in an instant. Terribly dangerous.'

'You're sending us out there knowing it could kill us?'

'Absolutely.' Shelley took a bite of her sandwich. 'Facing death builds character.'

'You're kidding.'

'Of *course* I'm kidding. You think I'm some kind of idiot? You should have seen your faces!'

Abigail let out a high giggle at the same time as Shelley cackled. Eve grinned, wanting to boom out a basso ho-ho-ho for a little contrast.

'You should go, Eve.' Shelley picked up an issue of the *Washington Island Observer* from her tray and glanced at Abigail, who'd become one with her phone. 'You'll have plenty of time to work later.'

Still Eve hesitated, until Shelley tilted her head meaningfully toward Abigail, her message clear: *Go for her sake.*

'Marx . . .'

'Marx and I will hang out. He's fine here.' Shelley held Eve's gaze. 'I was planning to take a walk later anyway.'

'Okay.' Eve sighed. Apparently she wasn't escaping the father–daughter mess that easily, though she had planned to have a look around the island at some point. 'I'm in.'

'Great.' Abigail's thumbs were flying. 'I'll text him that we'll be over after lunch.'

'Don't get too cozy too soon.' Shelley shook her spoon at the girl before dipping it back into her bowl. 'Give the guy a chance to adjust.'

Abigail bristled. 'He invited me. It was his idea.'

'You know what I mean.' Shelley continued eating, leaving Abigail to keep bristling or get over it as she saw fit.

Eve was impressed. The woman was a pro.

Abigail went into the kitchen and came back with food, disappearing back into her phone as she ate, while Shelley read her paper.

Eve finished her soup and sandwich leisurely, then stood to take her dishes into the kitchen.

The second she moved, Abigail's head shot up. 'Ready?'

Eve smiled. 'I need a cup of coffee and a change of shoes. *Then* I'm ready.'

The coffee took fifteen minutes. The shoes two. She came down to find Abigail standing impatiently by the door.

'Ready?'

'*Yes*, I'm ready.' Eve gave her a playful pat on the head. 'Cool your jets, babe.'

'Cool my . . . ?'

'A mother expression.'

Abigail's eyes popped. 'You have *kids*?'

'*My* mother.'

'Oh.' She opened the front door. 'Let's go.'

'Bye, Shelley.' Eve paused, waiting for a response from the porch. 'Want me to pick up something for dinner?'

'If you don't mind, thank you.' Shelley appeared from the kitchen, wiping her hands on an apron that had cats climbing all over it. 'I can finally finish off my Great-Aunt Lurene.'

Eve pretended shock. 'You're killing her?'

'She's writing about her.'

Eve looked at Abigail curiously. 'How do you know that?'

Abigail shot back a you're-so-lame look. 'She *told* me.'

'I'm working on my family history.' Shelley took off the apron and folded it. 'Seems like the thing to do when you reach my age.'

Abigail rolled her eyes. 'Oh, like you're over a hundred? C'mon, you're probably only a little older than my dad – than Glen.'

Shelley narrowed her eyes. 'Why, how old is he?'

'Forty-five.'

'Well.' Shelley was clearly tickled. 'I'll be sixty this summer.'

'Oh.' Abigail looked embarrassed. 'Well, you seem younger.'

'You do *not* need to apologize for thinking I'm forty-five.' Shelley made shooing motions. 'Now go have a good time getting to know your dad. But don't crowd him.'

'Yes, o-*kay*.'

Eve and Shelley exchanged grins as the door closed.

'I really like her.' Abigail leapt down the steps. 'She's kind of weird, but she's cool.'

'Shelley?' Eve patted her jeans pocket to make sure she had her phone. 'I like her too.'

'Last night she was telling me stories about her family. Like this Lurene she's writing about was the first ever female head of a library, somewhere in Canada. And her great-great-grandfather claimed he met the guy who shot Lincoln *after* he shot him, when everyone else said he was dead.'

'A ghost?'

'I don't know, but it was cool. Did she tell you about her life?'

'No.' For a brief moment, Eve was ridiculously stung that Shelley had opened up to Abigail, before she reminded herself that she hadn't been the one pestering her hostess with questions. Maybe she should start. 'Were you interviewing her?'

'Asking stuff.'

'You should be a journalist.' She gave Abigail a sidelong look. 'Like Clayton.'

Abigail looked delighted. 'That's it! I'm not nosy, I'm a professional. It's in my genes.'

'All in how you look at it.' They reached the end of the driveway and turned right.

'Anyway, Shelley's husband left her when she was pregnant with her third child, like she told us, and she went back to school for a teaching degree. Then her parents left her no money because they gave it all to her sister, so she had to go work in Boston as a corporate trainer for ten years so she could afford to retire here in this house. Her sister lived here first, but died. Apparently she was like a total loser.'

'Loser?'

'A drug addict, a mess.'

Ouch. 'Pretty harsh judgment, Ms Abigail.'

'Shelley didn't like her much.'

'Ah.' Eve had gotten the same impression, but decided this was a good time to change the subject. Addiction was a complicated beast, one Jillian Croft had wrestled with repeatedly, finally dying in defeat. 'Loser' wasn't the word Eve would use to describe that kind of heartbreak. Even for her mother.

She pointed up the street to Clayton's driveway. 'Look, he's got the truck ready and waiting.'

Clayton's arm rose on the far side of the cab in an exuberant wave, which Abigail returned. Almost immediately, Eve felt the familiar desire to turn around and go back to Shelley's. She hated the coward weenie inside her, totally out of her control, utterly illogical. What could possibly happen this afternoon that she couldn't handle? She never came up with an answer that would stop the feeling.

'Hey.' Clayton got out to meet them, striding up the driveway wearing a long-sleeved striped shirt rolled up at the sleeves over a black T-shirt, blue jeans and hiking boots. He moved easily, comfortable in his body, confident it would do what he wanted. Mike was also tall, but his large build meant he lumbered when he walked, as if he had to fight to move and constantly adjust to stay balanced.

Eve caught herself. On the verge of leaving Mike, she was being critical of how he moved? That was just not nice.

'Hi, Clayton.' Abigail bounced over to him. 'I got Eve to come.'

'I see that.' He smiled a greeting. 'Did it take a lot of effort?'

'Kicking and screaming,' Eve said.

'Cool! I've never been in a truck before.' Abigail ran over to the dusty red Chevrolet Colorado pickup. 'We have a Toyota Camry. A *white* one. My fa— Glen goes nuts over every speck of dust.'

'Ah.' Clayton gave Eve an I'm-not-touching-that-one look and opened the passenger-side door for his new daughter. 'Hop in. Unless you'd rather sit in back.'

'No way. Up front is cooler.'

They settled themselves in the truck, Abigail in the middle. Clayton climbed in and restarted the engine. 'First stop, the Stavkirke.'

'The what?' Abigail was playing cute; she'd just heard Shelley mention it.

'Coolest thing on the island.' He turned left out of his driveway. 'There were a lot of Scandinavian and Icelandic immigrants in Door County. In the early nineties, a bunch of Washington Island residents decided to build this replica of a church in . . . uh . . . Norway somewhere. The original was built back in the . . . somethingth century.'

'Oh *that* sounds accurate.'

'Hey, no harassing the tour guide.' He sent Abigail a quick grin. 'You can read the pamphlet when we get there.'

The interior of the island alternated between more of the same thick woods along the coast, and large fields, some looking wild and unclaimed, others clearly ready to be planted again in spring.

Just beyond a big red barn structure, which Clayton told them was the site of the island's first lavender farm, he pulled off into a parking strip along a forested portion of the road. Opposite the lot, on the other side of the street, stood what looked to Eve like an attractive but totally ordinary church – unless she had a completely wrong idea of somethingth-century Norwegian architecture. Her disappointment was cut short when Clayton took them further down the road, then through the trees on a wooden walkway that ended in a clearing.

There was the Stavkirke, exceeding all her expectations. The structure was small, about the size of a one-room cottage, and made entirely of wood. Several layers had been piled up, like a child's stacking-cup set turned upside down, topped by a cupola that vaguely resembled a steeple. Dragons' heads protruded from the upper levels, presiding over the scalloped-shingle roof and walls. It looked like a crazy witch's castle.

Eve loved it.

'Wow.' Abigail did a classic jaw-drop. 'That's not like any church *I've* ever been to. Ours is about ten times bigger.'

'Yours probably wasn't inspired by Vikings.' Clayton led the way up the front steps to the outer walkway, then into the interior of the structure, currently empty of people.

Inhaling the wonderful sweet wood smell, Eve grabbed a

brochure, and gazed around her. The complex knotty pine interior seemed to glow, light entering through small windows, enhanced by subtle sconces turning the wood golden. The walls were composed of vertical boards – staves – anchored in place by St Andrew's crosses. More of the crosses ringed the nave halfway up the space, suggesting a raised walkway or second story. Hanging centrally was a wooden model of a schooner with a full set of sails. Rows of simple chairs faced the wooden altarpiece, meticulously hand-painted to look like marble.

'It's amazing.' Abigail's face lit into new maturity. 'I can totally understand worshiping here. There's such a . . . feeling.'

'The place is mostly used for weddings these days.' Clayton drew his hand down one of the floor-to-ceiling beams supporting the roof. 'The worshiping is done across the street.'

'That's too bad.' Abigail lifted her head to gaze upward, expression peaceful and half smiling.

Eve stopped scrutinizing the church and started scrutinizing Abigail. The Braddock sisters hadn't been raised going to church. In her hometown of Jackman, Jillian had been taken every week by her mother and father, but left the institution behind when she fled Maine and her old life, though she kept her faith. Dad had been raised somewhat sporadically Catholic by well-meaning parents who were often too tired or too busy to take him on Sundays. In Beverly Hills, and after he and Lauren moved to Maine, he attended Easter and Christmas services, and occasionally taught the girls stories from the Bible. Other than that, Olivia, Rosalind and Eve were left on their own to decide what to believe.

Watching Abigail flower into radiant calm, Eve couldn't help wondering what it must be like to trust absolutely a being whose every aspect was so complicated and controversial. If Abigail's expression right now was any indication, it was rather euphoric.

She shifted her gaze to Clayton to find he'd also finished his examination of the church interior and was now examining her instead. Not wolfishly, but with a calm, thoughtful expression. Immediately she turned away. He gave her the unsettling feeling he could read her mind, and she didn't care for it. Mike was always in his own—

Enough comparing him to Mike, though she supposed it was normal to be doing a post-mortem on her relationship. Even one not quite dead yet.

The three of them left the church in silence in an unspoken agreement that it was time to go. Back in the truck, Abigail let out a blissful sigh. 'That was really cool. And for me, really important. I kind of worried I wouldn't be able to be with God anymore in a church. I stopped being able to hear Him in ours. I was getting in my own way with all my negative thoughts and fears. I mean obviously, right?'

'Sure.' Clayton started the truck and pulled out of the lot. 'Understandable.'

'But in there, I was able to feel Him again. It was wonderful. Like I was meant to be here to find that out. And like it's worth trying to find a new church wherever I . . . end up.'

'That's great.' Eve sort of understood what she meant, even if she wouldn't use the same terms. 'Had you always gone to that church?'

'No other choice. Glen and Mom insisted.' She peered right and left. 'Man, there's like hardly *anything* on this island. Where are we going next?'

'Schoolhouse Beach.'

'What's there?'

'A beach. No schoolhouse.'

She giggled, obviously a little manic. Eve worried that when she came down, she'd come down hard. 'Big thrill.'

'That's what we trade in here on beautiful Washington Island. Ex-*cite*-ment.' Clayton slowed, glanced both ways at the empty intersection, and turned right. 'I want to know something, if it's okay to ask a serious question.'

'Sure,' Abigail said.

'How did you cope having to go to this church once you realized who you were, and how the church felt about that part of you?' He spoke easily, as if he were asking about her taste in crackers.

Abigail turned abruptly to Eve, who nodded encouragingly. *Yes, she'd told him. Yes, he was fine with it.*

Visibly relieved, Abigail turned back to her birth dad. 'I got out of it what was good and ignored the rest.'

'Good plan,' Clayton said. 'But easier to say than do.'

'Yeah, I'd come out of some sermons wanting to throw up from the tension. I felt like there was a giant L on my forehead and that everyone would see it and throw me out, or worse, try to cure me.' She rolled her eyes. 'Trust me, if there was a cure, I'd be home now in my own bed, texting some girlfriend about hot guys.'

'You're probably better off without them,' Eve stage-whispered.

'Hey.' Clayton glanced at her. 'I heard that.'

Abigail snickered.

'You were brave to come out to your parents knowing they might not approve.'

'That's what Eve said.'

'Eve is very wise.'

'That's for damn sure,' Eve said. She wondered if Abigail was aware that she'd slid slightly toward her father.

'I wasn't going to come out to my parents.' Abigail tossed back her bangs. 'At least not while I was living with them. But then I met a gay woman in an advanced math class I was taking at UWM.'

'UWM?'

'University of Wisconsin in Milwaukee. She was out, totally comfortable with herself. She found me. I mean, she could tell, even though I thought I was doing a really good job hiding it. I wore dresses, makeup, jewelry, et cetera. We became friends. She was the first person I was able to talk to about . . . everything.'

'She encouraged you to tell your parents?' Eve asked.

'No, no, not like that. She respected my timing and my choices. It was how I felt with her and the things she said. Like, "Hate is in people, not in God. If God is love and love is good, how can He object to any of the love we feel?"' Abigail laid her head back on the seat, as if the speech had exhausted her. 'I chose to look at it that way. It helped. Except when my dad was screaming at me.'

'He *screamed* at you?'

Abigail sighed. 'Like a crazy person.'

'Hmm.' Clayton put on his right blinker. 'I'm thinking your mom should have stopped that.'

'I've been thinking that too,' Eve said, apparently too bitterly, because Clayton looked over at her, probably trying to read her mind again.

Abigail's head lifted from the seat. 'Hey, so what was my mom like when you knew her?'

'Leah? She was sweet, outwardly shy, but she had fire in her. Her parents were incredibly strict.'

'Yeah, Oma and Opa? Like *military* strict. How did you meet her?'

'We were in *Little Shop of Horrors* together. I was a sophomore, she was a senior. I was the voice of the man-eating plant. She was one of the narrator trio. Good voice. Talented.'

'She sings in church sometimes.'

'I was probably part of her teenage rebellion.' He nudged Abigail with his shoulder. 'We all have to stick it to our parents at some point.'

'What did *you* do?' Abigail asked him.

Eve was all ears, though she really hoped he wouldn't say *your mother*.

'Not much. I drank a bit when I was underage, smoked some pot, the usual stupid stuff. My parents weren't really around to rebel against. But *now*, I'm taking over the house, extending it, throwing stuff out . . . essentially changing the place into what *I* want it to be.'

Abigail drooped in disappointment. 'That is a really boring rebellion.'

'Ah, you wait and see. Someday you will think I am the *man*.'

'If you say so.' Abigail nudged him with her shoulder. 'I wish *you'd* married her, not Glen.'

Clayton didn't react. 'Your stepdad.'

'Talk about not a rebel.' Abigail's contempt was clear. 'He won't even cross the street against the light. Obeys every speed limit to the exact mile. Drives me nuts. Like maybe he should try being *more* rigid.'

'Hmm.' Clayton made a turn on to a road that cut between two halves of a graveyard. 'Coming out to a guy like that would be tough. But you did the right thing.'

She grinned at him. 'Thanks, Dad.'

'Uh . . .' He scratched his chin. 'Not sure I'm ready for you to call me that.'

'Okay, Papa.' Abigail smirked, then looked around. 'Wait, where are we going?'

'Beach is just through there.' He pointed. 'You can see the lake between the trees.'

'They have a *graveyard* by the beach?'

'It's best not to ask.'

Eve's laughter was interrupted by her phone playing the Killers' 'Ballad of Michael Valentine', indicating that Mike was calling. Her amusement died abruptly as it hit her that she'd have to speak normally to him in front of Abigail and Clayton, while in the back of her mind she was planning to do exactly what he'd predicted – break up with him and kick him out of her house.

Her stomach twisted. Where would he go? He'd be miserable. *She'd* be miserable.

'Who's that?' Abigail asked.

'My boyfriend.'

'You're kidding.'

'No, why?'

Abigail looked over at Clayton as if she needed permission to continue. 'Well, because you made a weird face.'

Clayton nodded. Of course he'd seen it.

'I thought it was, like, a telemarketer,' Abigail said. 'Are you mad at him?'

'No.' Eve felt herself blush and was even more annoyed that her face, which she thought she'd schooled into total inscrutability, had continued to share her feelings. 'If it's important, he'll call again. Otherwise he just wants to say hi. I'll call him later.'

'Okay.' Abigail was still studying her. 'How long have you been dating?'

'Three years. Don't you want to hear about my rebellion?'

'*Yes!* Totally.'

Clayton sent her an amused look to let her know he was on to her abrupt subject change. 'Let's hear it.'

'I went goth.'

'Goth!? *You?*' Abigail was so astounded, Eve was actually insulted.

'Black leather, eyeliner, triple-pierced ears, nose ring, the works.'

'Now *that* is a worthwhile rebellion. I bet your parents went crazy.'

'Dad and my stepmother were definitely not amused. They let it play out, though. I got bored of the look eventually, as they probably knew I would.'

They pulled into a parking lot bounded by cedars, beyond which were glimpses of the lake. Clayton turned off the engine and opened his door. 'Here we are. Washington Island's second-best attraction. Schoolhouse Beach.'

'Cool.' Eve and Abigail climbed down and walked toward the beach, stopping briefly beside an old phone booth on which had been mounted a white-corded push-button phone where the coin-operated metal one should have been. 'Wow. An antique.'

'Go figure.'

Abigail ran on ahead through the trees, then turned back at the edge of the beach, face showing total disgust. 'It's rocks!'

The cove was large, full of sunshine, and gorgeous. More cedars lined its horseshoe shape, their branches starting at the same height on each trunk so that it looked as if someone had taken a chainsaw and straight-cut them. The blue-green water was crystal clear and inviting, but the beach did indeed consist of rocks. White-gray rocks, most the size of a small potato.

The Californian *and* the Bostonian in Eve were likewise disappointed. '*This* is a beach?'

'Sure.' Clayton gestured around. 'Fabulous swimming spot. Very popular. It's a great beach. Trust me.'

Eve mimed stepping on an unstable, uncomfortable surface,

grimacing, arms flailing. '*Ouch, ouch, ouch*. Wow, you Midwesterners sure know how to have a good time.'

'Think of them as future grains of sand.' He put his hands on his hips, watching Abigail crunch her way down to the shoreline.

Eve took the opportunity to speak in a low voice. 'You're handling this well. At least you seem to be.'

He blew out a breath. 'I'm exhausted. I didn't sleep much last night. Finally just decided to act as if she were my niece. Then I realized my nieces are my age. So I decided she was a friend's daughter, and that this friend was on vacation and had asked us to hang out with her for a few days.

Us?

Eve decided to chalk that one up to enthusiasm and ignore it.

'Nicely done.' She lifted her face to the breeze, still missing the ocean smell, but enjoying the clarity of the air. 'How long is that ploy going to work?'

'Until it doesn't.' He picked up a rock and hurled it impressively far into the lake. 'Then I'll have to think of something else.'

'You can do that?' She threw a rock after his, not matching his distance, but not embarrassing herself either. 'Just decide something is other than what it is? That works?'

'Takes concentration, but yes. Kind of a survival mechanism. I used to tell myself my parents didn't *want* to live apart from me. That aliens were forcing them to. That every second they missed me as much as I missed them. It helped. Some. Eventually I stopped missing them, so that took care of that.'

'Creative. And poignant.'

He threw another rock, then stood looking after it. 'She needs to be back with her parents.'

'I know. I hope they come to their senses.'

'Poor kid.' He rubbed the top of his head, further mussing hair the wind had already been playing with. 'Eve, uh, I was actually thinking . . .'

Eve waved back at Abigail, who'd dropped down to inspect something. When Clayton didn't finish his sentence, she gave him a look. 'Why am I suddenly afraid?'

'Because you're a smart woman?' He grinned down at her. 'I was thinking that one solution is to drive Abigail back down to Wisconsin. See what her parents are really like, and whether her story checks out.'

Eve's smile dropped. 'You think she's lying?'

'No, actually. But . . . we only have her word.'

'True.' Something inside Eve rebelled at the idea that Abigail was putting on a show.

'You trust her?'

She nodded.

'So what do you think of my idea of taking her home?'

'It might be the best solution.' She watched Abigail balancing stones on top of one another. 'Do you think she'll agree to go?'

'I don't know. My guess is yes. As hurt as she is, she must want to go back. Sounds like before this she was decently happy. If they can just work out the great gay–church divide.'

'Hey!' Abigail called to them. 'Come look at my cairn.'

Eve took one step and felt Clayton's hand on her shoulder. 'Hang on.'

She turned back. 'What is it?'

'About this trip. If I go . . .' One corner of his mouth turned up. 'Oh, this is going to be good.'

'What is?'

'If I go, I—'

'Come see!' Abigail yelled.

'Just a second.' Eve looked impatiently up at Clayton. 'If you go, what?'

He made a face, as if gathering courage for a gruesome task. 'I want you to come with me.'

Chapter 11

July 15, 1980 (Tuesday)

Finally, it worked! The angel-bitch is going to have my baby! I am so impatient to start wearing the pregnancy costumes I ordered. Several months ago, one of the costume women from the studio showed up at an AA meeting and I wheedled out of her the name of the company they use for prosthetics. I ordered a range of fake pregnancy sizes under my real name. They are totally realistic and perfect! No one will know, even if they touch my belly, which I will avoid as much as possible. One of the times God put down His hand for me instead of making me cross the mud by myself.

Soon I will start 'showing' and being coy and blushing and happy, so in love with my husband at this special time, and so in love with the life growing inside me.

What will you name him or her? *Oh, I'll say, winking slyly, we'll surprise you on that one. They'll all be dying to know. They'll all be so very happy for us.*

We plan to give the story to People. *They'll be kindest.*

Pregnant, pregnant, pregnant at last! I'm going to have a baby!

I lie in bed at night and can't sleep and can't sleep. I haven't been this happy since I snuck on to the bus to leave Maine!

Since I met Daniel! Since I got my first part! I'm so happy I want to sing and dance all over the room all night!

Daniel turns over and tells me to take my goddam meds. He makes me laugh with delight, even when he's furious with me.

A baby!

'Come with you?' Eve couldn't believe he'd just asked her that. 'Clayton, I don't . . .'

Her father's expression had jumped into her mind: *I don't have a horse in this race*, though it probably wasn't a great idea to compare Clayton's daughter to a horse.

'Right. Never mind. Not your problem, I shouldn't have asked.' He took a step back, his gaze moving past her toward Abigail, anxiety creasing his brow.

He was right. Not her problem. Also right that it was wrong to ask her to become further involved.

Also right that she was enjoying a hippo-like wallow in thick, sucking guilt.

'So?' Abigail ran toward them, clattering over the rocks. 'What's our next stop?'

Bless her for the interruption. Eve could leave the question until she'd had more time to sort out her feelings.

'Jackson Harbor.'

Abigail wrinkled her nose. 'Is it more exciting than this place?'

'Nope,' Clayton answered cheerfully, apparently able to throw off his worry just like that. At least on the outside.

'Where *is* the exciting stuff?' Abigail rushed to fall in step with her father as he headed back to his truck.

'Isn't any.'

'Then why do people come here?'

'Guess.'

'I have *no* idea. Because they're boring?'

'Hmph.' He turned and waited for Eve to catch up. 'What do *you* think?'

She gave it some thought, grateful that he wasn't holding her indecision against her. 'I'd guess *because* there isn't any exciting stuff. More excitement would mean more people, which would mean having to build more houses and hotels, which would mean more stores and more restaurants, which would end up making Washington Island look more like the little towns I saw on the mainland peninsula, which are in danger of drowning in their own cuteness.'

'Bingo.' Clayton climbed into the truck. Abigail and Eve followed. 'Got it, Abigail?'

'Yeah, I get it. Sort of.'

Clayton started the truck and pulled out of the lot. 'I bet you'd go nuts for the cherry train.'

'Ooh.' Abigail was all ears. 'What's that?'

'One of those open bus things pulled by a truck.'

She snorted. 'That's not a train.'

'It sort of has cars. You've seen ones like it before, I'm sure.'

'Why would I go nuts for *that*?'

'Because it goes all around the island and you get to see every single not-exciting thing over the course of two hours, plus hear lots and lots of history of all the not-exciting things, *and* you get to eat and shop in our thriving downtown.'

Eve couldn't help a snort. 'Downtown?'

'Yes!' He pretended not to know why they were amused. 'A whole intersection! They call it "up the road".'

'You're right.' Abigail rolled her eyes. 'I would go nuts.'

'I'm sorry to have to tell you the train doesn't start running until later in the year.'

Abigail pretended to pout, then spent the next five minutes – all it took to get the rest of the way to Jackson Harbor – telling them about how she *really* went nuts, in a 'like, totally good way', when her class traveled to Chicago to see *Hamilton*.

As she was finishing, Clayton maneuvered the truck into a parking space at the small, charming harbor, mostly deserted. There was a fishing museum, an old ice house, and some of the strangest fishing boats Eve had ever seen. They looked like bizarre, clumsy above-water submarines, covered all over with metal sheets bolted together to block out the wind and weather.

'*Voilà*, Jackson Harbor. Rock Island Ferry takes off from over there.' He pointed to one side, and then ahead to a small island across a narrow channel. 'Cool place. Cliffs and a lighthouse on one end. Beautiful sand beach on the other.'

'Ooh, a lighthouse!' Abigail said. 'Can we go see that?'

'Nope. Ferry doesn't start running until May.' He switched off the motor and folded his arms. 'So, Abigail, I've been thinking.'

Her scowl dissolved into wary curiosity. 'About what?'

'What do you say to the idea of us driving to Wisconsin to have a talk with your mom and dad?'

Her eyes opened wide. 'But . . . Wow.'

'I can't guarantee anything will change. But we need to give it a try. That's your home.'

Her face clouded over. She looked down at her hands. 'Not if they don't let me live there.'

'I will not abandon you. But I have no experience of being a parent, and no legal rights to you as of now. Ideally, you are better and safer back with your parents.'

A tear dripped off the end of Abigail's nose. Eve put her arm around her, sending Clayton a look of sympathy and admiration. This was truly a brave and sane next step. 'I think he's right, Abigail. Much better than having to start your life over completely. New friends, new parent, new city. That would suck.'

Abigail dipped her head lower. 'What if Glen won't take me back?'

Clayton looked panicked.

Eve jumped in. 'I can't imagine he won't. Maybe your mom will come to her senses and give him a good guilt-thrashing. It's certainly worth a try.'

Abigail nodded. More tears dripped, splashing on to her hands and making crimson circles on her red sweatshirt.

'Will you come with us, Eve?'

Aaaargh. 'I . . . think I'd be in the way. And I have work.' She could hear herself making excuses and was embarrassed by her cowardice. 'But . . . I'll talk to Shelley, and maybe . . .'

Abigail twisted to look at her, face so hopeful Eve's heart nearly broke. She had no idea why she'd been turned into a comfort item for the teen. Why not Clayton, who was much warmer and fuzzier? Maybe his relationship to her was too fraught for Abigail to relax around him, and Eve could provide a buffer. Maybe Abigail just trusted women more. Eve wouldn't blame her. She did too.

'So?' Abigail wiped her eyes on the sleeve of her red hoodie. 'When did you want to go?'

'Soon. I'm waiting right now for responses on three writing projects, so probably this weekend. We should get in touch with your parents and find out what would work for them.' Clayton started the truck.

'Okay.' Abigail sniffed and wiped her eyes again. 'What's your job? I don't even know.'

'I write training and corporate manuals for an investment firm.'

'Oh, *jeez*.' Abigail half laughed, still sniffling, but obviously trying to return the conversation to normal. 'No wonder you think this island is exciting.'

'Just call me Mr Thrill-a-Minute.' He grinned and patted her shoulder, then turned the truck around and headed back toward the southeastern end of the island.

By the time they'd only gone a few hundred yards, Abigail had dug out her phone and was peering at it, apparently recovered. 'Are you close to your family, Clayton?'

'Not really. My parents live in Spain. My sisters in Seattle and Portland, Oregon.'

'That's far.' Abigail glanced at Eve. 'How about you?'

'I'm close to my sisters. Not so much my stepmother, though we're friendly. I love my dad, but he can be—'

'What about your mother, *Jillian Croft*?'

'Your mother's name was Jillian Croft?' Clayton was clearly amused at the coincidence.

Eve braced herself. 'Uh . . .'

'Her mother *was* Jillian Croft.' Abigail looked up in astonishment. 'You didn't know that?'

'No.' He glanced at Eve. 'I didn't know that.'

Abigail gasped. 'Why didn't you tell him?'

'Maybe she didn't want me to know.'

'It's not you,' Eve protested wearily. 'I don't want anyone to know.'

'Shelley told me,' Abigail said. 'If you didn't want me to blab, you should have said something.'

'I should have, you're right.'

'Why don't you want anyone to know?' Clayton asked.

'Because it's none of their . . .' Eve closed her eyes and leaned her head against the glass, embarrassed by her own reaction. She owed Clayton more than that. 'Because it's excruciating having to answer everyone's questions about her and about what it was like growing up as her daughter. I am not defined by my mother. I'd rather people think of me as my own person.'

'Okay.'

Silence in the truck.

Great. She'd killed another conversation. Someone should hire her out to end parties.

'I think society forcing biological families to live together is a mistake.' Abigail swiped at something on her screen.

'Why do you say that?' Eve asked.

'Too many families are made up of people who don't get along, or who don't like or even value each other. Like me and my dad. Like Clayton and his whole family. Like Eve and her mom. Even Shelley and her sister. We should pick our own families.'

'I'd forgotten Shelley had a sister.' Clayton slowed to a stop at another deserted intersection and moved on. 'She lived in that house before Shelley. My parents knew her. Kind of a sad person. Helen? Wasn't that her name?'

'Helen Phillips,' Abigail announced. 'Shelley told me about her. She died a long time ago. Like the early two thousands.'

Eve didn't move. She couldn't. Her hand was frozen gripping the door handle. Her neck had seized up. Shelley's sister, the druggie, the 'loser'.

Helen Phillips. Dad's payments to her stopped in April 2002.

The pretty, gentle, blond mother of Eve's imagination was abruptly replaced by a gaunt addict with wild hair, rotting teeth and sunken eyes.

Eve was staying in the house her birth mother had owned. She'd eaten in the same kitchen. Maybe slept in her room. Bits of her long-ago DNA might have mingled with Eve's in the air, on the porch . . .

But wait.

This meant Shelley Grainger was her *aunt*?

Eve closed her eyes, pushing the thought away. It wasn't possible. Coincidences this huge just didn't—

Lauren.

Rosalind had been able to confirm before she went to New Jersey that Leila was her birth mother's name, because Lauren knew. If Lauren knew about Leila, she probably also knew about Helen, and whoever Olivia's mother was. Which meant this trip had nothing to do with architecture. Lauren had sent her here on purpose, to stumble over information Eve hadn't wanted to find.

Did Shelley know? Was that why she'd confided in Abigail but kept Eve at arm's length? They were related – it wasn't hard to imagine they had similar coping skills. Or non-coping skills.

No wonder Shelley seemed so unconcerned with the job Eve was here to do, with how long the designing process took. No wonder she'd been so comfortable hiring a complete unknown from another state with next to no experience.

Eve's shock began to thaw into anger. Lauren and Shelley had no *right* to put her in this position without consulting her. No *right* to force her to confront this part of her past. Those decisions belonged to Eve, and *only* to Eve.

How could they have done this?

The dark burn of anxiety started in her chest. Crap. *Crap!*

Her attempts at deep breaths were useless. The panic took hold too quickly, spread through her body, out of her control.

She had to get out of this truck. She couldn't sit here. She'd totally humiliate herself.

'Eve.' Clayton steered the truck to the side of the road. 'What's the matter? Are you in pain? Sick?'

'I'm okay.' Her voice sounded too close inside her head and too far away coming out of her mouth. She pressed her lips together and did her best to smile reassuringly as she shoved the door open, heart racing, breath ragged. 'I need to walk. I'll walk the rest of the way.'

'It's over five miles.'

'No.' She climbed out and nearly fell, heard Abigail squeal in fright.

'I'm fine.' She staggered a few steps, vision sparking. Shit, shit, *shit*. She couldn't fool anyone. Way too late for that. They'd think she was a lunatic. She wasn't sure she disagreed.

'Easy.' Clayton's arm came around her. She bent nearly double. 'You going to faint?'

Eve nodded, aware of his arm, hearing his voice, the rest of the world starting to fade.

'Squat down. It forces the blood back into your head.' Gentle pressure on her shoulders, guiding her into a squat, then the feel of his jacket draping over her back. 'Breathe low in your belly. Your chest should stay still.'

'Is she okay?' Abigail's voice was high with fear.

'I don't know. Here's my phone. Dial 911 and—'

'*No*. Not necessary.' She did not want anyone poking and prodding and asking questions. Already her vision was clearing, blood coming back into her face and head, though her heart was still pounding much too hard, and she had to convince herself as well as Abigail and Clayton that she wasn't about to fall to pieces. 'I'm recovering.'

'Unexplained fainting can be serious. You should get checked out.'

'I know . . . what happened.'

'What?'

'*Nothing*.'

Clayton made a sound of frustration. 'Either prove to me you're okay in a way that convinces me, or I'm calling an ambulance. No bullshit.'

She raised her head to glare at him; he'd squatted in front of her so their knees were almost touching. 'I had a shock.'

He looked stunned. '*Electric?* In my truck?'

'Emotional.'

'What . . .' Now he looked bewildered. Poor man. After this, he would definitely change his mind about having her come with him to see Abigail's parents. He didn't need another basket case on the scene. 'We were talking about Shelley . . .'

Eve worked her mouth, trying to cope with her body's involuntary trembling. It was none of his business, but the words came out anyway, along with the realization that she could no longer handle this alone. When she got home, she'd call Joseph Simington. In the meantime, she had two rank amateurs she could apparently depend on.

Which meant a lot to her.

'Helen Phillips . . . is my birth mother. I knew her name, but I didn't realize until just now that she was Shelley's sister. My stepmother must know. She sent me up here. I had no idea.'

'Jesus.' Clayton put his hands on her knees.

'Jesus is *not* happy with the way you sling his name around.' Abigail knelt next to Eve and put her arm around her, radiating affection.

With wrenching sadness, Eve realized that these people she barely knew had proved themselves kinder and more empathetic than friends she'd had for years. Only her sisters offered such unconditional support – and she'd held them at arm's length all her life.

She'd surrounded herself with people who couldn't touch her.

In high school, boys had nicknamed her IP – Ice Princess. Eve had told herself they didn't understand. She wasn't cold, she'd just spent too long protecting herself from being Jillian Croft's daughter, holding her thoughts and feelings behind a shield, always aware of the extra burden of celebrity, the cruelty of gossip, of 'friends' who hung around only to bask in her mother's fame, even long after Jillian died. Even in Beverly Hills, where celebrity was common, her mother had been a force. Her addiction, her mental illness, her death whispered, rumored and pointed at. Her daughters as well.

While Olivia basked in and used the attention, and Rosalind forged through it with determined cheer, Eve had built layer upon layer of defense, the innermost doll of a Russian set with painted-on features and smile.

Or maybe she *was* cold.

'I'm sorry, Eve,' Abigail said. 'I had no idea what I was saying. I had no idea you were adopted.'

'Of course you didn't.' She forced her brain to back away from the emotion – a skill she was expert at by now, feeling her heart gradually slowing, the trembling in her body lessening. 'When did you find out?'

'Last summer.'

Abigail gasped. 'I knew it.'

Eve turned incredulously. 'How could you know that?'

'No, no.' Abigail shuffled around on her knees so she could face her. 'I knew there was a reason I was so compelled to talk to you at the coffee shop.'

Eve shook her still-foggy head. 'I'm not following.'

'God sent you. God knew you'd understand what I was going through.' She looked as Joan of Arc must have, standing in front of the French army, glowing with strength and purpose. 'It's His plan.'

Eve sighed. 'I wish He'd told me sooner.'

Abigail rolled her eyes, back to her snarky self. 'Special place in hell for you.'

'You feeling better, Eve?' Clayton squeezed her knee. 'You look better.'

'You were gray before.' Abigail got to her feet. 'I thought you were dying.'

'Sorry for the melodrama.'

'You're not allowed to apologize.' Clayton stood and offered his hand. 'Can you stand?'

'Yes, yes, I can stand.' She was embarrassed at how annoyed she sounded, embarrassed to have created such a ridiculous scene in front of people she barely knew. 'Thank you. Both of you.'

'We're having a hell of a time, all three of us.' Clayton put an unnecessary hand on her elbow to help her to her feet. 'Three people, three life-jarring surprises.'

'At the risk of you making fun of me again, God brought us together.' Abigail tossed her bangs and gave Eve a defiant stare. 'To help each other through all this.'

Eve managed a smile. 'Could He not have arranged a Caribbean vacation instead?'

Abigail grinned. 'We'll come through this better and stronger. You'll see. He knows what He's doing.'

'That would be nice.'

Eve made it to the truck, shaky and exhausted, wanting only her nice comfortable room at Shelley's with its view of the lake, and to say and feel nothing for the rest of the day. Except . . .

'Oh, wait.'

'What is it?'

'I'm cooking dinner for Shelley. I have to go to Mann's and—'

'No, you don't.' Clayton stood behind her, hands ready while she climbed into the truck, apparently still afraid she'd drop like a stone. 'Abigail and I will shop and bring dinner over. We'll leave you at Shelley's and go to Mann's right now.'

'Good idea.' Abigail beamed at him.

'That okay, Eve?'

'Thank you.' She sent him a grateful look. 'Bet you didn't know when you agreed to hire me that you'd have to be therapist, cook and caretaker in return.'

'No problem.' He closed their door and bent into the open window, his eyes open and warm. 'You okay now? Definitely?'

'I'm fine. Definitely. Thank you.' Eve felt a brief, improbable shock of attraction. The last thing she needed. She dropped her eyes. 'I'd appreciate it if you – if neither of you said anything about this until I can get my brain around it a little better.'

'Of course.' Abigail squeezed her hand.

'Absolutely,' Clayton said.

'Thank you. I owe you. In case you ever have a mental breakdown around me, I'm there.'

'I've already had mine.' Abigail rolled her eyes. 'More than one.'

'All you owe me is a sunroom.' Clayton tapped the top of the truck and went around to his side.

They drove the rest of the way to Shelley's in silence. Eve was grateful; fighting the last of the diminishing attack was taking all her energy. When they arrived, Clayton leaned forward to look her over. 'Want one of us to come in with you?'

'No, no. I'll be okay.' She managed to climb down safely, with both of them watching her as if one wrong move would trigger an explosion. She gave what she hoped was a cheerful wave, then let herself into the house.

First to greet her was a tail-wagging Marx, whom she'd shamefully forgotten in her list of beings offering unconditional love. Lucky beast, his brain wasn't big enough to grasp the messes humans got themselves into.

'Hello.' Shelley came in from the porch. Eve made every

effort to act normally, but since she never paid attention to how she was acting when she was relaxed, she had no idea what normally was. 'Did you have a good afternoon? Where's Abigail?'

'Yes. We had fun. Abigail and Clayton are going to Mann's to get dinner.' She did okay, sounding only as if she were being mildly strangled, trying to stare without really staring, taking in her aunt's features as if she were seeing her for the first time, comparing them to her own.

'Father and daughter getting along okay?'

'They are, yes. We had fun.' Ugh. She'd already said that. In front of her aunt, she felt utterly naked. Was Shelley watching her too carefully? Could she tell that Eve knew? Did she have pictures of Helen here in the house?

The last thought startled her enough that she had to bend to pet Marx. 'Did he behave himself?'

'He was a great companion. We just came back from a walk a few minutes ago. I might have to get myself a dog someday.'

'They are best friends for sure.' Eve stood too quickly and swayed as her head protested the abrupt change in position. 'I'm going upstairs to make some phone calls.'

'Sure.' Shelley cocked her head, frowning. 'You look pale.'

'Just tired. Crazy day.' To put it mildly. Two over-the-top emotional situations and it wasn't even dinner time.

'You did a great thing for that girl. Well done.' Shelley pulled a folded piece of paper from her jeans pocket. 'I got an email from Leah Oakes. Thought you'd like to see it, so I printed it out.'

Eve groaned silently. If this was God's plan, she wanted to reschedule. *Her* plan had been to call Rosalind to get her head back on straight, then call Lauren to dislodge it again.

'Thanks. Okay. I'll read it upstairs.'

She fled to her room, Marx bounding alongside her, and flopped on to the bright bed while he stood forlornly next to her, knowing he wasn't allowed up. 'Marx, pardon my language, but this day has sucked.'

He wagged his tail enthusiastically.

'Come here.' She wiggled closer to the edge of the mattress, petting his head and neck, burying her nose in his soft, fluffy fur, murmuring endearments until she felt strong enough to tackle reading the email.

Curious enough, anyway.

One look at the printed heading made her roll her eyes. Leah and Glen had a shared email address, which meant Leah wouldn't be able to write freely.

Dear Shelley,

Thank you for contacting me. I look forward to welcoming your family to our congregation. Attached are some materials outlining the church's mission and ministries, and a copy of our most recent bulletin.

During our chat, you mentioned that your husband had left the Church of Higher Faith in Michigan, and that his concerns linger as he considers the spiritual life of your baby daughter. I can assure you that were he to return to worship at our church in Mequon, he would only be enriched by putting his trust in Christ to forgive and to love.

If you have any more questions, please don't hesitate to ask. I look forward to meeting you and sharing with you the joy of God's word.

Blessings,

Leah Oakes

Eve tossed the letter on to the bed next to her, annoyance chasing away the last of her shaky weakness. What the *hell* did that mean? Leah wanted Abigail to come back, but . . . who had to do the forgiving? Abigail? Or Glen?

Why hadn't Leah opened a free email account and written anonymously so she could have sounded like a human with feelings?

At least it meant Clayton and Abigail wouldn't be tossed out the moment they showed up. That was good.

She guessed.

For the first time, the blue and yellow room made her crave the soothing muted shades of her Swampscott bedroom. She hurled herself over on to her stomach and pulled the blanket over her head.

Half an hour later, Eve woke with a start. She never napped. Her body and brain had obviously been exhausted to the point of shut-down.

She lay blinking for a few seconds, then dragged the elastic out of her hair and pulled her phone from her pocket.

Rosalind picked up right away. 'Hey, how'd it go?'

'Fine, actually. Clayton took it about as well as anyone could. But then . . .' She had no idea how to lead in gracefully, so she'd just say it. 'I found out that Shelley is Helen Phillips's sister. Shelley is my aunt.'

Rosalind made a few unintelligible spluttering sounds. '*What?* How could that *possibly* be?'

'Lauren sent me here. She and Shelley are buds. She must have known.'

'That's not like her, to be so sneaky . . . is it?'

Eve had been thinking it was *exactly* like her. 'What other explanation is there? Lauren has known Shelley since she was a girl. She must have known Helen, too. She knew your birth mother's name; why wouldn't she know mine? Dad must have told her everything.'

'Oh sweetie, that is grim. There's no reason she couldn't have just told you.'

'Actually, there is. A pretty simple one.' Eve rolled over and looked out at the lake. 'I wouldn't have come.'

'Oh. That.'

'Yeah.' She sat up, drawing her knees to her chest. 'It's funny. Lauren's been my mother for more than half my life, but I still think of her as this nice woman who married Dad.'

'Yeah, she holds herself pretty tightly shut. Not to mention she came into a house where the previous maternal figure loomed *large*.'

'Lauren looms tiny.' Rosalind's giggle provoked Eve's first smile in what felt like hours. 'I'll call her. Thanks for calming me down, Rosalind.'

'You're welcome. Oh, wait, have you read Mom's diary yet?'

Eve rolled her eyes. 'Oh yeah, because I really need more emotional upheaval right now.'

'I know, but you *should* read it. I've been thinking about this a lot. She was a piece of work, but you have always been the hardest on her. She wasn't all bad. No one is all bad.'

Eve felt the familiar rage building. Her sisters didn't know what had happened with Mr Angel. That was her own fault, yes. But it also meant they didn't realize how low their mother could go. 'I know that. But—'

'There are so many really great memories. So many stories and positive things along with the awful stuff. But you never talk about any of that. It's like you don't want to hear anything that might make you change your mind.'

Eve's mouth opened to make a retort, but all that came out

was a tiny puff of air. Marx looked up from where he'd been lying. His tail wagged.

Rosalind was right. Eve was clinging to her anger, and to her vision of her mother as the ultimate wicked witch of her childhood. It was easier than facing a more painful and complicated truth.

Which was probably the operating mode for Abigail's father, Glen, on learning that his daughter was gay.

'Yes.' Eve sighed. 'Touché.'

'Read it. Wait until the Little Orphan Abigail stuff and the Helen stuff calms down, but read it.'

'And the Lauren stuff.'

'Oy. That too. Be kind.'

'I'm always kind.'

Her sister snorted. 'By the way, I've been worrying about Olivia. It's her birthday tomorrow and—'

'Argh!' Eve smacked her forehead. 'Thank you, I remembered and then totally forgot. It came up so fast. I'll send her flowers or something.'

'Okay, good. I'm wondering if there would be a way for the three of us to get together again soon. On your birthday maybe, in May? Mine's too soon; you'll still be on the island next week, and anyway, Bryn is taking me to the Jersey Shore for a very chilly beach weekend.'

Eve's crabby mood perked up slightly. 'I would love to have you both come over. I'll be back in Boston by the end of April or early May.'

Back without a job. Soon to be single again. A celebration with her sisters would be exactly what she needed.

'Great. Now call Lauren, and good luck. I know it's hard to believe, but it's very possible this will all end with you in a happier place than you started. It certainly did for me.'

'I hope so.'

Eve ended the call and sat for a long moment composing herself, trying to devise a plan that would allow her to handle this discussion civilly, even though she felt like screaming.

Finally she decided she would never be ready, and it was probably smarter just to dial. She put her hair back into its ponytail and punched in her stepmother's number.

'Hello, Eve.'

Everything Eve had planned to say disappeared under a wave of anger. 'You knew about Helen and Shelley.'

A sigh came over the line. 'Yes.'

Eve jumped up and started pacing the room. 'You sent me here with no preparation, without asking if I wanted to know or not.'

'Yes.'

'Does Shelley know I'm her niece?'

'No.'

Small relief. 'Does Dad know any of this?'

'Which part?'

'That . . .' God, this was confusing. 'That Shelley is Helen's sister.'

'No.'

Eve stalked over to the window, pleased to see that a stiff breeze had blown clouds across the sun and ruffled the surface of the lake. It suited her mood. 'So you sent me here behind his back.'

Lauren let out a noise of exasperation. 'If you're trying to make me feel guilty, you can spare yourself the trouble. I did what I did for good reasons, and I don't regret it.'

Eve pictured her stepmother in the little cottage she shared with Dad, her blue eyes magnified by her thick silvery lenses, salt-and-pepper curls in the perm she'd adopted once middle age thinned her hair. The visual epitome of a plump, sweet, malleable woman – with a spine of iron and rules to match.

Olivia had already left home when Dad and Lauren married, and Rosalind escaped soon after to college, so it was Eve who bore the brunt of her stepmother's inflexibility. As much as she complained, once Eve had adjusted, the structure and routine had suited her personality a lot better than the wild ride of Jillian's moods and tempers. The house had been run with brutal efficiency, everything in its place. Dinner had been on the table at 6.30 every evening, and Lauren prepared it herself, saying she was not about to waste money on a cook when she was perfectly capable of handling a kitchen.

Lauren had been the bank teller at the branch Dad used when they summered in Stirling, Maine. The two of them had struck up a casual acquaintance until a year or so after Jillian died, when, lonely and looking for a friend, he happened to sit next to her at a church bean supper and invited her out for lunch. Their relationship had progressed from there.

Dad had become a new man after he met Lauren. A much happier man. In many ways, a younger man.

Eve's anger evaporated, replaced by a deep, exhausted sadness. 'Will you tell Olivia who her mother is too?'

'Not until she's ready.'

'*I* wasn't ready. Why did you do this to me and not her?'

'You are made of sterner stuff than you give yourself credit for, Eve. Shelley is a lovely person and worth getting to know in any capacity, architect, friend or niece.'

'Quite a coincidence that she needed a project done. Or did you manipulate that, too?'

'I'll answer the question when you phrase it more politely.'

Eve very maturely stuck her tongue out at the phone. 'How did it happen that Shelley needed an architect?'

'She was complaining about the noise when her kids and grandkids visited. I suggested the idea of the cottage. She jumped on it. The rest worked out in time. There's nothing sinister at work here, Eve.'

Eve grimaced, hating that her stepmother made her feel like she was still an unreasonable child. Especially when she had just acted like one. 'Except that you put me in this situation with no warning. This is all incredibly complicated and emotional.'

'A regular hot mess.'

The expression sounded so foreign and strange from prim, rod-straight Lauren that Eve burst out laughing.

'Now, no more questions. You have what you need. You're a bright girl.'

'No, no.' Lauren couldn't cut her off now. 'I need to know if you sent me my mother's diary.'

'What? No. Your father's awake. I must go.'

The line went dead.

Eve felt like snarling. Stubborn woman.

But at least she had the important answers. Shelley didn't know she was related to Eve. That could stay underground or come out as Eve chose, which was a huge relief, since all she wanted to do in the days ahead was put the drama aside and get some work done.

Abigail's boisterous voice sounded downstairs.

Oh. That.

She'd have to find some way to tell Clayton and Abigail that they were on their own for the trip to Milwaukee. If she thought Clayton would bungle the job or that her presence would be crucial in changing the outcome, Eve would go in a heartbeat.

Well . . . maybe two heartbeats.

She put her phone away, took a calming breath and went downstairs. Since she'd volunteered to make dinner then left the grocery shopping to other people, the least she could do was take over now.

'Hey, Eve.' The sight of Clayton's tall form in the gray kitchen surprised her at first, then seemed wrong, as if there wasn't room for his masculine vitality in Shelley's subdued home. 'Shopping delivered.'

'We got burgers and all the trimmings,' Abigail announced. She was flushed and smiling, but her eyes were shadowed and she looked exhausted. Like the rest of them.

'Nothing fancy.' Clayton took out a package of ground beef.

'You don't have to unpack,' Eve protested. 'I'll do that.'

'Clayton!' Shelley came into the kitchen, smiling so warmly Eve was taken aback. 'You'll stay for dinner.'

He glanced at Eve, then back at Shelley. 'Sure. Thanks. But only if you let me help Eve.'

'Fine by me,' Shelley said. 'I never have a problem letting other people do the work.'

Eve unpacked a container of deli potato salad. She'd kind of been hoping for one of Shelley's nice quiet meals tonight.

'I'll help too, but I've gotta pee.' Abigail headed for the downstairs bathroom.

Shelley huffed. '*Thanks* for keeping us posted.'

'Eve.' Clayton touched her shoulder. 'Got a second?'

'Porch is free,' Shelley announced. 'I'll finish here. Abigail can help me when she comes back.'

'Thanks.' He quirked an eyebrow at Eve, who put down a sweet onion and followed him, only because it would be rude to refuse. If what he wanted to say was even the least bit complicated or emotional, she'd explode into fragments all over Shelley's house.

Clayton strode to the center of the porch and turned around, waiting. Eve followed slowly. 'What's up?'

'First, you okay? Everything okay?'

'Yes. I'm dealing with it.' She heard the back-off message in her tone and was immediately contrite. 'Thanks again for the rescue. You and Abigail. It meant a lot.'

'No problem.' He grimaced. 'Kind of a unique situation.'

'Ya think?'

He half smiled, then sobered and rubbed his forehead. 'So, uh . . . I talked to Abigail.'

'Yes?'

'She thinks the trip is a good idea. She's ready to try with her dad. Maybe you could email or call her mom, let her know we're coming.'

'Funny you should say that . . .' She told him about Leah's email, watching his expression grow hopeful, then confused.

'So that's . . . good?'

She sighed. 'I have no idea. When are you thinking of going?'

'Saturday, so Abigail's dad will be home.'

'You're not going to try to see Leah alone first?'

'I thought of that.' He shrugged. 'But I decided it's better just to dive in and see what happens.'

Eve let out a silent whistle. 'You're a brave man.'

'Huh . . . yeah, about that.'

Eve squinted at him warily. 'What?'

'Abigail agrees with me.'

'That . . . ?'

'That it would be a really good idea for you to come with us.'

Her stomach jolted. 'Clayton . . .'

'I know, I know, it's not . . . it's not your problem. But Abigail thinks your being there would help. Her dad is less likely to go ballistic than if I show up alone, the guy who impregnated his wife.'

'Wait.' Eve looked at him suspiciously. 'You're not planning to pretend we're together, are you?'

'No, no, nothing like that.' Clayton actually blushed, surprising and sort of cute, though thank God her earlier attraction had returned to a safely platonic level. 'But you helped Abigail initially. Leah might trust you more. You'd help tone down the tension.'

'Hmm.' Her inner chicken was urging her to go through with her rehearsed no-thanks speech. But part of her thought it was time she stopped doing its every bidding. Time to think more about the entire situation and less about her fear. More about the other people involved, less about protecting herself. She was not the person in danger in this situation. Abigail was. Clayton was. Next to their courage, she'd look like a pretty piss-poor excuse for a human being if she turned them down.

Kind of an ice princess, actually.

'I'm thinking we'll drive down Saturday morning and come back the same night, stay overnight only if it seems like settling things will take more time.'

'And if the more time turns into more than one night . . . ?'

He put a hand to the back of his neck, rubbed up and down. 'Then Abigail and I will decide what will work out best for her.'

A rush of warm sympathy. Eve laid a hand on Clayton's arm. 'You have kind of a lot riding on this trip.'

'Nah, not that much.' He grinned ruefully. 'Just an abrupt, unexpected, massive life change.'

She squeezed his forearm, telling her inner coward to shut the hell up. 'If you really think it will help, I'll come with you.'

Chapter 12

October 5, 1980 (Sunday)

It's early, but I couldn't wait. I'm already wearing one of the pregnant tummies.

When I'm in public, I 'absently' put my hand to my stomach as if I'm protecting a real child in the empty, dry place inside me. I know people are watching – anywhere I go people are watching – and I know how the rumor mill works.

What is she doing? Does she have a bun in that very womanly and totally intact oven? Of course she does. America's most beautiful famous couple is destined to have famous beautiful children. The only question – why did they wait so long to start a family?

They must have wanted to be in a position to give their child the best of everything! We hear Jillian has taken a little break from filming in order to have the healthiest possible pregnancy. So conscientious! So caring! So loving! Ideal parents. How we wish we were them!

Of course I'm making myself sick with all that, but it's funny. Everything is funny! I laugh all day long. I am having one of the bedrooms made into a nursery. I'll have painters ready around the clock as due date approaches to do the room the right color. Yellow for a girl, teal for a boy. I have started a photo album of me in all the stages of my pregnancy, to show my child how beautiful I look as a pregnant woman, and so I can describe how excited I was that he or she was on the way. My child (children!) must never, ever know that Mommy isn't a real woman. No matter what I have to do. I'll kill whoever I have to, and I'm only half kidding.

Pregnantly yours,

Jillian

PS An extraordinary confusion. Christina, my baby sister, has gotten herself knocked up and refuses to marry the guy. Mom is apparently apoplectic, which doesn't surprise me.

But we've already entered into a contract with Angel Bitch (who I am delighted to report, is throwing up like crazy). I can't turn my back on Daniel's child, growing inside her. But neither can I turn down the one in a million chance to raise a child of my own blood.

I know myself well enough to know that I can't cope with two babies at once. I have to choose.

How can I choose?

For the first time in my life, I really have no idea what to do.

'You're doing *what*? What the hell, Eve?'

Eve sighed. Mike had been drinking again. She should have known better than to wait this long to call, but she'd spent the day completely free from any conflict, working hard on brainstorming and research, and doing a few rough sketches for Shelley's cottage. Maybe she was putting everything emotional on hold, but after what had happened the day before, during and after their Washington Island tour, Eve felt entitled to a relatively stress-free day. Forgetting the time difference, she'd thought late afternoon would be an okay time to call. Apparently, though, Mike had started early. They weren't going to be a couple for much longer, but she was still technically attached, and that meant letting him know about the trip to Milwaukee with Clayton and Abigail. She should have known he'd ignore every part of the story except that she was traveling with a guy.

'Mike, calm down. There is nothing—'

'Don't tell me to calm down. My girlfriend goes halfway across the country, meets a guy and now she's sailing off with him to shack up in Milwaukee.'

'We are *not*—'

'I know how guys think, Eve. He's trying to get into your pants. Trust me.'

'Why don't you trust *me*? I'm telling you there's noth—'

'I'm just saying, this looks bad.'

'For whom?'

'For *me*, who do you think? How would you feel if I went off to some motel with some woman after telling you a complete bullshit story about how she had a baby and didn't know it, or whatever is going on.'

Eve had explained exactly what was going on. Or tried to, amid the interruptions and outrage. She tried very hard to put herself in his place. Maybe she still owed him that much. 'I would probably be uneasy. But I wouldn't—'

'Uneasy my ass. You're not thinking—'

'Will you let me finish *one bloody sentence*? You don't even listen to what I have to say before you tell me I'm wrong. How is this a conversation?'

'Oh I see. Now it's *my* fault. Again.'

'Mike.' She closed her eyes. 'This isn't working. When I get back, we need to—'

'I knew it. I freaking knew it. You probably knew this guy before you left; now you're dumping . . .'

Eve took the phone away from her ear and looked at it disgustedly. There was no point when he got like this. The rants were usually at a colleague, some political figure or celebrity, or at a government policy. She let them go, knowing he'd get the anger and frustration out of his system, sober up, calm down. This was the way his family had functioned and it was all he knew.

The difference today was that she was stretched spider-thread thin, and she could see clearly that this wasn't the relationship she wanted, nor the type of conversation her personality was equipped to handle. When things were good with Mike, they were good. But relationships lived or died by how a couple handled the bad times. She and Mike had been lucky: aside from his depression last summer – not his fault – they hadn't had many bad times. But this couldn't continue.

'Mike. *Mike.*' She had to shout to get him to stop. 'Let's talk later, okay? We need to cool off.'

'Talk about what? I heard what you said. You're done. It's over. I'll move out. Thanks for the memories.'

Eve bit her lip. This was her chance. She could say what he wanted her to say: *No, no, stay, we need to talk more, face to face*. But she found she couldn't.

She'd had a hand in turning Mike into this raging, jealous beast she barely recognized. All this time, as her feelings had been changing – as he could *tell* they'd been changing – she'd said nothing, given him nothing. It had simply been easier not to. Now she could see that it had also been destructive and selfish, allowing him to fill in her blanks with his own version of the truth.

'I'm sorry, Mike. I don't know what changed. We were so damn good for so long, and then . . . we weren't. I didn't know how to get it back and it scared me. I started disappearing, and for that I'm really, really sorry. I regret it.'

'Wait, you're really . . . this is really it? You're really dumping me? I thought . . .'

She heard him starting to cry and felt her own tears coming. 'Aw, Mike.'

'I'm sorry.' He was sobbing now, drunk, sloppy sobs that were hard to find moving. 'I know . . . it's not good. It's not good between us anymore. I'm sorry. I'm sorry for what I . . . I'm sorry.'

The line went dead. Eve put her phone down and blinked at the cheerful blue and yellow walls of her room, then hung her head and let the tears come, resolute, relieved, and deeply sad.

Immediately, Marx sat up and howled, which made her smile even in the midst of her misery. She dragged herself over to him and gave him a hug. 'Just you and me now.'

Her throat convulsed and she chided herself. The worst thing when you were sad was to think pathetic thoughts that made the sadness worse.

She was not alone, just uncoupled. She had her sisters, her parents, and her friends, new and old. And maybe a new and improved understanding of herself. A path ahead on which to change, become a better person.

Good Lord, she sounded like the star of a Jillian Croft movie. Maybe she should cue a swelling soundtrack.

Marx licked her face.

'Eve?' Shelley knocked on the door. 'Shall I come in or go away?'

It was on the tip of her tongue to say, *Later, please*, but she stopped herself. Crying was not shameful when a relationship ended. She didn't need to hide. Add Shelley to the list of people she still had around her. 'Come in.'

'I heard the dog.' Shelley was holding a box of Kleenex. 'Thought I knew what that meant.'

'My boyfriend and I just broke up.'

'Oh dear. I'm sorry.' She plucked up a tissue and handed it over with a flourish. 'I suspected something wasn't right between you.'

Eve stopped halfway to blowing her nose. 'How?'

'You didn't talk about him. No bragging, no stories, no long, dull tales of all his adorable habits.'

Eve nodded and went for the nose-blow, then used a dry corner of the tissue to wipe her eyes. 'It's been bad for a while. I should have ended it sooner. Not over the phone, though, ugh.'

'Should have, shouldn't have, eliminate those.' Shelley waved them away. 'You worked it out when it was right for you.'

'I guess.' Eve managed a smile. 'Thanks. You probably didn't expect to play tissue-bearer to your architect.' And niece.

'You're human. You seem like a pleasant person. I don't mind. Unless you mope for weeks and I have to kick you out.'

'No danger of that.' Eve was surprised to find herself already rallying. She supposed she'd been grieving the relationship's slow demise for a long time. That or Shelley's appearance had interrupted her slide into true misery. Maybe it would come later. She'd take the moments of peace when she could.

'Want to talk more, or change the subject?'

'Change, please.' She accepted another tissue and blew her nose again. 'Nothing more to say on that topic.'

'All right. My topic is that I wrote back to Abigail's parents and told them that "Shelley Grainger" is coming with her darling little family for a visit this weekend. Leah answered almost immediately that Saturday is fine. I suggest you take a day or two to be miserable and then get going again.'

'Thanks, Shelley. I don't need that long. I was working today. Before this happened.'

'I didn't mean that. No hurry on that.' She paused at the door. 'Okay if I tell Abigail what happened? The howling worried her.'

'You should hear me bark at squirrels.' Eve undid her ponytail, thinking it wasn't such a terrible feeling to have this oddball assortment of people concerned about her. 'Yes. Go ahead and tell her.'

'All right. I'll keep her busy for a bit. You take it easy.'

'Thanks, Shelley.' Eve smiled warmly at her aunt, wishing Shelley could have been her mom instead of the two troubled, self-destructive ones she'd been given. Such a gentle, supportive and only slightly strange person. Maybe they could forge a genuine relationship . . . someday. Eve had plenty on her plate without worrying about her aunt's reaction if she told her they were related. Shelley might find Eve a welcome addition to her family or an unpleasant reminder of the sister she'd resented and lost. 'I appreciate this.'

Shelley shook her head – *don't bother thanking me* – and left.

Eve washed her face, put on minimal makeup to repair the damage and took stock. In the past three days she had gained and lost a mother, lost a boyfriend, gained an aunt and made two friends, one of whom was in trouble and needed her help, which would necessitate a long drive to confront a raging bigot and his wimpy wife.

For someone who wasn't best friends with complicated emotions, it had been a bitch. At least for the next few days she could work her ass off on the design projects. Familiar territory would help her regain her balance. Tonight after dinner she'd call Olivia to wish her happy birthday. Then she was going to sleep for about fourteen hours. If it meant that Marx had to pee on the floor, so be it.

The next few days Eve spent working on Shelley's cottage project, trying out floor plans on her computer in the office off the living room that Shelley had shown her the first day, sketching with pencil and paper on Shelley's porch when she felt stuck. She found it difficult to put together a plan that felt right, and had to call up reserves of sometimes shaky confidence in her talent. Plenty of projects she'd designed in school had bumps along the way; it was often part of the process. In fact, working out the issues, trying this, trying that, consumed with finding the perfect solution, was half the fun, even if she felt like all the progress she was making was in finding what *didn't* work. But in school, all that was riding on her success or failure was a grade. There was a lot more at stake here. Shelley's happiness. Eve's pride.

Lots of cozy private rooms sounded so enticing, especially given the island's long cold season, but all Eve's attempts so far had resulted in chopped-up cubby-hole spaces, without good flow or enough light. She certainly hadn't expected to find the perfect solution the first time, but this project seemed to be fighting her particularly hard. So? She'd fight particularly hard back, both for the project and against the deep-down irrational fear that she might never find a solution. There was always a solution.

While she worked, Abigail either hung out in her own room listening to music, or took Marx for long walks, or played piano and sang in a secure, clear soprano, an unexpected and delightful talent. She also spent time with Shelley, helping her pore over yellowing ancestor pictures and ancient letters in hard-to-read script. Clayton had received whatever approval he'd needed on one of his projects and was also hard at work, though he came over for dinner one night and took Abigail out another.

By Friday, Eve decided to switch her focus to Clayton's sunroom. Often taking time away from an intractable problem allowed her subconscious to keep working. When she returned, she frequently found a solution fairly quickly.

Within a few hours, she had made progress with a brilliant – if she said so herself – flash of inspiration. Given his house's situation on the side of a slope, she could tuck the new room under the current deck, reachable through the house's walk-out basement or from the staircase off the current deck.

Flushed with success, she did up a quick model on the computer to take over to show Clayton. Not a bad time to talk to him, given that they were leaving to see Abigail's parents the next day.

Oof. Eve would be fine if he suddenly decided this was about him and his daughter, so she could stay home with Marx and her design programs. Really.

He answered her text immediately. *Come on over. Rescue me from a day working on this boring project. How about after dinner?*

She smiled. *Dinner's at 5.30 here.*

Ah. How about 8.00?

See you then.

She hooked up her computer to her wide-format printer and rolled out a copy of her bare-bones sketch, then made a few changes and printed it again. He'd get the idea. Slightly unorthodox, but she loved the idea of the place being tucked downstairs, the view of the lake the same as up on the deck, but no extra real estate taken up.

Dinner was less chatty than usual – or at least what had become usual since Abigail had showed up. She seemed subdued. Given the shock she'd had at home, and the let-down after the initial high of meeting her father, plus what must be dread over the next day's trip, her relative quiet made perfect sense.

When the dishes were done, Shelley settled on the porch with her family boxes. Abigail joined her with earbuds in place. Eve went back to the office, intending to have one more look at the drawing, then told herself to leave it alone. She remembered a teacher telling her that when she was reduced to putting outlets in, taking them out, then putting them back in, it was time to call the drawing done.

She still had an hour and a half until she needed to leave. Downtime was when the grief hit worst; when she missed Mike, was queasy over whether she'd done the right thing, wanted most to pick up the phone and ask him to come back. Big changes were so hard.

She did pick up the phone, but instead of calling Mike, she dialed Olivia to check in on her, since her sister hadn't returned Eve's birthday call on Monday.

'Hey, Olivia.'

'Eve! I'm a terrible person. You sent me such beautiful flowers and you called me, and I've done nothing.'

'All is forgiven. Hope the birthday was—'

'It was fine, fine. Have you become the new I. M. Pei yet?'

Eve frowned. Olivia usually went over every second of her celebration in excruciating details. Obviously not her best birthday ever. 'Just about.'

'Things going well?'

'A bit . . . challenging.' She caught herself wanting to change the subject and rolled her eyes. This new sharing version of Eve was exhausting. At least she was under no obligation to tell Olivia anything about her birth mother, since her sister didn't want to hear it. So she told her briefly about Abigail and Clayton instead.

'Wow. It's like a soap opera up there.'

'No kidding.'

'Poor girl. I hope her parents take her back. Or maybe I don't . . .'

'It's probably best for her if she does go back.'

'I can't imagine being a parent and hating what your child is through no fault of her own. It's like, if she were born without a leg, would they hate her then?'

Eve squinted. She wasn't sure the logic held up, but Olivia's emotions were in the right place. 'I know. But that's what her dad learned growing up.'

Her sister started singing, and Eve recognized 'You've Got to Be Carefully Taught' from *South Pacific*.

'I was never a fan of that show.'

Her sister gasped, clearly appalled. 'I *loved* it. So did Mom.' Since childhood, Olivia had jumped on any possible similarity. It got old fast.

'Speaking of *South Pacific* . . .' Eve hummed a few bars of 'I'm Gonna Wash That Man Right Outa My Hair'.

'What? Wait, what are you saying?' Olivia's hopeful tone was salt in Eve's wounds.

'Mike and I broke up.' She still couldn't think about it without wanting to cry.

'*Hurray!*'

Eve gritted her teeth. Her sister meant well, but . . . 'Remind me to say the same when you divorce.'

'*Sorry*, I'm sorry, Eve.' She sounded it. 'I just . . . He wasn't right for you.'

'Apparently everyone knew but me.'

'You knew. I mean, deep down you must have.'

'I guess.' Eve wasn't so sure. Lately, maybe. Before that, she'd been pretty convinced Mike was Mr Right. 'What about you? How are things going out there? Any better?'

'Nope. Got my period on my birthday, woo-hoo.' Olivia gave a brittle laugh. 'Remember Derek said he was willing to go through IVF to get pregnant? Well, now he's showing signs of backing out. My show is tanking. I really think it's going to be cancelled. Then where am I? No career. No baby. I've failed at everything.'

'No, not failed.' Eve was so upset, she stood. 'Not failed. As a wise man used to say, "You only fail . . ."'

'". . . if you don't try." Thanks, Dad.'

'You're welcome. But seriously, Olivia. You've had incredible success. You had your *own show*. Cancellations happen all the time. You'll get back into acting, or get another show. Everyone's career goes up and down. Something will work out. You're gorgeous and talented.' She *was* fairly talented. A good presence on screen, though not a great actress. Still, careers had been built on less.

'Yeah, there is so much gorgeous and talented in this town it's not even funny.'

'But there's only one gorgeous and talented Olivia Croft.'

'That's true.' She didn't sound at all cheered up. Eve didn't blame her. Olivia was facing truly tough challenges. 'Maybe you should try surrogate parenting or adop—'

'There is *no* physical reason why I can't get pregnant. I'm doing yoga, meditation, trying not to be intense about it. But I just turned thirty-nine, I can't *help* being intense about it. All around me I swear women are getting pregnant by waking up and taking a deep breath.'

'Oh Olivia.' Eve plunked back down in her chair. 'I'm so sorry.'

'I'm whining. You have enough to cope with already. What's this Shelley person like?'

Eve considered how to describe her aunt, given that she couldn't see Olivia and Shelley ever being best friends. 'Introverted. Few words. Doesn't like people.'

'You must get along like a house afire.'

'Yeah, I like her.' She didn't bother calling her sister out on the comparison. It was true enough. What surprised her was how much her affection for this awkward, gruff woman had grown, as Shelley's generous, caring nature and goofy sense of humor had become more evident.

'So . . . you're single – is this Clayton guy single?'

Eve waved her hand back and forth, no-no-no, as if her sister could see her. 'Nothing is going to happen there.'

'Why? Not attractive?'

Eve rolled her eyes. Another reason she had happily left LA, land of perfect-appearance worship. 'Hideous. Missing half his teeth, half his hair and half his left leg.'

'Ew, stop.'

She couldn't help laughing. 'He's a nice guy. We both have a lot to deal with.'

'Something could happen.'

'You'll be the first to know.' A soft knock on the door. 'Hey, Olivia, I'm wanted here. Oh, listen, come to Boston! Rosalind mentioned getting together in May for my birthday. What do you think?'

'I'd have to check my schedule.'

'Come in.' Eve spoke over her shoulder, then put the phone back to her ear, waving at Abigail, who eased into the office. 'Do that. It would be fun. You need another getaway.'

Her sister signed off, promising to think about it.

Eve put her phone away. 'Hey, Abigail.'

'Whatcha doing?' She still looked somber.

'I was talking to my sister Olivia.'

'Cool.' Abigail picked up a stapler and turned it over. 'What's she like?'

'Glamorous. Very movie-star. A little attitude, but nice inside.'

'I wanted a sister really badly, but Mom didn't want more kids. That's what she *told* me anyway; who knows if it's true. It wouldn't surprise me if Glen can't get it up.'

'Oh *that's* nice.'

'I know.' She put down the stapler and leaned on the desk, arms folded. 'Is Olivia Helen's daughter too?'

'Not sure.'

'You're not *sure*?'

Eve gave her an impatient look, hoping she'd take the hint. 'We weren't told.'

'How did you find out then?'

'Too many questions, Abigail.'

'Okay, okay.' She leaned over the drawing. 'What's that?'

'Another question.'

'Aw, c'mon, a drawing isn't private.'

'I know, I know.' Eve moved the printout so Abigail could get a better look. 'A preliminary idea for Clayton's sunroom. I'm taking it over to him in a little while.'

Her eyes lit. 'Can I go too?'

Eve should have seen that coming. In addition to discussing the plan, she and Clayton would probably want to work on strategy for the meeting with Abigail's parents. And quite honestly, Eve had been looking forward to an evening of grownup conversation. 'Not tonight.'

Abigail's face fell; her lips set stubbornly. 'Why not?'

'Because . . .' Eve searched for something to say other than *because you're a kid*. 'This is a professional meeting.'

'You said I could learn about architecture. I'll just sit quietly, I swear.'

'I'm sure you would.' She kept a smile painted on, hoping to counter Abigail's mutinous pout, feeling totally out of her depth arguing with a teenager. 'But Clayton invited me.'

'You could ask if I can come.'

'No. I can't.' Eve tried to gentle her voice. 'Or rather, I'm not going to.'

Abigail's eyebrows rose in dismay. 'Why not?'

'Because tonight . . . I want it to be just us.'

Abigail's eyebrows crashed together in a scowl.

Eve groaned silently. Wrong thing to say. 'Not romantically, just . . . hanging out. Grownups. Friends.'

'Oh. Sure. I get it.' She turned to go in a massive huff.

Eve stood. If this was what altercations with adolescents were like, she pitied parents everywhere. 'Abigail, this isn't about you.'

'Yeah, I can *see* that. I have *nothing* to do with it.'

'That's not how I meant it.' Actually it was. Abigail had a really good point. 'I *meant* that it's not because I don't want you around.'

Abigail gave her a *yeah, right* look. 'Obviously you don't want me around or you'd let me go with you.'

Right again. How did one deal with these little beings? She should invite Shelley in, watch how she handled it and take notes.

The thought came out of nowhere. Take notes? For what? When Eve herself was a mom?

'I'm sorry. I have no more excuses. I like you. He likes you. This isn't a competition. You've spent time with him, I've spent time with him, you're not invited tonight. I am. That's all I've got.'

'Fine. While you're out trying to get into my father's pants,

I'll just sit home and watch freaking television with *your aunt*.' Abigail left the room and slammed the door.

Eve exhaled wearily. Soft-pedaling hadn't worked. Lies hadn't worked. Honesty hadn't worked. What should she have tried? Should she go after Abigail or leave her alone?

Honestly? Eve understood how Abigail felt. The foundation of her life had been badly cracked; now she was adrift and clinging poignantly to any rock she could find. Clayton seemed like a pretty great rock. Little wonder his daughter was so drawn to him.

And yet . . . in Eve's family, it was made clear from early on that no matter what Eve or her sisters wanted, no matter how insignificant or how much they deserved it, if they whined or pouted, they were out of luck.

Except one time. Eve sank back into her chair, remembering. She'd been nine years old. In the pages of an architectural magazine she'd spotted an ad for a drafting kit that came in a little black carrying case. Inside was a drawing board, pencils, rulers of various sizes and shapes, erasers – in short, everything a budding architect could need. Immediately the kit became her heart's desire. She'd begged and begged her parents to give it to her for Christmas that year, tortured by their response, a child's worst nightmare: *We'll see.*

Christmas came and went. Nothing. Trying not to cry from disappointment, Eve reminded them. Her mother had blanched. *Sorry, sweetie, Mommy and Daddy forgot. For your birthday, then.*

Her *birthday*!? But that was five months away!

Her father had corrected her impassively. *Four and a half.*

She'd been miserable, furious, started in on a teary rant, which her father had cut short. *There'd better not be another peep out of you. Or else . . .*

Eve's mouth had clamped shut. She knew what that meant. Or else . . . she'd never see the present.

On her tenth birthday, she was up at five, bristling with energy. For the entire day, in an agony of suspense, she was on her best behavior: at home, at school, during dinner – her favorite, hot dogs, baked beans and the brown bread that came in a can, foods never allowed except at their Maine summer house. She didn't even complain when her mother drank an entire bottle of wine after her double gin on the rocks and went to sleep on the floor.

After the cake – yellow, with chocolate frosting – it had finally been time. Her father had gently shaken Jillian awake.

The pile of presents beckoned. Eve tore into them, and discovered that her parents had forgotten again. This time her pent-up frustration would not be held back. She gave her father every ounce of her anguish and was sent to her room to cry out her misery.

The next morning, clearly in disgrace, she'd obeyed meekly when her mother ordered her into the car, not even asking where they were going, not even caring, except when they pulled up at Graphaids, an art supply store in Culver City. Even then, Eve suppressed her shriek of joy, afraid she was wrong. Afraid any noise or emotion could lose her the precious gift.

Her mother had swept into the store, immediately the center of attention. For once, Eve hadn't minded. Her mother was on this errand for *her*.

Back in the parking lot, with the kit in its handsome carrying case clutched in her hand, Eve had been taken aback when Jillian had bent down to her level, her beautiful face slightly puffy from the previous evening's drinking. 'Understand something. This is our secret. You don't tell your father. You don't tell your sisters. You go home and put this in your closet.

Don't play with it unless the door is locked. Okay?'

Eve hadn't even bothered to correct her – she wasn't going to *play* with it. Instead, she nodded so solemnly, her mother did the incredible: swept her daughter into her arms for a long, lilac-smelling hug and a quick kiss on top of her head, not in the store for the public's benefit, but here in the parking lot where no one was around to notice. 'Let's you and me go eat some ice cream. Okay, Eve?'

The case was still somewhere in her house in Swampscott, the board scratched and worn, the pencils and erasers exhausted, the rulers rendered all but useless by software. In spite of Eve's anger at her mother, she hadn't been able to throw it away.

Shaken by the forgotten memory, thinking of Rosalind's theory that she deliberately suppressed the good times, Eve spent an anxious half-hour staring at the sunroom drawing without seeing much. Eventually she gave up. It was nearly time to go. She'd poke her head out and see if Abigail had booby-trapped an anvil to fall on her head.

All was quiet in the hallway. On the porch, Shelley and Abigail immediately stopped talking when she appeared. Abigail was in tears.

'Hi.' Eve stood quietly, unsure how to proceed.

'You're off, then?' Shelley asked calmly.

'Yes.'

'We'll be fine here.' She patted Abigail's hand rather firmly.

'I'm sorry, Abigail. I didn't realize what a big deal this would be for you. If you want to—'

'I'm not going where I'm not wanted.'

Shelley nodded. 'That's right. Screw 'em. Because really, it's not like Eve owes you anything, right? She's proven over and over how selfish she is, and how little she cares for you and what you're going through.'

Abigail's scowl moved to include Shelley. 'Stop trying to make me feel guilty.'

'Yeah, because *you'd* never do that, right? To Eve? For wanting a nice evening with a friend? After you've been everywhere with him, including out to dinner?'

Abigail's eyes narrowed. She drew her knees up to her chest and lowered her head on to them. 'Go away and let me be evil.'

'That sounds like the perfect plan.' Shelley winked up at Eve. 'Have a good time. Be home by nine.'

Eve's jaw dropped. 'Nine?'

Shelley cackled. 'You should have seen your face. Go. Have fun. Tell Clayton I said hello.'

'Thanks.' Eve started to leave the room, then paused. Without allowing herself a second thought, she turned back and gave the startled Abigail a long hug and a quick kiss on top of her head.

Chapter 13

March 30, 1981 (Monday)

Oh, what incredible, life-changing, perfect happiness. I'm holding my beautiful baby girl as I write this. She is so tiny, so new, it's impossible to believe she'll grow so much, to be a teenager, an adult, an old lady. I can't wait to find out who she turns out to be. I can't wait to be part of that miraculous journey. This child will never, ever need to run away from the life Daniel and I will make for her.

I keep putting down my pen to stare at her. She is exquisite in every way. The funny, jerky, uncontrolled way she moves. The wonderful way she smells. She has Daniel's chin. I tell myself she has my eyes, and I almost believe me. In time, maybe I will.

Labor was hell, but nothing compared to the hell of having to take my daughter away from the woman who conceived, grew and birthed her. This is an awful, awful thing to do. I never realized, I never thought. I was so full of me me me and how much I wanted this perfect little baby in my life. Yet there was no other way to get what I needed in order to be complete.

I didn't think I could love anyone as much as I love Daniel. But this love for my child is so very pure, powerful and good, it must come straight from God. I was a fool ever to doubt His plan.

Welcome, Olivia Claudette Braddock. From this day onward, you are mine.

Eve strode down Clayton's driveway through the last bits of daylight, enjoying the mild temperatures, wishing she'd been able to be outside more during the day instead of in front of her computer. She'd been assured by Shelley that this weather was *not* the norm for this time of year, so she'd better take a heavy jacket because it could turn any minute. Amused and touched, Eve had allowed herself to be mothered and brought her jacket with her.

She rounded Clayton's house to the back and climbed the steep steps to the deck, lit softly by tasteful – of course – glass and iron sconces. Clayton was waiting, sitting in a comfortable-looking reclining chair he must have brought out for the nicer weather.

He stood when he saw her, face breaking into a grin.

Eve returned his smile, warmth blooming in her chest. She liked this guy. The one person she'd had contact with on this trip with whom she had an uncomplicated relationship. 'Don't get up; you looked so comfortable.'

'I brought these out since it was warm enough. I got them last summer. Have you ever sat in a zero-gravity chair?'

'Will I float off somewhere?'

'Try it.'

He waited while she draped her jacket over the chair back and tucked the sunroom plans in a slot on the attached tray, probably designed for holding a magazine. She sat. Comfortable, yes. 'Nice.'

'The best is yet to come.' Clayton leaned over her and turned small knobs attached to the chair's frame. The urge to shrink back disappeared when she caught his warmth and the scent of his aftershave. Nothing to fear.

'Now lie back some.'

She pushed back; at the same time, her legs went up, supported under the knees. Every muscle in her body relaxed, even a few she wasn't aware she had. It was as if she had no control over her response. The chair had decided for her. 'Oh my God.'

'Uh-huh.'

She turned her head the bare minimum to look at him. 'I'm never moving again.'

'Don't blame you. Would you like a glass of wine?'

'I'd love one. Just don't expect me to help, because I'm paralyzed with pleasure.'

Clayton chuckled on his way into the house. 'Don't worry, it's all ready to bring out.'

Eve shifted until every part was where it was meant to be, tempted to let out a moan of ecstasy but deciding it was not an appropriate noise to make. As soon as she got back to Massachusetts, she was buying one of these for her back yard.

One. A shaft of pain. Mike would love these chairs . . . He'd pull one out into the shady side of the yard on a lazy sunny Saturday afternoon . . .

And he'd sit and sit and sit, drinking too much and becoming argumentative and irrational.

The thought put an end to her pining, though not the pain. That would take a while.

'Here we go.' Clayton was carrying a tray on which stood a bottle of white wine, two glasses and a plate of small round cookies. He put the tray on the table between their chairs-from-heaven. 'This is Vin Santo, an Italian dessert wine. These are lemon shortbread cookies my mom sent from Spain.'

'Pretty fancy.' The combination of relaxation and grief made it hard for Eve to keep her voice light.

'My dad has a good wine collection up here. I have no problem raiding it.'

'I have no problem sharing it, thank you.'

'You're welcome.' He poured for each of them, then sat and held out his glass. 'Cheers.'

Eve clinked and took a sip. The wine was beautifully chilled, sweet but not cloying, with wonderful complicated flavors underneath. 'That is really good.'

'That's Dad.' There was a trace of bitterness in his tone. 'Good at everything he does.'

'Well, *that's* easy,' she scoffed. 'Just avoid things you're not good at.'

'I like that.' He offered her a cookie, took one as well, and moved his chair back into optimal position. 'How's Abigail?'

Eve bit into the shortbread, rich and crumbly, livened by the bright taste of lemon. 'Oh my God, these are good.'

'My mother's parenting method. Send kids postcards and stuff.'

'Ouch, sorry.' She shot him a sympathetic look. 'I can't remember the last time I got a postcard.'

'Yeah, nowadays it's more text messages.' He brushed cookie crumbs off his lap. 'Abigail?'

'Right, sorry. Got seduced by cookie.' Reluctantly Eve finished her last sweet bite. 'Abigail is . . . kind of upset tonight.'

'She is?' Clayton lifted his head to look at her, which must mean he was worried, because there would be no other reason to move, except maybe if he was on fire. 'Why?'

'She wanted to come see you. It was sort of cute. And also sort of not.'

'I think that's a sort-of-cute, sort-of-not age.'

'I think you're right. At the same time, she's been through some pretty serious stuff.'

'No kidding.' Clayton relaxed back into the chair of bliss. 'Should I do anything?'

'I don't think so. Shelley, the mom-expert, said she'll get over it.'

'It's funny . . .' Clayton gazed out into the darkness, one hand behind his head. 'I met this person who we assume is nearly a match for my DNA. I keep thinking . . . I should know her, in some deep, primal way at least. Every time I see her, I search for it. But there's nothing there. She's a nice kid. I will probably come to love her if I get the chance, but . . . you'd think in a relationship that profound and basic to who we are, there would be . . . something. Some link. Some recognition. It makes me feel defective, even knowing I'm probably being too mystical about it, and too tough on myself. It's hard not to be afraid that I'm like my parents.'

'No.' Eve shook her head emphatically, even though it meant disturbing her utter comfort. 'Trust me, you are not missing a single molecule of the caring and nurturing genes.'

'Thanks, Eve.' He turned to smile at her. 'I'm glad I met you.'

A lovely thing to say. Saying it back to him would create a perfect moment of trust and intimacy.

Only she couldn't do it.

'I know what you're saying.' She was babbling, stupid, ashamed. 'Shelley is my aunt. We have our similarities, but I haven't felt any deep connection outside of the little we know of each other. Don't know if that helps. Maybe I'm just a mess too.'

Yes. She was. And it had taken her twenty-nine and eleven-twelfths years to realize it.

'Well, good.' Clayton helped himself to another cookie and offered her the plate. 'We can be defective together.'

They sat in silence for a while, listening to waves gurgling up against the rocks, Eve processing her mortification at being unable to respond when he'd reached out.

She'd take his defective and raise him.

At least she could be open about one thing. 'Mike and I broke up.'

'No kidding.' His face was wreathed in sympathy. 'I'm sorry.'

'No, no. It was fine. I'm feeling . . . a little raw still, I guess, but okay. No regrets. It was the right thing to do.'

'You were together, what, three years? A little raw must be an understatement. I wouldn't be surprised if you had a breakdown every hour.'

'Except . . . I ended it, which is easier than being the dumpee.'

'Not by a whole lot, but yes.'

Eve took another sip of the lovely wine, savoring its lingering sweetness on her tongue. Clouds prevented any stars from being visible, but she could imagine the skies were full of them up here. Like in Maine. On warm nights, she and her family had often gone down to the rocks in front of their house to watch for shooting stars, particularly striking during the annual Perseid meteor shower. Her father had regaled them with scientific facts. Her mother had made up stories about Tinkerbell's sisters skating across the skies. The girls had competed to see which of them could spot the most. They'd lie in silence for minutes at a time, then there'd be a great chorus of *oohs* when a bright flash streaked across the heavens.

Somewhere in the woods behind them an owl hooted into the silence, a mournful, eerie sound that made Eve's skin prickle.

Clayton said nothing, just reached to lay a hand on her arm as they both strained to listen.

Another call, *whoo-whoo-whoooo*. Then silence.

'I'm glad I met you too.' The words were absurdly easy to say. 'Especially because we're both in such strange emotional places. It helps to be losing our minds together.'

'I agree.' He took back his hand. 'I feel like I could tell you anything. I've felt that way from the beginning.'

'Yes.' Her heart began to pound, she couldn't tell whether with anxiety or delight. The rush felt the same.

'Since we'll probably never see each other again after you leave, it's totally safe. Like having a beer with a stranger in an airport bar.'

Eve laughed, oddly disappointed. 'Only this wine is much better than beer, and there isn't even a scale for how much better this deck is than an airport bar.'

'Amen to that.' He turned to smile at her again. This time she smiled back, and though she caught herself blinking a couple of times, she managed not to turn away for a good two seconds.

Progress.

'God, you're beautiful, Eve.'

She made a face, appalled at the stab of pride and pleasure at his words. All her life, she'd watched Jillian – and then Olivia – treat beauty as an elite perk that qualified them for the best of everything and free rein to demand the center of attention. 'Clayton . . .'

'I know, I know.' He straightened in his chair and put his wine down. 'Enough of the serious stuff. Tell me your idea for the sunroom.'

'Here.' Somewhat relieved, she pulled out the drawing, feeling as if she were handing over a photograph of herself for judgment. *Not enough makeup. Complete non-hairstyle. Where do you get those clothes, honey?* 'Instead of putting the new room on the deck level, where it would stick out and compete with structures and design elements already here, I was thinking it would function better tucked underneath, with access from the existing stairs, as well as through the basement. It would still get as much air and light as it would up here.'

He took the drawing from her and studied it.

'It's still rough.' She could hear the apology in her voice and toughened it. 'I didn't want to put a lot of time into an idea you might hate.'

'Sure, sure.' He examined the sketch, then sent her a withering glare that shocked her. 'You realize what this means.'

'Uh . . . no?'

'In order to look at the site, I'm going to have to *get up*.'

'Oh!' She grinned her relief. 'As punishment, I'll come with you.'

It took her a few seconds to figure out which way to turn the knobs on her paradise chair, then she reluctantly pushed the seat upright and stood, grabbing her jacket. As Shelley had predicted, the air had turned chilly.

They went together down the steps to the lower level. Clayton folded his arms and stalked around the area under the deck, frowning in what she hoped was concentration rather than disapproval.

'There's plenty of space for a substantial room under here.' Eve motioned toward the lake. 'You get great views, and it can be air-conditioned on days when it's too hot to be outside. If that ever happens up here.'

'Not often.'

'You could also put a patio outside if you wanted, though the existing deck is already a great outdoor space.'

'Yes.' He paced the length of the imagined room, then turned, looking pleased. 'This might work well.'

'Yeah?' She tried not to sound too delighted. 'You could heat it too, and in the winter hang out here and watch snow coming down on the lake.'

'Nice. Yeah.' He walked the space again. 'Nice.'

'Wait a second.' She pointed to the blackness outside. 'The lake is freshwater. It *freezes*.'

He chuckled. 'Nearly every winter at some point, though some seasons more solidly than others. You need a run of really cold days.'

'So people are *stuck* on this island until it thaws?' How could they stand it? How did they get food? What if someone was seriously ill?

'Ah no, little one.' He lifted a finger, making a classic wide-eyed, raised-brow face of one about to reveal a stunning mystery. 'Ice-cutting ferry. Twice a day.'

'Whew.' She pretended to collapse into relief. 'I'd lose it.'

'Hey, this is Wis-*kahn*-sin. There's good fishing here, eh?' His accent broadened into a parody of the local flat vowels. 'A guy can get out there and catch lawyers.'

She couldn't figure that one out. 'The murdered ones bob to the surface?'

'It's a fish.' He reverted to his normal Chicago English. 'Supposed to taste like lobster, but I don't know about that. It's a bottom-feeder. Of course.'

'Therefore the name?'

'That and its heart is really close to its butt.'

It felt so good to laugh. Life had been way too intense in the past week. The past six months, really. 'Thank you for that image.'

'You're welcome.' He smiled at her and she sobered.

Something in his eyes – and then in her response – had changed.

Fabulous. Really. Just what she needed. A mushy moment with her first ever . . . no, her second client. She turned away abruptly.

'Eve.'

'Yes.' She didn't look at him.

'I like you. That was fun and funny, we enjoyed it together. End of story. Okay?'

'Yes.' She was embarrassed, but relieved. And constantly astounded by his radar for every emotion, and by his ease talking out whatever was necessary. She needed to study and learn. 'Thank you.'

'You're welcome. Come on, let's go back upstairs. There's lots of wine left. I'm sure you'll want to start our drive tomorrow with a raging hangover.'

'Absolutely.' She followed him back up to the deck, where darkness had settled definitively outside, and lightness had settled inside her. He liked her design. They were on an open and comfortable footing with each other. All good. 'So you want me to do up a formal plan of this idea?'

'Absolutely. I think it would work, and thank you for a great solution.'

Back in her ecstasy seat, Eve had another shortbread cookie and allowed Clayton to pour her another half-glass of wine.

'So.' He settled back with a contented sigh. 'On another topic, how do you envision this insane trip we suddenly find ourselves having to take?'

'I was thinking we should burst into the house, point at Abigail's father and shout, "You are wrong and bad."'

'Huh . . .' He pretended to consider. 'That's one possibility.'

'Got anything better?'

'Only one idea. I could take him aside for a man-to-man chat . . . and make a move on him.'

Eve nearly spit out her wine. 'Another good plan!'

Clayton shrugged. 'Seriously, I'm in over my head. This is my first confront-bigot-father-of-my-surprise-daughter encounter.'

'I vote we make it up as we go along. We don't know these people at all. We have no idea what to expect, so there's really nothing we can plan for. For all we know, her dad has changed his mind already.'

'I vote for that. Then we can watch the family reunite, applaud, and I'll take you out after to eat at one of Milwaukee's best.'

'Bratwurst and burgers?'

'What's that?' He put a hand to his ear. 'The screeching sound of coastal snobbery?'

'Oops.' She put on her best contrite look. 'Guilty.'

'We Midwesterners *really* hate that stuff.'

'Sorry.' A sudden breeze made her pull her jacket closer around her.

'You cold?'

'A little. But it's too nice to go in.'

'I agree.' Clayton put his wine down and climbed out of the chair. 'Wait here.'

He disappeared into the house, then reappeared carrying two blankets, one of which he tossed to her, then spread the other over himself.

'Oh, that is fabulous, thank you.' She was warm now, outside from the blanket, inside from the wine and the good company, and supremely comfortable in the chair of eternal delight.

'I was just thinking . . .' Clayton stared up at the sky, a few stars appearing here and there through thinning clouds. 'About the concept of family.'

'Gee, why *that* subject?'

'Came to me out of the blue.'

She turned so she could see his face, tucking her hood out of the way. 'What were you thinking?'

'You know that saying about how family isn't always defined by blood? You hear it and you think, "Well obviously, what else is new?" But when something like this happens . . .'

'Yes.' She didn't need him to go on, but she hoped he would. She liked the way his speech slowed and his voice softened and deepened when he was thinking something through.

'What you thought you knew, and took for granted, becomes this . . . totally remarkable truth.'

'Paradoxically one that takes a while to sink in. Even though you think you understand.'

'Yes. Exactly. Abigail and I, you and Shelley, my parents and siblings and I – we're blood but not family.'

'And my sisters and I are family but only half shared blood.'

'Yes.' He frowned. 'I don't know if that's profound or stupid.'

'Doesn't matter, because we're the only ones here. We get to decide.'

'Good point.' He sat staring out at the lake, which had started to whisper back to the rising wind. 'I bet Abigail's behavior tonight is part of that confusion too.'

'I'm sure it is. She's lucky to be young enough that she can pout and stomp her foot when she feels like it. I've wanted to do that many times.'

'Same here. Except I'd have to do something much more manly, like punch a wall.'

'Of course you would.'

They sat in companionable silence, gazing at the emerging stars, sipping the excellent wine, enjoying the evening. Eve couldn't think of another person apart from her sisters and Mike with whom she was comfortable in silence.

Actually, with Mike the silence was usually hers. He liked to talk.

She smiled affectionately up at the sky, even through another stab of pain. She hoped Mike would find someone to be happy with. Not too soon, or Eve would have to kill her, but eventually. She hoped that for herself, too. And for Clayton.

'Were you close to your ex-wife's family? Felicia?'

'Nope. She wasn't either.'

'But that means . . .' Eve sat up straighter and twisted toward him, 'you've never been part of a close family. Blood or otherwise.'

'Actually . . . Christie, my ex-girlfriend, her family was fantastic. They lived in Milwaukee. We saw them pretty much every week. I swear I miss them more than her.'

'I'm sorry.' She could imagine how hard that had been, to finally find and enjoy a family, then lose it.

'Yeah, it sucked. I admit that part of the reason I came up here, besides the apartment renovation, was to do some wound-licking.'

'Breaking up stinks.'

'It does. Can I ask what happened with you and Mike?'

'Sure.' She snuck her hand out from under the blanket and snagged another cookie. 'I was a lot of the problem.'

'Both people are always the problem.'

'True, but I wasn't – am not – good at talking about feelings. As things got worse, rather than work on the relationship, I shut him out. Fear, not hostility. I think I couldn't face that we weren't going to work out after all.'

'Saying nothing is easier. Half the world is guilty. And by the way, I think you're fine talking about your emotions.'

'It's simpler with you. As you said, nothing risked here.'

'Or he didn't make it safe for you.'

Eve sat thinking about that one. It was so important for Mike to be right, to be in charge, after growing up being constantly pounded on by his father. Her dad had been the same way. The combination had to make it harder for her to open up. It was difficult to share and then be told your feelings were the wrong ones.

'I want to become more like Abigail.' She washed down the rich cookie with a sip of the wine, whose gentle acid made it the perfect match. 'She wears her heart on her entire outfit.'

'True. At the same time, she's been ripped up pretty badly. Hiding her emotions probably isn't an option.'

'Sometimes I wonder . . .' Eve gestured self-consciously. 'This is really weird.'

'I don't care.'

She believed him. 'Sometimes I wonder when I'm walking around people how many of them I project these normal, happy, uneventful lives on, when in fact they have dark secrets they've never told anyone.'

He snorted. 'Probably all of them.'

'You think?'

'Sure. Don't you have a dark secret?'

Eve's first instinct was to shrink, wishing she'd never brought up the topic. Then she caught herself, and listened instead to what her not-chicken inner voice was saying. *Stranger in an airport bar*. 'It . . . bubbles up sometimes. Like when a nice park is built on an old landfill and toxic chemicals start seeping through the surface.'

'Ooh, *nice* one.'

Eve laughed. Clayton might be the only person on the planet who could get her giggling when she was thinking about the darkest, most terrifying moment of her life. 'I keep hoping the little bugger's safely buried, but it won't stay down.'

'Maybe because it's trapped. Like people on Washington Island in winter.'

'Bring on the ice cutters?'

He put his empty wine glass on the table and rearranged his blanket. 'Do you want to tell me?'

Subconsciously, she must. Why else would she have brought it up? Why else would she be jittery with nerves, wondering if she dared? Why did she trust this man so much, when she hadn't even been able to tell Mike? Or her sisters? Was it only because their relationship was temporary?

'Tell you what.' Clayton leaned his chair farther back, gazing up at the stars rapidly filling the clearing sky. 'I'll tell you mine, and if that makes it easier, you can go ahead. If not, no big deal.'

Eve was taken aback. 'Why would you tell me?'

'I'm not sure I have a definite answer for that, though I can guess . . . The story is old enough now, and I'm old enough, to realize that telling it can't hurt me. And honestly, the chance to unburden myself of lifelong dark secrets just doesn't come up that often.'

Eve snorted. 'People don't stop by your desk at work and ask?'

'Not too many.'

'Okay.' Her heart sped, familiar adrenaline warning that she was entering a dangerous situation. 'Go ahead.'

'When I was a boy, I snuck beers into my room to drink with a friend. We were looking at *Penthouse* or something, and got into a . . . mild situation, shall we say. We were both straight; just . . . there we were, and we got all worked up over the pictures, and it happened, and then it was over.'

He blew out a breath. 'There. I did it. Now quick, tell me you're not horrified.'

'*No*, I'm not horrified. Not even remotely.' She was, in fact, taken aback at how non-horrifying it was. She wasn't really sure what she'd been expecting. 'I'm sure it happens a lot.'

'Of course the kid and I barely spoke to each other the rest of the year. Ruined a good friendship.'

'And so . . . ?' Eve sat up and examined him carefully. 'How do you feel having confessed? Lighter? Better? Do I need to assign Hail Marys for the guilt or sing "Free at Last"?'

Clayton rotated his neck and felt his arms and legs experimentally through the blanket. 'You know what? I think I'm okay. No loss of hair, limbs or teeth. It was hard to say, but now I'm wondering why I thought it was a big deal. It's just one thing that happened a really long time ago. It doesn't define or control me in any way.'

His words sank in deep. And suddenly, the ugly story inside Eve, shoved down so deep for so long, rose up with a force that stunned her. She wanted a chance to tell. A chance to rid herself of this burden, of her mother and Mr Angel's power. Maybe it wouldn't work, but there was no risk. Clayton would never use any of her words against her. At worst, someday he'd tell the story: *I knew this woman once who* . . . That couldn't hurt her either.

'I was molested as a girl.' She blurted out the words, waited for the world to explode, but heard only Clayton's sharp inhalation.

'God, I'm sorry.'

'Yeah, it was awful.' Awful, but not impossible to share with him. Containable, not threatening to swallow her, panic her. The presence of another body here on the dark deck made it safer. Or maybe it was the presence of this man's body.

'A friend of my mother's. She did nothing to stop him.'

'*What?*' The horror in his voice made her regret telling him. 'She was *there* when this happened?'

'No, but she let me go upstairs with him. He wanted to see one of my presents, a dollhouse I could design and build myself.' She couldn't hide her bitterness. 'At a holiday party with no other children, this childless unmarried guy wants to see my dollhouse? He gave me the creeps. I asked my mother to come with me, told her I didn't want to be alone with him. She said not to be silly, she had guests to take care of. That I was too shy and needed to get over it. That Mr Angel was harmless.'

'Mr *Angel*?'

'Sickening, huh.'

'Sacrilegious.'

'He was a producer.' She hadn't planned to go into this much detail. But once she'd started, the words poured out and she couldn't – didn't want to – stop, even though her voice and body were shaking with tension. 'He was dangling a role Jillian wanted.'

'No.' Clayton's chair rose upright. 'She couldn't have done that.'

Eve blew out the air in her lungs as if they'd collapsed. 'No. Maybe. I don't know.'

'*Jesus*.'

'Don't say Jesus.'

He didn't even acknowledge the joke. 'What was she thinking?'

'I have no idea.' Eve gestured and let her arm drop to the chair. 'I hardly ever knew what she was thinking.'

Immediately she remembered the diary. In Shelley's closet. In her suitcase. Along with Joseph Simington's card.

'How did you connect the abuse with the role your mom wanted?'

'Mr Angel told me she had been sad lately because she wanted to be in the movies again. He said he wouldn't hurt me, but that if I was quiet and nice to him, I could make my mother happy again.'

'Eve.' His voice was hoarse.

'Afterwards, up in my room, I was crying. I remember so well because we were having a rainstorm, which didn't happen often, and I felt like the city was crying along with me.' She couldn't believe she was telling him all this, but the words wouldn't stop. Details she couldn't normally bear to remember were coming back and pouring out of her mouth like Niagara Falls. Her mother's yellow gown. The crimson triangle of Mr Angel's handkerchief. The alcohol on their breath. 'That sounds so ridiculous.'

'No. It doesn't.' His low voice was warm. 'No judgment. Not from you or me.'

Eve pulled the blanket up under her chin. His permission made her nervous, self-conscious. She needed to make sure she could tell this objectively, because otherwise . . .

Otherwise what? She'd get upset in front of him?

'I told my mother that he'd touched me and . . . gotten himself off.' By now they were just words. Painful, but just words. 'She said, "It is always up to you what happens to your body. But you are a beautiful girl. Men are going to want to touch you your whole life. It must have been scary the first time, but he didn't hurt you and he could have. Right now, you can either collapse and be a victim, or you can recognize that as a beautiful woman you have remarkable power and can use it to get what you want. I want you to be strong, but it's your choice."'

Silence from Clayton. Instinctively she understood he was trying to rein in the outrage. No judgment.

'I told her I hated her. She said I'd get over it, and that someday I'd realize she was right and we'd laugh together about how sad and weak men are and how easy to manipulate. A week later, when she learned she hadn't got the part, she killed herself.' Eve's voice broke in spite of herself. 'So we never got to have that super-special grown-up-girl moment together.'

She closed her eyes and relaxed in the chair-that-heals-all. It was done. She'd told, and did feel lighter, though whether it was a permanent change or just relief at having gotten the story out, she couldn't tell yet.

'It's amazing how we expect our parents to be parents when they are just people. Some become good parents and do the right things. Some become shitty parents and we get hurt. I'm sorry that happened to you, and that you didn't get the support you deserved.'

'Thank you.' She was getting some of it now.

'And? How do you feel having told me?'

Eve took in and let out a slow breath. 'I feel sad. For me and for her. She was not a happy or well woman.'

Clayton's chair creaked as he got up and held out his hand. Eve stood, awkwardly, and let herself be pulled into his solid embrace. She rested her cheek against his shoulder. His shirt smelled pleasantly of detergent and Clayton. The wind buffeted them, chilling her back, but where they intersected there was only warmth.

It occurred to her that the last time she'd spent this long in the embrace of a non-lover, the arms around her had been Jillian's.

Chapter 14

May 7, 1981 (Thursday)

I hate being a mother. It's relentless drudgery. I look like hell and I smell worse. Daniel and I despise each other thanks to this screaming, demanding, never-satisfied creature. Why did I want this? Why does anyone want this? I've been up thirty-six hours straight. She's only a little over a month old! There is no end in sight. I want to give her away to anyone who'll take her, just so I can sleep.

PS Olivia just smiled at me. On purpose. At me, at the simple fact of my face being close to hers, and her knowing that I'm her mother. I melted. That smile must be the first thing babies are programmed to do, because otherwise parents would hurl them out of the cave and let the wild animals have them, and our race would have died out long ago.

When she's old enough to travel, I will take her to see my parents. I won't tell them I'm coming. They might tell me not to. I'll just show up. I haven't spoken to them or heard from them in thirteen years.

It's time.

Eve let herself into Shelley's house feeling as if she had boulders attached to her feet and shoulders. Wasn't she supposed to be uplifted and free after letting loose such a weighty burden? Maybe after she got a good night's sleep. Right now, she was exhausted, not regretting sharing necessarily, but a bit uneasy. She was still convinced she'd set nothing free that could turn back and bite her. But she also couldn't help feeling as if she'd let a stranger see her naked bits. Which, considering her story, was a rather apt way to phrase it.

Either way, the deed was done. She couldn't re-cage the beast.

'You back?' Shelley's voice boomed out from the porch.

She was still awake. Eve sighed and headed through the living room, letting her fingers trail silently across the piano keys that Abigail had been having so much fun playing. A talented girl.

'Yes, hi.' Eve stepped out on to the porch. Shelley was sitting with a wooden box on her lap containing three-by-five index cards. There were more spread out on the table, showing precise writing or tiny yellowed newspaper clippings attached with age-browned tape. 'Recipes?'

'Yes.' Behind her lenses, Shelley's eyes were unusually bright. 'I found my grandmother's file, buried in a box. Look at these.'

Shelley's grandmother. Eve's great-grandmother.

Good Lord.

Eve shrugged the boulders off her shoulders and dragged a chair up next to her aunt. 'Which grandmother?'

'Mother's mother, Janet McDonald. She was Canadian. Listen to this recipe. "Put chopped cold meat, egg whites, cucumber, tarragon and scallions in a tureen, then mix mustard powder, sugar, cream, egg yolks, an *entire bottle* of wine and a quart of sparkling water and add it to the tureen." That's soup!'

Eve did a double-take. 'More like a cocktail. How funny.'

'And this.' Shelley squinted at a yellow clipping, then held it farther away and tried again. '"Even with meat rationing, you can still entertain! Here's how to fix a delicious meal to serve twelve guests for as little as fifteen points. There's no fuss or flurry when you fix beef tongue."'

'Beef tongue!'

'They tell you to boil it in plain water for *four and a half hours*.'

'Eww!' Eve cracked up, glad she'd come in and not made excuses. She hadn't seen Shelley this animated since she arrived. Connecting to her past, to the people it contained, must have given her a boost. 'Can you imagine serving that today? There'd be a dozen people scrambling for the back door.'

'Exactly.' Shelley passed the card to Eve, who took it reverently and scanned the tiny print.

'This is history, right here. We read about rationing in school, but it hits home when you see something like this. Fifteen points. For tongue.' She handed the card back, wondering what her mother and father had kept of their ancestors' lives. All she knew was that her father's parents – both dead before she was born – had been New Yorkers, wealthy from a family shipping business, and that her mother's family was from Jackman. There must have been something in one of the boxes she and her sisters had sorted through when Dad and Lauren sold the Maine house. Where had it all gone? When she got back home, she'd try to trace it. In the meantime . . . this was her family too.

'People think the war was all overseas, but there were German subs patrolling the eastern coast of this country. My mother told me they had to black out their windows at night. Story goes a couple of Nazis landed in Hancock, Maine, which isn't all that far from where Lauren and I grew up. They walked right through towns as if they belonged there. People noticed them, all dressed up in dark suits, but no one stopped them, and they disappeared. Who knows what mischief they got up to?'

Eve watched her animated face, thinking this was an entirely new version of Shelley. 'Do you miss Maine?'

'Sometimes. The smells, the sounds, the ocean. But my life there . . . had its difficulties. I wanted away from it.'

'Difficult because . . . you had to raise your kids alone?'

'That's part of it.'

Eve stared at a recipe for home-made wine made with rice, sugar, water, raisins and yeast, which she could happily spend the rest of her life not tasting. She wanted to ask Shelley more questions, but felt as if she'd be trying to get a butterfly to stay on her shoulder. Push too hard and she could crush it.

She put the card down on the table with a snap. Abigail asked any questions she felt like asking, and Shelley had yet to flit away. Eve was the one afraid of being crushed. 'Was . . . did some of the difficulties have to do with your sister, Helen?'

Shelley laughed, not her happy cackle, but a low, painful bark. 'Not all, but you might say she caused a lot of them.'

Eve wedged her hands between her knees. 'Would you like to tell me about her?'

'Would I *like* to?' Shelley barked again. 'No, but it's strange you asked tonight. Gave me a shiver, actually. As if her spirit is particularly strong in the air.'

'What do you mean?'

'The anniversary of her death is coming up. April fourteenth.' She shook her head. 'Such a waste. She was an extraordinary beauty. Like you are.'

Eve couldn't help a bizarre, Tourette's-like spasm of movement. She was suddenly desperate to see a picture.

'You look like her, you know.' Shelley closed the box in her lap, gripped it on both sides. 'I noticed it the first time I saw you. I thought God had brought her back to me.'

Somehow Eve was still managing to breathe, though she had to loosen her knees or her fingers would have fallen off from lack of circulation. 'That would be nice.'

'Maybe. I suppose she'd deserve another chance.' Shelley put the recipe box on the table next to her and folded her arms across her plump chest. 'I imagine in Los Angeles women who look like you are a dime a dozen, but in Machias, Helen was like something descended from heaven, and boy did she know it. She used her looks to her advantage, on my parents, on her friends, and most especially on men. She was a black hole of need, could never get enough reassurance that she was loved.

'Later in life, in her mid twenties, she got into drugs. She stole, she lied. She had horrible, abusive boyfriends. She laid waste to her life and most of my parents' money, spent trying to help her. A good deal of mine as well.' Shelley's voice sharpened. 'I took her in and she repaid me by stealing. Everyone who tried to help her got burned. This house was in appalling shape when I moved in.'

'But . . . there must have been times when she was better, right?' Eve was embarrassed how desperately she wanted to find something maternal and admirable in this person.

'Define better.'

'I guess sober? Clean?'

'In between her bouts of self-destruction, she did clean up, yes. A couple of times she went to some fancy rehab place. My parents must have paid, though I have no idea how they afforded it, or how she afforded any of the other ways she lived her life. As far as I know, she never worked a real job. Here and there she'd pick up a part-time something, but she always hated it, felt it was beneath her.' Shelley chuckled harshly, shaking her head. 'What did she expect, a CEO position? My parents had nothing left when they died. Maybe that's where Helen got the money she lived on. It seemed to keep coming from somewhere. I don't know if she was dealing, or selling her body, or both.'

Eve made a sympathetic sound through clenched teeth. She'd opened this Pandora's box, and wanted nothing more than to glue the lid back on. Then nail it. Then put a million-pound weight on top. She knew where the money to fuel Helen's addiction had come from. Paid by Eve's dear mother and father, for sexual services provided.

Unlike Rosalind, who'd found something of a soulmate in her birth mother, Eve wasn't going to get to replace Jillian Croft with a better materfamilias.

'Well.' Shelley absently traced the outline of the rose painted on top of the recipe box. 'I've tried to forgive her. I've often thought I've managed it. Then in moments like this the anger comes back.'

Eve picked up another index card and read the title distractedly. *How Sauerkraut May Be Cooked Without Telling the Neighbors*. She knew exactly how Shelley felt. Incredible that she and Clayton had just been talking about this same thing. Or maybe the experience was common enough that the conversation could be had with just about anyone off the street. 'How many people have you told about Helen?'

Shelley looked startled. 'Not many. I guess not any. My kids, some. There didn't seem to be any point painting her as she was. Let them enjoy the Aunt Helen of their imaginations.'

'Do you think it's possible that kind of anger sits inside us until we let it out?'

Shelley snorted, scratching her elbow. 'Sounds like a load of hooey to me.'

'Hooey!' Eve burst out laughing, relieved to be able to. 'Mumbo-jumbo?'

'Absolutely mumbo-jumbo.' Shelley grinned. 'And balderdash.'

'Listen to this.' Eve brandished her recipe card, happy to change the subject. 'To keep sauerkraut fumes from disturbing the neighbors, you should put it in an electric grill, which you then stuff into your fireplace, so the smell goes up the chimney.'

'Now there's a tip.' Shelley started gathering up the cards. 'We should put together a meal from some of these recipes. When everything calms the hell down.'

'That would be fun.' Eve handed her a stack, thinking she would very much enjoy settling in here with nothing to worry about but the job she'd been hired to do.

'I should get to bed. It's late.' Shelley secured the stack with a rubber band. 'Did you and Clayton figure out a plan?'

'Yes, we did.' Eve stood, smiling cheerfully. 'It's called "Make It Up As We Go Along".'

Shelley interrupted a yawn with a smile. 'Probably as good as any. What ferry are you aiming for?'

'Seven o'clock if we can make it. Clayton's coming by for us at six thirty.'

'I'll be awake.'

'Okay.' Eve laid a hand briefly on her aunt's shoulder, then turned to go upstairs. 'Goodnight.'

'You should talk to Abigail before you turn in.'

Eve held back a groan. Shelley was right. Eve would have to keep her big-girl pants on a little longer. She'd probably sleep better having made sure things were okay between them again. 'I will.'

Upstairs, she hesitated outside Abigail's closed door, listening.

When she could hear nothing, she stooped to see if there was light coming from under the door.

There was. Still awake.

She rapped lightly. 'Abigail?'

'Yeah.' Her voice was low and dull.

'I'm back.'

'I could tell.'

Eve growled quietly. Kids were the most obvious reason not to have kids. 'How do you know I didn't send my voice back ahead of me?'

'Ha ha.'

'I take it you don't want to talk to me.'

Silence.

'Tell you what. You don't have to talk. Just . . . If it's okay for me to come in, blink three times to let me know.' A faint snort at the lame joke gave her permission. She pushed open the door to find Abigail in bed, lying on her side, one arm wrapped around herself, the other holding her phone to her face.

Maybe easier if teenagers had the screens implanted in their eyeballs . . .

Eve went over and sat on the side of the bed, encouraged when Abigail moved her legs to make room. 'So.'

'So?'

'So . . . you're still pissed at me.'

Abigail shrugged. 'Shelley said I'm being a pain in your ass.'

'Really? She said that?'

'Only she said neck.'

'That sounds more like her. And? What do you think? Are you?'

Abigail finally moved the phone. Her eyes were puffed and swollen. Eve's heart ached for her. So much trauma in such a short time for such a young girl. Her own had been of a different type, but the sense of parental betrayal must be the same. She didn't envy Abigail the mess ahead, though Abigail was bolder and more self-aware than Eve had ever been, which would help her through.

'I'm entitled to my feelings.'

Eve nodded, letting the moment sit for a while, not wanting Abigail to feel she was being contradicted. 'I had a teacher who used to say, "All feelings are okay, but not all behaviors." You feel what you feel, nothing you can do about that. How you react to those feelings is the important choice.'

Abigail made a face. 'I guess.'

'But look. You're a kid who's been dealing with some tough stuff, so it's to be expected. Even grownups in your shoes don't do so well. Look at your dad. Glen.'

She shrugged again.

'Your shoulders talk more than you do.'

Abigail put the phone down and sat up, leaning against the iron headboard. 'I felt like you and Clayton were excluding me.'

'Because we were. But we had a right to, okay? I mean, you don't have to get invited to everything all your friends do, do you?'

She looked down at the domed ridges her legs made under the quilt. 'No. It just hurt.'

'I'm sorry. That wasn't what we were trying to do.'

'What did you talk about?'

'You. The entire time. What a pain in my neck you are.' Eve stuck out her tongue to show she was kidding. 'We talked about his sunroom. I had an idea for tucking it under the existing deck.'

Abigail put on a *huh?* expression. 'That's weird.'

'Why?'

'Kind of like hiding.'

Eve paid her back with a rude shrug. It felt pretty good.

'What else did you talk about?'

'The trip tomorrow.'

'What are you going to say to my dad?'

'No clue.'

Abigail drew her knees up to make a mountain and rested her chin on the highest peak. 'I have to tell you something.'

'Okay.' Eve waited silently, wanting to shriek that it had better not be anything huge or she was going to pitch herself through the window.

'My dad didn't exactly throw me out permanently.' She wrapped her arms around her leg-mountain. 'I mean, he did tell me to get out, but he said I should go stay with my friend and come back in a few days when I'd calmed down.'

The last sentence hijacked Eve's anger over her lie. 'When *you'd* calmed down?'

'Well, I . . . I also didn't tell you that I said some stuff I probably shouldn't have.'

'Like . . . ?'

'Like . . . that people who hated gays the most were often gay themselves.' She wrinkled her nose. 'Only I didn't say "gay themselves".'

'What *did* you say?'

Abigail hung her head. 'I said, I don't know, something like "everyone knows people who hate gays the most are the ones who really want it up their—"'

'O-kay, got it, thank you.' Eve had to fight to stay serious. In her to-remain-private opinion, Glen deserved at least some pushback. 'I think that was a little harsh.'

'It was not my best moment. But it was right after he called me a filthy stain on the family, and an abomination in the eyes of the Lord.'

'So he did say all that.'

'Yes.'

'And you wanted to hit back.'

'Yes.'

'No turning the other cheek.' She kept her face deadpan. 'I mean . . . the one on your face.'

The bed shook with their giggles.

'We're awful.' Abigail's tears weren't entirely from laughter.

'We're allowed. Black humor can be healing.' Eve patted Abigail's leg. 'Is there anything else?'

Abigail scowled and ducked her head.

Eve sighed. 'Let's have it.'

'Before I left, I kind of chucked a bible through the living room window.'

Again Eve struggled desperately for control, and again she failed. She would *never* be a good parent. 'You *kind of* chucked it?'

'Pretty much chucked it.' Abigail's blushing face was so much cuter than when she'd been pouting.

'Did it *pretty much* break the glass?'

'It pretty much landed in the bushes outside.' She sobered. 'It was a stupid thing to do. I've prayed a lot for forgiveness.'

Eve shook her head. 'You were acting out of terrible pain.'

'I guess.'

'So . . .' Eve managed to put on a suitably adult face. 'Why didn't you tell us this sooner? You've let us believe this whole time that your parents didn't want you back, when in fact they expected you home after a few days. You essentially ran away.'

Abigail bunched up her mouth, ducked her head and mumbled something.

Eve raised an eyebrow. 'You thoggered full surry or firmy?'

'I thought you'd feel sorrier for me if you thought I'd been locked out permanently.'

'Why would we need to feel sorrier for you? The real story was horrible enough.'

'Because I was afraid if you knew I was a runaway you'd just call the police, and I wasn't ready to go back, and I don't know. It just seemed like a better story.'

'You lied to people who trusted and cared for you, including your birth father.'

Abigail stared sullenly at the bed. 'I didn't think past getting food and somewhere to stay. And help meeting my dad.'

Typical live-in-the-moment teenager. Eve had never been like that; she'd always had a plan. Get away from her family. Be an architect. Marry Mike. Now she felt as in-between and adrift as Abigail. And, she suspected, Clayton, though he hadn't said as much.

'Haven't *you* ever lied?' Abigail's hostile tone meant she'd mistaken Eve's silence for censure.

'No. Not ever. Not once. Everything I have ever said since my very first word was the absolute truth because I am perfect.' She stood when Abigail rolled her eyes. 'That's not the point. The point is that we could have gone to Milwaukee and blasted your father for something he wasn't guilty of, which would have taken a lot of the power out of our outrage.'

'That's why I told you now.'

'Is there anything else? You promise now that we have a clear picture?'

'Yes.'

'See, this is the problem with lying. Now I don't know if I believe you.'

'You can believe me.' Abigail hugged her knees and rocked forward and back, then stopped abruptly, as if the movement had once been a habit she wanted to break. 'Are you going to tell Clayton? Tonight?'

'No, you are. First thing in the morning.'

'Do you think he'll be mad?'

'He won't be thrilled. But probably not mad.'

Her eyes filled with tears. 'I screwed up.'

'Yeah.' Eve sat down again and put her hand on Abigail's shoulder. 'But who doesn't? And don't cry, or the dog will sing.'

That made Abigail smile, but only briefly. 'Will you tell my parents about the lie?'

'Uh . . .' Eve felt her eyes go wide with panic and had to force them to their normal size. How the hell did parents make snap decisions like this? 'I'll get back to you on that.'

'Please don't tell them. It will just make it worse.'

'Yeah, it probably would.' She pushed hair back from Abigail's bent head, then repeated the gesture when her bangs obeyed the laws of gravity and fell forward again.

To her astonishment, Abigail tipped her head, laying her cheek against Eve's palm. Eve stayed still, savoring the moment, feeling a deep, tender happiness different from any she'd felt before.

'Thanks, Eve. For everything.'

'You know . . .' Eve half rose and gave Abigail a hug, afraid she'd start bawling, 'if a few weeks ago someone had told me I'd have to face this whole situation up here, I would have told them I'd fall completely apart. So as much as you are a pain in my ass, I owe you thanks also.'

Abigail wrinkled her nose. 'That's weird.'

'Aww, you're just saying that.' She patted Abigail's head a little less than gently and moved to the door. 'Try to get some sleep. Tomorrow will be a *super*-fun and relaxing day. But I'm counting on a happy ending.'

'I hope so.'

'I'm sure so. Goodnight, Abigail.'

Eve left the room and crossed the landing into her own, standing for a long time without turning on the light, needing the darkness, the chance to be protected and alone with her thoughts.

She was changing, finding new parts of herself she'd thought missing, shedding the old protective armor to grow a new, more tender, pierceable suit, like the young lobsters she and her family devoured in late summer in Maine.

Out on the lake there was a pinprick of light, representing the only visible part of a boat traveling the blackness. Beyond that, invisible people, with lives spreading and entangled and complex. Like the merest sliver of moon representing an entire mysterious landscape.

And in her closet, a diary representing the equally mysterious terrain of her mother's mind.

She slid back the door, opened her suitcase, pulled out the book and smoothed her hand over the cover, thinking about the conversation with Abigail, the unexpected revelations, the need for instantaneous decisions on the messages important to convey to a child and the messages important not to.

Then the conversation with Clayton, out under the stars. The way it felt to tell her story, the understanding as he'd said that by now it was just a story, long past, though the scars legitimately lingered.

Okay, Jillian.

She tossed the diary on to her bed, cleaned up in the bathroom and crawled under the comforting blankets, adjusting the pillows under her head, wanting to feel totally warm and safe before she started to read.

Part way through, she reached an entry in which her mother

described dealing with a predatory male: *If I have a daughter . . . I will teach her at the youngest age possible never to feel she's a victim, but to look down on these pathetic men who come to us because we are goddesses and they are nothing. I will teach her how to handle herself, how to detach emotionally, how in those situations she can use her beautiful and fully female body as a weapon of triumph.*

Eve slammed the book and squeezed her eyes shut. She couldn't read any more. Not tonight. Maybe not ever, though she couldn't make that call now.

But hearing this much of her mother's true voice – if an actress like Jillian could be said to have one – had opened up a new and deep curiosity.

She reached for her phone to call Rosalind.

Chapter 15

October 2, 1981 (Friday)

I took Olivia to Maine and saw my mom and dad. They were stunned when I knocked on the door. Dad was there first. He just turned and called for Mom. When she showed up, she locked her cold eyes on me and reached to shut the door in our faces. Just in time Olivia let out the most adorable coo ever made, which stopped her. She stared at her granddaughter. It was clear everything lay in her hands.Then she said, 'Well, come in, then' in her cranky way, and we came in. I cried. We all cried. Then Olivia did too, which made us laugh. My parents love their granddaughter. Either they've mellowed, or they loved me that much too, when I was that little and couldn't talk back yet. It's hard to imagine, but I'd like to think it's true.

It was a shock how much older they looked. Other than that, they seemed the same. Mom was unable to say much that was pleasant, and Dad was unable to say much of anything. But they doted on Olivia and didn't throw me out, which was all I'd hoped for.

Maybe I'd hoped for more. Maybe I'd hoped for some verbal forgiveness for ignoring me for so many years. But that was asking for a miracle.

Nothing was mentioned about how I'd managed to have

a baby, especially one who looks enough like me to be convincingly mine, but there's no point going back to that old pain. It was so great to be in Maine again, smelling those wonderful tree and lake smells, and enjoying the quiet. Even Jackman, the nowhere nightmare that is my hometown, looked beautiful. Maybe it's changed; maybe my memories were colored by my unhappiness.

Daniel had never been to Maine and loved it. After we left Jackman, we explored the coast and decided to buy a house somewhere fairly remote. It will be the perfect place to pretend for a time every summer that we're an ordinary family, where we can watch the water without anyone watching us, take walks, cook our own meals, have clambakes . . .

I am excited to have another child, but I want to wait. I'm content for the first time in a long while. I suppose I won't need to write in this diary very much anymore.

Mom-Jillian

Eve woke early after a fitful sleep full of dreams about exams she wasn't prepared for and a bizarre monster chasing her that looked a lot like her Grandma Betty.

Before falling asleep, she and Rosalind had talked for an hour – or mostly Rosalind had talked and Eve had listened, hearing in a nutshell the contents of the diary her sister had received.

Jillian's childhood, or rather Sylvia Moore's childhood, since she hadn't yet chosen her screen name, had been chilling. Grandma Betty had told her daughter nothing about her physical condition, letting her discover her infertility and lack of adequate vagina only when she first tried to have sex with her then-fiancé, Daniel Braddock. Worse, when she'd had surgery at age sixteen for the undescended testicles she'd been born with, Grandma

Betty – and the doctor! – had led her to believe they were some form of pre-cancerous growths.

Rather than tell her daughter she had a rare but benign condition, Grandma Betty thought it was a better idea to let Sylvia think she had cancer?

There wasn't enough empathy in Eve's entire brain to understand the motivation behind that, even factoring in a different, less enlightened age, one more hesitant to discuss not only issues of gender but the basics of sexuality. Rosalind also suspected that the trauma of being diagnosed with complete androgen insensitivity as an adult could conceivably have triggered her mother's bipolar disorder. If Jillian had known from puberty why she wasn't like other women, would it have made her life easier? Saner? Impossible to tell.

But for the first time, maybe ever in her life, Eve had felt sympathy for her mother. As a little girl watching Jillian self-destruct, she'd reacted with a child's ignorance of the iron grip of addiction and mental illness, and out of her own need for a stable, loving mother.

One day she would make herself read the rest of the diary Lauren had sent – Eve still assumed it had come from her stepmother. But she needed more time to internalize and process the information Rosalind had given her.

Definitely not today. Today would be complicated enough.

After a quick shower, she put on that one nice outfit she'd packed – good maternal advice after all – and forced her unwilling stomach to eat a mostly silent breakfast with Abigail. They were just finishing the cleanup when they heard the sound of Clayton's truck pulling into the driveway.

Eve pointed to the front door and fixed Abigail with a stern look. 'You go first. I'll be out in five minutes. He'd better know by then what you told me.'

'Okay, okay.' Abigail pulled out the handle of her suitcase to engage the wheels, shouldered her backpack and trudged to the front door.

'What was that about?' Shelley wandered into the kitchen wearing an oversized T-shirt, short greying hair sticking out in wild clumps. The rumpled sight of her made Eve want to smile.

'Last night Abigail kindly let me know that while her dad did order her out, he sent her to a friend's house and made it clear he expected her back in a few days. She stayed away to piss him off.'

Shelley's thick eyebrows rose. 'Well.'

'Yeah.' Eve found herself wiping down a counter she had already wiped. 'Changes things. Not a ton, but enough.'

'I'd say.' Shelley went to the refrigerator and took out the bottle of not-from-concentrate orange juice Eve had bought. 'That makes your job easier, then. They'll definitely take her back.'

'I hope under good terms.'

'Meaning?' She poured her juice.

'That her father can make peace with who she is.'

'Most people can't even do that with themselves.'

Eve took a turn raising her brows. 'Well.'

Shelley grinned, lifting the juice to her mouth. 'I'm right, though, admit it.'

'Maybe.' Eve glanced at her watch. 'Two more minutes and I'm going out there.'

'You look quite nice.' Shelley gestured to her blue patterned tunic over black pants. 'I've only seen you in jeans.'

'That makes two of us.'

Shelley snorted. 'I never took to getting dolled up. Those years in the corporate world, I felt like I was in costume every day. But I don't have your looks.'

'Oh, but Shelley, you are beautiful *in*side. That's where it *counts*.' Eve gave a vapid smile.

'All right you. Get out of my house.' Shelley pointed to the front door. 'I'll expect you back tonight unless you're not, right?'

'We'll let you know either way.'

'Good luck.' Shelley walked toward her with her arms straight out, but just as Eve was thinking she was going to hug her, her aunt clapped her twice on the shoulders. 'You're doing a good thing. My guess is this Glen has done a lot of praying and figured things out. Or at least he's willing to listen. It's much easier to hold on to principles when nothing is testing them.'

'I hope you're right.'

'If I'm wrong, well . . .' She gestured toward Eve. 'You and Clayton will have to raise her together.'

Eve gasped, then realized a split second before Shelley's trademark laugh that she'd been had. She was even able to recite Shelley's next words silently along with her.

'You should have seen your face!'

'That's it. I'm outta here.' She grinned at her aunt. 'Thanks for the good wishes. We'll probably need them. C'mon, Marx! Let's go.'

Marx's tail announced that he was more than ready; in fact, had been ready for quite some time and what was taking her so long? Eve picked up her bag, gave Shelley one more smile and a flash of crossed fingers, then stepped outside into the chilly gray morning.

Clayton and Abigail were seated in the truck, staring straight ahead. In silence? She couldn't tell.

She opened the door and climbed in. 'Hello. Been having a fun chat?'

Abigail sent her a daggered look.

'Learn something every day.' Clayton turned on the motor and put the truck into gear. 'How'd you sleep, Eve?'

'Like crap.'

'Same here. Abigail?'

'Three of us.'

'The perfect way to start a long drive.' He headed to the end of Shelley's driveway and made a left turn to skirt the southern edge of the island on their way to Detroit Harbor.

They made the 7 a.m. ferry in plenty of time, and reached Northpoint Pier at the tip of Door County half an hour later. By the time they had exited the peninsula on to I-43 at Green Bay an hour and a half later, there had been about four sentences exchanged, mostly banal comments on the businesses they were passing.

'Hey, guess what?' Abigail spoke up suddenly from the back seat, where she'd insisted on sitting with Marx in his crate.

'What?' Eve glanced back to see her grinning and felt encouraged.

'I just made up a hymn for Glen. It's called "Jesus Came to My Heart".'

Clayton glanced at her in the rear-view mirror. 'Let's hear it.'

'Okay.' Her sweet soprano filled the space.

'Jesus came to my heart today
But left when He heard that I was gay
Glory to God at heaven's gate
You only get through if you lie that you're straight.'

A couple of beats of silence while Eve tried desperately not to laugh, and failed. Clayton was apparently the only grownup in the front seat.

'What do you think?'

Clayton shook his head. 'I'd save that one for later. Maybe forty, fifty years from now.'

'Yeah?' Abigail pretended disappointment. 'I thought I had a sure hit.'

'You can't go into this only in your own head, Abigail. Glen's not all bad, you're not all good, right? You tried to frame it that way to us, but you had to lie to do it. It's not that simple.'

Abigail's huff could be heard from the back. 'I thought you were on my side.'

'That's exactly what I mean.' He found her in the mirror again, his face grave. 'It's not about sides, who's right, who's wrong, who's the perpetrator, who's the victim. If you go into it that way, all you get is an argument. It's about figuring out how to get along with the people you love and that you're stuck with.'

Abigail grumbled something under her breath Eve was sure they were both glad to miss.

'On the other hand.' He changed lanes to pass a slower car. 'That was definitely the funniest hymn I've ever heard.'

'Cracked me up,' Eve said. 'But I'm easy that way. And you're only stuck with your parents another two years. After that, you get to make your own choices.'

'I'm not going to give up what I believe and who I am just to make Glen happy.'

'I'm not suggesting that,' Clayton said. 'The conversation today will be hard. But the payoff is that over the next two years, you and your parents could grow closer and understand each other better, even if you can't agree. If you just stick to your side, because you're right and he's wrong, then yeah, two more years of misery counting days until you're sprung.'

'How come you're so smart about all this when your own family sucks?'

'Abigail . . .' Eve turned to give her a look.

'Sorry,' she mumbled.

'You do have a point, however.' Eve ignored Clayton's sound of protest. His words had hit home for her too. If her mother had lived, would Eve have been able to give her an opening toward reconciliation and understanding? 'I screwed up with my parents too. Think of it as us giving you a chance not to turn out as messed up as we are.'

'Huh?' Clayton glanced over in amusement. 'Is that what we're doing?'

'Ugh, I can*not* let *that* happen.' Abigail shuddered and crossed herself.

The mood changed after that. Abigail regained what seemed to be her natural cheer, and suggested they play the alphabet game: find the letters in order on signs outside the truck as fast as possible, and whoever reached Z first won. After that, they moved on to invent a story, each of them providing one sentence in turn, making themselves giddy at their silliness.

Granted, they were all a little out of their minds.

They stopped near Sheboygan for a bathroom break, caffeine and a snack before continuing, this time with Abigail's phone blaring songs by her favorite bands, accented either by her running commentary or by her singing along.

When highway signs started showing fewer and fewer miles remaining to Milwaukee, the mood shifted again full circle to the low-energy tension of the trip's origin.

By the time they pulled into Abigail's driveway in Shorewood, the truck engine was the only sound. Then that cut out too, and left only the metallic intestinal ticks and gurgles of the cooling motor.

The house was a modest white-shuttered brick bungalow on a shady suburban street, not too different in size or design from those around it. At least an hour went by before anyone spoke. Or it seemed that way. In reality it was probably all of thirty seconds.

'We appear to be here,' Clayton said.

'We do.'

Another pause.

'Everyone ready?'

'*No!*' Eve and Abigail spoke simultaneously.

'Me neither.' Clayton pushed open his door. 'But someone's gotta be the man around here.'

'Ha.' Eve got down from the truck, then opened the back door to let Marx out of his crate. While he went to water the Oakeses' grass, she went around and opened Abigail's door, since the girl hadn't moved.

'Hey.' She held out her hand, surprised when Abigail took it and clung for a few seconds, eyes large in her pale face. Given her intelligence and confidence, it was hard to remember she was a child, with so much on the line.

'Think they heard us?' Clayton waited on the front walk for them to catch up.

'I'm sure they're listening.' Eve saw no one at the apparently newly repaired living-room window, but couldn't imagine Abigail's parents had been doing anything but waiting tensely all morning. She put a hand on Abigail's shoulder, prepared for the shrug-off, surprised it didn't come. The three of them started up the steps just as the front door opened.

Glen looked so exactly the way Eve had pictured him, she nearly snorted. Tall, thin, receding reddish hair, large ears and earnest eyes. He wore a blue polo shirt and, yes, brown slacks with loafers. The only thing missing was the Mister Rogers zip-up cardigan.

Behind her husband – why did Eve get the feeling she

spent a lot of time there? – was Leah, dark, younger, very pretty, face set in an apprehensive smile.

Abigail took a step back, bumping into Eve, who kept her hand on her shoulder. Next to Eve, Clayton closed ranks, sending a clear message: *we are Abigail's people.*

'Abby.' Leah started to cry and made a move to pass her husband, but he stuck out his arm. Clayton made a hissing sound that was nearly scary. Abigail's body turned to stone.

'Wait, Leah.'

'Hi, Mom. Dad.' Abigail's voice sounded so thin and wobbly, Eve squeezed her shoulder, though she was suddenly terrified. Beyond Clayton's brief lecture in the car, they hadn't coached her in what to say. What if she sang the hymn? 'I'm back. I'm sorry if I worried you. This is my friend Eve. And this is my birth father.'

Well done.

Glen's gaze jerked to Clayton. '*What?*'

Eve groaned silently. Apparently Leah had failed to let him know Clayton was coming.

Clayton walked up to him, hand extended. 'I'm Clayton Marshall. Your daughter is a remarkable girl.'

Glen turned to his wife. 'How did Abigail find out about *him*?'

Eve waited, watching Leah's panicked expression, willing her to say: *I told her, you dickhead.*

'I wanted her . . . to have somewhere safe to go.'

'*Safe?* With a man she doesn't know, and we don't either? Safer than with one of her friends or home with us?'

Abigail let out a growl of frustration. Eve got the feeling she did that a lot around her father. 'Dad, I'm fine. Clayton is a good guy. Mom knew that.'

Leah said nothing, just stood there staring with tearful longing at the daughter she'd been forbidden to approach.

Clayton held his position, hand still extended.

Obviously embarrassed into acknowledging him, Glen finally gave a perfunctory shake and dropped his arm as if he might catch something.

'Please, come in.' Leah beckoned to them. 'I have iced tea and lemonade. And lunch later, if we . . . if we . . .'

'. . . haven't killed each other by then,' Eve murmured, causing Clayton and Abigail to laugh softly. A tactical error she immediately regretted when she saw Leah and Glen's expressions. Unwittingly Eve had made the three of them a unit of snarky popular kids and Glen and Leah the vulnerable geeks on the outside. She'd need to be more careful.

Glen stood back, holding open the storm door. Abigail went straight into her mother's arms, where she stayed so long, Eve started misting up, not surprised to see Clayton blinking repeatedly. Glen didn't even try to hide his tears. He got points for that.

'Please, come in.' He gestured into the house, his voice husky. 'Leah, let the others past.'

Leah moved indoors, still clutching her daughter, releasing Abigail only to give Clayton a shy smile.

'Thank you for bringing her back.'

He touched her shoulder. 'You're welcome. She's a great kid.'

'Yes.' Leah nodded rapidly as Marx introduced himself by nudging her thigh. 'Oh look at the pretty dog! I miss dogs. I grew up with them. But they're so much work, and we never found—'

'Leah?' Glen was still standing in the doorway. 'Did you say you had lemonade for everyone?'

'Yes, of course. I'm greeting our guests. Hello, Eve.' She took Eve's outstretched hand in both of hers. Up close, her lovely eyes and brow showed the stress of the previous week. 'My goodness, you are so beautiful.'

'Thanks.' Eve hated when people complimented her looks. As if they were something great she'd accomplished. All she'd done was be born. 'You are also.'

'Oh no. Not like you.'

'*Lemonade*, Leah?' Glen had crossed behind them to stand awkwardly near Abigail, who angled her body away from him.

This would be a super-fun morning.

'Yes, Glen, I'm sorry. I'll get it.'

'I'll help.' Abigail followed her mother toward what must be the kitchen.

Which left Glen, Clayton and Eve cozily alone together. And Marx, of course, who set about exploring his new surroundings, glancing back at Eve once in a while to reassure himself he was in the right place.

'Come in. Come in.' Glen led them into the oddly shaped living room, long and narrow, dominated by a brown puffy leather couch that looked overinflated and a couple of beige armchairs. Over the fireplace, a print of haloed Jesus pointing to his chest, where his heart was blasting red and blue beams of light out in front of him. Over the couch, a vividly colored painting of a bird's-eye view of Christ on the cross, and another watercolor of a mountain church by a lake, making pleasing and unusual splashes of color in the otherwise muted room. 'Lemonade will be out in a minute. Have a seat, have a seat.'

Clayton and Eve lowered themselves on to the obese brown giant. Marx sniffed at Glen and wagged his tail when the father of the house gave him a distracted pat on the head.

'Nice house.' Clayton crossed, then uncrossed his legs. 'I love the leaded glass.'

Eve shoved him discreetly. Low blow.

'Thank you.' Glen moved a wooden chair from the dining room in front of the fireplace and sat with his hands clasped in his lap. 'Brilliant German craftsmanship. Can't buy quality like this anymore. No, you can't.'

'No, you can't.' Clayton glanced at Eve with amused eyes. How was he keeping so calm in this situation? She felt ready to break. 'How long have you and Leah lived here?'

'Since we married.' Glen's face reddened. He must realize they were picturing him at the altar next to Leah carrying Clayton's daughter *in utero*. 'It needs some work. New roof in the next year or so.'

'That'll be fun to pay for, huh?'

'Yes. Yes. Quite expensive. We've had to save for it.'

'Better than a leaking roof.' Eve couldn't let Clayton suffer the miserable conversation all by himself.

'Yes indeed, indeed.' Glen chuckled politely and gestured to Marx, who'd decided to sit nearly on Glen's feet and put his furry head in Glen's lap. 'Nice dog. What's his name?'

'Marx.'

'Marx. Ah. Great. That's great. *Leah?*'

'Here I am.' She entered the room holding a tray on which sat five glasses of iced lemonade, trailed by Abigail holding a plate of what looked like home-made sugar cookies. They passed the tray and plate around, and for an excruciatingly long time the living room was silent except for the tinkle of ice cubes and the crystalline scrape of cookies being removed from the plate and crunched.

'Well.' Leah sat on the other armchair, eyes manically bright. 'Isn't this nice?'

'No,' Abigail said emphatically.

Leah deflated. 'You're right. I said it out of habit. Stupid.'

'It's fine.' Eve reached a hand toward her, even though she

was across the room. 'Totally understandable. We're all tense. These cookies are delicious, by the way.'

'Thank you.' Leah beamed and rubbed her hands together. 'It's my mother's reci—'

'May I suggest a short prayer before we talk?'

'Or a hymn . . .' Abigail suggested sweetly.

Eve put up her hand to vote. 'I pick prayer.'

'Same here,' Clayton said.

Abigail shot them a look and bowed her head meekly.

Sassy girl.

'Lord, we welcome our daughter back into our midst and ask that you bless her, uh . . . biological father, Clayton, and his wife . . .'

'Friend,' Abigail corrected.

'. . . his friend, uh . . . uh . . .'

'Eve,' Eve supplied.

'. . . Eve. We ask for your love and guidance in discussing our family and the current . . . difficulties under which it labors, and we ask for your blessing on whatever solution we discover together. Amen.'

'Amen,' from the chorus.

'I'll speak first.' Glen stood and cleared his throat, making Eve wonder how long he'd rehearsed this speech and taken it for granted he'd lead the show. 'First, I want to thank Clayton and Eve for bringing our daughter safely back to us. And to tell you, Abigail, how glad I am to have you home again.'

Abigail's head was still bent from the prayer. Leah reached over the table between their chairs and put a hand on her shoulder. She didn't move.

'Also, Abigail, I want to . . . apologize . . .' he put a fist to his mouth and coughed, 'for the way I spoke to you that day. I am deeply sorry.'

Clayton and Eve exchanged glances. Something a little uncomfortable about witnessing a public apology over a private matter. But maybe Glen found it easier that way, avoiding the true intimacy of being alone with his daughter. At least it was a step in the right direction.

'I hope you will forgive me.'

'Yes.' Abigail still wouldn't look up. 'I'm sorry too. For what I said to you. And for the window.'

Glen flashed a goofy grin, taking two rapid breaths that sounded like a wheezing fit, which Eve decided to interpret as happy relief. Another good sign. Almost endearing.

'You were both very upset.' Leah turned placatingly from husband to daughter and back. 'But what matters is that we're together again.'

'What matters . . .' Abigail hunched her shoulders, 'is that we respect each other for who we are.'

Glen cleared his throat again. 'We respect you. Your mother and I both respect you. But . . .'

Abigail finally looked up, straight at him, eyes defiant. 'But?'

He sat down, knees together, body bent forward, staring at the ground for several long seconds. Then he raised his head. 'But we have our beliefs, and they too must be respected.'

'Glen . . .' Leah pleaded.

'I will not budge on that point.'

Abigail stood up. 'Even if you lose me?'

'Glen. Leah.' Clayton stood as well. His height and build made him seem a tower of solid strength in the narrow room. Eve's heart gave an unwelcome flip. 'I think it would help if we talked in specifics. Abigail is gay. Your religion keeps you from being able to . . . condone that. Yet she's your daughter. I can appreciate the terrible conflict this has caused you, pulled by the two things you care about most deeply. Love of and obedience to God, and love of and need to protect your daughter.'

Eve was pretty sure the open-mouthed admiration on Leah and Abigail's faces was reflected on her own.

Glen's not so much.

'So how about each side starts with what he or she can or can't tolerate.' Clayton glanced around at his audience. 'If it makes it easier, I'll start. I'm prepared to—'

'Excuse me. You have no say in this. It's my name on her birth certificate.' Glen got to his feet again, a head shorter than Clayton, his face turning red. 'You are not part of this family.'

'By blood I am,' Clayton said kindly. 'Abigail is my biological daughter. Morally, I certainly am. I can also easily establish paternity, then legally I will be as well.'

The two men did the classic stare-down, Glen's chest puffed out, Clayton's arms folded. They couldn't help themselves, the testosterone ran so deep. Even Marx stood, looking around the room, wagging his tail uncertainly.

'I want to hear what Clayton has to say,' Abigail said.

'So do I.' Eve wasn't part of the family, not by blood, morally *or* legally, but she thought Clayton was brave as hell and wanted to support him.

'Thanks.' Clayton sent his daughter a smile. 'I want Abigail to live here. It's best for her. You are the parents she knows, and this is the life she belongs in. But if it means she will be treated as if a basic part of her needs fixing, then I am prepared to open my home to her.'

'*What?* Oh no. No.' Leah clasped her hands to her chest and looked pleadingly at her husband. 'Glen.'

Attagirl. Eve waited for her to go further, but one glare from Pious Carrot-Top and she lowered her eyes, already defeated.

Extremely annoying.

'Glen, I think we have a pretty clear idea where you stand.'

Clayton took his seat again. 'But tell us what's negotiable for you.'

'The word of God is not negotiable.'

'Which means what, specifically, in this case?' The tiniest bit of impatience had crept into Clayton's voice.

'Abigail is welcome in this house as long as . . .' Glen swallowed with such effort his torso jerked forward, 'as long as she obeys the word of God.'

'Which *means* . . .'

'Which *means* I can be gay but I can't act it.' Abigail laughed bitterly. 'Gay as long as I don't do anything that would define gayness. Which is the same as saying I can't be gay in this house.'

'It's *not* the same,' Glen said. 'You are welcome in our house and in God's.'

'As long as I leave my attraction to women at the door?'

Silence.

'See?' Abigail laughed again, a biting and poignant sound. 'It's the same.'

Eve glanced at Leah, who was wringing her hands. At least she did not look totally at peace with her husband's argument.

Say something.

Glen took a step toward Abigail, so much pain on his face that Eve felt some of it herself, in spite of her vicious opposition to his views. 'Abigail. This . . . aspect of you does not define you as a whole person. God created you and loves you in spite of that . . . part.'

'Which part is that, Dad? My brain? My spleen? My vagina?'

'Abigail!' Leah pounced on that offense, while still staying silent over the worse one.

Glen's face grew redder. 'The part of you that is not part of

God. The sinful part He gave you as a challenge, as He gives out any sickness or disorder of the body or mind. In order that you fight against it, that you pray for His healing. Even if you are not fully healed in this short life, if you continue to seek God's glory, afterward you *will* find healing, total wholeness and peace.'

Despite what he was saying, the way Glen spoke gave Eve hope. It was as if he were repeating words he'd heard somewhere, not ones he felt deep in his soul.

She wanted to think he was on the edge, still hanging on for dear life but ready to drop.

'So if I suppress my essential self and don't have feelings for or sex with any women while I'm alive, I can go to heaven?'

Glen turned on her. 'Homosexuality is not natural.'

'I was born this way; how can it not be natural?'

'It's not *normal*. It's not what God intended us to be.'

'He *made* me this way!'

'*He also made serial killers.*'

Marx's tail stopped wagging. Eve had had enough.

'I'll tell you what's not normal.' She got to her feet, surprised to find herself steady as a rock. 'Throwing your child out of your house isn't normal. Betraying your responsibility to love her unconditionally is not normal. Telling a beautiful, talented, smart kid that something she can't help is terribly and sinfully wrong with her is *not normal*, and it sure as hell can't be what God intended.'

Silence.

Clayton scratched his head. 'Gotta say I'm with Eve on that one. I think it was George Bernard Shaw who said, "All great truths begin as blasphemies."'

More silence. Eve turned to Leah, pleading with her eyes. *Support your daughter. Say something. Help her.*

Leah looked away, hands fidgeting in her lap. 'Would anyone like more lemonade?'

That did it. Eve bent and snatched up her glass. 'I would. What's more, I'll come with you to get it, and we can have a nice *chat*. Okay?'

Leah's lovely eyes shot wide with apprehension. 'Oh no. I can manage.'

'No trouble. Come on.' She waited while Leah stood slowly and, after an I'm-off-to-the-gallows glance at her stone-faced husband, led the way to the old-fashioned kitchen, which probably hadn't been updated since the house was built in the first half of the twentieth century. If Eve wasn't so furious, she'd enjoy exploring.

'Eve, it's awfully nice of you to want to help, but I—'

'Do you agree with your husband that Abigail can't live in this house as a gay woman?'

'She's . . . still a girl.'

'Gay girl, then.' Eve put her glass on the tiled counter. 'Do you agree with him?'

'I . . . He has thought about this very hard, and—'

'I'm not interested in what he thinks. I'm interested in what *you* think.'

Leah's eyes hardened for an instant before relaxing back into passivity. 'I'm not going to let you come between my husband and me. If that's what you're after.'

'I'm asking you to protect your daughter from being thrown out of her home. From living with a stranger. A very nice one, but a stranger. Giving up her friends, her town, her school. You think that's what God wants for her? For any child? Is that what *you* want for her?'

Leah turned her back, opened the door of the white refrigerator. 'The church is very clear about—'

'Screw the church. What about *you*? Do you have a thought in your head that was not put there by your husband or the church?'

Leah whirled around, eyes blazing. 'Of course I do.'

'Then let's hear it. Your daughter is at stake. Your *daughter*. Not just now but for the rest of your life and hers. I know this because I've lived it, and I have never, ever forgiven my mother for sitting on the sidelines while I got hurt.'

Leah clutched the lemonade pitcher to her chest. 'You're also . . . gay?'

Eve rolled her eyes. '*No*, I'm not gay, it was something else entirely. She could have protected me, but she didn't. I still have emotional scars. Don't let that happen to Abigail. If you believe that your husband is even a little bit wrong, *say something*.'

Leah picked up Eve's glass and filled it, her hands shaking. 'It's complicated. I'm caught between my love and respect for my husband and my love and respect for my daughter. I don't know the right thing to say.'

'I think you do. It's just easier not to say anything.'

The words hit Eve hard.

Easier for Leah to conceal from Abigail that she wasn't Glen's child. Easier for Jillian and Dad not to tell their three daughters they were born to different mothers. Easier for Eve not to tell Mike their relationship was on its deathbed. Easier for Grandma Betty not to have to talk to her daughter about her condition. Easier for Jillian to send young Eve upstairs with the man who could remake her movie career than risk insulting him over something that might not happen.

All that 'easier' created so damn much difficulty.

Leah stood for a long time, head bowed over the pitcher. 'I guess it is easier. I'm not a strong woman like you are. My feelings seem right to me, and then Glen starts talking and I get confused and not sure anymore. Who am I to say anything about what God wants or means?'

'Don't you think He speaks to you too?'

Leah half turned, revealing her troubled face. 'I've been learning, lately, some . . . other ideas about God that are also beautiful. I just don't know which one is right.'

'There are probably as many ideas of God as there are people. You don't have to accept Glen's as the only truth. Not accepting it doesn't mean anything except that you differ on this one interpretation. No two people can agree on everything. Right?'

'For Glen it will mean more than just one little disagreement.'

'Is it worth sacrificing your daughter to that?' Eve hated herself for pushing so hard, but she was utterly sure that she'd hate herself more if she didn't.

Leah stayed leaning against the counter, holding the lemonade glass in one hand, clutching the handle of the pitcher with the other. Her dark floral dress had a scooped back, revealing the whitened knobs of her vertebrae, then hugged her to the waist and flared to below her knees. She evoked Eve's idea of a 1950s housewife, dressed up in the kitchen, chained by her lemonade and pitcher, free to keep house as she wanted but not to think for herself.

Apparently the 1950s still thrived in some places.

Leah put the glass on the counter within reach of Eve and let her arm drop to her side. 'Take your lemonade. I'll be in soon.'

'Okay.' Eve picked up the tumbler, wrapped her arm around Leah's shoulder for a brief, impulsive hug, then went back into the living room, where Clayton was discussing with Glen the merits of Washington Island versus the rest of Door County, Abigail hunched and glowering in her chair, Marx back to lying adoringly on Glen's feet.

Both men broke off and looked at her.

'Everything okay?' Clayton asked.

'We'll know in a little while.'

Glen frowned. 'What does that mean?'

'It means your wife is taking some time to think for herself.'

'About something you told her?'

'About what she believes is right.'

Glen half rose, making Marx stand also. 'What did you say to her?'

'Not your business.'

'She's my wife.' He straightened proudly. 'We have no secrets from each other.'

'I'm *not* your wife, so I have many.'

She glanced at Clayton, saw him cheering her on with his eyes. His silent support made it simple to stand here and calmly say what she thought, not caring how Glen reacted, not minding if he didn't agree with her. She'd discovered she did have a horse in this race after all, and she was intent on riding it to victory for Abigail's sake – and for her own in a way she hadn't expected.

'Glen.' Leah came back into the room. 'I have something to say.'

Abigail lifted her head. Eve crossed her fingers.

'About what, Leah?' Glen spoke gently, as if Leah was a brainless rebel about to be shown the error of her ways.

'I've thought a lot about all this.'

'In the kitchen? In two minutes?' He glanced to see if anyone was laughing at his joke.

No one was.

Leah shook her head. 'Since I started suspecting Abigail was gay. When she was twelve.'

'Twelve!' Glen's smile dropped off his face. 'You said nothing to me about this.'

And *voilà*, the perfect moment for Eve to throw the we-have-no-secrets line back in his face. Pointlessly cruel, but she would have enjoyed it.

Leah glanced at her. 'I guess it was . . . easier not to. And I wasn't sure. Not really. I did a lot of reading, though. And I met a . . . gay person at the library, a gay man. He goes to a different church. His faith is beautiful, Glen, and runs deep into his life, as deep as ours. We've talked many times.'

Glen looked as if she'd just socked him in the solar plexus. 'You should have told me this right when it started. I should have been there with you.'

Leah's lips parted, but it took a while for words to come out. 'So you could prove to him he was wrong? Or so you could listen and learn?'

Glen pressed his lips together so firmly it looked as if he were trying to turn himself inside out. 'Do you agree with what this man says?'

Leah moved to the back of Abigail's chair and laid her hand on her daughter's still head. 'It's very hard to see how he could be a sinner. It's very hard to see my daughter as a sinner. I believe our church is acting on pure faith, but I'm . . .' She swallowed convulsively, visibly trembling. 'Glen, I'm coming to wonder if it's the right way.'

Glen drew himself up straight. His nostrils flared, his face turning red again. If it wasn't so awful, it would be funny. 'You're all against me, then? Against God?'

'Dad,' Abigail said quietly. 'We're not against you *or* God.'

'Come with me sometime and talk to him, Glen.' Leah had all the power in the room now, still gentle and soft, but newly infused with authority, reminding Eve of her daughter's face in the little Norwegian church. 'He is willing, but I was too afraid to approach you. That was a mistake. I'm sorry.'

'Leah, I don't know what has happened to you, but it was wrong to shut me out of this. Wrong to . . . to choose this other path without . . . without me.'

Eve held her breath, praying Leah would not apologize.

'It is wrong to shut my daughter out.' Leah still spoke calmly, standing tall, hand gentle and relaxed on Abigail's head, radiating what could be nothing else but God's glory, and how could Glen think otherwise? 'Do not make me choose between you again.'

'Mom,' Abigail whispered. She rose from the chair and put her arms around Leah's waist, burying her head against her breast. Mother and daughter burst into tears.

Eve broke down. Clayton's arm came around her, his eyes filling too. The room filled with the damp sounds of weeping.

And Marx started to howl.

Chapter 16

May 16, 1984 (Wednesday)

I was right, my dearest diary, I have neglected you! Life has been up and down, but when you're bipolar, that's normal. Is that funny? Probably not.

Woman #2 has dropped into our laps. She showed up at one of Daniel's book signings right here in LA. She is beautiful and a performer, with lovely brown eyes we trusted right away.

I thought it would be easier this time to let Daniel go to her. You'd think it would be, that I might have gotten used to the idea, be more at peace with it, understanding what joy the result brings. Not at all. It was worse this time. Woman #2 is beautiful, sophisticated and talented, the kind of woman he could fall in love with. Instead of being a loving, supportive wife, grateful that Daniel was willing to take part in this crazy charade of mine, again I wanted to kill him when he got home from being with her. I screamed and threw things at him. It was all I could do not to start drinking again. I got so upset that I called Dr Townsend, who prescribed me more lovely, lovely Valium, even though I'd managed to stop for a while. I promised I would just take it for a week. It helps so much with this agony. With Olivia to think of – my darling, impetuous, always cheerful girl who looks up to me with such worship – I can't go to pieces. Life is no longer just about me.

I must find some way to keep myself together.

I try to focus on the baby. Maybe a boy this time? Maybe another girl. I don't care, as long as he or she is here with me soon.

The silence in the car as Clayton and Eve drove away from the house in Shorewood was inevitable. What was there to say after such a draining experience?

After Leah's ultimatum to her husband, talk had continued over ham sandwiches and potato chips, a few times veering again into emotion, but then returning to objectivity. Gradually the power ebbed from Glen's insistence that Abigail would have to renounce any 'practice of homosexuality' in order to remain in the house. By the time Clayton and Eve left, it appeared some path was possible that would not force anyone to compromise his or her beliefs.

Sort of a family don't-ask-don't-tell policy.

Fabulous in theory. Eve could only hope they would all resist the temptation to keep demanding change from one another.

Clayton had been grudgingly granted visitation rights. Abigail would spend time with her birth father on Washington Island in the summer, and during the school year in Chicago – a short train ride from Milwaukee – when their schedules meshed. Clayton had promised her at the very least a Cubs baseball weekend at Wrigley Field, which had horrified the whole Brewers-loving family.

At least Abigail was back home with that family. Marx had stayed with them for the evening so Clayton and Eve could enjoy themselves in the city. Going back to pick him up would also allow them a second chance to check on Abigail before they left. Eve dreaded the eventual separation. Clayton of course would see his daughter again, but for Eve, the prospect was less certain. She'd miss Abigail like crazy – her bravery, her wisdom, even her adolescent attitude.

'If it's okay, I thought we'd head for the East Side.' Clayton slowed to exit the highway. 'I'll show you around a bit there – some great houses along the lake. Then, have you seen the Calatrava addition to the art museum?'

Eve hit 'send' to deliver a text to Shelley, bringing her up to date. 'I've read about it, haven't seen it. I'd love that.'

'Great. Do you like oysters?'

'Love them.'

'Beer or champagne?'

She pretended to look surprised. 'Is that even a choice?'

'Umm . . .' He looked at her speculatively. 'I'm guessing champagne?'

'My mother insisted. If you were going to spend that much on a mollusk, you'd also better splurge on what you drank with it.' The first time Eve had tried an oyster, Jillian had insisted she sip champagne along with it. At the age of seven or eight, Eve had found both flavors repulsive, which had amused her mother and made Eve scowl in embarrassment. 'She also mandated that the only, or at least the best, place for both was in a café or bistro in Paris.'

'Did you ever do that?'

'No, sadly. The only time I ever went to Paris, I was *in utero*, when the family—' Eve broke off, crestfallen.

Her mother had never been pregnant with her.

She'd never been to Paris.

'I lied, apparently.' How much more of her life would she have to rewrite? 'I've never been to Paris.'

'We'll go!'

'What?' She looked at him as if he were crazy, which he obviously was.

'We'll fly over, have oysters with champagne, then fly home.'

'Oh, *infinitely* doable.' Eve laughed, grateful to him for helping her out of her mood slump. 'Have you ever been?'

'I've been everywhere.' He turned right, off the commercial street they'd been traveling, into a residential area. 'It was the only way to spend time with my parents. This is Lake Drive we're on now. Pretty desirable real estate.'

'No kidding.' She assumed the lake was on their left, but while on Washington Island it was bordered by modest homes and a country atmosphere, here it was lined with an impressive array of mansions.

After another mile or so of house-gawking, Clayton got into a left-turn lane and headed for the lake, which revealed itself as they approached, the view here unimpeded by structures.

'We can go to Harbor House after the museum; it's practically next door. A fancy seafood restaurant with a fabulous lake view. They have an oyster bar there. Then we can go somewhere else for dinner. One of Milwaukee's nicer places.' He threw her a mischievous look. 'Unless you prefer bratwurst or burgers?'

'No, thanks.' Eve grinned, so comfortable around Clayton, and so looking forward to the evening. Mike was intimidated by higher-end restaurants, making Eve mildly anxious that they'd be one of those couples who sat opposite each other across a white tablecloth silently eating course after course, avoiding each other's eyes because they had nothing to say. She wasn't worried about that today.

'And then we'll need to find a hotel.'

Eve started, then blushed, totally unnecessarily. Spending the night in a hotel – in separate rooms – was a purely practical step, but the idea still felt intimate. Goodnight, sleep well, then hello, good morning over breakfast, hair still wet from the shower . . .

'Right. One that takes dogs.'

She could handle it. After what she and Clayton had just been through, the bar was pretty high for what constituted an awkward situation.

They followed a long, curving hill down to the lakefront: parks and unexpectedly beautiful sandy beaches that stretched for miles, the city's modest skyline gaining height as they neared.

'I had no idea Milwaukee was such an attractive place.'

Clayton sighed loudly. 'You coastal people have no idea.'

Since he was undoubtedly right, she kept quiet.

A few miles later, they emerged from an overpass to see the museum addition on their left. Eve had first read about it as a teenager in *Architect* magazine – a breathtaking space that evoked a sleek yacht with sails that opened into the sky, a fantastical brise-soleil, or sun-breaker, shading the building beneath, providing a signature monument for Milwaukee's lakefront.

They parked in a garage across the street and entered the majestic, high-ceilinged white marble space, a fantastically colorful and whimsical glass sculpture by the artist Dale Chihuly providing brilliant contrast to the surrounding monochrome. White floors, white ceiling, white walls, relieved only by enormous windows overlooking the endless lake.

Bolstered by a cup of coffee from the downstairs café, they took their time touring the museum, keeping a similar pace in the remarkable range of rooms, both in the new wing and the original older space, three floors with wide staircases and lovely parquet flooring. After the exhausting morning at the Oakeses' house, Eve found the quiet contemplation of art, sculpture, photography and antiques exactly what she needed to recharge.

Human beings could be so draining – but look at what all that complexity could produce!

When they'd seen enough, Eve requested another stroll around the Calatrava addition, where she studied again the unexpected lines and spaces, the ways in which solids played with light and captured its reflections. A remarkable piece. She couldn't help thinking that even her architecturally conservative father would like it.

Back outside, in bright sunlight that had broken through clouds scudding in front of a stiff breeze, Eve felt like a new person.

'Think you'll design one of those someday?' Clayton directed them south, walking at a brisk pace that felt good after so much stop-start meandering.

'Nope. I appreciate its brilliance, I enjoyed being inside and out, but it's not remotely me.'

He pointed ahead to a rectangular white building whose length ran perpendicular to the lake and whose upper floors gave the impression of being suspended over a glass-enclosed first floor. 'Discovery World, a hands-on science museum, lots of fun. Straight ahead, past where we're going, the Summerfest Grounds.'

'Summerfest . . .'

'Ten- or eleven-day music festival. Something like eight hundred bands. It's huge.'

'You're *kidding*.'

'Nope. They also have ethnic festivals on the grounds all summer. German Fest, Polish Fest, Festa Italiana, et cetera.' He turned on to a street running between the museum and Discovery World. 'There are others all around the city. It's a happening place.'

'I had no idea.'

Clayton smirked. 'Of *course* you didn't.'

'Right, right, the sin of being coastal.' Eve paused for one more view of the museum addition, the brise-soleil wings reaching toward the sky, the structure full of motion, seemingly about to take off, or swim, or roll in and crash on to a beach. It was imaginative, daring and thrilling.

Something started nagging at her, disturbing her contentment.

Professional jealousy?

Unlikely. She wasn't out to make breakthrough artistic statements with her work, preferring to look back instead of forward in terms of style, and to make people comfortable rather than challenge them. It was one of the reasons she'd moved from LA to embrace Boston's more traditional architectural bent.

But something about this structure was calling her. Something . . .

'Getting ideas?'

Eve turned abruptly, realizing she'd been standing staring for a while. 'Picturing wings on top of your house.'

'Uh . . .'

One more look, then she snapped a couple of pictures with her phone and turned to follow Clayton past Discovery World toward the lake, lit vivid navy by the descending sun.

When it looked as if they'd have no choice but to dive in, he turned left. 'Harbor House, right here. Should be happy hour specials at this time of day.'

'I like being happy.'

The place was already crowded – Eve would keep her comments about early-eating Midwesterners to herself – but they found places at the oyster bar where they could watch the cooks preparing various shellfish and arranging them on ice-mounded trays.

After a dozen oysters and a glass of excellent bubbly, Eve

could safely say that yes, she was happy. She and Clayton chatted about what they'd seen at the museum, then about possible places for dinner – he couldn't decide whether to choose Braise, Crazy Water or Goodkind, which led to the sure-why-not idea of going to each one in sequence until they were either too tipsy or too full to continue.

'You know.' Clayton looked down at his empty glass, turning it idly. 'I wouldn't have expected to be planning such a fun evening after that day with Abigail's family.'

'Yes.' Eve hunched her shoulders. 'That was hard.'

His dark eyes met hers. 'I want to tell you how grateful I am that you were there.'

She looked away. 'I'm glad I was there too.'

'Wait, really?'

Eve laughed. He was so good at making intense moments easier. 'I needed to yell at poor Leah.'

'You did a great job, apparently.'

Eve took her last sip, a delayed drop that had accumulated in the bottom of the flute. 'I hope it works out for Abigail. For the whole family.'

'I do too. It's hard to change a lifelong conviction. But even harder to end a lifelong relationship because of it. I don't see that happening.' He picked up an oyster fork and dragged it through the cocktail sauce. 'I was trying to say . . . I'm going to make a mess of this.'

Eve frowned, for a second thinking he was talking about the sauce. 'A mess of . . . ?'

'I was thinking . . .'

'You say that a lot.'

'It's what I do.' He swiped more sauce and put the fork between his lips. 'What I escaped to Washington Island to do. Figure out who I was, what I needed, egocentric as that sounds.'

'It sounds healthy. It sounds smart.'

'Oh, and I also wanted to clean out the garage.'

'Just as important.'

'So I thought about my relationships. About Christie, and Felicia, and my high-school girlfriend before that, and my middle-school girlfriend before that. I have always been with someone. Not that I regret any of the relationships; they were all important.' He plunked the fork back on to the tray. 'I believe there are no mistakes in life, only second chances to learn what a screw-up you are.'

The pretty blond waitress interrupted to pick up their oyster platter. 'How are you two doing? Need another glass?'

'Just the check, please.'

'I'll be right back with that.' She hoisted the tray and disappeared behind them.

'So I was saying . . .' Clayton scrunched his brow, looking uncharacteristically nervous. 'What was I saying?'

Eve put on her sweetest expression. 'That you're a screw-up.'

'*Right*, thanks.' He turned in his chair so he was facing her. 'I want to take relationships slowly from now on, understand why I'm attracted, make sure I'm dating someone for the right reasons, not just out of fear of being alone.'

She loved that he could confide in her. She'd never had a male friend with whom she could talk out deeply personal stuff like this. Her friends had been female; the men she got close to invariably became lovers. This was nice.

'You're very smart.'

'I thought so too. It was the perfect plan. Take a year just to be me. Longer if that was how it worked out.' He lifted his eyebrows, looking vulnerable and – she wasn't sure how it happened – absolutely adorable. 'And then I met you.'

Eve stopped moving. That was not what she'd expected. Not

what she wanted. They had been such friends, had functioned so well without the stupid complications of . . .

God, he was hot.

How had she not noticed? She was feeling fizzy, and not just from the champagne.

'Clayton . . .'

'I know, I know, not returned. It's okay. Truly. I'm fine being friends. It's what I want too. I'm sticking to the plan. I just . . . maybe it was today, all those feelings so close to the surface. I got tired holding everything in.' He rubbed the side of his head, which made him look even cuter.

Anxiety blocked Eve's words. She stared at the counter, unable to sort out her thoughts, no idea how best to respond or even what she genuinely felt. Too soon after Mike. Crazy idea. Last thing she needed. How did you say that to someone you'd come to care about so deeply in such a short time?

The waitress brought over the check. Eve bent to fumble for her purse, but Clayton was ready with his credit card.

'Thank you,' she said lamely. 'I'll get the next round.'

'Sure.' He turned back to her, old relaxed grin in place. 'So with all that me-me emotion out of the way, what do you say to some dinner?'

She could accept his change of subject and go with it. Get out of jail free. No obligation to share her own feelings. He was making it easy for her.

'Here's what I want to know.' Eve clutched her purse in her lap. 'For someone who grew up alone so much, you are an effortless communicator. Is that genetic, or did you practice?'

'I was never really alone.' His slow grin made her want to grin back, even though he hadn't said or done anything funny. 'I had an imaginary friend.'

'Really?' She slung the purse over her shoulder. 'I don't think

I've ever known someone who had one of those.'

'No one who'd admit it. Mine was Barney – no, not a purple dinosaur, or even inspired by one. Remarkably, we thought *exactly* alike. My stories and games and obsessions never bored him. We shared so many of the same interests, it was downright eerie.'

'Ooh.' Eve rubbed her arms, still uneasy over having let him down. 'Goose bumps.'

'Here you go.' The waitress handed Clayton the receipt. He signed it with a flourish and laid down the pen.

'Ready to go?'

'Yes. Thank you.' Eve stood, determined not to leave his confession dangling out there. They had the rest of tonight and the trip back tomorrow. On the better-late-than-never theory, she'd take time to work out some appropriate response. She certainly owed it to him. And to herself.

Outside the restaurant, twilight had taken over. They walked in silence until the art museum was in view, its wings folded now, but still reaching up and out, silhouetted against the vast sky.

Eve stopped, staring again, as if the sight of it hypnotized her.

Reaching up. Reaching out.

The idea that had been nagging at her emerged front and center.

She was planning small, private rooms for Shelley. She wanted to tuck away the sunroom for Clayton. Everything about her designs closed in and closed out, while the structure in front of her opened up, invited in.

'Beautiful, isn't it?' Clayton stood close behind her, making Eve want to lean back and feel his chest against her shoulder.

Without her planning them, the words came freely.

'I met Mike three years ago. We didn't fight. We liked many of the same things and were willing to tolerate or try out tastes we didn't share. I felt I'd never fit so well with anyone. Then over the past year we started to drift apart. We found less and less joy in each other and the things we did together. When I broke up with him, it was the first relationship I'd ever ended.

'Before Mike I had two boyfriends I considered serious. The first broke up with me because he was graduating high school. The second dumped me because he was graduating college. In both cases I was sad, but their reasons made sense and I got over it. Within a few days in all three cases I was feeling well enough to function.

'Now I am starting to understand that none of them was ever vital to me. None of them truly touched me or became a part of me. Otherwise, why would I have been able to let go so easily? I thought it was them, that they just weren't right – which they weren't – but now I think I was half the problem.

'I've spent my life blocking people out, trying to stay whole, not to get fractured by feelings or vulnerability. Even the designs I came up with for you and Shelley were inward-looking, hiding.' She took a deep breath and willed herself to have the courage to say what she wanted to say. 'And then I met . . .' a convulsive swallow that nearly made her cough, '. . . you.'

He put his hands on her shoulders, chuckling deeply. 'I thought you were going to throw up saying that.'

She turned and looked up at him. Meeting his eyes was powerful and terrifying, but she made herself do it. 'It was hard.'

He touched her cheek. 'I meant what I said about not wanting to be involved right now.'

'I don't either. I'm still rebounding. It would be stupid for me, too.'

'Okay, then.' His warm, dark gaze was wide open, inviting hers to connect in a way that terrified and enticed her. Big nose? Big teeth? She no longer saw them. He was tall, had fabulous dark curls, was totally masculine and smelled really good.

Clayton held out his arm. 'There's nothing left to do but go to dinner in several restaurants, drive back to Washington Island in the morning, and spend a couple more really fun weeks getting to know each other even better. Then we'll decide whether we say goodbye or see ya later.'

Eve linked her arm with his. Another emotionally vulnerable and difficult moment gotten through, and this time she was not only intact, but refreshed and exhilarated.

'That sounds to me like the perfect plan.'

Chapter 17

April 8, 1985 (Monday)

Rosalind Greer Braddock is beautiful. Not stunning like infant Olivia was. She has fat baby cheeks and a stocky body and hardly any hair. The second she came out of Woman #2, she started screaming like a banshee. Even the nurse looked startled. I hope there's nothing wrong with her. Rosalind, I mean. I don't care if there's something wrong with the nurse!

It was easier taking my baby this time. Woman #2 looked sad and hungry for her, but not like I was taking away part of her soul. I will never forget that look on Woman #1's face, not for as long as I live. It keeps me humble and grateful for their sacrifices.

More humble. I'm too much of a diva to do a lot of that stuff.

I'm coping as best I can with the idea of having two children, afraid of the times when it's too much for me, when I can't get out of bed, or when Olivia's voice seems to drill holes in my skull. Daniel wants to hire a nanny, but I refuse. These girls will never feel that I didn't want them, or that there's something wrong with the way they are. I try to tell them I just get tired sometimes. I try to be patient with Rosalind's crying and Olivia's moods and endless pleas, 'Mommy, watch this! Mommy, watch this!' When does what they want you to watch get interesting? I'm so terribly tired, and it's only just started . . .

Me

Eve let herself and Marx into Shelley's house, checking her watch. Quarter to six. She'd texted Shelley that she'd be bringing dinner. On their way back from Milwaukee, she and Clayton had stopped in Sister Bay, one of the last of the adorable towns on the Door County peninsula – the last one of any size – and picked up groceries at the Piggly Wiggly, including a bottle of nice red wine and a steak, some mushrooms and spinach, and from the fabulous Door County Bakery, just south of the town, a fantastic-smelling loaf of multigrain bread.

In Milwaukee, Clayton had taken her to a round-robin dinner at a series of really good restaurants – yes, Ms Coastal Snob had been pleasantly surprised – and had found rooms for them in the downtown Hotel Metro, which allowed dogs. They'd picked up Marx from the Oakeses' house when they were finished stuffing themselves, and said a big-hugging, tight-throated goodbye to Abigail. Eve couldn't manage a single word on the drive to the hotel for fear of sobbing, and Clayton seemed similarly afflicted.

Spending the night turned out not to be awkward at all, and they'd enjoyed a late breakfast and further exploration of downtown along the Milwaukee River on the city's RiverWalk, chatting as if they'd known each other their whole lives.

Now she was back at Shelley's, feeling changed. Yesterday had been a day of epiphanies, of difficult conversations and grown-up solutions. As much as it had exhausted Eve, it had also inspired her. Having understood the destructive power of holding back, she was determined to share the story of her birth and the nature of her relationship to Shelley, before not doing so became a stumbling block to their friendship.

Remarkably, the idea made her only mildly terrified.

Progress!

'Shelley?'

'Welcome back.' Shelley appeared from the living room in her uniform of jeans and flannel shirt. Marx rushed over to receive his due of adoration. 'Mission accomplished?'

'Yes, thank goodness.' Eve pushed the door closed behind her. 'It may take a while for Abigail's dad to come around, but having met him, I feel pretty confident he will.'

'You did good.' Shelley relieved Eve of one of the shopping bags. 'You didn't have to bring dinner, you know. I always keep plenty of Spam and ketchup for emergency meals.'

Since Shelley was looking right at her, Eve controlled her horror. 'Oh. Well. I hope you don't mind. It seemed like a good night to—'

'Spam!' Shelley slapped her thigh.

Eve groaned. 'I know, I know, I should have seen my face.'

'Priceless.' Shelley examined her, still enjoying leftover mini-cackles. 'You look a lot happier than when you left.'

Eve bypassed her aunt's inspection and hoisted the bag of groceries on to the counter. 'It's a relief having Abigail home where she belongs.'

'Uh-huh.' Shelley sounded skeptical. 'Clayton couldn't make it for dinner tonight?'

'No, he's got work to catch up on.' The minute the words were out, she realized she'd just admitted to inviting him.

So? They were friends. Shelley could think what she wanted.

'Too bad. He's good company.'

'I also have work to do.' Eve kept the steak out to come to room temperature. 'In Milwaukee I got inspired to do a completely new set of drawings for your house. And for Clayton's sunroom.'

'What was wrong with the old ones?'

Eve smiled mysteriously. Since she wasn't yet sure exactly how she'd change the plans, she didn't want to say too much. 'You'll see.'

'Can't wait.' Shelley pulled out the bottle of wine. 'My goodness, this looks lethal.'

'It's a Cabernet. You'll like it.'

She hoped.

Shelley did. So did Eve. In fact, between the two of them, they finished all the steak and almost all the wine, which meant Shelley actually talked during dinner, telling stories of Kate, Kenny and Keith Junior's accomplishments, faults, talents, illnesses, emergency room visits and escapades, adorable and otherwise. Eve ate it up. These were her cousins, after all. She'd like to get to know them someday.

They were washing the dishes when Shelley finally took a breath. Eve jumped in. 'Do you ever get lonely up here?'

'Oh no. Not after what I went through raising those three by myself. I like being alone.' Shelley picked up one of the chunky wine glasses to wash by hand and gave her a sidelong look. 'What about you? You planning on being married someday?'

'I suppose.' Eve stood ready with the dish towel, refusing to blush. 'I don't want kids, though, so I'm in no hurry.'

'That's too bad. Kids are a great way to know yourself, and understand your strengths as well as your—' There was a splintering crash. The glass had slipped through Shelley's fingers. '*Oh*, look what I've done.'

Eve rushed over to help. 'Did you cut yourself?'

'No, no, I'm fine. Serves me right for drinking all that wine. Made me clumsy.' Shelley stared down at the shattered mess in the sink, bits of the gold *G* still shining bravely. She sniffed. Wiped one eye. 'Funny, I *hated* these glasses. Look at me, all sentimental over a gift for a doomed marriage given by people I didn't care for and who never cared for me.'

'They were part of your past.'

'I suppose I got used to them. Maybe even enjoyed them for their hideousness.' She got out the garbage, and she and Eve started gingerly picking up the larger pieces of glass. 'I think sometimes I haven't tried hard enough to forgive my husband or his parents. And I don't mean for the glasses.'

Eve grinned. 'I figured.'

'I know the Bible says to forgive, but I wonder if it's truly possible.'

'I don't know.' Eve winced as a sharp edge nicked her fingertip. 'You can tell yourself to forgive someone, but if your subconscious doesn't go along with it, I don't see how. Not if the reason was true cruelty or betrayal.'

'Have you had to try?'

'Yes.' Eve fought the familiar urge to retreat. 'Not very hard, though, I admit.'

'Hmm.' Shelley picked up a largish piece of glass and tossed it in the garbage. 'Who's yours?'

Eve gave a weary blink. 'My mother.'

'Ah. Parents.' Shelley laughed. 'There are things every kid won't forgive a parent for. My children have a list, I'm sure.'

Eve wasn't going to clarify. Hers wasn't an ordinary you-wouldn't-let-me or you-always-made-me complaint.

They finished cleaning up the glass in silence. Shelley wiped a wad of paper towels around the sink to remove any remaining fragments, while Eve surreptitiously pressed bits of paper napkin to her bleeding fingertip.

When the sink was clean, Shelley picked up the second glass

and looked at it, running her thumb over the gold, then unceremoniously dumped it in the trash. 'Done. Let's go out and sit for a bit.'

'Sure.' Eve poured two glasses of water to counter the wine and took them out to the porch, where Shelley had started the heat since the night had turned chilly. Marx followed, wagging his tail, glad to be back. Clearly he'd grown fond of Shelley.

'Nice night.'

'Yes.' Eve sat down in the wicker love seat, Marx on the floor next to her. She put a hand on the dog's soft back, needing the comfort and support for what she'd promised herself to do tonight. 'Shelley.'

Shelley looked over, obviously alerted by her tone that something out of the ordinary was coming. 'Yes?'

'I don't know if you knew, but I was adopted.'

Shelley blinked. 'Adopted? But . . . I remember reading that your mother was pregnant. Don't I? Or was that with one of your sisters?'

'My father is my biological father. But my mother . . . couldn't have children. So she used . . . she found women. I mean, she and my father hired women to carry Dad's babies, while Jillian pretended to be pregnant. They never told anyone.'

'Good heavens.' Shelley's jaw was practically on her chest. 'That is . . . I don't *know* what that is.'

'It's a lot of things. Cowardly. Selfish. Slightly mental.'

'It . . . Well . . .' She seemed not to know where to look. 'Unusual, certainly.'

'I still can't believe they carried it off. My mother was obsessed with no one finding out she was infertile.'

'That's too bad.' Shelley shook her head, lips pressed in a line. 'I guess in those days women were more sensitive to that stuff. I haven't ever thought about it. I was pregnant before I knew it. Most of us take having kids for granted.'

'Right.' Eve drew up her shoulders, then let them drop, relaxing her hand when she realized she was gripping Marx's fur as if she might float away without him as anchor. 'I'm telling you this because . . . when my mother and father decided to have a third child and went looking for another surrogate, they chose your sister. They chose Helen.'

Shelley's eyes went totally round. 'That's not possible.'

'No?' Eve waited, understanding that it would take a while for the facts to sink in, hoping Shelley would react well.

'Helen was . . . I saw her fairly regularly. She couldn't have . . .' Shelley's brow furrowed. 'How could she have met Jillian Croft? Why would they choose someone like . . . Are you *sure*?'

Eve nodded solemnly. 'I'm sure. You said I look like her, remember?'

'Good God.' Shelley stared at her as if she were an alien. 'Good God.'

'I don't know the details. We vacationed in Maine every summer. They must have come across her somehow. Did she ever go to Stirling? Or I'm sure my parents were in Machias. They loved to eat at Helen's Restaurant.'

'Her namesake.' Shelley was shaking her head, gripping her wrist as if she were afraid her hand would fall off. 'Helen was a waitress there.'

'Maybe that's where they found her.'

Shelley was silent for a bit, clearly lost in thought. 'She was so beautiful. I suppose they couldn't resist her any more than anyone else could. She was probably clean then, too. I'm sure they'd have checked. Though she could have sold anyone any story to get what she wanted.'

Eve stared out into the blackness of the lake, wondering if in different circumstances Helen could also have been an actress instead of a thief and a con artist.

Shelley gasped suddenly and turned to her with a wide grin. 'But this means . . . you're my *niece*.'

'Yes.'

'My goodness.' Her eyes filled with tears, which made Eve's eyes do the same, then the two of them were sitting there laughing as the tears fell.

Eve sniffed. 'Don't let Marx know you're crying . . .'

'Right.' Shelley dabbed at her eyes. 'I can't believe it. You're my sister's child.'

'I didn't find out until last week.'

'*What?* But you came up here to . . . I thought . . .' Shelley's face cleared. '*Lauren*. She sent you to me.'

'Yes.'

Shelley folded her arms across her chest. 'She should have *told* me. Told *us*. That's years and years we could have had.'

'Dad swore her to secrecy. I'm guessing she sent me here hoping we'd figure it out without her having to break her promise.'

'Ah.' Shelley shook her head slowly. 'She always was an operator.'

Eve's eyebrows went up. That didn't surprise her. What had struck her was that she'd had three mothers, Helen, Jillian and Lauren, and *all* of them could have earned that description. 'You have stories?'

'Oh yes. We were inseparable.' Shelley absently rubbed her elbow. 'I remember once her brother had been drinking and wanted the car. Instead of confronting him, risking a scene, Lauren slipped outside and let the air out of his tires. Then she snuck over to my house to spend the night so he wouldn't take it out on her while he was drunk.'

Eve was ashamed to realize that she knew next to nothing about Lauren as a kid; had always taken her presence for granted and never pushed through Dad's domination to ask more than superficial questions about her life.

'Another time a girl had been bullying me, calling me a dyke and so on. One day in assembly, in front of the whole school, this girl was demonstrating Irish dancing. In the middle of all that hopping and stomping, her costume started falling off. She had to leave the stage half naked. I happen to know that Lauren was wicked good with a needle.' Shelley chuckled, wiping her eyes. 'Never figured out how she managed it, but I'm sure it was her. I miss her. Sneaky devil.'

'Why didn't you ever come visit us?' Eve couldn't remember seeing Shelley around.

'I can't stand your father.' The words burst out of her, and she caught herself. 'No offense.'

'He can be tough to love.'

'And she'd never leave him to come see me.' Shelley shrugged, but her voice betrayed her pain. 'I don't have much use for women whose only mission in life is catering to their husbands.'

'No.' A flash of intuition made Eve wonder if Shelley had been hopelessly in love with Lauren and never quite got over it. The story made her pray harder that Abigail would make her way safely through the world and find a wonderful woman to share the journey with her.

'So. Enough about that.' Shelley rose from her chair. 'I'll get you a picture of Helen.'

She stepped into the house, Marx following her with his eyes, leaving Eve in a state of breathless anticipation. She wasn't sure she was ready to meet her mother – in the only way she could. But she had sworn not to avoid difficult moments anymore. So she'd look at the picture of her dead mother and face whatever emotions came along with it.

'This is a good one.' Shelley stepped back on to the porch holding a plastic-framed photo in one hand, a large brown album tucked under her arm. For all Shelley's protestations of not being able to forgive her sister, she'd come back to the porch quickly, which meant the picture and album weren't buried in a box, but easily accessible.

Helen was indeed beautiful. Blond, with slightly wavier hair than Eve's dead-straight strands. Her eyes were similar in shape, as were the height and prominence of her cheekbones. But her mouth was a perfect Cupid's bow, while Eve had her father's wider lips, the bottom slightly more prominent. They shared an oval face shape and a delicate chin.

Hi, Mom.

'Pretty, isn't she?' Shelley spoke with a combination of exasperation and pride. 'I told you.'

'Yes.' Eve couldn't take her eyes off the photo, studying every millimeter as if she could pull out some reality of the woman from what was nothing more than a chemical reaction captured on paper.

'This was taken before she got in too deep. In her early twenties. She'd been in a little trouble with alcohol and pot, but got clean. Clean enough to finish a college degree, though she never did much with it. Probably when . . . Well, when were you born?'

'Nineteen-ninety.'

'Helen would have been . . . twenty-four. So yes, this was taken a year before that, probably not long before she got pregnant with you. One of her boyfriends took it, one of the better boyfriends, who didn't get her in trouble. He imagined himself a photographer. I think he did end up opening a studio in Bangor.' Shelley was frowning, gazing off into the distance. 'What month were you born?'

'May. The eleventh.'

'I remember her then. I went to see her not long afterward. She'd left Machias several months earlier, and had just come back. She'd told us she'd been living with a man, but she must have been hiding her pregnancy. She claimed the guy kicked her out.' Her voice rose, her words accelerating. 'My God, this all makes sense now. She was staying in some fancy cabin on the coast in Machiasport – I remember wondering how she could afford it.'

'My dad.'

'Yes. Yes, I'm remembering this now.' Shelley retook her chair, sitting heavily as if the weight of the memories was too much. 'She'd gained weight and was terribly depressed. She kept crying, saying what I thought were the strangest things. "It was such a loss." "I hadn't expected to feel so empty." "I hadn't expected to love so much."'

Eve didn't move, afraid to break the spell Shelley seemed to be under, in case she stopped talking.

Her mother had loved her. Giving up her baby had been devastating. Not a cold business deal. Not a way to earn money for drugs. *I hadn't expected to love so much.*

'I thought she was talking about a man. I was disgusted and snapped at her to get over it. She looked at me as if I'd . . .' Shelley's eyes refilled with tears, 'as if I'd made light of her losing a child.'

'No, no, don't blame yourself for that.' Eve could only come up with a whisper, hating that her parents had created so much pain for so many people. 'You couldn't have known.'

'No. I suppose not. But it haunts me.' She raised her glasses to wipe her eyes and her plump cheeks. 'Soon after that, she started drinking again. Then drugs. Bad ones, then worse. I was so angry at her. She tried half-heartedly to break free once or twice, but was never clean or healthy again.'

'I'm so sorry.'

'Well.' Shelley replaced her glasses and folded her hands tightly in her lap. 'Maybe I understand a little better now.'

Eve bowed her head, furious with her mother and father for their selfish meddling, a game only the highly privileged could play. Helen would have understood from the beginning what was required, and bargained willingly with the devil duo, but she couldn't have foreseen the emotional costs.

'I made that after Helen died.' Shelley pointed to the photo album she'd brought out with the framed portrait. 'Back when I was so furious with her, I was almost tempted to throw it away, but I figured one day I'd regret it. If you'd like to look, you're welcome to. I'll just warn you, it's not all pretty.'

'Thank you.' Eve picked up the album and started leafing through it, studying some pictures more closely than others, trying to get a sense of Helen Phillips. From the very earliest photos she was strikingly lovely, her toothless grinning baby shots eerily similar to those Eve had seen of herself. Then a grubby, beaming toddler holding up a tiny fish she must have helped catch. A little girl in her Sunday best, pink bow tied in her blond curls that matched one on her pink gingham dress. Next to her an older girl, unsmiling in matching blue gingham, the shape of her dark head clearly outlined by a blunt, undecorated pixie cut.

'This is you.' Eve pointed to the picture.

'That's me.' Shelley snorted. 'Tomboy to her angel.'

'You're both adorable.'

Shelley rolled her eyes. 'Mother made those dresses. Every year we got new matching outfits for church, hers always pink, mine always blue. I loathed every one of them. I let my own kids wear whatever they wanted, within reason.'

Eve continued turning pages, watching her birth mother grow from a sweet little girl into a stunning young woman. Her poses became more calculated, her smiles less genuine. Then the pictures became fewer, as the addiction took hold and her health deteriorated. She lost weight and the shine in her eyes. Her skin became blotchy, and in the last few photographs, taken at Christmas, there were lesions on her forehead and she was missing some teeth.

Eve closed the album. 'Thank you for showing me this. It's very . . . honest.'

'I don't sugarcoat who she was. Not even for you.'

'There's no need.'

Shelley stood suddenly. 'Would you like to go visit her?'

That didn't compute at all. 'What?'

'Would you like to visit your mother? Her ashes are buried on the property.'

Eve wasn't sure how many more shocks her body could take before it just imploded like a demolished building. 'Helen is buried *here*?'

'She lived and died in this house. Moved here in 1995 and died in 2002.'

Eve put a shaky hand to her forehead. 'You know . . . I thought I was coming up here to design a house.'

Shelley threw back her head and let out a laugh that startled Marx and made Eve giggle when she wouldn't have thought laughter possible.

'And look what you got. Poor thing. Come on. We'll go through the kitchen and get a flashlight. I'll introduce you to your mom.'

Helen's grave wasn't far from the site on which Shelley's

house would eventually stand, in front of a beautiful clump of birches whose pure white trunks reflected the beam of the flashlight. A plaque sat at the base of the trees, surrounded by greening grass that had been obviously well cared for. Breezes blew, and the lake made faint lapping noises. It was an idyllic spot.

Eve approached the grave, close enough to read the plaque, a pretty oval with a wandering leafy vine chiseled around its edges. The words were simple and poignant: *We are all like the bright moon, we still have our darker side.*

'That's . . .' she swallowed hard, 'a lovely quote.'

'Khalil Gibran, the Lebanese philosopher.'

Eve bent to touch the plaque. 'How did she die?'

'Brain aneurysm when she was thirty-six. Her body couldn't take the abuse anymore. She wasn't found for a week.'

Eve sighed and pulled back her hair, holding it in a ponytail before letting it go. The money Daniel had paid for Helen's silence had enabled her self-destruction. A sad life.

'You said she went to college. What was her major?'

'Music, over my mother's objections. But she got a full ride to the University of Maine at Orono, so Mom had no leverage to stop her. She probably also knew there was no point keeping Helen from something she wanted.'

Music. Eve knew immediately. 'She played piano.'

'Yes. She bought that one second-hand from an estate sale. She wrote and told me about it. One of the few emails I got from her after she moved here. She was talented, but nothing came of it. She liked to draw, too, mostly abstract patterns. I probably have some of those in the attic if you'd like to see.'

'I'd love to.' Eve wrapped her arms around herself. Did her drawing talent come from her mother? She shared Daniel's love of form and logic, of practicality over sentiment. She'd never found much of anything to connect her to Jillian.

No wonder.

'We were talking about forgiveness earlier.' Shelley bent down and picked off a leaf that had blown on to the plaque. 'After Helen died, I read everything I could find about addiction. I suspect she was mistreated by men, so I read about abuse, trauma and depression. Understanding those pieces of her helped. You've given me an even clearer picture of her, which I imagine will help too. I don't know that I can ever forgive her for stealing from me, or for some of the hurtful things she said. But most of the rest I was able to put to bed.'

Eve thought of Leah, coming to terms with her daughter's sexual orientation after talking to the man in the library, gaining some insight into what Abigail might be feeling. 'I think I see what you mean.'

'How well do you understand your mother? Jillian, I mean?'

The question resonated. In a moment of remarkable clarity, Eve realized how, in a strange reversal, she had failed Jillian. And how easy it would be to fix her mistake.

'Not at all.' She smiled at her aunt; their eyes held for a long, affectionate moment. 'But I think it's time I changed that.'

Chapter 18

June 3, 1989 (Saturday)

Life is so lovely! I have a wonderful husband, a still-fabulous career, and a perfect house. I'm clean, going to AA, taking my meds, all the good things wrapped up in one. Best of all, I have two charming, smart girls everyone thinks came out of my body and from my DNA.

Olivia takes after me in all things. She is strong, passionate, crafty and stunning. She is my heart. Rosalind is energetic and sweet and determined. I love her as only a mother can love a child who is a complete mystery to her.

I want another. Just one more. I want to feel that deep animal tenderness for a tiny, tiny new creature, the feeling so strong you want to take her into your body because there is no way to keep her close enough. Oh, how I fell in love with my girls on sight.

One more, just one more! Daniel says no, but I know I can change his mind.

If it's a boy this time, I'll call him Clark Gregory after Gable and Peck. If it's another girl, I'll name her Eve Grace after Arden and Kelly.

We'll have to find another mother.

This is the part I hate.

* * *

The night after her graveside talk with Shelley, Eve stayed up for hours reading and rereading the rest of her mother's diary. It was painful at times, heartbreaking, infuriating, shocking to discover that Aunt Christina could be Olivia's birth mom, though Olivia might never want to know or care to investigate. It was also honest, hilarious and, ultimately, devastating.

But it was her mother, in a way Eve would never have been able to know her otherwise. There was a good reason kids weren't allowed into their parents' most intimate thoughts, and several times Eve felt she was trespassing unforgivably. And yet, as Shelley had predicted, seeing the world, however incompletely, through her mother's eyes – as much as she didn't agree with the view – had helped her at least to begin to bridge the awful divide. Jillian Croft had never been the kind of woman Eve admired or wanted to emulate, and she still wasn't. But coupled with the snippets Rosalind had told her about Jillian's life in Maine, and the emotional fallout of her physical condition, this was a way to graze the surface of understanding.

The next morning, Eve had woken strangely refreshed after not sleeping much, and had jumped out of bed for a morning run. Barring any other major life-altering discoveries, she felt optimistic that she'd now be able to work solidly on the two projects that had brought her here.

Frankly, she couldn't wait. Goodbye to wrenching emotions, hello to the inanimate beauty of space and line and form. Her architectural and personal epiphany at the Milwaukee Art Museum had sent her brain in entirely new directions, and she was anxious to get started.

Ideas were still murky, but she envisioned a more open concept for Shelley's house: light, air, and room to move, a place of color – lots of color! – and motion. Clayton's design still presented problems, but at least Eve knew that hiding the room under the existing deck wasn't going to cut it.

For the next three weeks, when she wasn't having a meal with Clayton or Shelley, or both, or texting with Abigail, who had so far not killed either parent – always a good sign – she ate, breathed and slept the two designs, interrupted in the first week only by necessary and extremely painful communications with Mike over his move out of her house: what he was taking, what he wasn't, all the horrible logistics of an unraveling relationship. With her new courage, Eve made it through his few attempts to guilt her over his temporary homelessness. Happily, a friend from his group therapy agreed to take him in until he found a place, sparing Eve the temptation to offer him money for an Airbnb.

However, the reminders of life in Boston made her even more determined to finish and be on her way back. She'd miss Shelley and Clayton, but would certainly be back to visit when construction started. After quitting her job and the breakup with Mike, she needed to feel solidly planted in a new life before she could think about furthering the relationships she'd started here.

Luckily, unlike her first design attempts, which had only made her more and more insecure and confused, this time Eve gradually became more and more certain, not only that the plans would work for both Shelley and Clayton, but that she was totally up to the job.

The more convinced she became, the more passionate and unstoppable she was, getting up early, working late. Ideas didn't so much as occur to her as demand her attention, sometimes in the middle of the night, when she'd roll over, blinking to focus, grab her phone and record the idea – or at least a fragment to remind her – speaking in a thick, groggy voice that would make her laugh when she listened to it the next day. When she got stuck on one project, she'd turn to the other, though Shelley's house started consuming more and more of her attention.

Two weeks into her marathon, she finished the plans and presented them to her aunt on the chosen site. The weather was warm, in the low sixties, spring clearly arriving, crocuses and daffodils blooming or on their way, tree branches showing a mist of reddish-green buds. Apart from her morning jogs and a few brainstorming sessions on the porch, Eve had been hermited in the office. Getting out felt like she was emerging from winter as well.

With Shelley looking on, Eve unrolled the plans on a flat rock and described how she'd altered the space. The exterior was still traditional, designed much like the larger house: white with black shutters, and dormers on the lake side. Inside, most of the lower floor stretched all the way to a vaulted ceiling, with open kitchen and dining areas flowing into a living space. Large windows looked through a screened-in deck to the lake beyond. Next to a natural stone hearth and fireplace, a spiral iron staircase led upstairs to a bedroom suite, underneath which was first-floor storage space and a bathroom.

Shelley looked at the drawings carefully, listening to Eve's description, then studied them on her own. Finally, when Eve was holding back shrieks of impatience, she inhaled deeply and let out a long sigh.

Was that good?

'Well.' She looked up and met Eve's eyes, her own crinkling into pleasure. 'I love it.'

'Really?' Eve let out a goofy rush of relief. 'Hurray!'

'I loved the other one too. It was like this.' Shelley hugged her arms around herself, expression wary. 'Cozy and small. It was exactly what I thought I wanted. But this one . . .' She spread her arms and lifted her face to the sky, beaming.

'That's it.' Eve nodded way too many times and had to

make herself stop. 'I'm so glad you like it.'

'I love it.' She surprised Eve by wrapping her arms around her. 'Thank you, Eve dear. For everything. I'm going to miss you when you go.'

Eve closed her eyes and returned her aunt's hug. 'I'll miss you too. But I'll be back. I'm family now. And I still have another week here.'

'I know. Just dreading the inevitable.' Shelley released her. 'You have to meet my kids. I told them, and they're happy to know about you. Kate is coming in June. Then they'll all be here in August with their families.'

Eve kept smiling, pushing away instinctive dread at the idea of this quiet refuge thronged with three families of strangers. Maybe Clayton would let her stay with him. 'I'd love to come up when they're here, if I can.'

'Good.' Shelley laughed down at Marx, who was nudging her for attention. 'Yes, you can come too. We'll introduce you to Princess Leia, my daughter's cat. Throw you together in a room and see who comes out alive.'

'Oh, great idea.' Eve rolled her eyes, getting used to her aunt's dry sense of humor. 'Another pelt for his collection.'

'He'll be so proud.' Shelley held out her elbow. 'This calls for a celebration. Let's go inside and have a glass of something. What do you think?'

Eve grinned and linked arms. 'I think that sounds like a great idea.'

It *was* a good idea, as was going out to dinner at KK Fiske Restaurant, where they ate freshly caught lawyers and traded childhood stories, then laughed over the contrast with that first silent dinner the night Eve arrived. She'd found an anchor, friend and parent in Shelley – plus cousins to spruce up her spindly family tree.

She'd also rediscovered the joy of pouring herself into a project and having her work and ideas validated. Not that every job would be a slam dunk. She still had to see what Clayton thought. But for now, she was feeling like a proper architect, and it felt really good.

Over the next week, she resumed her feverish pace, working obsessively on drawings for Clayton's sunroom, hitting snags here and there, but ultimately convinced that the new concept was sound and that she would make it work. As April drew toward its close, grass green, flowers blooming and birds returned from their migration, as much as she enjoyed Shelley and Clayton's company, Eve found herself increasingly anxious to get back home to Swampscott.

Late on the morning of Tuesday the twenty-eighth, she took a final look at the design for the sunroom and experienced the magical it's-there moment. No more outlets that needed taking out and putting back in, figuratively speaking. She hit print and called Clayton.

'Eve!' His voice was so warm, she felt herself melting just a little. Their time together – all-too-quick lunches, drinks and the occasional dinner – had been fabulous. She was having to work harder and harder not to fall head over heels. What was the point? Their lives were in separate cities and would be for the foreseeable future.

'I'm finished. You want to see?'

'Of course I want to see. What are you, crazy?'

'Not quite yet.' God, it was good to hear his voice. They'd had lunch the previous weekend, but he was on crunch time revising an employee manual and had been similarly holed up. 'I'll bring them right over.'

'No. Wait. Not now.'

'No?' She couldn't help being disappointed.

'Tonight. Six o'clock. For dinner.'

'Oh.' She broke into a wide grin, no longer disappointed. 'I'll check with Shelley, but that sounds delightful. What can I bring?'

'Drawings. And yourself.'

'I won't forget either one. See you later.'

'Wait.'

She put the phone back to her ear. 'Yes?'

'I lost track. Does this mean you'll be leaving soon?' His voice was so wistful, her happy bubble burst.

'Yes. I need to get back to my life.'

Or what was left of it. She'd need to rebuild, get a job, forge a social life both by making the effort to meet new people and by continuing whatever friendships survived the breakup with Mike. Maybe she'd finally get a subscription to the Symphony so she'd go more often. Try new restaurants. Get herself into therapy. Eventually, date . . .

Ugh.

Clayton sighed. 'I'll need to do the same.'

Eve mixed up his words with her thoughts and for a strange, stomach-roiling second thought he was saying he needed to date, too. Her stomach didn't get any calmer when she realized that though Shelley would always be here when she visited, this was only a sometimes place for Clayton. It would be hit-or-miss seeing him again unless they made specific arrangements, which they weren't quite ready to do.

She forced her voice to stay cheerful. 'We can only hide here for so long. Too bad.'

He snorted. 'I'm the one hiding. You've been assaulted by reality on every side.'

'Not for the last few weeks.' She emerged from the office into Shelley's living room, no longer able to stand the small space. 'I can't wait to show you what I've done. It's weird, but I think you'll like it.'

'I bet I will. See you at six.'

She ended the call feeling as mournful as she'd been feeling giddy before. She'd miss him horribly, no point pretending otherwise.

If only they lived closer to each other.

By six o'clock, Eve had packed everything of hers and Marx's and loaded the car in a sprinkling rain that turned from a nuisance to a downpour just as she finished. She put the folded drawings into a manila envelope protected by a couple of plastic bags, snuck the package under her raincoat and made it to the car, dripping but dry inside.

At Clayton's house, she repeated the dash to his door, which he opened so quickly she wondered if he'd been standing behind it waiting for her.

'Hi there.' His eyes went past her and his welcome grin faded. 'Your car's full.'

'Yes. It was horrible packing in the rain, but I need to get an early start tomorrow.'

'*Tomorrow?* That's abrupt.'

'Not really.' His accusation surprised her. 'I finished the work. And I told you on the phone that I was leaving.'

'You said "soon".' He looked more upset than . . . well, than she wanted him to.

'But . . . I mean . . . I'll be back to see the . . . I guess it didn't seem . . .' She sighed and waved her dripping arm. There was no way out of this conversation except to dig herself deeper into it. 'I'm sorry. I should have said something sooner. I wasn't thinking.'

He pushed a hand through his hair. His eyes looked slightly puffy, as if he'd been staring at a screen all day. Exactly the way hers looked. 'We've both been busy. It's just that . . . well, you and I are in a strange place – not involved, but not exactly uninvolved either. Would that be a fair description?'

Why couldn't she just say something that obvious that easily? 'Friends without benefits.'

'That's it.' He looked suddenly taken aback. 'Would you like to stand out there in your miserable wet coat while we have a long discussion about this?'

'Not super much.'

'Sorry. I thought I'd have you here longer, that's all. Come on in.' He moved aside to let her into the house. 'Let me see what you came up with. I wish we could sit outside, but . . .'

They convened in the living room, where at least the sunroom site would be visible. Eve rolled out the drawings on the antique-looking coffee table, thinking as she always did how the decor didn't fit him.

'Here.' She pointed to the new room. 'Instead of hiding it under the deck, I'm proposing that we enclose the entire existing deck and build another deck beyond it. It's a little strange, I know, and when I first came up with it, I was actually scared. But the more I thought, the more I decided it would end up being a very livable and attractive space.

'For one thing, you'd be able to enter the room from anywhere along the back of the house. Living room, master bedroom, and kitchen. Get up in the morning, go outside to watch the water. Bring a book out from the living room. Take breakfast out through the kitchen. It sort of unifies the back of the house, one big room that everyone has access to.'

She stopped talking. Usually she felt the less said the better. Let the drawing speak for itself and let the clients' imagination do the work of figuring out how the proposed space would suit their lives.

Today, she was nervous. She wanted Clayton to like this. More than that, she wanted him to respect her talent and choices.

'Hmm.' He looked from the drawing to the existing deck, seen through the raindrops trickling down the windows. 'That is . . . interesting.'

'Yes?' Her heart sank. Was it wrong both to love and admire his honesty and right now want him to lie through his teeth?

He looked down at the drawing again. Back outside.

Eve watched the uneven planes of his face and her chest tightened with how much he'd come to mean to her. They hadn't known each other long, but had leaned on each other through some pretty extraordinary circumstances.

'Actually . . .' he looked up abruptly and caught her staring, which probably would have mortified her a couple of weeks ago, 'I think it might be genius.'

'Ah.' Eve tried to hide her delight, then couldn't figure out why she'd do that and broke into a huge grin, clapping her hands together. 'Well, of *course* it's genius.'

'I mean seriously.' He stared down at the lines she'd worked so hard to make form a coherent and practical aesthetic. 'It would completely change the character of the house.'

'And that's a good thing, right?'

'That's an incredibly good thing.' He looked around as if he was seeing the place for the first time. 'Here I've been cleaning up outside, and it's inside that really needs it. The house has always felt . . . I don't know the word.'

Stuffy? Unwelcoming? Stilted? 'Like it needs to relax a little?'

'Yes.' His gaze came back to her. 'It needs to relax. Open up. Feel communal. Did I mention that you're brilliant?'

'I'm so pleased you like it.'

He pored over the drawing for another minute or two, then tapped it sharply. 'Sold. Let me look some more later on, and we can talk it over. I don't want to waste time with you on your last . . .' He frowned. 'Shouldn't you be with your aunt?'

Eve shook her head. 'Shelley practically shoved me over here. I think she's matchmaking.'

'Aww. That's nice. I wish I knew someone to fix *her* up with.' He moved toward the kitchen, beckoning. 'Can I offer you a glass of wine from another excellent bottle I stole from my dad?'

'You may.' Eve followed him and leaned against the counter, watching him uncork the wine. The kitchen was warm and smelled of rosemary and sausage. Along with the rain pelting the roof and windows, it made the severe space seem almost cozy.

'I'm going to miss you.' The words came out unguarded, brave as hell, straight from her heart.

'Same here.' He met her eyes briefly, then resumed pouring. 'I think we're going to have to see each other again somehow.'

'That does not sound like a terrible idea.'

'Then here's to two great ideas.' He handed her a glass and picked up his own. 'That one and the new sunroom design.'

'Cheers.' Eve lifted her wine and sipped. A smooth red with depth and character. She was going to have to stop her habit of grabbing the same old bottles from the same old supermarket. 'Oh yum. What would we be drinking if you hated the design?'

'Dirty water.' He opened a cabinet and got out a tin of cashews. 'Want to go informal and just camp out here at the table?'

'Love to. Can I help make dinner?'

'All I have to do is boil water for the pasta. And that won't take long because I had it boiling before you came.' He turned the water on under a pot on the stove. 'Sauce is already made.'

She sat at the little table, remembering how nervous she'd been when they'd eaten Somali chicken soup in the same chairs what seemed like months ago. 'How did you have time?'

'To boil water?' He sat opposite her.

'Ha . . . ha . . .'

'The sauce was frozen.' Clayton grabbed a few cashews, tossed one up and caught it in his mouth. 'I made it last month.'

'Aren't you the clever one.' She threw a nut in the air and opened her mouth. It bounced off her front tooth. '*Ow!*'

'So I was thinking . . .'

She searched for the cashew on the floor and pounced on it. 'Again?'

'Can't help it.' He tossed and caught another nut. 'Chicago has been my home for a really long time. I told myself I belonged there, that someone without a real family should always belong somewhere. I went to college in-state. I've turned down job offers in other cities. New York, Boston, Seattle – which felt right at the time.'

'And now?' She tossed up a second cashew. '*Ow!*'

'Now I think I've been hiding down there, same as I've been hiding up here. A lot has changed over the past month. Meeting Abigail, having to face her and myself, made me realize what I want more clearly.' He looked down at the table. 'And getting to know you.'

Eve had no idea what she was afraid of, but her entire being went on red alert. She put down the cashews and picked up her wine.

'And . . . so . . . what is it that you . . . want?' Immediately she buried her nose in her glass so she wouldn't have to react until she processed his answer.

'Eve . . .' His eyes turned melting and sincere. A little too melting. 'I want to move in with you in *Swamp*scott, so we can have enough children to fill both this house and Shelley's.'

Eve's gasp drew in enough alcohol to throw her into a movie-worthy coughing fit. When she could speak again, she pointed accusingly at his mad grin. 'That was horrible.'

'I know.' He got up and added salt and a couple of fistfuls of whole wheat spaghetti to the steaming pot. 'But all I was doing was starting to talk about moving out of Chicago, and you looked like I was about to leap over the table and strangle you.'

'Okay, okay, so I have issues.' Eve thumped her chest and managed a normal breath, embarrassed to have been caught being so paranoid. 'I'm working on it. Where will you move to?'

'I hadn't gotten that far.' He set a timer. 'My job is sort of portable, but I'm thinking I might want to change that too.'

'And do what?'

He planted his hands on his hips, the picture of comic outrage. 'Jeez, all you do is hound me.'

Eve put her hand over her mouth until she had safely swallowed her wine. 'Why haven't you figured this all out?'

'Yeah, not sure of the timeline yet. I might sell my apartment and rent somewhere for a while. Longer term, a lot depends on where Abigail goes to college, where she settles.' He stretched, working his shoulders, which must be as stiff as hers from sitting all day. 'It is strange suddenly having to include a daughter in my plans.'

'What about marriage?'

'Are you proposing?' Her cashew bounced off his chest. Incredibly, he caught it. 'Marriage would be another thing to consider. I don't seem to be in any hurry about that either.'

Eve raised her glass. 'Here's to your new life.'

'Thanks.' Clayton came back to the table to retrieve his wine. 'How do you think you'll do with *your* new life? New job? New boyfriend?'

'*Jeez, all you do is hound me.*'

She loved his laugh when he really let it loose. 'Tell you what, Eve. When I decide something about my life, I'll let you know. When you do, you can do the same.'

'Agreed.'

'In the meantime, we stay in touch, yes?' He lifted his eyebrows, and for once, under his cool, she sensed tension.

'Yes.' She hoped that wasn't a mistake, hanging on to a long-distance friendship that might not have the chance to turn into more. But she couldn't imagine cutting him entirely out of her life.

'All right.' He got up to set the table. 'Enough terrifying you.'

'You're not . . .' Eve rolled her eyes and got up to help. He could tell. Why bother denying it?

Dinner was delicious. Eve usually found whole wheat pasta was better used as packing material, but Clayton's sauce was composed of Italian sausage, tomatoes and rosemary, whose strong flavors subdued it perfectly. With the pasta, a simple tossed salad, and for dessert, a genuine Door County cherry pie he'd bought on a mainland trip and thawed for the occasion.

They talked while they ate, they talked while they did the dishes, and while they sat in the living room sipping tiny amounts of brandy in tiny snifters. Eve had reached the point where she realized she could happily keep talking to Clayton for hours and hours, maybe days or years, and there would never be a time when she would say, 'Okay, finished, nothing more to say.'

So she might as well leave now, even though it made her feel shaky and sad even to contemplate it.

'I should go.' She put her snifter on the coffee table and managed to get up from the couch. 'I want to say goodbye to Shelley tonight in case she'd like to sleep in.'

'Sure.' He stood, looking uncharacteristically lost.

'Thank you for having me to dinner.' Eve's throat closed in spite of her effort to sound cheerful. She gestured to the drawings. 'I'll leave those with you. Let me know about any changes or questions.'

'Okay.' He walked with her to his front door, their steps slowing the closer they got. 'Any chance you'll be coming back up later in the summer to see some of the construction? Maybe when Abigail's around?'

'I'd like that. I already told Shelley I'd try to come back in August when her kids are here.' She opened the door to find it had stopped raining. Damp air moved gently through the trees, causing drops to fall with a pleasant plopping sound. 'And if you're ever in Boston . . .'

'Sure.' He opened his arms and she went into them, not entirely surprised to feel sadness welling in her chest, cramping her throat. As the cliché went, he'd been her harbor in all the crazy storms of the past weeks. 'Let me know you got back home okay.'

'I will.' She took a small step back, looking up at him, wanting to find the perfect thing to say that would let him know how much his friendship had meant to her.

He leaned down so quickly she had no time to react. The kiss was deep and lingering, and shot her through with an undeniably sexual thrill.

Aw, hell.

He pulled back, looking as sad and hopeless as she felt. 'Drive safely.'

'Thank you.' Eve lifted her hand in an inane wave. 'For everything.'

She managed to make it to her car before the tears started, and drove away, toward her new life, feeling as if she'd just left part of herself behind.

Chapter 19

August 3, 1989 (Thursday)

Daniel found Woman #3 here in Maine. She was our waitress when we went to dinner at Helen's in Machias. Funny how that kind of thing happens just like that. She is very, very beautiful, but there's something terribly empty and sad in her eyes. Daniel liked her and trusted her, but I'm worried. This one could be trouble. We had her sign the contract, but agreed to wait a bit until we start trying. Daniel is worried about me drinking again. I can handle it this time. I'm sure. I haven't had more than two or three in weeks.

I had to cut short our time in Maine, which I hate. I'm filming a western with Burt Reynolds! I'm totally in love with him, in a platonic way of course, since Daniel is my whole heart. I have had to learn how to ride a horse. There is absolutely nothing natural about all the horrific bouncing up and down. How I'll be able to keep a smile on my face and manage to speak lines I have no idea. My inner thighs are screaming in pain, I've got bruises everywhere – just the sight of the animal makes my body hurt. But I will keep at it. This is for my art. I'll do anything to get it perfect.

Mom and Dad showed up for a visit at our house here in Stirling last week. Nearly a four-hour drive – they must have felt as if they were going to the other end of the planet! And what a strain to be around them. I don't know how they manage to enjoy life. If something ever made them happy, it would be like matter meeting antimatter, and they'd spontaneously combust. Olivia and Rosalind chattered away, which helped fill the awkwardness. Maine is where the best times happen for our family.

Fingers crossed I can keep it together when Daniel is out screwing Woman #3. I'll need to be strong for the girls' sakes.

Love,

Jillian

Marx was thrilled to be home. He raced immediately into the back yard to chase all the squirrels that had taken advantage of his absence. Eve lugged her stuff and his into a house that seemed horribly empty and still without Mike. Most of the furniture remained, but a few pieces Mike had taken would have to be replaced, and her closet and the bathroom cabinet were positively ghostly. Eve shed a few tears, couldn't help it. She'd loved him and he was gone. But life was stretching out ahead of her, a blank slate she had solid plans to fill.

On Washington Island she'd scored her first professional credits, both successes. She'd take a couple of weeks here at home to fill empty spaces, add more color, more liveliness, and then look for another job or see if she could develop an online presence and try for more solo work. She'd call Joseph Simington and see if they were a good match or if he could recommend another therapist. She'd get in touch with friends from graduate school, find out if they'd be up for going out this week, or next. Or both. She'd see movies, go to museums, plays, concerts. Oh, and she'd send Shelley the fancy tea, maybe a silver frame for the picture of Helen, and a long, heartfelt thank-you note. For so many more things than just trusting her to design a cottage.

She'd also text Clayton to let him know she was back safely, as promised, though hearing from him might make her want to jump in the car and go back.

If only she could feel geared up and excited about starting fresh, instead of vaguely uneasy, as if something still wasn't in the right place.

On her first full day home, she woke early, at first thinking she was still on the island, then realizing her walls were no longer bright blue or yellow, and that she was home.

She threw off the blankets, greeted Marx, lounging in his bed by her door, and got ready for her run. Looked like a beautiful day. Spring had fully sprung in her absence, which was cheering.

Back from the run, she poured herself a glass of juice and noticed a missed call on her phone. Clayton?

Mike. No voicemail. Just a call.

Deep breath. Okay. She could do this. But first a shower and some breakfast. Talking to him again would be emotional, and she didn't want to be smelly and rumpled.

After cleaning up, she dressed in black jeans and the brightest top she owned – teal with black stripes. Downstairs she ate toast, yoghurt with too-early-in-the-season strawberries and granola. Made a cup of coffee. Drank half.

Then couldn't stand the suspense anymore.

Mike didn't pick up.

Too early for him to be on his way to school. Maybe he was in the bathroom?

A minute or so later, she was on her way to the sunroom to finish her coffee, followed by Marx, when he called back. Eve took a moment to relax and remind herself to sound cheerful.

'Hey, Mike!'

'Hi.' His deep voice made her heart melt just a little. They'd been together a long time. It was so familiar to be talking to him, it seemed she should be able to turn around and find the house the way it had always been. 'Welcome back from the wilds of Wisconsin.'

She frowned and drifted over to the window, noticing that the green-streaked late-blooming tulip plants she and Mike had planted the previous fall were open. 'How did you know I—'

'I don't have much time to talk. I want you to hear it from me. I'm . . . seeing someone.'

Eve turned abruptly from the tulips. 'Well. That was quick.'

'Yeah, I . . . yeah. I've known her for a . . . while, actually.' He sounded miserable. Or ashamed. Or guilty. Or all three.

Eve connected the dots, breakfast turning sour in her stomach.

Oh Mike.

'You were seeing her while you and I were—'

'*No*, not like you think. There was nothing going on. Give me some credit. Jesus, Eve.'

'Don't say Jesus.' The words came out automatically. Absurdly, even through the pain, she found herself having to keep from giggling. 'When did it start?'

'Ah, Eve . . . don't do this.'

Crap.

No more giggling. Not even close. She started pacing the length of the windows, preparing for the blow. 'I just want to know.'

'I met her in group therapy last summer. We spent time together. But I swear, nothing physical happened until you left.'

Nothing physical. But a whole lot of emotional. Was there really much difference?

Then the truth hit her. *Group therapy?*

'You're living with her now. She's the one who offered you a place.'

'I . . . wanted you to know.'

'Gee, that's noble of you, Mike.'

'Now you're pissed at me.'

'Would that be so shocking?' She turned back toward the yard and the flowers. Peonies, daisies, rhododendrons, roses – it would be a mass of color in a month or so. 'All that time I spent wondering what had gone wrong with us, trying to fix it, worrying about you, blaming myself, and you were on to someone new?'

'*No*, you're not *listening* to me. Back then she was a friend. A good friend. I still loved you, but you were acting all weird and distant. I needed someone, Eve.'

Even now, his self-centered cruelty stunned her.

'Weird and distant? Maybe because my father had a massive stroke that nearly killed him and then I found out I was *adopted*? But *you* needed someone?'

'I did, and I found a friend. I don't think that's a crime.'

Eve stopped pacing, took a deep breath. What was the point? He'd always done this to her. Nothing was ever his fault, nothing ever would be. She had no need to tie herself in knots trying to explain herself or fix a relationship that was over. Not her problem anymore, except to work out in therapy, make sure she never, ever chose another Mike.

'Okay. I'm happy for you. Truly. Just having a bad moment.'

'Ah, Eve. I know. This is hard for me too.' His voice was kind, full of regret. Human.

Eve bent down to pet Marx, then knelt and gave him a hug she undoubtedly needed more than he did. 'Take care. I hope you—'

'Whoops, I gotta go.' His voice had dropped to a whisper. 'Patty doesn't want me talking to you. I had to sneak this call.'

That was so delightful that Eve actually laughed. 'This sounds *really* promising, Mike.'

'Eve . . .'

She hung up and let Marx outside before she cried, to spare herself the doggy duet. When she finished – not that much later – Eve felt profound relief that she wouldn't have to claw her way through any more of those bewildering and infuriating Mike-centric conversations. And profound sadness that she'd ever thought that was an acceptable way to communicate.

Drying her eyes, she vowed that she was not going to cry again for at least the next six months. Then she picked up the phone once more and called Joseph Simington.

A week later, Eve felt like a new person, with one session under her belt and the distance of time between the ex-boyfriend she no longer missed and the people she did miss on Washington Island – though texting with Clayton and Abigail and emailing Shelley was better than nothing. Or rather she felt like the old person, but not quite so lost, though maybe a little manic. She'd gone out dancing with a friend at a trendy downtown club, and decided that at one week shy of thirty she could finally admit that she hated trendy downtown clubs and would rather dance in her own living room, where she wouldn't go half deaf, she had room to move, there were no creepy guys, and the floor wasn't sticky.

Another evening she had better luck having dinner with Barbara, her former colleague from Atkeson, Shifrin and Trim, who reported that morale at the office was at a new low, and that Robert was a terrible choice and everyone wanted her back.

Ha! Enjoy!

All week long she'd been visiting flea markets and antique stores, and had not only found furniture to replace what had belonged to Mike, but also donated a lot of her old stuff to Habitat for Humanity and gone crazy redecorating. Gone were shades-of-gray and olive. Newly arrived were navy and red and teal and white. Flowers in vases all over, just because they made her feel good. Bright throw pillows and rugs that had her smiling every time she walked into the room. Even Marx had a new collar, in vibrant royal blue, to remind her of her room at Shelley's, but also because it made him look extremely handsome.

Bravest of all, Eve had gone to a salon and gotten a new haircut, a chin-length style that cupped her face and made her feel even more like a new person.

Thirty was a week away, and she was going to be ready for it.

Tonight, blissfully alone on a Friday evening, she was planning on getting takeout, putting her feet up on her new glass and brass coffee table, opening a bottle of better wine than she used to buy, and watching a movie, maybe calling Clayton to say hi. She missed his voice. She missed his . . . everything. How long before the longing calmed down enough for her to be stable and happy alone? Enough for her to trust that her feelings weren't just a result of meeting a nice guy at a lonely and needy moment?

Feeling a bit reckless, not to mention hungry, she ordered sushi, probably more than she could eat. The woman taking her call said thirty minutes, but it was more like twenty when the doorbell finally rang. Starving, Eve nearly ran to fling it open.

Her mouth dropped. '*No way.*'

'Happy birthday a week early!' Olivia threw her arms around her. 'Ooh, I *love* the new do! So elegant.'

'Happy birthday! We brought the surprise party!' Rosalind held up a bottle with a yellow bow stuck to one side. '*Un peu de champagne*. Bryn recommended the brand, which means it will be really good.'

'Oh my gosh, *thank* you!' Eve couldn't stop grinning. 'I can't believe you're here.'

'We wanted to come next week for your real birthday, but

Olivia couldn't make it.' Rosalind poked her sister accusingly.

'It's Derek's mother's birthday weekend too.' Olivia made a face. 'I would much rather spend it with you than have to celebrate the birth of Mrs Satan.'

'I'm so glad you came.' Her sisters! Eve wasn't sure when she'd been so happy to see them. She felt she'd been through the wars, a victorious returning soldier with a touch of PTSD. Her evening with sushi and Netflix was revealed for the peaceful but lonely time it would have been.

'Hey, you've changed things.' Rosalind was looking around, taking in the colorful additions, the new paint, new furniture. 'A lot of things. Wow, it looks fantastic.'

'Thanks.' Eve smiled at the newly revitalized first floor. 'It had started to feel drab.'

'Because it was.' Rosalind hugged her, looking endearing in her characteristically bizarre outfit of yellow harem pants with a pink sparkly top, in sharp contrast to Olivia's black-and-white chic. 'So good to see you.'

'Well. New hair, new apartment, no more Mike.' Olivia nodded approvingly. 'Looks like you're starting the new decade with a vengeance.'

'Yes.' Eve took the champagne from Rosalind and led the way into the kitchen. 'I am.'

'Good for you.' Olivia started opening cabinets, always the first to make herself at home. 'I should think about doing the same when I hit the big four-oh next year. Glasses?'

'There.' Eve pointed to the cabinet where she kept her crystal champagne flutes, thinking nostalgically of the horrible chunky glasses in Shelley's house. 'Are you staying with me?'

'God, no, we wouldn't do that to you.' Olivia took down three flutes. 'We're booked into the Coach House Inn in Salem.'

'On a witch hunt,' Rosalind said.

'Ha ha.' Olivia twisted off the wire cage and popped the cork. Champagne started foaming up over the neck of the bottle. 'Eek!'

'You never do it right.' Eve shoved across a glass to catch the precious foam. 'You're supposed to—'

'I *know* what I'm supposed to do. But it's more fun this way.'

Rosalind exchanged a smiling glance with Eve. 'Old dog. Old tricks.'

The doorbell rang.

'My takeout's here.' Eve rushed to get it, glad now that she'd ordered so much. It would absorb some of the champagne and make the perfect appetizer.

They took the wine and food out to the sunroom, delayed because Olivia insisted on arranging the sushi on assorted Limoges plates inherited from their dad's parents that she discovered in a high cupboard, and that Eve had totally forgotten about.

Rosalind and Eve plopped on to the couch. Olivia dragged a matching upholstered bamboo chair up to the opposite side of the coffee table.

'So tell us, Eve.' Olivia put an edamame pod between her whitened teeth and squeezed out the beans inside. 'What the hell happened to you in Wisconsin that made you break up with Mike, change your hair and redo your entire house?'

Eve felt herself shrinking. 'I'm not sure, really.'

'Oh, come on.' Olivia tossed the empty pod on to her plate and grabbed another. She was still too thin, making Eve decide that if nothing else, they were going to feed her this weekend. 'You must have some idea.'

'It was complicated.' Eve stared thoughtfully at her champagne. 'Being away from Mike made me realize—'

'That he was stomping out your life spark?'

'Let her talk, Olivia,' Rosalind said gently.

'That we brought out the worst in each other instead of the best.' Eve thought of who she was around Clayton and sent him a silent prayer of thanks. She'd tried very hard all week not to miss him. It had only sort of worked.

'Very diplomatic,' Olivia turned over a piece of salmon sushi to dip the fish in soy sauce before she stuffed it into her mouth.

'Mike called me when I got back.' Eve's features tightened. 'He's already seeing someone else. Someone he met last summer. Living with her, in fact.'

Rosalind and Olivia froze, Rosalind with a piece of tuna roll halfway to her mouth.

'Oh shit,' Olivia said.

'Sweetie, I'm sorry.'

'Actually, it's okay.' The words came out sincerely, beneath them only minor agony. 'He had somewhere happy to go. I didn't feel like I was destroying him.'

'You are *much* too nice,' Olivia said. 'I would have strung him up by his—'

'You are much too judgmental,' Eve countered.

'*Down*, girls.' Rosalind refilled their glasses. 'Wait, speaking of which, where's Marx?'

'Asserting his manhood over the squirrels.' On cue, Marx appeared, dashing across the yard after a fluffy-tailed streak of gray. 'I'll let him in to slobber all over you when the sushi's gone.'

'Oh goody.' Olivia licked her fingers and dried them on a cocktail napkin. 'I love me a good slobber.'

'Olivia.' Eve was struck with sudden guilt that she'd been so deep in her own problems, she hadn't been keeping up with her oldest sister. 'What happened with all those parts you were auditioning for?'

'Nothing. No one wants me. My show is being cancelled. I'm

about to give up on having a baby. My husband hates me, and I'm not so fond of him either.' She beamed as if she were talking about great successes. 'Basically my life is fucked.'

Rosalind's expression turned queasy.

'Oh Olivia.' Eve put her champagne down, guilt turning sharper with grief. It wasn't fair that her beautiful sister should suffer like this. She needed to kick her life to the curb and start over. Eve knew first-hand how hard that could be – Olivia would have to want it for herself. All they could do was line up behind her and shove as hard as they could.

'No, no! This is a celebration! No pity. For God's sake.' Olivia jumped to her feet. 'I'll get the presents. They're in the car.'

She disappeared into the house, striding confidently on heels that would have sent Eve to the emergency room in ten seconds.

'How bad is this?' Eve asked quietly.

'I think bad. I'm not sure.' Rosalind shook her head, clearly worried. 'She looks skeletal. I'm wondering if we need to stage an intervention.'

'I was wondering the same. Let's start by ordering a house-sized pizza with pepperoni and extra cheese.' Eve reached for her phone. The food was her sister's favorite. She'd beg for it every time. Jillian never gave in, either commissioning the cook's soggy-crusted version or ordering out with only healthy toppings: half the usual cheese, broccoli, mushrooms, spinach . . .

'I think that's a great idea.'

Eve's favorite pizza place, Cindy's, answered right away, and she managed to place the delivery order just before her sister returned.

'Here we go!' Olivia came in lugging a Dolce & Gabbana bag, which she dropped at Eve's feet. 'Happy thirtieth, baby sister!'

'Thank you! This is such an amazing surprise. It's so great to see both of you.'

'We wouldn't have missed it.' Rosalind sent her a loving smile.

'Amen.' Olivia sat and drained her champagne. 'Now stop being so sweet and open your presents.'

'Yes, ma'am.' Eve pulled out a small package first, wrapped in cream-colored paper with a swirling gold design.

'That's from me.' Olivia waited proudly as Eve unwrapped a fabulously sexy minuscule black lace bra and panty set with Dolce & Gabbana tags, which had probably cost more than Eve spent on lingerie in a year. Her only other Gabbana had been gifts from Olivia as well. 'To celebrate a new era of your life.'

'Oh, wow.' Eve held them up admiringly. 'These are stunning, Olivia. *Thank* you.'

'Ooh.' Rosalind smirked suggestively. 'Didn't you also give her sexy underwear when she started seeing Mike?'

Olivia sent her a *well, duh* look. 'You can't wear the same sexy underwear for two different men!'

'Oh.' Rosalind lifted her eyebrows, clearly amused. 'I had no idea. So is there someone I don't know about? Like maybe—'

'Clayton?' Olivia finished for her.

'Nope. He's a great friend. But I love these. Totally hot.' Eve told her brain to stop imagining Clayton's reaction if she wore them for him. Which wasn't something a 'friend' would imagine, but she didn't want the special and confusing situation with Clayton to be up for sisterly dissection. 'Thanks, Olivia.'

'You're welcome.' She poured herself another glass of champagne. 'We brought two bottles, right, Rozzy?'

'We did.' Rosalind and Eve exchanged glances.

Olivia pointed to the presents. 'Next one.'

Eve reached for another package.

'This is from me.' Rosalind was having trouble keeping a straight face.

Eve eyed her suspiciously as she unwrapped . . . a tube of cream for vaginal dryness. Olivia nearly sprayed champagne around the room. 'Whoa. What do I get when I turn forty, diapers?'

'Gee, Rosalind. Thank you *so* much. Really. Best present ever.'

'You're so welcome.' Rosalind blinked sweetly and hoisted her glass. 'Here's to ya, babe.'

'Moving on . . .' Eve rolled her eyes and reached into the bag again.

The next gift, from Olivia, was a photo album covered in beautiful soft green leather with Eve's name stamped on the cover in silver script.

'Look inside,' Olivia instructed.

Eve turned a few pages. Family pictures, all of which included Eve, from babyhood on. A record of her life with her sisters and parents.

'Oh wow. Olivia, this is amazing. And such a perfect gift for such a complicated year.' Eve clutched the album to her chest, beaming at her sister, who had taken an amazing amount of time out of her busy life to put together such a sweet gift for her. 'Thank you so much. I will really enjoy this.'

'Come.' Olivia got up and joined them on the couch so Eve was in the middle. 'Let's all look.'

They sat together, blond, brunette and redhead, bound by a lifetime of memories, leafing through the pages of pictures, pointing, laughing, telling stories, some of which Eve – the baby of the family – didn't know or hadn't remembered.

Throughout the album were pictures of Jillian Croft,

sometimes glammed up in her celebrity persona, but more often dressed down, smiling with her daughters, holding them as babies, caught by the camera kissing their fat cheeks.

'Aw, Olivia.' Eve leaned warmly into her sister. 'This is really special.'

'I think we all needed this.' Rosalind sniffed suspiciously.

'Oh no.' Olivia shook her finger. 'Don't go getting all emotional on us. You'll drag me down too.'

'Sorry.' Rosalind wiped her eyes. 'It's been a hell of a year.'

'No kidding.' For once, Olivia wasn't being sarcastic.

Eve turned another page and stiffened. The party. A picture of her in that awful blue strapless dress, posing with her sisters and Jillian. The photographer must have taken that one.

'Oh wow, one of the holiday parties!' Rosalind said.

'I *loved* those parties. They were so incredible, so elegant, so *Hollywood*. They made Mom so happy.'

Eve couldn't speak, staring at her shy-girl smile in the picture, knowing what was about to happen to her.

'Hey.' Rosalind nudged her gently. 'What's up? You look like you've seen a ghost.'

Eve hunched her shoulders, breathing accelerating, preparing for the inevitable attack.

And then, as if he were standing beside her, she heard Clayton's voice.

It's just one thing that happened a really long time ago. It doesn't define or control me in any way.

'Eve?' Olivia leaned forward to look into her face. 'What is it?'

It doesn't define or control me.

Eve put her glass back on the coffee table, then took both her sisters' hands and a deep breath. She wasn't ready to tell all of it. Not the part about her mother ignoring her plea for help, or about Jillian's reaction later that night after Eve told her what had happened – that she should get used to being assaulted and become tougher. For one, it would be so hard for her sisters to hear, and for another, Eve no longer believed it was as simple as her mother being cold or cruel or selfish. Her mother was herself.

'Do you remember Mr Angel?'

'Sure.' Olivia examined Eve's face. 'The producer.'

'The jerk who practically promised that role to Mom and then gave it to whatsername,' Rosalind said.

Olivia bristled. 'He was not a jerk!'

'He said he wanted to see my Christmas presents. He took me upstairs.'

'Eve . . .' Rosalind sounded terrified.

'Yeah. It was bad. Could have been worse, just touching and creepy stuff, but bad.' Even all these years later, her voice came out thick with grief, but the panic stayed away.

Gasps from both her sisters.

'Mr *Angel*? Are you *sure*?'

Eve turned a withering stare on Olivia, who immediately clapped a hand over her mouth. 'I can't believe I said that. It's like when you hear someone died and you say, "No, no, I just *saw* him!" I am so sorry.'

'You must have gone through hell.' Rosalind put an arm around Eve. 'Did you ever tell Mom and Dad?'

'I told Jillian.'

'I can't believe it.' Olivia screwed up her face. 'Shit, I'm doing it again. It's just . . . I liked him. He seemed so sweet and so . . .'

'Disgusting?' Rosalind supplied.

'So . . . interested in what I was doing.' Olivia looked faintly ill. 'So anxious to get me alone . . . *ugh*. Oh my God, you poor thing.'

'Sweetie.' Rosalind squeezed Eve's shoulder. 'I'm so glad you told us. That must have been hard to do.'

Eve blew out a breath. 'It was not the most fun I've ever had.'

'Really?' Rosalind was still hugging her tightly. 'I'm stunned to hear that.'

'It sucks that in that type of situation *we* are the ones who get the shame and the guilt and the misery for years and years, when *he* deserves it all. I am *proud* of you for telling, Eve.' Olivia got up and lifted her glass. 'Here's to being able to admit you're screwed up.'

'She's not screwed up,' Rosalind said.

Olivia rolled her eyes. '*Everyone* is screwed up.'

'Okay, but if you *know* you are, at least you're in the right place to get better.' Rosalind took her arm away and joined Olivia's toast. 'It's the people who *don't* know they're screwed up who are *really* screwed up.'

That got a giggle out of Eve. She was able to relax her shoulders too. She had told Clayton. She had told her therapist. Now she'd told her sisters. The world hadn't ended. The panic hadn't materialized. The abuse was something terrible that had happened to her, something she'd still have to contend with for a long time, in therapy and out. But she was no longer going to let that night control her.

Maybe that was all her mother had been trying to tell her.

The doorbell rang, announcing pizza. Olivia's face when they lifted the lid and the aroma hit her was priceless. She fell on a piece like a starving tigress and didn't stop until there were only three slices left, the second bottle of champagne was gone, and they were all groaning and clutching their stomachs.

'Please tell me there's no cake,' Eve said. 'I am never eating again.'

'No cake. But there's one more present. From me.' Rosalind drew a book-shaped gift from her purse. 'Olivia, close your eyes.'

'Why?'

'Because it has to do with the subject you won't talk about.'

Olivia looked mystified. 'There *is* no subject I won't talk about.'

'Mom's infertility,' Rosalind said.

'Oh, *that*.' Olivia sighed heavily. 'Go ahead. I'll erase it from my brain later.'

Rosalind handed the gift to Eve. 'You might not be ready yet. But when you are . . .'

Eve unwrapped a home-made book, nicely bound. On the cover, a simple title: *Sylvia*, and a sweet inscription in her sister's freaky-perfect handwriting. Eve looked inside, scanning the printed pages until realization hit. 'You typed up her diary.'

'Whose diary?' Olivia asked.

'Mom's,' Rosalind told her. 'From when she was a girl to when she was diagnosed with—'

'Lalalalala.' Olivia's hands were over her ears.

'Oh, for . . .' Rosalind looked exasperated. 'Eve, I think you'll find it . . . well, I know it will be hard, but I hope you give it – and Mom – another chance.'

'Thanks, Rosalind.' Eve held the pretty little book in her hand, still reeling from her new insight into Jillian's words that awful night.

Maybe it was time. Maybe she would.

The rest of the weekend was a fabulous mix of fun and conversation. Somehow Olivia had snagged a Saturday-night reservation at one of Boston's best restaurants, Alden & Harlow, where they had a fantastic meal that Olivia insisted on paying for – and cake for dessert. They spent a few chilly hours shivering on the beach, did much too much shopping, saw a tearjerker movie they had to recover from with ice cream in Harvard Square, and in general, apart from the occasional mild squabbling, enjoyed being sisters in a way they hadn't been able to for far too long.

They parted on Sunday swearing they would get together more often.

Eve sincerely hoped they would.

Back home, she curled up on the sunroom couch with Marx at her feet, tired from all the socializing, as any good introvert would be, but uplifted. The girls had encouraged her to strike out on her own professionally. She'd think about it, though right now she didn't feel ready. Still, the possibility, one she hadn't allowed on her own, definitely had her feeling pumped, like a really good life could be within her grasp.

Impulsively she picked up the book Rosalind had given her, still on the coffee table where she'd first unwrapped it, and started reading about Sylvia Moore's struggles with knowing her body was different, without understanding how or why. Her struggles with her difficult and ignorant mother, who withheld the diagnosis from her. Her subsequent escape from home, her initial acting successes, and her meeting and falling in love with the man who'd become father to her three adopted daughters.

Hours later, Eve closed the book, deeply moved. She lay quietly on the couch for so long, Marx came over and nudged her hand, as if checking to see if she were still alive.

And in a flash of inspiration, Eve reached for her phone. She knew exactly where she wanted to spend her birthday.

Chapter 20

October 5, 1989 (Thursday)

Mother #3 and I are pregnant, thank God. It took forever again. I wanted Daniel to give up and find someone else, but he wouldn't. It was total torture, though I did better controlling myself this time. At least I didn't launch anything at him when he came home, though I had trouble being welcoming. There are worse things to worry about now.

I think Daniel is having an affair. I don't know if it's with Mother #3 or someone else. Part of me doesn't blame him. My body isn't what men want. I try to understand that he needs to be with a whole woman. It's how God meant the world to be. I helped create his hunger by asking him to have these children for us. How could he help but want more? But it hurts, hurts, hurts, sometimes unbearably. I have started drinking too much. I was wrong that I could handle it. And I can't stop taking my lovely pills. I'm afraid I will have to get help again. People will know again. People will talk again. I'm about to turn forty. The work is not going to be around much longer. I can't let addiction be a bigger legacy than my art.

The only thing I hate more than having to drink is having to stop.

May God help me and everyone I love.

* * *

Jackman, Maine, the self-proclaimed 'Switzerland of Maine', whatever that meant, home to Eve's Grandma Betty, was a small town – roughly the same population as Washington Island – in the west of the state on Route 201, nearly to Canada. If one thought of Maine as a raised head on the body of the country, Jackman was at the nape of the neck, nestled in the state's densely forested Longfellow Mountains, where there was as good a chance of spotting a moose as a person. Maybe that was an exaggeration. But its most famous resident, Sylvia Moore, grew up there before she escaped to seek fame and fortune as Jillian Croft, and found both.

Eve hadn't been back to visit Grandma Betty in a long time. Estranged from her elder daughter for years, Betty hadn't reached out to her granddaughters much either after the reconciliation – awkward if the diary was any indication – and the girls had taken their cue from their mother and spent a bare minimum of time in her rather unpleasant presence after Jillian's death. Olivia had gone the most frequently, visiting every year on Betty's birthday – eighty-nine years and counting. The eldest Braddock daughter was the clear favorite, and the means by which Jillian had eventually made something close to peace with her mother.

Apparently this concept of having to make peace with your mother hadn't skipped a generation.

Eve wasn't sure what she was after, only that when she read the diary Rosalind had been sent, she'd felt Betty could shed light on her daughter's life, and maybe her death. In addition, though the Braddock family had successfully kept it a secret from the world, Jillian Croft's ashes were buried in her hometown. The girls had fought long and hard with their father over this. Why bury her somewhere she hated so much? Why not on their property in Maine, which she'd loved, or in LA, where people could come and pay their respects? In the end, Daniel had compromised somewhat, buying an empty plot in LA and providing it with a headstone, while insisting his wife's ashes belonged in her home.

Given that the girls had sold the Candlewood Point summer home not long after Dad's stroke, Eve supposed Jackman was the best resting place after all.

The drive from Swampscott was about four and a half hours, a comfortable distance with a stop for lunch and a couple of chances to let Marx run around. As they approached Jackman, Eve strained for glimpses of Wood Pond, which bordered the town. She had to pass the turnoff to Grandma Betty's house for the full view, but it was worth it to see the lovely fir-tree-bordered lake and the mountains rising gently in the distance. It seemed smaller than she remembered. Or maybe her recent acquaintance with Lake Michigan had colored her impressions.

Backtracking briefly, she turned left on Murtha Street, then left again on Bartley, where her grandmother still lived in the bright white house with forest-green trim where Sylvia Moore had grown up.

Eve pulled into the short driveway, picked up the items she'd brought with her, and stepped out, inhaling the lovely mountain air. Perfect weather. Summers could be horribly humid here, and winters severe, but spring was a gorgeous if still chilly time of year.

Marx jumped out of the car and, like her, immediately started sniffing. Maine smelled so good. Eve always crossed the soaring bridge from New Hampshire into the southernmost part of the state enjoying the feeling of coming home, a place where she'd known more happiness than anywhere else she'd lived.

Behind her, the house door squeaked open and banged shut.

'Hello, Eve.' Her grandmother's voice was raspy and low, as if she'd spent her life smoking and drinking. One of life's strange tricks: Betty was a teetotaler who couldn't stand the smell of smoke.

Eve mounted the front porch steps to where the old woman stood leaning on a cane, looking exactly as she did in her granddaughter's memory. How long had it been? Three years? She supposed the difference between eighty-six and eighty-nine wasn't going to be dramatic.

'Hi, Grandma.' Eve hugged Betty's thin frame gingerly, worried about unbalancing her, and kissed her soft wrinkled cheek. Her grandmother's eyes were still dark; her white hair still looked as if she'd picked up kitchen scissors and hacked away until it no longer bothered her. She was dressed in a faded pair of blue and white plaid pants with a white blouse worn nearly transparent under a beige sweater that had seen better days.

As always, it was nearly impossible to connect this shrunken relic of a woman with the stylish, larger-than-life mother Eve had known. Betty's other daughter, Christina, had rated somewhere between her glamor-eschewing mother and her glamor-greedy sister. She'd been co-conspirator with Jillian and Daniel as midwife for all three Braddock girls, but largely ignored the sisters afterwards, remaining in Maine until she died of complications from diabetes in 2010.

'You look great, Grandma.'

Betty arched a gray eyebrow, though her mouth curved slightly. 'You need your eyes checked.'

That was Grandma Betty in one of her better moods.

'I had a good drive up. I'd forgotten how beautiful it is around here.'

'You think so? Your mother didn't.'

'Nope. She hated it.' Eve's calm response was rewarded with a quick startled glance. She held up the small package she'd brought with her from Massachusetts. 'I got you a present, Grandma.'

'What is it?'

'Let's go inside. I'll give it to you there.'

'All right.' Betty turned and led the way, letting Eve handle the door for herself. Maybe when Eve was in her late eighties she'd decide to look out for number one and let everyone else fend for themselves.

But she hoped not.

The front door opened right into the sitting room, whose furniture was probably purchased when Betty and Arnold got married in the 1950s. The sagging couch had been draped with a crocheted blanket in browns, golds and greens. In high-traffic areas the grubby carpet was worn down nearly to its supporting structure. Eve was pretty sure Jillian had sent money fairly regularly. The room was a visual depiction of Betty's stubborn pride. Eve didn't know where the money had gone, and didn't care.

Grandmother and granddaughter sat together on the lumpy couch, Betty lowering herself part way then letting her body drop. 'So where's this present?'

'Here you go.' Eve handed over the package and watched Betty tear into the paper.

Eve had copied a picture from Olivia's album, taken on a family visit to Jackman when Eve was a baby. Everyone was in it. Betty, her husband Arnold, the three girls, Jillian and Daniel, and never-married Christina, standing in the kitchen with frozen smiles on their faces. It was a great picture. Three generations of Moores and Braddocks.

'Hmm.' Betty shoved the picture toward Eve, who was taken aback until she realized her grandmother needed both hands to pat various articles of clothing and find her glasses – sweater, lower right pocket – and put them on. 'Let me see again. Oh. Well. My goodness.'

'I wasn't sure you had any pictures of the whole family.' Eve's mother or father might have sent some, but if Betty did have them, she certainly hadn't put any on display.

'No. I don't.' She continued to stare at each face, no expression on hers. 'Thank you for bringing this. It's very nice.'

'You're welcome.' Eve wasn't fooled by Betty's apparent impassivity. The picture had pleased her. But it brought home how foreign Jillian must have felt in this house, a girl whose every emotion was constantly – relentlessly – on display, a trait that followed her into womanhood. Betty must have found her unfathomable. And as Eve remembered him, Arnold wasn't much different from his wife.

'Who took it, do you recall, Grandma?'

Betty was still examining the photo. 'I expect it was Phoebe. She was a good friend of Christina's, then a good friend to me until she moved to New York to marry a man she met online. Do you want some lunch?'

Eve glanced anxiously at the clock. It was 2.30. 'No, no, I've had mine. You didn't wait for me, did you?'

'Of course not. I'd starve to death.'

'Right.' There was a reason none of the girls scheduled frequent or long visits with Betty. 'We're fine then.'

'You want something to drink?'

'A glass of water would be nice. I can get it.'

Betty looked highly offended. 'I can certainly get my granddaughter a glass of water in my own house.'

'You certainly can. I'll come with you.'

She accompanied Betty into the small kitchen, Eve's favorite room in the house, though worn down from her girlhood memories. From the red and white checked tablecloth, now stained, to the curtain fabric decorated with bunches of faded cherries, to the bowl of dusty wax apples and the cheerful decorative plates on the walls, the room had been the epitome of her fantasy of grandmotherly comfort. On some visits there was even a pie on the shelf under the window, fragrant fruit cooling beneath tough tasteless pastry. When Eve was growing up in Beverly Hills, coming here was like visiting the pages of a Laura Ingalls Wilder book.

With bad food and without the pig-bladder balloon.

Water in hand, she sat at the kitchen table. Betty pulled out a tin containing from-scratch oatmeal cookies, which Eve knew without trying one would be overdone and odd-tasting. Her grandmother should stay out of the kitchen. 'You're still baking?'

Betty scowled. 'Why wouldn't I be?'

Because you're so damn old? 'I just thought . . .'

'I still cook for me. I still bake for other people. I'm not dead.' She put a few cookies on a plate, mumbling to herself, and set it on the table before sitting opposite Eve, letting her body land with a *whump* that blew air out of the vinyl-padded chair cushions. 'How are your sisters?'

'They're fine.' Eve dutifully helped herself to a cookie. 'We just celebrated my birthday together.'

Betty looked panicked. 'I missed it?'

'No, no.' She managed to swallow her first bite. At least the raisins were good. 'It's tomorrow.'

'That's what I thought. I got mixed up and sent your card to your house. I forgot you were coming.'

'I don't mind.' She smiled at Betty, wondering if the card

would contain a dollar this year, or a five, or nothing. It varied.

'I don't bake cakes anymore.'

Thank God. 'I don't need a cake.'

'Nobody *needs* a cake. I can do you a pie.'

'You don't need to . . . have to.'

'Of course I don't *have* to. I do it because I want to.'

'Right, thank you.' Eve forced down the rest of her cookie, took a gulp of water and a deep breath. She might as well jump to why she was here, because there was no point waiting for the miracle of her grandmother becoming gracious and attentive. 'Rosalind gave me a birthday present this year. A diary Sylvia wrote when—'

'Why do you call her by her first name?'

Eve pressed her lips together. 'A diary my mother wrote in high school.'

Betty didn't look surprised. 'She was always writing, always about herself.'

'She talked about her condition.' Eve forced herself to keep going. 'Complete androgen insensitivity.'

'Ah.' Betty's mouth snapped shut. 'Have another cookie.'

'Thanks.' Eve took another, hoping she could find some way to avoid eating it. 'She says you never discussed it with her.'

'Is that what she wrote? That I didn't *discuss* it?'

'Not that word. But that you wouldn't talk about it with her.' Eve put down the cookie. Her legs were shaking under the table but she would not back down from what she wanted to know. 'Or help her understand.'

'What was there to discuss? God gave her a deformity. There was nothing I could do to fix it. She was too young to understand.'

Eve's eyes narrowed, stomach twisting in revulsion. 'Did you really just say that?'

'What could I have done?' Betty's eyes had turned darker,

her gaze fierce. 'You have no children. You tell me.'

Eve wasn't sure if it was worth trying to sound patient. One thing this visit had accomplished already, better than the diary, better than probably just about anything else, was to make her jump to her mother's defense against what seemed like a greater enemy. 'You could have explained. You could have helped her understand what was happening to her body. Or what wasn't happening.'

Betty dropped her eyes. 'We didn't talk about those things then. My mother never told me about . . . any of it. We simply didn't mention them.'

'You could have asked her doctor to explain.'

'She was too young. I was waiting until she was older, ready to be married. She was still a child. Then she left without a word. Not one word to any of us, not even her sister. I don't need to describe what it's like when your child disappears. I can't tell you how much sleep I lost, imagining the worst, and then worse than that. Only to find out she was having the time of her life in the big city, happy as you please.'

Eve sat in silent horror at the level of anger coming out of her grandmother. After all these years, and all Jillian's gifts and attempts to reconcile. Jillian had suffered too.

'I dealt with that child the best way I knew how. She was a handful. More than a handful: she was my private misery, and often my public misery too. If you'd heard some of the phone calls from school! The terrible gossip! I'm sure people thought it was my fault, that I was a bad mother.' Betty shook her head, loose skin under her chin wobbling over her high collar. 'It was not my fault. She was born with some demon inside her that I never understood, and could never exorcize, no matter how hard I tried.'

'She had a mental illness, Grandma.'

Betty flinched and gave a quick shake of her head. 'It's no excuse for what she did. Through all my praying and all my begging God to help me, the only thing I could never forgive was that she left this family without a word.'

'She wrote to you,' Eve said quietly. 'She wrote to you every week for thirteen years, and you never responded. Not once.'

'Is that why you came up here?' Betty demanded. 'To blame me for your mother's unhappiness?'

'No.' Eve laid a hand on her grandmother's arm and stood. She wasn't going to win any battles here. Betty had taken her position decades ago, and if the death of her child – both children and her husband – hadn't softened her, nothing would. It was possible she'd lost some mental acuity, and fixated on this one aspect of her loss. Or she could simply be a narcissist, who literally couldn't feel anyone's pain but her own. 'I came up here to see her.'

St Anthony's Cemetery lay north of Jackman, on what used to be called Route 201, now fittingly called Old Route 201. Eve pulled to a stop opposite the graveyard, several miles from the actual church of St Anthony's, which had been torn down and rebuilt a decade earlier, much to Betty's dismay. She'd loved her old church, had grown up, gotten married and christened her daughters in it.

Eve sat for a moment, then turned to Marx, who was grinning at her from the back seat, ready for anything. 'Hey, boy. I'm going to let you stay in the car, okay? No offense, but this could get a little emotional. You do have a lovely voice, but . . . I think I'll go it alone.'

She pushed open her door and walked over the field, fresh and pliant from the spring rains, following Betty's directions to the location of her mother's ashes. There had been no formal ceremony here, and Eve had never been interested in driving over on previous trips to Jackman, but the headstone was easy to find, polished gray granite with a rounded top, no fancy engraved picture or decoration, simply her mother's name, Sylvia Moore, and the dates: October 17, 1950–December 31, 2001.

A car passed, but otherwise the atmosphere was quiet, reverent, the way graveyards should be. Eve moved to clear a fallen leaf off her mother's grave, then knelt and laid her hand on the stone, warm from the sun.

'Hi.' She felt fairly stupid talking to a rock and thinking her mother could hear her, but something had compelled her here, so too bad. 'I stayed away before. I'm sorry. I was angry.

'That night at the holiday party . . .' She stopped. Looked down at her fingers twisting around each other. 'That night . . . I needed . . . You were . . .'

Aw, hell. She'd discussed this with Clayton, with her therapist and with her sisters, but she couldn't tell a rock?

The memory came back again. Her mother in the yellow gown. Mr Angel in a tuxedo with a crimson handkerchief in the jacket pocket. Her fear. His hands. The sticky mess on her thigh. Her mother in the dark of her room that night, bending over her as she cried.

And she realized why she was having trouble finding the right words. Why the tears weren't coming. Why there was no panic and only distant pain.

There was nothing left to say. Not because everything was fixed – that would take time and more therapy – but because the issue was Eve's and didn't belong to anyone else.

She could let her mother rest in peace.

A quick burst of laughter surprised her. Tension uncoiled in her chest, then a swell of energy. She sprinted over to the car, flung open the back door and let Marx spring out on to the field.

They ran together, chasing each other through the gravestones, Eve leaping and dancing and whooping, Marx barking and bounding, both of them completely nuts.

Finally she called him over to her mother's grave and flopped down on to it, glowing with the fun of their wild rumpus, her cheek on the grass, her arm over Marx's heaving flanks.

Eve would call Grandma to let her know she wasn't going back to Jackman. Betty could stew in her own narcissistic rage tonight. Then she'd call Dad to see if he and Lauren could handle a visitor in Blue Hill. She could spend her birthday with them tomorrow, take them out to dinner to celebrate. Maybe she'd call Clayton, too, see how he was doing, how he felt Abigail was doing. In her texts, Abigail had sounded cheerful, often hilarious, which Eve took as a good sign. Clayton might know more.

And while they were talking . . . she might just ask whether he'd like to come visit her some weekend, see the sights in Boston. That would be really nice.

When her breath calmed, she pulled up on to her elbows. Marx sat up as well.

'Hey, boy. I should have introduced you. This is Sylvia Moore, also known as Jillian Croft.' Eve gestured toward the stone, lit by the descending sun, a still and peaceful monument to such a turbulent life. 'Also known as Mom.'

Chapter 21

May 11, 1990 (Friday)

I'm naming my last daughter after my heroine, the wonderful Ms Arden. But also after the world's very first woman. Eve Grace Braddock was born early this morning. She is so precious, I weep just looking at her. So small, so fragile. How this cruel world will hurt her! So little I can do to keep her forever safe as she is now, snuggled against me as I write, making sweet baby noises on her very first day of life on the outside. All I can do is teach her to be strong, and pray to God to send her only happiness.

How I love you, little girl, more than you will know, until you gaze down at a new child of your own. Only then can you understand how huge this feeling is, even the third time around.

Welcome to this ugly, flawed world, my beautiful, perfect Eve.

Want more of the intriguing family secrets and compelling romantic entanglements of the Braddock family?

Look for Rosalind's story in *Private Lies* and Olivia's story in *Honest Secrets* – the other enthralling titles in the Fortune's Daughters trilogy.

Hidden Truths

Bonus Material

Taking a trip to Washington Island

When you mention Door County, Wisconsin, most people think of the peninsula protruding into Lake Michigan, a popular summer destination of cute towns and plenty of opportunities to hike, bike, shop, laze, and swim. Washington Island is a 35-square-mile island four miles off the tip of the peninsula, which already feels like the end of civilization. The ferry to the island really does cross a channel called Death's Door after all the grisly accidents that happened there.

The island is quirky, sparsely populated and, frankly, there's not a lot to do. You have to like what's available, and you have to be a special kind of person to appreciate its laid-back charms. My husband and I once stayed at an inn on the mainland, but decided one day to hop on the ferry and bike around Washington Island. When we told the innkeeper our plans, he looked alarmed. 'Have you visited before?' We assured him we had. He looked relieved. 'Then you know there's nothing up there.'

When you get off the ferry on to the island mid-May through early September, you'll see what's called the Cherry Train. For one thing, it's not a train. For another, while cherries are grown (commercially) in abundance on the Door County peninsula, to my knowledge there aren't cherry orchards on the island. Be that as it may, Cherry Train riders are treated to a running commentary in a thick Wisconsin accent while they're driven around to visit the six things there are to do. Hint: one of them is a farm museum.

I'm exaggerating, of course, mostly so none of you will go crowd the place for the rest of us who love it. My husband's parents went to Washington Island on their honeymoon in 1950, and his family (he has four brothers) has visited several times, including trips involving three generations. Mark took me there for the first time on a September long weekend only a few months into our relationship. I was smitten with him for sure, but not yet convinced he was The One. We knew we had a lot in common, but on the island we discovered our daily rhythms and moods matched perfectly. On the way home, we enjoyed more shared passions: listening to Mahler's 4th Symphony followed by a baseball game. Half a mile from my house, he unexpectedly detoured to a spot overlooking the lake. Before we went back to our separate homes and children, he wanted to kiss me one more time in a beautiful place. That did it. I was a goner.

Washington Island might not be for everyone, but it means a lot to me. I had a wonderful time sending Eve there, so she could fall in love as well.

Clayton's Spiced Fruit Bars

These are chewy, delicious and not too bad for you as cookies go. A perfect way to sneak fruit and whole grain flour into sugar-craving kids.

Ingredients
1¼ cups (150 grams) all-purpose flour
½ cup (60 grams) whole wheat flour
1 teaspoon cinnamon
1 teaspoon ground ginger
½ teaspoon baking soda
½ teaspoon salt
½ teaspoon allspice
¼ teaspoon ground cloves
½ cup (113 grams) butter, softened
¾ cup (148 grams) brown sugar
1 egg
½ cup molasses
1 cup (125 grams) walnuts or pecans, chopped
6 oz (170 grams) chopped dried fruit (I use apricots, dried cranberries and raisins)

Method
Preheat oven to 350°F/177°C.

Grease a 10 x 15 x 1 inch baking pan.

Mix dry ingredients (flour through cloves) in a bowl.

Cream butter and sugar together in mixer until light and smooth. Add egg, beat to incorporate. Add molasses.

Add dry ingredients, mix slowly until very little dry flour remains, then add nuts and fruit. Mix only until evenly distributed. The dough will be stiff.

Drop dough by spoonfuls on to the prepared sheet. Oil your hands and press it gently into a smooth layer.

Bake for 25 minutes. Let cool in pan. Cut into bars.

Private
Lies
Three beloved sisters.
One unimaginable secret.
Muna Shehadi

Hidden
Truths
A secret to shatter a family.
Or heal a broken heart.
Muna Shehadi

Honest
Secrets
Her mother lived a lie.
Will the truth set her free?
Muna Shehadi